LEVIATHAN

Books by Warren Tute

THE CRUISER

THE ROCK

LEVIATHAN

⚓⚓⚓⚓⚓⚓⚓⚓⚓⚓⚓⚓⚓⚓⚓⚓⚓⚓⚓⚓⚓⚓⚓⚓

LEVIATHAN

by
Warren Tute

Little, Brown and Company

BOSTON   TORONTO

⚓⚓⚓⚓⚓⚓⚓⚓⚓⚓⚓⚓⚓⚓⚓⚓⚓⚓⚓⚓⚓⚓⚓

PRINTED IN THE UNITED STATES OF AMERICA

AUTHOR'S NOTE

There was, I know, a liner called *Leviathan* — the ex-German *Vaterland*, as a matter of fact — and for some years she lay moldering in New York harbor before being scrapped about the time the *Leviathan* in this book was launched. So, in order to avoid any confusion at all, I would like to stress firmly that the ships and characters in this book are entirely fictional and that no resemblance whatsoever is intended to anyone, dead or alive, connected with the shipping world.

LEVIATHAN

⚓⚓⚓⚓⚓ I ⚓⚓⚓⚓⚓

It BLEW half a gale the night before the launch. Any further worsening of the weather conditions, and the elaborate arrangements for launching the huge ship would all have to be abandoned. Peter Beecher nodded to the gatekeeper and slipped into the shadowy dockyard. By this time he was known to most of the guards and night watchmen. They thought the company's naval architect a little eccentric, perhaps, with his habit of midnight walks round the hull of No. 379; they reckoned he was harmless, though, so far as their own jobs were concerned, and if one of the higher company officials chose to waste good sleeping time in such brooding that was his affair.

Peter himself could not discover a logical reason for this restlessness. It had possessed him from the moment his plans for the monster had been passed and the decision to build what would be the largest ship in the world had been taken by the Transoceanic Steamship Company with Government backing. "Monster" indeed! — he frowned and shook his head at his involuntary use of the word. No. 379 was no monster to Peter Beecher, she was by far the comeliest of the many ships he had already designed for the company. She would be other things too, of course. She would have luxury, speed, and size as no other ship had ever had before. She was to epitomize the grandeur of the British Mercantile Marine, which was already in this troubled year of 1936 reaching up to new heights of achievement. She was to be the greatest ship the world had ever seen.

He walked past the mold loft, where section after section of the ship had been laid out on the scrive board, past the platers' shed, where red-hot steel had been shaped to form the gigantic hull now cradled on the launch way, past the furnace and along the dark cobbled approach road he had come to know so well. Gusts of wind and rain battered his face as he turned a corner and there suddenly she was, newly startling in her immensity even though he was looking up at her for perhaps the thou-

3

sandth time and the element of surprise should long ago have disappeared.

But surprise — or rather a kind of impersonal wonder — took hold of him as he stared up at the stem flanked by the tiered launching platform where tomorrow the King would watch his sister-in-law name the ship by releasing the traditional bottle of wine against her bow and sending her slipping down to the oily waters of the Clyde on the next stage of her career.

"Well, Beecher, are we going to have to postpone it?"

He jumped at hearing the familiar gritty voice behind him. There was only one person with that autocratic approach, only one person who pronounced his name "Bitcher," only one person with oddities far more highly developed than his own.

"Good heavens, sir, what are you doing out here on a wet and windy night like this?"

Sir Josiah Flint, chairman of the company, ignored this question and pressed on as he always did with the problem in hand.

"What are the chances? Can we launch her in a wind like this?"

"I wouldn't like to risk it."

Strictly speaking it was nothing whatever to do with the company, nor would it be until the ship had been completed and delivered. The launch of the hull of Job No. 379 was certainly a shipyard matter, for which MacDonald, the builder's naval architect, would answer. It was his job to calculate the slope of the launching way, just as the trim and stability remained the responsibility of the yard until the ship's trials had proved or disproved Peter Beecher's designs. Neither Flint nor Beecher, in fact, had any right to be where they were at that particular moment. However the company had been having its bigger ships built at this yard for over seventy years and there was a solid basis of experience and mutual understanding upon which their business relationship lay.

"She'll be launched on time tomorrow if *I* have anything to do with it," Flint remarked tersely, and without further ado wandered off on another perambulation, his hands crossed behind his back, his pince-nez tucked away in a waistcoat pocket, his gray spats just visible beneath the striped black trousers he

4

perennially wore. No one quite knew what went on in his head. He had made a point of being unpredictable. Physically accessible he might claim to be, in fact in the Liverpool office the Chairman's door was always left slightly ajar both to foster this idea of accessibility, and also to permit a draft to blow directly upon any visitor rash enough to take advantage of the invitation. But Josiah Flint was remote in himself with a sort of puckish habit of darting after ideas or suddenly leaving them cold and neglected. No one could call him dishonest, yet no one was ever quite sure of his real opinion, especially where other people were concerned.

Peter took a torch from his pocket and examined the daggers, or steel triggers, which held the ship in position pending her launch. Next morning hundreds of workmen, swinging their hammers in unison, would ram home innumerable finely tapered wedges. These would lift the hull a fraction of an inch above the position in which she had been built. Then when she was resting firmly in her cradle, that cradle which would slide down to the water with her and fall to pieces as she floated for the first time, the launching triggers would be cocked. From then on there would be no going back. Those six steel fingers were the earth's last hold on the ship and it would be those six triggers that the Duchess would release the next day when she pressed the button. Thereafter the ship would belong to the sea.

He had not expected to find anything wrong nor did any detail excite attention. But the insomnia he had now had since *Leviathan* had first been mooted (and only he and a handful of others knew what she was going to be named) would not yield to this one short midnight expedition. If he turned in now it would be six o'clock before he would get any sleep and he refused to take the drugs so frequently urged upon him. There was no bar or club on Clydeside at this hour of night where he could get a drink. He had no wish to bump into Flint again and he had just decided to walk slowly back to his hotel in the center of Glasgow when his eye caught sight of a lick of flame through the window of No. 2 Paint Shop, a mere fifty yards from the ship.

Jerked into action as if by a string, he ran yelling "Fire! Fire!" at the top of his voice. The swirling smoke from the shed filled him with fear and foreboding. A fire of any size at this time and at this place could be disastrous to *Leviathan*. Yet even by the time he reached the door of the shed, he realized that the blaze was already out of hand. There was a fire extinguisher by the door; this he upended and directed into the flames, but it was like throwing a teaspoonful of water on to a bonfire. Choked by the smoke and the fumes, he staggered out into the open air.

By this time one of the night watchmen had raised the alarm and help was converging from a number of different directions. Within ten minutes two fire brigades had arrived, followed by Sir James Gorston, the head of the shipyard, MacDonald, the architect, and Phillips, the chief engine designer.

As the fire grew in intensity, more and more firemen poured into the yard and it seemed to Beecher that the scene took on a prehistoric quality as though cavemen were executing some sort of ritual fire dance beside a slain brontosaurus. The great gaunt shape of *Leviathan* towered above the scene as the roof of the paint shed fell in and a fountain of sparks and flames plumed up into the night sky. By chance the wind was blowing away from the slipway but should it veer even for a few minutes it was obvious to Beecher that no human intervention could save the ship.

So he stood and watched, silent and helpless, while a tender, almost maternal feeling possessed him as he thought back over the growth of the great ship, springing as it did from a single idea in his brain. Surely she was not to be smitten at this critical point in her life? Wordlessly from his heart he began praying that *Leviathan* should be spared, and in the meanwhile firefighting forces continued to race into the shipyard from all over the Clyde.

Then at last the blaze reached its own climax and, almost as if it had suddenly lost interest, allowed itself to be doused and brought under control. Within another half hour the paint shop had burnt itself out, the fire had been prevented from spreading and the news of this event was on its way to the four corners of the earth. At that point it was discovered that *Leviathan* had claimed her first victim.

From out of the charred remains of the building, the firemen carried the dead body of old Wilfred Clawston, for fifty-five years the carver and decorator of special fireplaces, commemorative boards, and the like. Up in his cubby hole, and all ready for the morrow, was found the beautifully chased mallet in its carved casket which would be presented to the Duchess after the launch. Old Wilf had apparently run out of varnish and had gone down to burgle a fresh supply from the paint shop. He must have stopped, as he so often did, to relight his pipe, never for a moment paying any heed to the fire regulations which he had never agreed with and which he was in the habit of calling "a lot of fuss and poppycock for irresponsible apprentices."

By the time the fire broke out in the paint shop Josiah Flint had walked from the starboard side of *Leviathan*, underneath the stern with its four propellers, each of them weighing thirty-five tons, and up along the port side with the huge dark bulk of the ship between him and the rest of the shipyard. He had not been pleased to find Peter Beecher "messing around," as he put it to himself. Though possibly the most loyal and zealous of all his team, Flint saw his architect's midnight prowling as almost an intrusion into his own preserve. Like any experienced leader, Flint knew there was room only for one at the top, and he intended to keep it that way. He relished the seclusion. He was never lonely. It had taken forty years and a hard fight to gain control of the company. Now that he had had it in his bony hands for the past twelve years, he did not allow anyone to approach the throne too closely. He had very few friends. His wife had died five years ago and they had not had a family.

He stood now in his characteristic stance, his hands behind his back, his wing collar almost aglow in the darkness, gazing up at the ship which more than any of the others had been a special child of his own. He was aware of a lot of problems seething about in his mind. Yet he did not worry. Indeed, had he ever let anxiety plague him for long, he could never have survived up to now. Unlike Beecher, he could sleep soundly whenever he chose. But when more problems tried to press in than he had time or energy to cope with, he went round shutting doors in his mind after first peering quizzically into each room where the matter was duly contained. Then like a housekeeper with her bunch of keys, he would go jangling off down the corridor to another part of the building.

The hull of the ship loomed above him, a black shape set against a stormy night sky. On a sudden impulse, Flint decided to go on board. He never analyzed these whims. People thought him odd, even a little crazy. He didn't care. All through his life he had obeyed his instinct first and his reason second. It was the golden thread. It brought him sudden opportunities, energy, people the company needed, and fresh ideas. One needed courage to follow some of his ideas, but in their train came the success and the wealth which was all that the world ever saw or bothered about.

There was a working ladder up some scaffolding and this he began to climb. Even at seventy-one his body still had a wiriness which had long been its strength. About halfway up the ship's side the scaffolding came to an end and from there a rope ladder with wooden cleats led on up to the port side of the fo'c'sle. Already some fifty feet from the ground, Flint hesitated a moment before trusting himself to the swaying rope ladder for the final forty-foot climb. "Ridiculous foolhardiness," he could hear his general manager saying after portentously clearing his throat. "What did the old fool think he was up to this time, climbing about like a monkey in a tree?" The vision of Fabian Mitchell's paunchy, well-fed expression at those interminable board meetings gave him the impulse to go on, and braving the strong wind which roared gustily along the exposed flanks of the ship, Flint went up hand over hand till he reached the upper deck of the ship, the better part of a hundred feet from the ground.

He enjoyed the feeling of exhilaration the climb had given him. As he levered himself up on to the deck, a loose stanchion suddenly wobbled and for a split second he felt he would fall.

But he held on tight, poised half over the side, until the panic left him and he had full command of his muscles again. Then no longer surprised by the uncertain hold the stanchion afforded him, he pulled himself up and on to the fo'c'sle, dusted off his black overcoat and almost instinctively brought out the famous pince-nez spectacles which gave his attention such a concentrated look. High up there, with the lights of Glasgow below him, the wind and the rain buffeting his face, he felt both a sense of occasion and a drawing into himself of power, as though a number of separate pieces were coalescing into one whole, a unity greater than its parts. *Leviathan* was *his* ship at that moment as it never would be in quite the same way again.

He walked up to the stem and looked down on the launching platform with its glassed-in partition some fifty feet below. Tomorrow at two-thirty what scenes there would be! The King, the Duke of York, and the Duchess of York, who was to name and launch the ship, Queen Mary, and other members of the Royal Family would all be there. To organize their presence on the Clyde at that time had been no mean feat in itself. The Court was still in mourning for King George V and now there was this gnawing, creeping scandal about the King and that American woman which was still only mentioned in whispers in England, although the American papers were playing it up. Flint shrugged his shoulders in the darkness and looked down the sloping length of the ship to the oily glinting river beyond. The King's private life was his own affair. So long as *Leviathan* was properly launched on the morrow, the King could do as he pleased. Tomorrow it was *Leviathan* and the company that mattered. Nothing, nothing on God's earth was going to stop that.

He looked out into the darkness trying to discern the banks of the Clyde. In some of those fields even now people would be sleeping in their cars. The police reckoned two hundred and fifty thousand people at least would be watching the launch. Every bed, every settee in Glasgow, and for miles around, would be occupied this night. Old Mother Cathcart had told him that and many other titbits of local news, when

he arrived to stay in her murky rooms which he always preferred to the luxury hotel or the lavish shipyard hospitality he
was entitled to receive.

"The Lord love us, Mr. Flint," she had greeted him, eyeing
him in the old aggressive way as the chauffeur brought his
bags in from the Rolls, "it's a good thing you came now. I was
just going to let your room go for four times the money you'll
pay me. To a Jewish gentleman, too, in the jewelry trade."

"I've a title now, Mrs. Cathcart," Flint had answered severely, giving her hand the one abrupt shake it habitually received since his apprentice days when "Mother" Cathcart's
boarding house was the only home he knew. "It won't do you
any harm to call me Sir Josiah for the few remaining days of
your life."

But old Mother Cathcart had folded her arms and looked
down on him impassively from her eighty-three years.

"The day I indulge in that piece of folly, Mr. Flint," she retorted to the private enjoyment of the chauffeur and of the
neighbors peeping from behind their lace curtains, "you can
sew me up in a shroud and take me to sea in one of your oily
great hulks. Come on in now, I've your tea ready for you in
the kitchen. No doubt you'll be cold and hungry now from
your journey."

Colleagues like Fabian Mitchell with his comfortable Dorking home, his public school background, and his first class
season ticket could never understand him going back to his
old digs in one of the poorer quarters of Glasgow. They regarded it as inverted exhibitionism, or gave it some other such
fancy title, simply because Flint never had been and never
would be "one of them." But then almost all his colleagues on
the Board of the company had been "their fathers' sons." Outwardly, they gave him lip-service loyalty; inwardly, they resented him. They could not understand what it was like to be
born in a Glasgow slum, to be brought up an orphan, and
finally to rise through hard work, guts, and sustained brilliance
to the top of the most famous steamship company in the world.
But Mother Cathcart knew what it meant. The twinkle in her
eye had long been one of the few things which gave a deep

meaning to his life. In return, and in token of the distance he had come since his apprentice days, Mother Cathcart would be there tomorrow on the launching platform among the great of the land, her old-fashioned hat slightly askew, her robust old heart full of pride. She would be "Mr." Flint's most special guest.

He started to walk aft down the sloping deck, slippery and treacherous from the rain. His other directors, and in particular his "inner team," came one by one to mind. First of them, of course, was Fabian Mitchell, waiting to step into his shoes with those polished good manners Flint both admired and detested. Then there was Captain Masterton, the Marine Superintendent, gruff, sound, his judgment weathered by a lifetime at sea, full of prejudices, even if they were "the right ones," and instantly on guard against any outside civilian interference with the Navigating Department.

There was Renshaw, the Engineering Superintendent, even more jealous of his "private empire" than Masterton. Flint played one off against the other as a matter of routine without either of them being particularly aware of Flint's role in the struggle. Indeed, Masterton and Renshaw merely personified at the highest company level the unceasing war between engine room and deck which has raged with varying intensity since steam first went to sea. Peter Beecher, the naval architect, was a law unto himself, superficially the easiest of any of them to bully or coerce, in actual fact far more surely grounded in technical know-how than either Masterton or Renshaw, even though, being still in his early forties, he was the youngest member of the inner cabal.

Then there was Frederick Fox, the Chief Catering Superintendent, upon whom the company's superb reputation for good food and luxurious living so largely depended. There was Max Laban, the American Director, whose nervous energy and skill was responsible for so much of the company's transatlantic passenger trade. Max Laban with his mania for publicity would be there tomorrow, as usual irrepressibly full of impossible schemes promoted with what Fabian Mitchell called "that embarrassing push," and aided in London by that little hunchback Quilly whom he had once persuaded Flint to accept as assistant to the General Manager, but whose loyalty, Flint had concluded, lay in the first place with Laban in New York and only after that with the Liverpool and London offices. In fact, Quilly was Laban's spy on this side of the Atlantic. Mitchell, to whom he was directly responsible, disliked him intensely and had done his best to dispose of the little man from the moment the appointment was mooted. But Quilly knew his way around on both sides of the Atlantic. Over in New York he had worked in the hotel business, and for a time had run a travel agency. He was at home in a number of circles which did not normally touch each other. Flint had studied him for a while, had supported him against Mitchell's most violent attacks and by thus subtly guaranteeing his position had transferred to himself a part of the loyalty Quilly gave to Max Laban. This had proved to be a very shrewd move on Flint's part. Now Quilly was not only the New York spy, but also acted as an unofficial, one-man intelligence system for the benefit of the Chairman.

In another few hours all of them would be there to watch "Flint's Baby Hippo," as Mitchell had once called the ship, take to her natural element. Soon there would be an end to those discussions and arguments, stretching back almost to the time Flint had been made Chairman of the Company, as to whether two giant ships for the transatlantic service were equivalent to or better than three vessels of medium size. Soon the facts would be established, the answer known.

There was a lull in the wind, and suddenly Flint was startled to hear the clang of the fire engine from down in the yard. It came from the starboard side, and as swiftly as the slope of the deck allowed, he ran across, just skirting the gaping hole where one day a hatch cover would be. From where he stood he could not see what was happening, but presently he saw flames darting up from one of the sheds; there was a smell of burning paint, and, far below, men were running in different directions. His period of reflection was over. This was no time to be high up on the fo'c'sle of a half-built ship. He did not relish scrambling down that rope ladder in a hurry. Then, as his brain began to react, he remembered there was a midships gangway over which he could perfectly well have walked. He determined to find it, and at that moment *Leviathan* claimed her second casualty.

As he began to make his way cautiously aft, his foot caught in a ring bolt causing him to stumble, slip, fall over, and then roll with terrifying speed towards the black mouth of the hatch. Instinctively he clutched at the coping and it must have been this deflection of momentum which saved his life. Instead of falling eighty feet to the bottom of the ship, by some extraordinary quirk his body caught on the deck below. The shock of the fall stunned him and his left leg was struck hard just above the ankle, the bones splintering with a sickening crack. With an expiring cry of pain Sir Josiah Flint, K.B.E., Chairman of the Transoceanic Steamship Company, lost consciousness in the darkness of the deck below, his whereabouts unknown to anyone in the outside world.

Four of the sleepers on the "Night Scotsman" were occupied by Fabian Mitchell and his family, and three more by their friends the Spicers. "Pity we didn't simply take a coach to ourselves," Susan Spicer had said, as they had installed themselves at Euston to the usual accompaniment of fuss from her mother and the throwing-about-of-weight of her father. How she hated these scenes! Just because her father was an M.P. and a Director of the railway company, there was no need to behave like an outraged *prima donna* when a mistake showed up in the bookings. And whenever the Spicers traveled, mistakes and misunderstandings sprang out of nothing. They all seemed designed to prove how important and powerful a man Sir Henry Spicer had made himself and how pointless it was to oppose him in anything great or small.

There was a rap at the communicating door between her compartment and the next, followed by Joan Mitchell's husky seventeen-year-old voice.

"Hey! Sue, are you asleep? Can I come in?"

A moment later her friend slipped in and perched herself on the foot of the bed.

"I'm fed up with counting sheep. I wish we had a gramophone, don't you? We could have a party. I know Alan's got a bottle of gin hidden away. Shall I go and fetch him?"

Joan was always bursting with little ideas, dashing here, dashing there. They were the same age and Joan was perhaps her best friend. They had grown up virtually next door to each other, gone to the same school, shared the same passions and crazes. Alan, Joan's nineteen-year-old brother, had fallen in love with her, fallen out of love with her, and had now reverted to being a sort of honorary brother of her own. But already their paths were beginning to diverge.

"Yes, go and drag him along if you want," Susan said as she reached for her dressing gown, "but he's not to start laughing. You know how Mummy goes on about our not being kids any more." She dropped into an imitation of her mother: "You let Alan come into your room *in pajamas?* Really, Susan, it's high time you realized you're no longer a child."

A few minutes later Joan returned with her bulky, tousled-haired brother and the bottle of gin. Alan had been asleep but the idea of any sort of party never failed to arouse him. He was like his father, large, good-natured, rather slow, addicted to rugger, "Oxford bags" (he was in his first term at St. John's), and the wearing of overlong club mufflers. He was also persevering with a pipe, though as yet this was a somewhat awkward and unmanageable toy. They shshed each other into whispers, poured out the gin and enjoyed the illicitness of the occasion.

"If they surprise us," Alan said, "we'll all climb into Susan's bed and then really shock 'em."

"No, thank you," said Susan. "The first man to do that will be there because I invite him and for no other reason."

"Lordy! what a prude!" Alan remarked getting out his pipe and the inevitable box of matches. His consumption of matches ran at about a box an hour. "You virgins are all the same — no finesse."

"Where on earth did you pick that word up?"

"Well, anyway, I think the three of us in one bed is a rather jolly idea." He relit his pipe and looked over at his sister.

14

"There's nothing like a bit of incest for brightening up the night train to Scotland."

Susan smiled at him, took a sip at her drink and drew her dressing gown more tightly around her. He was a nice boy, but she wished he wouldn't show off in that oafish way. She supposed they must really be growing out of each other, growing away into that area of "incommunicability" which adults seemed to inhabit. And this she did not want to happen. The three of them were far too "thick" just to drift apart in that way.

"Is that what comes of reading classics?" she asked. In her mind the ancient Greeks were always getting up to extraordinary nonsense with each other, and always for the most obscure reasons.

"Well, of course the Greeks knew what they were doing," Alan said as if he'd been commenting on some piece of modern politics, "so did the Romans for that matter."

"I dare say, but look where it got them."

"Human nature doesn't change." He enjoyed trying to shock them. "Do you mean to say your father's never made a pass at you yet? You're pretty enough."

"Don't be disgusting, Alan," Joan cut in. "Susan's father is a Member of Parliament. And a Tory to boot."

"They're the worst of the lot. We know all about *them* up at Oxford. The trouble with our parents' generation is that they don't know the first thing about sex. Ours never mention the word, do they, Joan? And I'll bet they haven't been to bed with each other for donkeys' years."

"Well, mine have separate rooms," Susan put in, "but I don't see that proves anything at all."

Neither of the girls really liked that sort of talk and Joan seized a chance of changing the conversation.

"I've got a wonderful idea," she said. "After the launch tomorrow, why don't we stow away in the ship and whiz over to America? I'm mad about America and you're always hankering to go to sea, Alan."

"How like a girl!" Alan remarked loftily condescending, "you think a ship is launched and that's that — she just chugs

15

off to sea. Job No. 379 hasn't even got her engines yet. She's nothing but an empty shell. She won't be completed for another eighteen months."

"Then what's all the fuss about now?"

"The launch of a ship is always the most critical time; she's the biggest ship in the world; there's never been anything like her before."

"But you *do* want to go to sea in her, Alan?" Susan asked. He did not immediately answer, first finishing his drink and then relighting his pipe. He had brown eyes and she liked the way they wrinkled up when he smiled. For a moment she thought he wasn't going to reply. Then he shot her a shy, almost secretive look through the smoke, as if he was judging how far he could trust her.

"That's always been my idea," he said, "but as you know I didn't get into Dartmouth when I was thirteen, and Father wouldn't hear of my going to one of the Merchant Service training ships like the *Conway*, so here I am — having just scraped through matric. And I suppose I'll just scrape through Oxford."

"And then?"

"The dear old Civil Service, I fancy. At least that's Father's idea. I'll never get into the I.C.S., but I might just make the Home. Father thinks I ought to go in for something safe and secure."

There was a faraway look in his eyes. For a moment or so they sat listening to the rhythm of the wheels, the little compartment full of blue smoke. Susan liked both of them best in this sort of mood. Joan so obviously doted on her brother, and now she was leaning her head against his shoulder lost in her thoughts. The three of them were very close to each other at times like this.

"Why don't we all go to sea?" Susan asked suddenly, a little astonished at herself.

"All of us?" Joan echoed blankly.

"Yes. You can be a nurse — that's what you've always wanted to do. I can be a stewardess, and I bet I'd make thousands in tips, and Alan — what could Alan do? He could run the ship."

"That's just what I couldn't do," he said sadly. "I've missed my chance of becoming a deck officer. And anyway, you're miles too young to be a stewardess."

"Well, then, I'll be something else. They do have women on board. All sorts of girls go to sea. Someone has to run those shops for instance. And then don't they have female pursers? I once heard your father say the company was introducing purserettes as an experiment. Of course I'd need shorthand and typing, but I could easily mug that up in eighteen months. It's a wonderful idea."

"I'd like to be a Nippy in a liner," Joan said. "Why don't they have waitresses, I wonder? Then all the passengers you didn't like you could slosh the food in their faces. Feeling seasick, madam? Try our nice greasy onion soup! Just the thing for bilious old bags."

"You're making a joke of it," Susan said quietly, "but I'm serious. I want to do something with my life. I'm not going to sit around at home, being a deb and suffocating at all those dreary, dreary hunt balls. Everyone has a job nowadays — look at Amy Johnson and Amelia Earhart and all those others. Well, that's what *I'm* going to do."

"I'd like to hear what your parents say to such an idea," Alan said, but she knew his mind was already exploring the possibilities. "At least our father doesn't talk very much — but Uncle Henry's really got the gift of the gab. I suppose he has to when you think of it — after all, he's a politician."

"I don't care what Father says," Susan said impatiently. "It's *my* life; I shall do what I like."

"Hear, hear!" Joan said, sitting up. "Just look what a mess *they've* made of the world. Do you know Mummy said the other day that after the war she and Daddy *actually believed* in the League of Nations. They were so green they actually *believed* it was the war to end all wars. Huh! *now* look at the bog our elders and betters are making of it all. Look at Spain. Look at Hitler, and dear sweet old Musso with his castor oil.

I agree with you, Sue. We ought to find out what *we* want to do with our lives and then do it."

"Well *I'm* going to go to sea in the biggest ship in the world, I'm going to be part of it and I'm going to help to run it. I don't know how — but that's what *I'm* going to do. What about you? Are we making a pact? The three of us — somehow or other?"

Joan looked at her brother and her brother looked at Susan. It was odd how Susan had always been the real leader of the three. It was always Susan who first had the ideas, Susan who gave them the vital push into doing whatever it was they'd dreamed and drifted about.

"All right," Alan said, shaking her hand. "I don't know *how* any more than you do, but it's an aim — it's a pact. In any case, so far as I'm concerned nothing could be worse than the Civil Service — even if I do end up as a greaser in the hottest boiler room of the ship."

Part of Quilly's power in the company lay in his instant availability at all hours of the day or night. He was flexible. He had no set routine. In a company as old and with as many ramifications as the Transoceanic, to have someone very near to the top who was equally at home in the crew "pig" aboard one of the Company liners or in the Savoy Grill lunching an important client, who had a quick shrewd brain hiding behind a timid, almost servile personality, who always had fresh ideas and was not afraid of seizing an opportunity on his own initiative, but who always took good care to credit it to the man who should have had those ideas himself, in fact a character who apparently did not want anyone else's job but who was content to be the interpreter, the confidant, and repository of secrets — to have such a man, who was also a hunchback so that he could be looked down on and patronized either openly or in secret, was an invaluable asset to the company.

People said Quilly must have a sixth sense in that he was always first with the news; and if not on the spot when something happened, could be there in a matter of minutes. However, they never considered what lay behind such an ability. A good portion of Quilly's not very generous salary (the company being "the Company" paid its servants as little as it could get away with following the Victorian precepts of Joshua Tunney, its founder) went on tips, rewards, and remembrances. This was not the sort of thing to be justified on an expense account claim. If anything unusual happened, it was always, "Run and tell Mr. Quilly, there'll be half a crown in it for you" — or five bob or a dollar or, more rarely, and for something very special, a crisp one-pound note.

The evening before *Leviathan* was launched Quilly had been on board another of the company's liners, the *Pluto*, which was being refitted in a nearby yard. He was visiting with the American Director, Maxwell Laban, and his wife who, on Quilly's recommendation, had crossed the Atlantic a couple of weeks earlier on board the *Pluto*. This crossing had not been without its motive. Laban had wanted to travel in a bigger liner, whereas the *Pluto* was one of the company's slower ships. She was usually employed on the Canadian run, but she also happened to be commanded by Quilly's unlikeliest friend, Captain Basil Bellerophon Banks, one of the most striking characters in the North Atlantic, and indeed in the whole British Mercantile Marine. It was this man whom Quilly had privately decided should command the *Leviathan*. Seagoing personnel matters were, of course, none of Quilly's business, and in any case "Bible Banks" was still a junior captain by company standards. But Quilly took a delight in pulling strings behind the scenes that nobody knew about, and then in keeping quiet when the result he had planned came about.

Quilly, moreover, was an old hand at oblique lobbying, as he put it. He was not afraid of planting a seed and then giving it time to germinate while he got on with other things. He knew that Flint, guided by his Marine Superintendent, had already decided upon the *Leviathan*'s first captain, and that once that appointment was made a general post would take place in which Banks at best could only move up a notch or two.

But he also knew that Flint detested the principle of "Buggins' turn next," as he cordially loathed the Civil Service outlook in any shape or form. Flint had an eye for the men he wanted and no company regulations would stop him putting such a man where he should be once his mind was made up. Yet he would take advice. Thus Quilly set about subtly publicizing his protégé, who himself had not the faintest idea of Quilly's machinations, to the various high-tension personalities in the company such as Maxie Laban, who might one day be consulted by the Chairman in passing and, as it were, casually. Hence the Labans' trip in *Pluto;* hence the return visit on the eve of the launch, when Quilly, the Labans, and Basil Bellerophon Banks all chanced to be in Glasgow at one and the same time.

The Labans and Quilly were just being seen off the ship by their bearded host when Flint's old chauffeur, white-faced and panting, came running up the gangway.

"Oh! Mr. Quilly, sir, thank heavens I found you. There's a fire in the yard and Sir J.'s disappeared."

"How do you mean, disappeared?"

"Well, sir, you know how he likes to walk about near the ship. I always wait outside for him in the car. Well, tonight he was longer than usual and I was just getting properly worried when a couple of fire engines went tearing into the yard. I locked up the car and ran in after them. First person I saw was Mr. Beecher shaking like an aspirin. 'Have you seen the Chairman?' he asks me. 'I think something may have happened. Come on, we'll look around No. 379.' So we do that, but there isn't a trace. Then at the foot of a ladder up the side we find one of those chamois leather gloves Sir J. always wears. That did it. 'He's gone up that ladder,' Mr. Beecher says, 'and he's out of his mind. Go and find Mr. Quilly,' he says, 'and you'd better get an ambulance and a platoon of doctors . . . and a strait jacket,' he yelled as he started clambering up. So here I am, Mr. Quilly, sir, and could you come quick? I've got the car alongside now. Oh! dear, sir, and No. 379 being launched in a few hours' time."

Quilly turned to Captain Banks.

"Captain Banks, I suppose your doctor isn't aboard by any chance?" The beard twitched and the eyes twinkled like angry stars.

"You suppose entirely wrong, sir. All my officers are aboard until after the launch. I've already sent for the surgeon."

A few minutes later Quilly, Laban, and the young Irish doctor from the *Pluto* were on their way round to Job No. 379. Captain Banks had promised to send Mrs. Laban back to their hotel in a taxi and he had said something to the doctor which Quilly could not overhear before they went down the gangway. Whatever it was had put young Doctor Kelly into a continuing chuckle at some private joke, and in a moment or so Quilly could not resist asking if the Captain had given any last-minute instructions.

"Instructions!" Kelly retorted. "He told me I was slow off the mark, said I wasn't properly dressed and that he'd like to see me in his cabin on my return. Glory be! He'll have us all Admirals in the R.N.R. before he's through with this ship."

"You don't think that's a good idea? It's discipline which has made this company what it is."

"I think it's a splendid idea," Kelly said with a wry smile, "but it so happens I'm already in the Reserve. I'm all for being kept on my toes, but there's no one like Captain Banks for falling back on the Bible when he wants to ram home a point."

"How do you mean?"

"Just as I followed you down the gangway, buttoning up my coat, he called after me: ' "The sluggard is wiser in his own conceit than seven men that can render a reason." Proverbs twenty-six, Mr. Kelly. Remember that next time there's an emergency call.' "

"It doesn't seem to worry you much," Quilly remarked.

"Well, I'm Irish for a start," Kelly said, as the car drew up alongside No. 379. "Then, you see, Captain Banks happens also to be one of the finest masters it's been my luck to sail with so far. If he wants to shout the Protestant Bible into my sinful ears, what should I care? We'll be converting him yet."

Ethel Laban returned to their hotel in a reflective mood. She was dreading the launch the next day with all its British pomposities. She hated Glasgow and had enjoyed their evening's escape aboard the *Pluto*. The pocket Captain Bligh, as she called him privately, though it would need some pocket to contain his mountainous body, had become quite a friend over the years they had known him. He was certainly a personality. Something of a bully, she supposed, though anyone of force and character who used his authority in these milk and water days was accused of being a bully.

But bullies were so often snivelers and flatterers when the coin was reversed, and there was none of that in Captain Banks. She saw it all the time now that Max was a director of Transoceanic in charge of the American side, and since they were also Jewish, the insincerity of the flattery, the barely disguised hypocrisy of those who bowed their stiff heads in order to progress up the ladder, disgusted her. It was the same in the theater. Ethel's father had owned three theaters in New York, and now her brother ran them instead. So many people said one thing and quite obviously thought another. It was refreshing to come upon a man like Captain Banks who lived his life by certain principles and made no bones about it.

She wondered if anything had happened to Flint or whether it was a false alarm. Knowing her husband's taste for the headlines she fully expected a call from the Press. They must be around in strength for the morrow's launch, she imagined, and any mishap to the Chairman of Transoceanic, who himself hated publicity, would be manna from heaven. She undressed and creamed her face. Sometimes Max was a difficult man to be married to; he really believed, which Ethel certainly didn't, that all publicity was good for the company. His life was the company. Well, a man had to have his work and Max had certainly come a long way since his days as a fifteen-dollar-a-week clerk in a tramp shipping firm, owned by a friend of her father's. He had got as far as he was ever likely to do with Transoceanic. Approaches from other firms had now become frequent. The money offered was always far in excess of the salary he drew from Transoceanic.

But Max loved the company. Having jeered at and fought the principle for years, he now openly preferred the lesser salary plus the honor of serving Transoceanic to the much greater rewards he could very easily get from other companies. To her husband, she admitted with a sigh as she climbed into bed and began reading a book, the launch of the greatest ship in the world would finally prove him right. *Leviathan* and, later on, her sister ship were to be the apex to all his ideas. *Leviathan* was to be the greatest flowering of the greatest liner company in the world.

She was just going to turn out the light when her husband arrived back and, with characteristic energy, began undressing, talking, gargling, and brushing his teeth more or less all at once. He was in high good spirits.

"What a story, Ethy, what a story it nearly was! A reporter arrived about five minutes after we did. I gave him all he wanted to know. Can you beat this? Old man Flint had climbed a rope ladder in *that* gale and at *his* age all the way up to the fo'c'sle; he'd tripped up and then very nearly fell all the way down again to the bottom of the ship. Talk about luck! Somehow or other he managed to stick on the deck below. His left leg's a nasty mess, though. But think what headlines it would have made if he *had* been killed in *Leviathan* a few hours before the launch. Made me think of the *Great Eastern*, but of course they never did launch her. They had to float her off sideways into the Thames. Boy! I hope that doesn't happen to us."

Ethel could not remember what the *Great Eastern* was and had to ask.

"She was Brunel's ship," her husband called out between gargles in the bathroom, "the great Victorian engineer. She was for years and years the biggest ship in the world. About twenty thousand tons. Well, they're supposed to have walled up a man accidentally in the double bottoms when she was being built. So all her life she was carrying a corpse around inside her hull. And that ship had some life, I can tell you. She lasted about thirty-five years. Gosh, Ethy! Suppose the same thing had happened to *Leviathan* — only the corpse had been Flinty!"

"So he'll miss the ceremony tomorrow?"

"Not Sir J.; not the Chairman. He must have been in great

pain but he directed the whole operation of having himself carried off the ship in a stretcher. Said he'd be at the launch even if it meant coming in a hospital bed. He'll do it, too."

"I suppose Quilly was hard at his 'Yes-man' act?"

Max stuck his head out of the bathroom and looked at his wife.

"Quilly's O.K.," he said. "Why do you take on about him so much?"

"I don't trust him. He's too liable to stick a knife in your back."

"*I* trust him. Nobody else does — except Flint. The result is, if he's loyal to anyone it's to the two of us. I keep telling you, Ethy, in a company the size of this one there has to *be* a Quilly. If he didn't exist, we'd have to invent him."

"I don't see why."

"Well, I'm not going to start in on all that at this time of night."

"Why do you think he enticed us aboard the *Pluto* tonight?"

Laban stopped for a second to think.

"I think it was my suggestion," he said. "Anyway, Biblical Banks is an old favorite of ours."

"Quilly would like you to think it was your idea," Ethel retorted. "That's how he works. You want my opinion, Max? Quilly keeps bringing you and Captain Banks together because he wants Banks appointed captain of *Leviathan*."

"For the love of mike, the Navigating Department is nothing whatever to do with Quilly, or with me for that matter. Neither of us have control of that side of things."

"I dare say Florence said that of the Borgias — or the German army of Hitler."

"You're letting your romantic ideas run away with you, honey. In any case, suppose you're right — it's all for the good of the company."

"Is it?" Ethel said with a yawn. "I wonder if Captain Masterton or Mr. Mitchell would agree. We could ask them tomorrow."

"We could do no such thing," Max Laban said as he turned off the light and climbed into bed beside her. "Tomorrow is the day of days."

"Wasn't there a fire as well?" she asked sleepily as she cuddled in closer.

"Oh! that was nothing," Max murmured already halfway asleep. "Some old fool workman lit his pipe in the paint shop or something. There was never any danger to *Leviathan.*"

By noon the next day the gale had blown itself out, being replaced by a gray autumn drizzle. It was somehow appropriate, Peter Beecher thought, as he stood watching the final preparations, that the Clyde in November should not be bathed in improbable sunshine. This was no Ascot meeting. He had never known a doctor drool over the birth of a human being — nor a naval architect over the launch of a ship. Both were highly practical matters. A great deal could go wrong.

The experts, of course, knew the process that should happen, but it was what lay outside the calculable that one had to remember. The launching of a ship was like the sounding of the first note in any great human enterprise — an act of faith. No one could foretell what the future of a ship or a human being would be, but in making the most meticulous preparations for either event an instinctive trust in a divine and guiding Providence was, in a way, inevitable. And if not, Peter thought with a mental shrug, then what hope is there for any of us in anything we do?

By this time the royal party had arrived at Ibrox Station and the civic formalities had already begun. The route to the shipyard had been lined solid since early dawn. Grubby children waved damp Union Jacks, their mothers with bright scarves over their heads shouted at them to keep out of the way of the familiar yellow and green trams until these, too, ceased to run and the wet cobbled streets, drained of their normal traffic, contained only bright-eyed Glaswegians, marshaled good-naturedly by the police with their checkered cap bands. Aged crones, muffled to the mouth, leaned out of tenement windows, hawkers sold souvenirs and balloons, a bearded prophet in a dirty macintosh paraded a sandwich board which said, "Repent, for the Kingdom of Heaven is at hand."

Elsewhere, on both sides of the river, every point of vantage from which the ship could be seen was packed with people. The estimate of over a quarter of a million visitors to the Clyde must have been well exceeded. Almost no work would be done on the river that day. By two o'clock the stream of guests arriving inside the shipyard rose to a peak. The launching platform, with its glassed-in royal partition containing a raised dais and the four gilded chairs, and behind them the seats for important personages, had now all but filled up, leaving only the four royal chairs empty and expectant. To one side of the dais was a twelve-foot model of *Leviathan*, showing the launching cradle, the ways and the drag chains which would bring her to rest once she was afloat. The bottle of wine to be broken at the naming ceremony hung outside, gaily bedecked with colored ribbons, and ready to be dropped against the stem as the ship moved down the shipway.

Standing selfconsciously on another side of the launching platform, their gray hair plastered into unusual tidiness, their old bodies encased in dark Sunday-best suits, stood a head foreman engineer, a brass finisher, a boilerworks machineman, an assistant shipwright foreman, a plater, and a riveter, each with over fifty years' service to the shipyard to his credit. Elsewhere on the launching platform Cabinet Ministers, leaders of public life in Scotland, representatives of the shipping world, of Lloyd's, and of the City of London now stood with their wives and families. Susan Spicer and her father and mother were next to the Mitchells. Near them stood the volatile Max Laban and his wife, within whispering distance of Quilly, who, in turn, had his eye on a platoon of Press photographers awaiting the royal party's arrival.

Special arrangements had had to be made for Sir Josiah Flint whose will-power had beaten his doctor into agreeing that he could attend in a wheelchair, his left leg stuck out and encased in plaster, his movements watched anxiously by old Mother Cathcart in her best Sunday hat. He looked pale and still suffering from shock, as indeed he was, but the striped trousers still had their impeccable crease, his chamois gloves made a spot of yellow against the surrounding black and his pince-nez sat at their usual business-like angle on his narrow, pointed nose. In another place stood Captain Basil Bellerophon Banks, resplendent in his uniform with the D.S.C. and Reserve Decoration prominent among his medals, his beard handsomely combed, a small pocket Bible in his left hand and his eyes fixed almost hypnotically at the thousand-foot length of *Leviathan's* hull, at her narrowly tapered bows, at the whole vast ship he had every intention of one day coming to command.

Suddenly a sigh growing into a murmur, which in turn became hoarse, frantic cheering announced the arrival at the special gangway of the King and the royal party. Peter Beecher, waiting to be presented, surrendered himself almost with astonishment to the surge of pride and loyalty generated by thousands upon thousands of people waiting there patiently for the launching of this vast ship, the child of his brain. Peter Beecher lived so much in his thoughts that emotion often took him by surprise.

As His Majesty stepped out of the car, as the band played "God Save the King" and the thin drizzle continued to blow in his face, Peter remembered, at a speed beyond his control, the hundreds and hundreds of drawings, the endless discussions, the to-and-fro, hammer and anvil process by which a workable compromise had been achieved in the design of the ship. He remembered the day the keel had been laid; then the framing as rib by rib the hull took shape, to be followed by the plating in a daily crescendo of riveting. More vaguely, since he was not directly concerned, he remembered the other problems the giant ship had occasioned — the finance and the Government guarantee, the placing of the construction risks insurance, and the negotiations of the scores of subcontracts the ninety-thousand-ton ship entailed. Now, in a few short moments, *Leviathan* would take to the water, his work on her largely over. He found his train of thought abruptly broken as the Chairman of the shipyard presented him to His Majesty King Edward VIII.

Proceeding up to the Royal Pavilion, the King, Queen Mary, and the Duke and Duchess of York took their places on the dais. Sir Josiah Flint was wheeled forward in his chair, other directors and officials of the shipyard and the Transoceanic Steamship Company were presented together with the long-service shipyard workers. Fabian Mitchell, in place of Flint, read a loyal address to which the King, with somber face and hesitant voice, replied.

It was now very nearly time. The sky had darkened and as the King spoke a sudden squall beat down upon them all. Though women's hats and coats were being ruined, no one seemed even to flinch; Peter Beecher, watching the scene, his eyes continually drawn back to *Leviathan*, marveled at the power which royalty — or at any rate British royalty — had to subordinate any outer and temporary misfortune to the inner radiance of fine and noble ideas. "The very sight of this great ship," the King had said, "brings home to us how essential it is for the welfare of man that the arts of peaceful industry should continue — arts in the promotion of which Scotland has long held a leading place. The city of Glasgow has been for Scotland the principal doorway opening upon the world. The narrow waters of the Clyde have been the cradle of a large part of Britain's mercantile marine. So that it is right that from here should come our foremost achievement in that connection — the greatest of the ships that ply to and fro across the Atlantic, like shuttles in a mighty loom weaving a fabric of friendship and understanding between the people of Britain and the United States. It is altogether fitting that the noblest vessel ever built in Britain, and built with the help of her Government and people, should be dedicated to this service. This great ship has been planned, and rightly planned, for success. Indeed to plan for anything short of success must inevitably lead to failure. We wish this ship God speed and a long, a prosperous, and a happy life."

As these words were spoken there was a flash of lightning, a rumble of distant thunder and a slight increase in the light rain now gustily and almost playfully counterpointing the ceremony. By this time the six chosen apprentices had run up to the Managing Director of the shipyard with the safety pins from the daggers holding *Leviathan* in place. It was high tide and the moment had come.

Thousands of people held their breath and sent up a prayer as the Duchess stepped forward, touched the launching button and declared in a strong clear voice, "I name this ship *Leviathan* and wish success to her and all who sail in her." At the same time she released the bottle of wine which swung and broke against the ship's side. As this happened *Leviathan* herself seemed to quiver, as though she had in fact been brought alive. There was an apprehensive gasp from the crowd followed by a shout in unison "She's away!" as the ship began slowly to move.

It was a deeply impressive spectacle. The initial trembling was scarcely perceptible, yet everyone so anxiously watching knew instinctively that it had taken place. A sense of immense inevitability dominated the thousands upon thousands of spectators. As the great ship gathered speed, her movement took on a cataclysmic quality, the unexpected awesomeness of her mass in motion causing people to hold their breath. People were crying and people were swallowing and people were smiling bright-eyed at one another as if to extend a common human comfort in the face of an experience far outside the normal workaday range of emotion.

Smoothly and gracefully down the ways she slid to be greeted as she touched the water by a deafening chorus of steam whistles from all the other craft in the river. This, in turn, was almost drowned by the rattle and thunder of the drag chains, the swirling cloud of dust from which rose up and all but hid the ship and the river from the launching platform. *Leviathan* was afloat.

The tension broke, and the vast crowd, from being one coagulated mass, began to split up first into groups and then into individual men, women, and children. *Leviathan* was securely borne on the oily waters of the Clyde. The ceremony was over.

As soon as it was seen that the vessel was safely launched, the waiting tugs steamed out to meet her and the next process of nosing her into the fitting-out basin began. Back on the launching platform a lone figure in a wheelchair remained looking down on the now empty ways. Silent and still Flint sat there brooding on the great event which had come and gone. Behind him stood the monolithic figure of Mother Cathcart in her hat, and in the background his chauffeur — none of them speaking or moving until long after the royal party had left the shipyard and the crowds had largely dispersed.

By now some people would be catching London trains, while others would be trudging back to Clydeside homes. Up in the mold loft high tea was being served to all who had been concerned in the launch at which the Chairman of the shipyard proposed the health of *Leviathan* and for which he was given three rousing cheers. It was here that the only public mention was made of old Wilfred Clawston, the carver, to whom *Leviathan* had meant the loss of his life.

As the cheers died away, a quiet voice at the back said, "And here's to old Wilf. May his soul rest in peace." There was a murmur of assent followed by a momentary hush. Then as if a machine were being started after suddenly stalling the celebration tea went on. If, as the popular superstition had it, the dark powers controlling the ship demanded a sacrifice in return for the successful launch, then for the present they seemed appeased.

Some time before the last guest had left the yard, the delicate operation of securing the ship in the fitting-out basin had been completed. The next stage in her life had already begun.

⚓⚓⚓⚓⚓ II ⚓⚓⚓⚓⚓

Over the next eighteen months, while *Leviathan* grew into a fully completed passenger liner, the world in which she was to function alternated between hope and a growing despair. A few weeks after her launch, King Edward VIII abdicated and his brother ascended the throne. By the time *Leviathan*'s engines were installed, the national mood of dismay and confusion had changed to one of traditional joy and celebration at the Coronation in May 1937.

By the autumn when the decks were all in place, the outlook was darkening again. Franco had gained control of Northwest Spain, and nine Powers with deeply opposed interests signed the Lyon agreement in a hypocritical attempt to contain (or foster) the Spanish Civil War. On 28th September Hitler and Mussolini addressed a mass meeting in Berlin's Olympic Meadow. In the Far East the Japanese had all but captured Shanghai; Jean Batten had broken another record by flying solo from Australia to England in five days eighteen hours and fifteen minutes; and the French liner *Normandie* had gained the Blue Riband of the Atlantic by a west to east crossing of just under four days. This so far as *Leviathan* was concerned was a more important item than all the others added together.

With some five million pounds at stake in *Leviathan* the directors and officials of the Transoceanic Steamship Company watched with particular care the world setting in which the ship would make her début. The North Atlantic is the most keenly competitive ocean in the world. France with the giant *Normandie*, Germany with the *Bremen* and *Europa*, and Italy with the *Rex* and *Conte di Savoia* all challenged, if they did not seriously threaten, British supremacy in the North Atlantic. They made the running, and since all liners of fifty thousand tons or more had perforce to be subsidized or sponsored by governments, the drift toward war through crisis after crisis made the transatlantic passenger trade a most sensitive barometer of world affairs.

Flint watched it all from his office in the old Transoceanic Building in Liverpool. So did Laban in New York and Mitchell in London. These three, together with the heads of the passenger and freight departments, with the tireless Quilly diplomatically weaving between them all, really formed the heart of the company so far as its direction, its policy and its connections with the outside world were concerned. Captain Masterton and other heads of technical departments were more concerned with the internal running of the fleet.

Meanwhile *Leviathan* was in process of changing from a simple hull to a complex ship. Countless skilled workers in every conceivable trade were involved, through the hundred and fifteen subcontracting firms, in the supply of thousands of different pieces of equipment, from windlasses, capstans, and warping winches to mincing, dishwashing, and butter-pat machines, from anchors and cables to lifeboat davits, from forced-lubrication pumps to propeller-shaft liners, from fuse-boards to bled-steam air heaters. Sometimes, when a supply problem had reached up as far as the Chairman before being settled, Flint would stare up at the dark Liverpool sky through the top of his office window (the bottom was of frosted glass to ensure privacy and concentration upon one's work) and re-flect on the increasing complications of building a modern ship. His predecessors had had it much easier in that respect.

Although Transoceanic, after nearly a century in the North Atlantic, now had a wealth of tradition forming, so to speak, the veins of its body, the ordering of a new liner such as *Leviathan*, of a size for which there was no previous guide, meant pioneering in all sorts of unforeseen directions. For instance there was only one dock in the country big enough to take her, and that happened to be the largest in the world. This was the King George V graving dock at Southampton. *Leviathan* would be using Southampton instead of Liverpool with its archaic facilities.

The Company had always been based at Liverpool, a port Flint had cursed and fumed against most of his working life. The move to Southampton — at any rate for liners on the New York run — was a step in the right direction. But here again there was a snag. *Leviathan*'s great draft made it essential for her to enter and leave Southampton only at high tide. Other lesser liners could take advantage of Southampton's four tides a day and virtually make schedules to suit their own conven-ience.

Then there was the question of staffing the ship. Here Flint in his cheeseparing mood had come up against all three of his departmental chiefs — the Marine Superintendent, in uneasy alliance with the Merchant Service Officers Association and the National Union of Seamen, refused to budge on the number of navigating personnel needed for the ship; the Chief Engineering Superintendent was able to make out a cast-iron case for his ninety-six Engineer Officers, and it was only Mr. Fox, the Chief Catering Superintendent, whom he was able to browbeat over the steward complement.

"To say you need eight hundred and fifty in the servants' hall out of a total crew of twelve hundred, Mr. Fox, is frankly absurd," Flint had said, adjusting his pince-nez and glaring at his "hotelkeeper," who by now was used to this treatment. "I've worked out your figures. A good man can look after twelve cabins standing on his head."

"Excuse me, but no, sir," Fox said with as much firmness as his normal servility allowed. "Begging your pardon, an exceptional steward working with an equally expert stewardess might manage twelve, possibly even thirteen or fourteen, but that would also depend on his passengers. The *average* for *efficient* service," and he stressed the words as though they were some sort of talisman bringing him strength in his argument, "would be very much less — more like eight I'd say, at the very outside."

"Would you, Mr. Fox?" Flint said with an edge to his voice. He had always had a peculiar and instinctive hatred of the "servant" side of a ship. It was not logical. Perhaps it arose from his own humble background but it was by now a well-known facet of the Chairman's personality that he regarded the whole tribe of stewards and stewardesses as "tip-grubbing scum." This thought, converted into one of his invariable arguments for getting more work out of any man in a given situation, now presented itself to him as the obsequious Mr. Fox bore with him, outwardly patient, privately longing to pick the Chairman up by his scraggy neck and shake him hard.

"They'll make more tips the more cabins they have," Flint said, craftily, after a pause.

"There's a certain point beyond which they'll make no tips at all, sir," Fox retorted. "It's no good encouraging the passengers to expect impeccable service if the bell doesn't get answered when it's rung. A man can't be in two places at once.

Dilute the stewards too much and with the best will in the world, sir —"

"We're not talking about 'best wills' in any 'world,' Mr. Fox. The Company cannot afford those extra salaries. You must make do with seven hundred and fifty — so kindly reorganize your scheme on that assumption."

"Very good, sir," Fox said, in no way revealing his feelings. Hard facts would tell in the end. The old man might declare unctuously, as he so often did, that to mollycoddle a man was to corrupt his soul — and a man's soul was far more important than his under-exerted body, but Fox knew very well the practical capabilities of the men in his department. He had been a steward himself, which Sir J. had certainly never been. He would be proved right in the end.

Fabian Mitchell's point of view over this differed radically from the Chairman's, as indeed it did over an increasing number of problems these days. There was no doubt about it, the old man was getting very set in his ways. Flint had matured in the solidity of Victorian commercial life. He had harsh nineteenth-century principles. He had a formula for success. Those ideas had got him where he was. Unshaken by either the Boer or the Great War in neither of which had he fought — for after all it was only the aristocracy and the "gentlemen" whose world had been cleft from top to bottom, not the sacred principles on which British business had been founded — the Chairman still believed that however tough the going might be he had only to hold on to survive and then later on bend the world once more to his will.

But now it was early 1938. Fabian Mitchell had been in his mid-twenties in 1914 when the war broke out. His maturing had been speeded up by the R.N.V.R. He had come back to civilian life in the turmoil of the 'twenties. His dominating father had been one of the biggest shareholders in Transoceanic, and Fabian had been born in a big house in Blackheath. He himself now lived in Dorking in the style appropriate to a City man of his standing. All this added up to a point of view progressively different from Flint's.

He had never liked Flint. He thought his life crabbed and

mean. It had been Fabian's father whose vote had put Flint where he was and although the company had certainly prospered, surviving the slump in a way no other steamship company had done, Fabian had never forgiven his father for what turned out to be the last autocratic act of his life. Six months after Flint had been made Chairman and Managing Director, Fabian's father had died, his fortune being split up among a large and scattered family. Fabian thus found himself number two to a former protégé of his father's, without the necessary share control to do anything about it, and in private disagreement with "the little man" on almost every topic he cared to think up.

Fabian regarded himself as a man with a lot on his plate but someone who was eminently fair. He had to admit that Flint knew the company and the business in a way impossible to himself. It was one thing to be "put through" the various departments when your father was one of the principal shareholders in the background, quite another to have fought your way up through those same departments as an orphan from a Glasgow slum. Fabian had been groomed for the top but he lacked Flint's bitter practical experience as a half-starved apprentice in a yard and later on as one of dozens of competing clerks in a shipping office.

The main difference between them though, Fabian considered, lay in their treatment of the men and women the company employed. Flint was dictatorial, ruthless, exact. Commercially speaking he was heartless: a defective piece of machinery and an ineffective man were one and the same and must be replaced without sentimentality or delay. He would pay, and pay well, for quality if he had to, but he was merciless toward failure or the second-best. Fabian, on the other hand, while he fancied himself as having the same high ideals of giving and receiving value for money, had been changed forever by his period in the R.N.V.R., where he was taught to look after the men under his command much as a father has responsibility for his children.

As a result, he would always listen sympathetically to hard-luck explanations. He would give a man the benefit of the doubt at the expense of the company. When staff had to be sacked, he spent sleepless nights trying to find another way out of the tangle. Brought up to lead and to consider himself one of the governing class, which was certainly not one of Josiah Flint's ideas, Fabian Mitchell looked on himself as kind, wise, tolerant and understanding. In private he gave himself high marks for power of command and officer-like qualities. In public he tended toward the club tie and the genial approach. One of his favorite remarks was "The troops would always rather be led by a gentleman, even if his technical knowledge isn't as good as your ranker's. The ex-lower deck officer is all very well but he can't command the respect a gentleman can. I'm not being a snob, I'm simply stating a well-known fact." It was always astonishing to Fabian, and somehow disturbing, that even when all this had been pointed out people still seemed to admire the tough, mean little Chairman of Trans-oceanic, even when in some cases they'd come up against his rough side and had lost their jobs. He was also forced to admit, when he thought about it, that the world was moving as far away from his own ideas, as it was from Flint's Victorian approach.

"I don't understand the young people of today," he confided to Masterton after one of their staff conferences in Liverpool. "They seem to have no guts, no pride, and certainly no patriotism. They're all after fair shares and a cushy job. Where's the spirit of adventure these days?"

"But I thought your son was going into the Civil Service, Mr. Mitchell," Masterton said, unable to resist a sly dig.

"Only because he couldn't get into anything else. I'm not going to have him waste his education," Fabian replied hastily. He was always catching his foot in his own trap.

Masterton lit the famous corncob pipe that had gained him the nickname of "Popeye" throughout the company's Fleet.

"They're all right once you get 'em to sea. The stock's just as good as it always has been. It's the homes, Mr. Mitchell, that's where the trouble is. Once they've had a bit of discipline brought back into their lives they shape up much as ever they did. It's the parents I'd like to get after."

"Meaning me, I supppose," Fabian said with a smile. "Well, possibly you're right. I don't think we were either very severe or particularly lax, but I just don't know what to make of my son, Alan, these days. He's picked up some rum ideas at Oxford. Won't die for King and country, he had the nerve to tell me the other day, as wars are simply a racket made by the armament barons, if you please, and we're all of us dupes. Yet in the next breath he talks about dashing off to fight for the Reds in Spain. Of course he's a Socialist. I don't know who isn't these days."

"I don't think my Johnny is," Masterton said through a cloud of blue smoke, "but then he's set on getting his first mate's ticket and I don't think he has much time for brooding about politics and the like."

A sudden stab of jealousy made Fabian pause. It was absurd, of course, for him to be envious of this white-haired sea captain with a son already, at twenty-one, a third mate in the P. & O. He had more wealth, a better education and a higher position in the world than Captain Masterton ever had or wanted to have; yet here he was, a stranger to his children, while in the Masterton family, as he well knew from watching them together, it was as if there was a freemasonry between them, as though the son really was a new sprig on the old trunk, as though here was an instance where the heritage of the sea had a practical meaning.

"Discipline is the answer," Masterton went on reflectively. "The young always hate it to begin with but they learn to bless it later on. Old man Tunney was on to that a century ago. *He* knew you can't provide a service without discipline. And we've never lost a passenger yet."

This was true and a fact which always made Fabian marvel. It was never a boast, the superstitions of the sea being what they are, but it greatly sustained the pride they all felt. Except in the war, no company ship had been lost since 1846 when Joshua Tunney's first cockle of a steamship began its regular passenger service from Liverpool to New York. Transoceanic had the finest safety record of any of the liner companies operating in that most treacherous of oceans — the North Atlantic.

After Mitchell had left his office, old Popeye remained for a time puffing at his pipe. He knew what Mitchell was trying to say. He had as grave doubts about the future as any of them there. He did not like the way the wind was blowing. There was an apathy, a sourness, and a lack of spirit these days which was infecting them all. He looked back on his own long life and counted himself lucky. He had had the luck to be in a disciplined service where things were in order and everything had its place. The system would see him through, he thought, but already the seeds of decay had begun to germinate in this woolly, disorganized England of 1938.

He had told Mitchell he did not think his son, Johnny, had socialistic ideas, but now that he remembered some of the arguments they had had on his last few leaves he wasn't so sure. All that fuss about sticking up for the union, as though life at sea could ever be effectively under union control! "And get out of your head," he remembered nearly yelling at his son, "that all men are equal. They're not, never have been — never will be. How could you man a ship if your able seaman is supposed to be just as good as your captain? It can't be done, Johnny, it can't be done."

But his son had mumbled something about all men being the same when they're born and when they die and how it seemed to be a splendid world for those who did the ruling but not so hot for those who carried out the orders. To which Masterton had retorted that if he felt like that, he had no business to be at sea. There was no point in striving to get a command of his own if, when he got it, he didn't really wish to command.

"I can get you a job ashore, Johnny, any time you like. As a matter of fact there's a vacancy in the Accounts Department this very week if you're interested in totting up a ledger for your daily bread."

But his son had only burst out laughing.

"You're incorrigible, Father," he'd said, and that was certainly not a word Masterton would have used himself. "I've only been pulling your leg. I may vote Labor at the next election, but I'm damned well going to be Master of *Leviathan* before I'm through. I've told them that at the P. & O. They quite understand. They say the whole of the rest of the British Mercantile Marine is going to stand on end in wonder and amazement when your hippopotamus puts to sea." Then he had bowed very low, winked at his mother and gone off to see his girl friend on that far too powerful motorbike of his.

Masterton thought about it a moment or so longer and then put it out of his mind. Command of ships at sea over a large number of years had given him the ability to concentrate and the will to shut things out of his mind whenever he chose. He could be as single-minded as Flint if the need arose. Now there were the day's letters to sign, two more drafts to prepare on the company's "intermediate services to Montreal," and on the roster of personnel in the Freight Service running to Mediterranean and West African ports. Finally, there was a matter never very far away from his waking thoughts — the final list of officers and men for R.M.S. *Leviathan*, whose trials and acceptance date now lay only a few weeks ahead.

Over in New York Maxwell Laban followed progress on the great ship through company reports, the Press, and in private letters from Quilly. Every day his personal enthusiasm and excitement grew. The opinion of travel agents in the U.S. who mattered was that *Leviathan* would skim the cream off the transatlantic trade, and indeed the advance booking was phenomenal. It seems that anyone who was anyone intended to travel to Europe that year in *Leviathan*. This could certainly be expected during the ship's first season, when her curiosity value was at its peak. The *Normandie*, the *Bremen*, and the *Conte di Savoia* had each of them had their years. But *Leviathan* was designed to do more than this. As the largest, most comfortable and possibly the fastest ship the world might see, *Leviathan* was to consolidate the already enormous share the Company had of transatlantic passenger traffic.

Ethel, who had "the giant wonder" rammed down her throat morning, noon and night, had developed an allergy to the ship. She tried scoffing and she tried turning the conversation. But there was no refuge from Maxie's consuming obsession. "So she's to be the greatest load of scrap iron the world ever saw,"

39

she would say when Laban launched off on yet another of his eulogies. "Does that mean she can stop Hitler doing what he likes? I tell you, Max, if I have to sit on any more Refugee Welfare Committees, I'll get a permanent cramp."

These tactics quite often worked. Max would grunt some sort of casual reply and withdraw into his study. Ethel kept telling him that *Leviathan* had eaten into his life. So what did he care? This was his life. He returned to his brooding. An exceptional ship called for exceptional measures. He was determined that her maiden voyage should end in a triumphal reception in New York such as no other ship had ever before received.

"Of course, *Leviathan* is *absolutely* my *favorite* word nowadays," Ethel told her brother when they were lunching one day at Sardi's. "I'll certainly light a candle the day we get through with her first voyage — when I can sit back and tell Max she's just another floating Waldorf-Astoria and not to make all that fuss. Some days I can't even get him to laugh. Give you an example. Did you know *Leviathan* was strictly kosher? I went and looked it up in the encyclopedia. *Leviathan* was a Jewish Devil-god. And do you know the only thing Max said when I told him? 'There are six separate kitchens aboard *Leviathan*, Ethel,' he said, 'and one of those kitchens is reserved exclusively for kosher cooking. What more can the company do?' 'Well, I certainly hope you don't get a sudden rush of Chinese,' I said. 'Which of the six kitchens is going to cater for them?' But he just glared and muttered something about some people having to take things seriously some of the time. As if *I* didn't know that! I'd just laugh like hell if the goddam ship struck an iceberg . . ." she stopped abruptly and put her hand over her mouth. "No, I wouldn't; I've gone too far and I take that back. But, Olly, don't you think a small rubber iceberg dropped in *Leviathan*'s path might get rid of a little of this starry-eyed voodoo that seems to be building up?"

But her brother, whose mind was as full of the next production at one of his theaters as Laban's was of *Leviathan*, patted her hand and told her that if she hadn't realized by now that all men had special toys of their own then she was in for a thinnish time over the next six months. "*Leviathan*'s not just any old ship," he said, and "Oh! God!" Ethel had commented, bringing the discussion abruptly to a close. There was no doubt about it, she thought ruefully, men had an unbreakable understanding among themselves whenever the sacred importance of their jobs came in for a little critical attention from a woman.

Susan Spicer, alone of the three, had done something practical about their "pact." Against the combined opposition of her father and mother she had gone to London, taken a bedroom in a friend's Chelsea house and had enrolled for a course of shorthand and typing. She had carefully kept her ulterior motives well hidden. There had been trouble enough getting away from home at all and this had been one of the few occasions when a brother or a sister of her own would have been an asset.

Indeed, as an only child she still felt a little guilty at leaving her mother to battle on by herself against the pretentious emptiness of her father's life. But after all, Mother married him, she thought. I'm only his daughter. And, of course, within a few weeks her father was already assuming that Susan would in due course become *his* secretary — at first as a trainee under the long-suffering Miss Perkins, then as a somewhat cheaper replacement, though in all conscience he paid Miss Perkins little enough. But Susan had other ideas.

She duly went home at week-ends, forcing herself, as part of the price of escape, to take a more than normal interest in local affairs and almost overdoing her "model daughter" act. Secretly she knew her mother was on her side but her father continued in private to bluster at the unreasonableness of her leaving home and then, wearing his "public" face, would show her off proudly at cocktail parties and take her along to his political meetings.

As the weeks and the months had gone by, she had often had bad bouts of conscience, but her father would never understand how suffocating she found the country life into the fringe of which she had been born, the inane idle young men, the fatuous, lumpy girls all in a small exclusive world of hunting, of the social calendar, of week-ends in each other's houses, of dwindling incomes and disappearing servants, of a life as out of touch with what was really going on in the country and the world as any French aristocrat before the Revolution. If it had not been for the Mitchells, as much on the perimeter as the Spicers, she would not have known where to find a safety valve by dinner time each Saturday night.

In April 1938, just before *Leviathan* began her trials, Susan passed her shorthand-typing exam, and on a sudden impulse decided to do something drastic at once. With her certificate of proficiency, birth certificate, and passport (in case of sudden emergency), she packed a small overnight bag and set off for Liverpool without any clear idea in her head of what she would do but with a prayer to the Almighty and a determination to go to sea in *Leviathan* one way or another and to achieve this herself. She was just nineteen.

No sooner had the train left Euston than a mood of doubt and despair laid hold of her. She must have been out of her mind. What could have been easier, in fact, than to go and see "Uncle" Fabian at his London office? A word from him and no doubt all sorts of paths would have cleared in front of her. But somehow that wasn't the way. And he might have told her father and . . . Well — it was always possible to catch the next train back.

However, by the time she reached Liverpool, just before lunch, she had regained her spirits and this foray to Merseyside had once more become an adventure. Leaving her bag at the station, she went straight to the Transoceanic offices and asked to see Sir Josiah Flint. The commissionaire, with four rows of medals on his chest and a wary mind inside his baldish head, asked if she had an appointment. She said no but that nevertheless she wished to see the Chairman straight away. The sight of a pretty fair-haired girl in a trim black coat demanding audience with Sir J. did not occur every day in the company's marble entrance hall, and the commissionaire scratched his chin in perplexity.

"You'd better see Mr. Johnson, I think," he said, and was

then astonished to see a new pound note slipped over the desk and under his hand. A pound was a lot of money to Susan and it was certainly a shock to the commissionaire.

"But I haven't come all the way from London to see Mr. Johnson," Susan said, her blue eyes at their most innocent and appealing, a smile round her rather wide mouth that would have melted a cannon ball.

"Suppose you just knock at his door and show me in yourself. I haven't got a bomb in my pocket. Please!"

But the commissionaire shook his head firmly.

"I'm sorry, miss, it can't be done." He gave her back the pound note. "I can't let you in to see Sir Josiah without a proper appointment."

Then one of those accidental strokes of luck happened to Susan by which whole lives can sometimes change their direction. A heavy mahogany door down the corridor opened and the Chairman appeared. As usual he was dressed in his wing collar, black coat, and striped trousers with the gray spats showing above highly polished black shoes. His pince-nez sat at their accustomed angle and he walked slowly toward the front door, limping slightly as he had done since his accident on board *Leviathan*. Susan's heart beat wildly. She knew this was a moment not to be lost and despite a warning from the commissionaire, she went forward to meet him.

"Sir Josiah," she said, unable to suppress a frantic and embarrassing blush, "I'd like to ask you to lunch."

The Chairman stopped abruptly, looked first at her and then at the commissionaire.

"This young lady's been asking to see you, sir," the commissionaire began but found himself cut short by Susan who said, with a control which astonished herself, "I'll explain to the Chairman, thank you very much." She gave him a brief smile and then put the commissionaire out of her mind. "I'm Susan Spicer," she went on to Flint who, as always when something unexpected occurred, was standing absolutely still and intensely watchful. "I want you to give me a job, so — if you don't mind being asked by a woman — I think it's only fair I should invite you to lunch."

43

"My dear young lady," Flint said after a pause, "I don't know who you are, I don't give away jobs, and I already have a luncheon appointment."

He began to walk down the steps to the big front door. Because of his leg he had to manage them one at a time and on a sudden instinct Susan took his arm and helped him downstairs.

"You know you should really use a stick," she found herself saying, and then before Flint could get in a word she went on, "but of course if I'd seen that rope ladder hanging down *Leviathan*'s side I'd have climbed it myself. I suppose in a funny way that's what I'm doing now. Only *I* shall look where I'm going when I get to the top instead of falling down some mingy old hole in the deck."

By now they were out in the street and the old chauffeur was holding open the door of the Rolls, astonished to see Sir J. come out on the arm of a most attractive young girl.

"Thank you," said Flint with a momentary softening in his voice which Susan instantly noticed, "I can manage quite well by myself." He dropped his arm but did not shake himself free.

They walked across the pavement to the car. It had begun to rain. Susan shivered, and a sudden premonition of total humiliating failure took hold of her. By the time they reached the car all her bravado had vanished and she felt like bursting out crying.

"I'm sorry," she said leaving hold of his arm and blushing scarlet. "I shouldn't have tried to rush you like that. It was just an idea which hasn't come off. I apologize, I'm . . . very sorry."

Whether it was the unusual proximity of an attractive warm and very alive young girl, whether he was suddenly touched by her crestfallen, childlike appearance or whether he had been secretly impressed by her fearless approach, Flint never knew, but something at that moment stirred in his heart. An unspoken, so very easily crushed appeal seemed to emanate from her body as she stood by the car, her head hanging down, her eyes on her toes. He looked at her for a split second and smiled to himself. The unexpected had always played a big part in his life. He had never been afraid of taking a risk; perhaps now he should spare a moment for someone else who was beginning the same long path.

"Why don't you get in the car?" he said in as gentle a tone as his crisp Scottish voice would allow. "We can't stand here forever in the rain."

Susan looked up startled, past the long pointed nose, past the crooked pince-nez straight into the old granite eyes.

"But you said you had a luncheon appointment?" she faltered.

"Och! I go every day to the club," he said as he climbed in ahead of her, beckoning her to follow. "I shall rather enjoy being taken to lunch by a charming young lady. Where are we going?"

"The Adelphi," Susan said firmly, "but you may have to lend me some money."

Leviathan herself was now all but ready. A month previously the "black squad" had virtually finished their work, the structure of the ship was complete and she was now in the hands of a small army of electricians, joiners, woodworkers, painters and decorators. Dock trials of the two hundred thousand horsepower propelling machinery had been satisfactorily carried out. At first the engines had been run with the propellers uncoupled; then one day the four huge screws had been connected and for a spell water was furiously churned up in the basin while experts made intent readings of vibration detectors and reported an almost complete absence of that particular nuisance.

The principal first class dining saloon was now graced with its huge decorative panel, twenty-six feet by fourteen, depicting a mythical dragon breathing fire in the middle of the Atlantic. Frescoes were being painted on the walls of the Veranda Grill. The ballrooms, the smoking rooms, the libraries, bars, and shops had all been painted and otherwise embellished. The cinemas, the tennis and squash courts, and the two large swimming pools were installed. The ship's siren had duly been tested, its deep bass blast being heard over a wide area of Glasgow, although its note would be so adjusted that "passengers on board would suffer little or no discomfort from its sound."

Beds and mattresses were in place in the hundreds of staterooms in the three classes the ship would carry. Hundreds of miles of electric wiring and of salt and fresh water plumbing had been installed. The electric bakery that would soon be manned throughout the twenty-four hours had been given a trial. The lift from the engineers' accommodation on the sun deck down eight decks to the engine room was functioning, as were the six gilded elevators for the passengers in different parts of the ship.

The two great funnels were in place, painted vermilion with the two pearl-gray bands which were the company's markings, lifeboats hung at their davits, masts and derricks had been rigged, the wheel house and full navigating equipment had been installed, the intricate radio and radio-telephone equipment was aboard, and *Leviathan* was at last ready for her trials in the record completion time of seventeen months.

"When *Leviathan* leaves her builders' fitting-out basin on Tuesday," *The Times* remarked, "she will then undertake the most adventuresome, momentous and ticklish voyage of her life so far. The Clyde has never before seen such a vast ship sail the fifteen miles down to the Tail of the Bank off Greenock, where the river opens out into the Firth. At many points the river is only just wide and deep enough to let the vessel clear. Three tricky bends must be negotiated, the first soon after she leaves the dock at Dalmuir, the next some four miles farther down, at Bowling, and the last near the end of the trip as she swings round under the Renfrewshire shore at Port Glasgow, just above Greenock. *Leviathan* will undoubtedly provide the spectacle the many thousands of visitors to the Clyde are expecting. The whole nation wishes her a safe and successful journey."

To the hard-pressed police and civil authorities, it did indeed seem as if the whole world was descending upon the Clyde. The week-end before she sailed *Leviathan* was thrown open to inspection by the public. First the workmen who had helped to build her brought their wives and families to see the great ship, then fourteen thousand senior pupils from Clydeside schools followed by sixteen thousand of the general public were shown round the ship, the crowd marshaling in queues eight deep from early forenoon till eleven at night. Since the day of her launch, over a quarter of a million visitors had been aboard. Gifts of all sorts had been showered on the ship, from a silver rose bowl for the Captain's table given by the Queen to a whale's tooth paperweight for the Purser's office, alleged by its owner to have come from "that other Leviathan, to wit the Great White Whale, or Moby Dick."

By this time the ship's principal officers had either been earmarked or had already joined. *Leviathan* was, of course, still in her builders' hands and their house flag would remain hoisted until the trials were satisfactorily concluded; but Sir Norman Coxley, the Commodore of the Line, was standing by the ship together with key officers such as the Chief Engineer, the Purser, the Chief Steward and one of the three doctors *Leviathan* would carry. This, as it happened, was Michael Kelly. He would, in fact, be the second medical officer in seniority but it was a move up for him from the *Pluto*. Bible Banks, too, had left the *Pluto* and now had command of the fifty-thousand-ton *Juno*, one of the other liners sharing the New York service with *Leviathan* until her consort could be built and the service run with two giant ships.

Though Quilly had failed to get Banks in ahead of the promotion line, he had succeeded in another direction. The Purser, Dudley Fitzpatrick Mott, was undoubtedly young for the job, being only forty on his last birthday, but he had long been starred in the confidential reports his various captains had compiled on his twenty years' service to the company. Indeed, one of the best of these reports had been sent in by Banks when they had been together in the old *Vulcan*, the twenty-thousand-ton pre-war liner which had made such a success of the cruising craze of the early 'thirties.

"Mr. Mott," Banks had written, "combines tact and courage to an unusual degree. He has a well-trained memory, an excellent power of command over his subordinates, and a cheerful

47

disposition. On this cruise we were blessed with some of the most pernickety, vain, selfish and sparrow-brained passengers it has ever been my misfortune to carry" (this particular report had done little to advance Captain Banks's own career) "but throughout the three months the ship has been away from the United Kingdom I have not once seen the Purser ruffled, either in public or in private, despite two attempted suicides, the quitting of the ship by an eccentric millionaire in Cape Town, and a cocktail party for two hundred and fifty given by Mrs. Van der Eisenberg which ended up in a brawl. This Purser will go right to the top and stay there; I am sorry to be losing him now to another appointment."

Though marked for the top from almost his earliest days at sea, not all his reports had been as good as that. One earlier master he had served wrote tersely "This Purser has received the dubious blessing of a public school education and shows it." Another commented that "he appears more interested in the comfort and welfare of the younger female passengers than in attending to his ship duties such as captain's rounds. Never short of a good excuse for avoiding work he does not like or considers unnecessary. Perky to the point of cheek, he has several times fringed on insubordination. Would benefit from a spell in freighters to improve his sloppy paperwork. Drinks more than he should."

This latter remark was not altogether fair. Part of the Purser's job is to entertain the passengers and the more successful the parties given the more a reputation for conviviality becomes a two-edged weapon. Mott enjoyed himself. Indeed, that was part of his success as a host. The dour Captain making that report drank a good deal too, but no one had seen him smile. In any case Mott had survived. He had the gift of resilience and an almost total lack of resentment. As a youngster, if some blow had felled him to the ground he would pick himself up with a rude and expressive noise and get on with something else. Now with this appointment to *Leviathan* well ahead of his turn — thanks to a word dropped here and there by Quilly — he faced the biggest challenge of his whole career.

48

The Tuesday at the end of April chosen for *Leviathan*'s passage down the Clyde was no accident. This would be the highest tide for six months. "The Ark Monstrous," as one paper called her, extended a thousand feet in length and drew thirty-five feet. If she grounded and stuck, the consequences could be very serious, especially since she was too long even to lie across the river at Clydebank. Indeed, she could only be turned on leaving the basin thanks to the presence opposite of the tributary river, the Cart, and even then she would come so near the low, flat banks that spectators could throw stones on board without effort if they chose.

High tide that day was at two P.M. By nine-thirty in the morning most of the large official party was aboard, and by eleven o'clock seven tugs were easing *Leviathan* out into the river and maneuvering her stern up river. Fifty-three special trains had poured a mass of people into Clydeside, hundreds of motorists had slept overnight in their cars, and farmers were reaping an unexpected harvest in car parking fees. Refreshment marquees had been set up in the fields, postcard and souvenir sellers were doing a roaring trade, and it was estimated that over a million men, women, and children had gathered to watch the greatest ship in the world go down to the sea.

Susan could scarcely believe her good luck. Her presence there on the curved forward apron of the sun deck — one of only half a dozen women on board — and the steps by which this had been achieved were so astonishing as to be in her opinion miraculous. Beside her stood Leonard Quilly, the hump on his back somewhat muffled by his overcoat, his uneven teeth protruding in a little smile, his eyes darting ceaselessly round the concourse of officials, experts, personalities, and Press now clustering at vantage points on the different decks. There were a lot of people he would have to have a word with but in the meantime he thought it expedient to keep his eye on Miss Spicer. She looked "controllable," but the Chairman's latest whim might land them all into trouble if she were left too long to her own devices.

He studied her out of the corner of his eye whenever her attention was elsewhere. The old man must be going soft in the brain, he thought, reflecting sardonically on the extent to which one man's will could affect so many lives. Since when had the company needed a "Social and Publicity Assistant" in the form of a nineteen-year-old girl? She was certainly an arresting creature. His lips curled in resentment. The cheek of it! He resented her youth, her freshness, her vitality, and her sex.

Automatically this resentment rang a warning bell in his head. For his normal inner detachment to be affected by some-one like Susan Spicer, with her clear skin and her white teeth, was a sign of hidden danger to Quilly. He must proceed with more than his usual care. She was certainly unpredictable. He had observed the fearless way she tossed her head and squared her shoulders when facing something she did not know. A lit-tle number like that could make him a great deal of trouble. That was why he had decided to be especially kind and atten-tive. "Trust old Lenny Quilly" the whole of his approach seemed to say; "Leave it to Len, he has your best interests at heart." He took good care to suppress that foxy glint he often observed in his eyes as he shaved his poor misshapen face. "Trust dear old Uncle Len," he thought, smiling to himself at this unexpected new role he found himself playing. The ship's double-bass siren blew a long steady blast, answered by two of the tugs. The voyage down to Tail of the Bank had be-gun.

In view of the narrowness of the channel, it had been de-cided that the tugs would maneuver *Leviathan* down and past the most acute bend at Bowling, and that not until that hazard was passed would the ship be under her own power. On the very first bend, however, just below Clydebank the engine room telegraphs were suddenly put at full speed astern. No one on deck knew of this since *Leviathan* was unusually free of vi-bration, but a few moments later the great ship was aground.

Luckily the mud was soft and high tide was still two and a half hours away but it took ten minutes to get her off and a hemp hawser to one of the tugs parted under the strain. " 'At no point of the journey,' " Fabian Mitchell remarked sarcastically, reading from an advance description of the route given in one of the papers, " 'will there be less than four feet under *Levia-*

than's keel.' As of eleven-thirty-five A.M. there's a slight inaccuracy in that statement." Captain Masterton, next to whom he was standing, grunted and frowned. He did not care for civilian comment on navigating matters, even though Mitchell had been in the R.N.V.R. and was one of the colleagues he got on best with.

"She's too big," he muttered almost to himself, "we're overreaching ourselves when we build a ship of this size."

Peter Beecher, on Mitchell's other side, heard this remark, lit another cigarette, and battled with a recurring urge to do something even though he knew perfectly well there was nothing he could or should do. He wished he was anywhere else than where he was now. One side of him was inordinately proud of the ship which, now that she was built, had fulfilled everything he had hoped for and planned, another and instinctive side was full of dark thoughts such as Masterton had just expressed. Everything had a right size, there was no doubt about that. He thought of the *Great Eastern* and of the *Titanic*, he thought of the *Graf Zeppelin* and the *R. 101*, he thought of the long-extinct dinosaurs and of Babylon the great — hell's bells, there was no end to the uneasiness you could feel if you let your thoughts loose in the dark. He rattled the small change in his trouser pocket and drew on his cigarette. Then he caught sight of the back of Susan's head and was struck by how well shaped and proportioned *that* was.

"Who's Rigoletto's girl friend?" he asked Mitchell. Fabian, who knew nothing of Susan's new job, looked where Beecher was pointing and promptly went aground, so to speak, with a shock of his own. "Good heavens!" he said walking over to where they stood gazing down on the tugs. "Good heavens above!"

"Hello, Uncle Fabian," Susan said a moment or so later. A delicious, somehow illicit thrill tingled her nerves.

"What are you doing here?" he asked rather sternly. It might be deuced awkward if she had managed to smuggle herself aboard into this most exclusive party under false pretenses.

"Oh! Didn't you know?" Susan said with well-stimulated, wide-eyed innocence. "I'm on the strength."

"You're *what?*"

"The Chairman's given her a job," Quilly put in silkily from her side. "She's a 'Social and Publicity Assistant.' And she's going to help the Purser with his duties once *Leviathan* goes to sea."

"Good God!" Fabian exclaimed. "What on earth does that mean?"

"It means I'm going to sea — probably as a purserette. Until then I'm working in Sir Josiah Flint's office."

Slightly behind her back, Quilly smirked and winked at Fabian. He could not help relishing old Pomposity's discomfiture. Fabian pointedly ignored him. He felt anger rising inside him.

"Why on earth didn't you come and see me?" Fabian asked. "Especially if you were using my name."

"But I wouldn't have dreamed of using your name without asking you," Susan said gently. "I wanted to do this myself, and I did."

"She took the Chairman out to lunch," Quilly put in, "and came away with the job in her pocket."

"Huh!" Fabian said, rounding on him, "then why wasn't I told? You're supposed to keep me informed of such things."

"I'm so sorry, sir," Quilly answered smoothly, "I had no idea you would be interested in Miss Spicer." This was a lie, since Quilly knew all about the Spicer and the Mitchell families, but he was also aware that such knowledge could never be proved.

"Well, this is certainly a surprise, Susan," Fabian remarked severely, as a murmur went up around them of "she's away." "You'd better come and have a yarn with me as soon as we're through with all this. If you're looking after her, Mr. Quilly, perhaps you'd bring her along."

"Certainly, sir," Quilly agreed. "I'll see to that, provided the Chairman can spare her, of course."

Fabian managed a frosty smile at them both and then walked back toward Masterton and Beecher. Susan gave this a moment's thought, and then ran after him, catching him by the sleeve.

"Don't be cross with me, Uncle Fab," she said, using the old familiar nursery name. "I wasn't trying to upset you. I didn't want to ask any favors, that's all. I wanted to do it myself — if it could be done."

Fabian stopped and looked at her intently.

"I'm not 'cross' with you, Susan. I think it's a little odd, that's all, when you've known me all these years. And how long is the whim going to last? You can't play ducks and drakes with a company like Transoceanic, you know."

"It's not a whim."

He looked at her reflectively, his mouth set in a wry smile.

"What do your parents say?"

"I don't know. I'll be telling them this week-end. I expect Daddy will have other plans. He usually has."

"Well . . ." Fabian said dubiously, "I can't see it's much of a career for a girl of your background but — if you really want to make a go of it, Sue, then of course I'll help as much as I can."

"Thank you, Uncle Fab."

"I should be careful how much you confide in the gentleman you're with, though. He's a rather tricky customer."

"Oh! yes, I got that right away. But he does seem to know an awful lot about things."

"He knows a damned sight too much about everything."

This time the smile was warmer as they parted and Susan returned to Quilly with less misgiving. She was glad the air had been cleared over that. She felt somehow that despite every right in the world she *had* gone behind Uncle Fabian's back. She knew his feelings had been hurt. She knew also that he would be afraid of Joan catching a similar and irresponsible independence. And why shouldn't she? Susan thought with a toss of the head. The days for young ladies and gentlemen to sit around twiddling their thumbs were gone forever.

By this time *Leviathan* with her seven attendant tugs had emerged from Glasgow's thick pall of smoke, leaving behind the clanging of hammers and the machine-gun rattle of riveters. She was going "doon the watter" in fine style, one of the delights and indulgences about which there was no argument in

Glasgow. Now, followed by a flotilla of pleasure craft, *Leviathan* was sailing through rich open country on the boundary between Highlands and Lowlands. On her starboard hand the northern banks of the river rose steeply. Passing the fashionable suburb of Bearsden, with the Kilpatrick hills behind, the Highlands were beginning to stack up as far as the eye could see.

The most acute bend of the river at Bowling caused speed to be reduced to the minimum. At the previous Dalmuir bend the ship had taken an uncomfortable sheer but had not grounded again, and once round Bowling it was a smooth glide down past Dumbarton where, through a break in the hills, Ben Lomond could just be seen, down past Cardross Castle where Robert the Bruce had died, down past Port Glasgow on the southern bank, down on the widening river to Greenock.

At two-thirty off the spit of land known as Tail of the Bank, where forty years before the *Great Eastern* had lain, and later on the ill-fated *Lusitania*, where two years previously the burned out hulk of the French liner *L'Atlantique* waited pathetically to be broken up, *Leviathan* came proudly and easily to anchor, her ninety thousand tons already being maneuvered with the ease of a picket boat. Cormorants, perched on nearby buoys, watched her with indifferent curiosity. To the north side the high hills and the mouths of the many lochs looked forbidding in the cold, dark weather. There had been a few minutes of feeble sunlight on the trip but these had soon been chased away by rain clouds scurrying in and out of the hills. In front of *Leviathan*, her path dotted with islands, lay the still invisible open sea.

Farther down the Firth lay the measured mile where new ships are put through their paces. *Leviathan* was to undergo handling trials the next day but these would be largely improvised and informal, so that navigating and engine room personnel could get the feel of the ship. Then would come a five-hundred-and-fifty-mile trip to Southampton for docking, so that eighteen months of underwater growth could be scraped off her bottom. Then, and only then, would she return to the Clyde for her full acceptance trials.

The official party on board now made their way down to the first class restaurant for a champagne lunch. The great ship had successfully completed the first stage of her journey from her birthplace into the outer world. "I shall not pass this way again," Fabian declaimed in his Irving manner as he sat down next to the general manager of the Shipbuilding Yard. Across the table, to the surprise of others besides Fabian, Susan was placed next to the Chairman. As the late luncheon got under way, Fabian could not resist looking round at the company's lady superintendent. No doubt she would have something to say about Susan. He wondered how she would take it — if indeed it would bother her at all — but she was in earnest conversation with the smiling indefatigable Quilly.

⚓⚓⚓⚓⚓ III ⚓⚓⚓⚓⚓

OVER in New York the Labans were finding it more and more difficult to keep *Leviathan* from swamping their days. The Transoceanic Company had a fleet of twenty-one liners and cargo vessels under its direct operation, and another ten ships managed by a subsidiary, the old Tunney-Faversham Line. Though the North Atlantic passenger trade was the heart of the company's business, there was also a flourishing trade to Mediterranean and Indian ports and what was rapidly becoming an all-the-year-round program of cruises.

By any standard there was plenty to do and now that *Leviathan* was entering the field, Ethel seemed to see less of her husband than ever. Now more than ever before, she regretted their joint decision not to have a family. Her brother Oliver's mixed brood of five made up for it a little by proxy, but fond though she was of her nieces and nephews they did not quite fill the gap which up to now she had never fully acknowledged.

There was a bond of affection between Max and her forged in his early struggles and now fully tested by the passage of time. They were devoted to each other. He was there in her thoughts — sometimes in the front, sometimes at the back of her mind, almost every hour of the day. She supposed that Max forgot her more easily and more often, but then he had more to do, and there were phone calls, flowers, and little presents at unexpected times which consoled her in a quite disproportionate way. In addition, she had a few firm friends, an ever changing Christmas card list and a brother through whom she could keep in touch with the Broadway theater world in which they had both grown up. But with all this, there seemed these days to be a growing emptiness in their lives.

Now, as she packed in readiness for their crossing to England to return on *Leviathan*'s maiden voyage, as friends phoned or wrote wishing them good luck and envying the prospect before them, Ethel's heart was heavy. There was a pointlessness in it all. Life had given them what they wanted and the taste was sour. It was like being part of a beautifully painted, smoothly running machine which moved but was dead.

She knew Max did not feel the same way. It was private to her — this solitary confinement in success and plenty. Max was still fascinated by his life. He could still play with his toys. Moreover her distress was largely incommunicable. Indeed, what was there to complain about? So you don't feel satisfied with material things, her friends would remark, so go to Church; that's what Churches are for. She'd tried that too. She'd tried working for charity. Indeed, a good part of each week went on the committees and functions such interests always entailed. But what was it all about? At the end of her life what would she have to show?

Luckily every day there was a great deal to do, and she drove herself willingly to do it for Max's sake. They had never moved from their West Side apartment high up over the Hudson (so that while he shaved Max could see what was going on in the port). Most of their friends now had moved over to Park Avenue and the East River; but the Labans stayed put in their roomy, old-fashioned penthouse, the money for which had originally been loaned them by her father.

Ethel liked the apartment. She had been very happy there

with Max. Though servants were increasingly hard to get, they still had Annie Maugh, the Scottish cook-housekeeper who had been with them fifteen years, and Eliza, the colored daily woman, who did the rest of the housework. Both women were as interested and intrigued by *Leviathan* as Max himself, Annie because she, too, came from the Clyde, Eliza because *Leviathan* would be "the most high and mighty" ship in the world.

Eliza's mother had come from Jamaica and she lived now in Harlem in a house full of other British West Indians. "My folks are saying . . ." Eliza would begin in the morning, and then would follow some highly sensational statement, arrived at with a fine disregard for accuracy but colored with an admiration and awe usually reserved for the King of England. Eliza had never really recovered from being told that *Leviathan* if stood on end would reach as high as the Empire State building — "Now every time I catches sight of that building, I sees that old *Leviathan* lying up the side of her." "Och, away with you, Eliza," Annie would retort. "Will you not give your imagination the rest it deserves?" But a few minutes later there would be something else. "My folks are saying nobody going to get seasick on board that old *Leviathan* on account she's so big she's going to flatten the sea in front of her, it don't matter how raging the storm. She's sure going to be known as the best flattener the Atlantic Ocean ever done see." Attempts to explain to Eliza that any ship both rolls and pitches failed to dislodge from her mind the impression that *Leviathan* would run from New York to England as if on invisible rails just below the surface of the sea.

Whenever the Labans entertained, Eliza would come and, in one of her mother's old uniforms which gave her a kind of dated grace, would serve at table. Since every Transoceanic Captain had at one time or another dined at the Labans' apartment, Eliza had met and studied them all. Favorite of the field by a long way was Captain Basil Bellerophon Banks, who bore some resemblance in Eliza's mind to the prophet Isaiah. Perhaps it was the beard, perhaps it was the piercing blue eyes, perhaps it was simply the man's great bulk and the air of authority with which he even unfolded his napkin — whatever the immediate causes in her mind, the lasting effect was of wonder and veneration amounting almost to reverence.

When Eliza discovered that the Labans were traveling over to Europe in R.M.S. *Juno* with the prophet Isaiah in command, she declared that this was the best omen yet. Eliza was a great one for portents and auguries. Old Wilf Clawston's death in the fire and the Chairman's accident the night before the launch had, in Eliza's opinion, darkened *Leviathan*'s prospects, indicating a perpetual danger of fire and the possible presence in her of a devil from the scorching inferno which had not been properly exorcised and propitiated. This theory was offset to some extent by *Leviathan*'s successful launch and her subsequent speedy completion, though a small fire in the bakery when it had first been tested, followed by the grounding on her passage down to the sea, proved to Eliza the continual presence of one of the dark spirits unwilling to let go its hold on the ship. Her remedy was simple and it would have delighted Quilly.

"Make Captain Isaiah to command that old *Leviathan*," Eliza declared, "and Beelzebub's going to be kept in his rightful place, stoking in the boiler house. Captain Isaiah — he's no man to stand truck from no satanic powers."

Both Max and Ethel had found it a hopeless task to explain why Captain Banks must wait his turn on the seniority list. Eliza would have none of that. It was Isaiah and success or a lesser man and disaster.

"But what have you got against Sir Norman Coxley?" Ethel asked her one day. "He's the commodore of the Line, he's been here to dinner too, and he's the most experienced captain in the company's service."

"I ain't got nothing against the gentleman," Eliza answered. "I'm just saying there ain't been no guest in the house who said grace before sitting down to his dinner like Captain Isaiah."

So there the matter was left. Two days later Ethel Laban embarked in the *Juno* with her husband to find a stateroom filled with flowers. In one hand she clutched a fistful of good luck telegrams from their friends and well-wishers, and in the other a hideous celluloid text embellished with roses which read "The Lamb of God is Risen" and which was a present from Eliza to her Captain Isaiah.

By the time R.M.S. *Juno* sailed from New York for Southampton with Captain Banks and the Labans aboard, *Leviathan* had already begun her very first journey south through the Irish Sea. The previous day she had completed various experimental turns over the measured mile, returning to the Greenock anchorage in the evening, when her hull was floodlit for the benefit of the scores of pleasure steamers circling her until late at night. Already the massive ship had caught British and, indeed, world public opinion. The papers had been full of her journey down the Clyde. Any item of news from the ship was certain of a place.

"And perhaps that's where you can be of assistance, Miss Spicer," Flint had dryly remarked as they took a turn round the sun deck. He was enjoying the presence of this lively young woman, the more so since it was costing the company and himself so little. The training and habits of a lifetime had not deserted him on Susan's irruption into his affairs. The girl had invited him to lunch and he had let her pay. She had asked for a job and he had given her one, but on an apprenticeship basis. She would get her keep and perhaps later on a small pocket-money allowance but that was all her present services were worth, despite her much flaunted shorthand-typing certificate. Flint knew an employee's value to a penny. Very few people grew rich working for the company. Unless, of course, they were stewards.

"But you have a Press representative," Susan answered, "and he looks on me with great suspicion as it is."

Flint shot her a penetrating look.

"It's quite right that he should. You'll have his job away from him in a trice if he doesn't watch out."

"If I thought I could do it better — which I certainly couldn't."

"Exactly. Well, over the next few weeks you can supplement Mason's work. He's always asking for an assistant. You can get to know the ship: you've got sharp, young eyes and I've no doubt a fairly active imagination. You've also good taste, which is more than Mason has ever had. Give them the 'human interest' items they keep yammering for — those paragraphs we're always being pestered about."

"I thought this company shunned publicity."

She could see him ruffling his feathers like an angry crow.

"Do you want an opportunity when it stares you in the face or don't you?" he said sharply. But by now Susan was getting his measure. She was already daring the one thing almost no one ever did these days — she stood up to him and answered him back.

"You're always telling me you loathe and detest your name in the papers, that you're not a showman like Donald Currie and a whole string of others. You can't have it both ways. Either we go out and use this unique occasion for all it's worth or we keep as mum as a Victorian bank manager and treat *Leviathan* as any other old ship creeping anonymously about the Atlantic. This is the most glamorous ship in the world. We ought to be standing up and yelling about it."

"You're a very saucy, impertinent slip of a girl," Flint remarked with asperity. And you're a mean and spiteful old man, Susan thought. One day she would tell him so. At present, though, she must bow to the wind.

"I'm sorry," Susan said. "I'm only saying what other people haven't the courage to tell you."

"You've been with us less than a month, Miss Spicer. You're getting a little ahead of yourself."

"Just as you say," Susan answered, with an impatient shake of the head, "in any case you're paying me so little it can scarcely matter at all. What you don't pay for, you don't respect."

A sour smile touched the old man's face for a moment or so.

"You've been talking to that rascal Quilly," he said and then abruptly turned and walked off in the direction of his state-room. "I'll be ready for a game of chess in ten minutes' time if you're in a more amenable mood."

Susan turned up the collar of her coat and walked thought-fully to the guard rail. There was a choppy sea, and a stiff breeze. *Leviathan* seemed scarcely to be moving yet she must be doing at least twenty-five knots. Susan had no means of judging but she had overheard one of the stewards talking to another that the ship had already bettered her service speed of twenty-eight and a half knots for a couple of hours that morn-ing. She looked down at the sea and thought back on her last few days with the Chairman.

Perhaps she was "getting ahead of herself" as he said. It was an extraordinary situation with unknown rules. What was her job? What was her position? To tell Uncle Fabian that she was on the strength as a "Chairman's assistant" or "future purser-ette" was one thing, to be sure about it herself was another.

Yet she knew the old man liked having her around. He would scarcely let her out of his sight. One day, almost shyly, he had asked if she played chess and when she answered that she knew the moves, he had immediately proposed a game, saying he would teach her. Naturally he won but both were surprised that she could even give him a game. Instinctively she had come to sense ways in which she could drive him pro-vided she played innocent and did not consistently overdo it.

The pattern had been set by that first lunch, which already seemed to have taken place such ages ago. He responded to daring. He enjoyed watching the ease with which she handled a sudden crisis such as coming to the end of the meal at the Adelphi with not enough cash in her bag. To her this was a big matter; to him of no importance at all. He could without thinking have signed the bill himself or have loaned her the money as she had suggested he might in the car.

But he made no move, curious to see how she would react to the situation. Just before the coffee was served, she had ex-cused herself ostensibly to powder her nose. In fact, she had walked straight into the Manager's office, interrupting a meeting, had made her position clear in three or four sentences and had asked if she might sign the bill and later cash a check. The Manager, accustomed to making snap and usually negative decisions about credit, gave her one look and said "Yes." Then she had returned to the table and in due course had signed the bill, as if it had been the most casual thing in the world. Flint watched but made no comment. Then, in the afternoon when Susan had gone back to London, he had rung the Manager himself to find out what had happened.

It was a simple enough problem in all conscience, but the deft way she had faced it decided him finally that an exceptional young fly had walked into the spider's parlor and that it would perhaps be worth the company's while to employ her, after training, in a more permanent job. But that could wait. A more permanent job meant paying the girl a salary and that Flint had no intention of doing if he could get her services for a song in return for the glamour and kudos of working for the Chairman of the most famous steamship company in the world.

The founder would certainly have approved. Joshua Tunney had always preferred the grant of an extra privilege or two, a piece of gold braid or a medal to an award of hard cash from the company's coffers. The more ambitious and idealistic they were, the longer it took them to think about money. Miss Spicer still had her eyes on the stars. That would keep her going for a while.

Susan shivered and was just turning to go down to her stateroom on A deck when a cheerful voice behind her said:

"Good afternoon, Miss Spicer, are you coming to the Purser's party this evening?"

She found herself talking to an officer with two and a half gold rings on his sleeve, his cap at something of a "Beatty" angle and a broad smile on his freckled face.

"I don't think so," she said. "I haven't been asked."

"Oh! I'll ask you, if I may. I suppose Motty thinks you'll be up in the cuddy with the high and the mighty. I'll tell him you're coming. He'll be delighted. He's one of the best, is old Motty."

"How did you know my name?" she asked curiously, "and who are you?"

"Good Lord, everyone knows your name," the officer answered. "You've become a sort of mascot already in the wardroom. If they're all as gorgeous as that, they say, *Leviathan's* going to be glamoured up inside *and* out. My name's Charles Beecher — I'm a cousin of Peter Beecher who designed this great hulk and I'm a Junior First Officer for my sins. I can go on if you like but you look desperately cold. Why don't we go and have a cup of tea down below?"

"I'd love to but I've got to go and play chess with Sir J."

"You've got to play *what?*" the officer stopped and then burst out laughing. "That's really a gem."

"I don't see why," Susan said with as much reserve as she could muster, "and you're not to laugh at me like that — or give me away."

"All right, I'm sorry, Susan — may I call you Susan?"

"If you want to," she said as coolly as possible.

"Ah! now don't take it wrong. I'm sorry if I sounded a bit forward and rude. But the idea of a girl as pretty and attractive as you solemnly sitting down to play chess with old crabber-nose on our first day at sea just struck me as funny. I'm sorry," he made a mock little bow. "And I apologize."

"Ought you to be calling the Chairman old crabber-nose to total strangers?" Susan asked. "After all, I might be his daughter."

"That's the most preposterous idea of the lot. The mere thought of the old prickly pear having a daughter — well, it's almost obscene. And if I told you some of the other names he gets called, I would be obscene." He gave her a sudden sharp look. He had rather nice gray-green eyes, she decided. "Now *you're* not going to give *me* away and I won't let on about the chess," he said, "and we'll meet up in Motty's cabin on A deck square about seven-thirty tonight. All right?"

"All right," Susan said and smiled.

"And you're never to take offense at anything I say. Except on watch and on the company's service," he sprang to attention, "I'm totally unreliable and hopeless. But I must say," he added, "you do have a lovely smile and some pretty good teeth. Oh! and I like your hair, too — if that's of any interest at all."

He gave her a cheerful wave of the hand and was gone. Susan walked along to the Chairman's stateroom with one or two new thoughts in her head.

An ample twenty-four hours had been allowed *Leviathan* for the five hundred and fifty-mile passage from Greenock to Southampton. Even with an average speed of only twenty-three knots she would still have been on time. As it was, long before she rounded Land's End it was evident that she would be well ahead of schedule, and therefore speed was reduced. It was an unusual trip — one of the very few empty ones the ship would make in her whole life. Except for directors and senior officials of the Builders and the Transoceanic Company, there were no guests on board. Navigating and engine room personnel were almost at full strength, but the catering department only had a skeleton staff. The hundreds of staterooms in the three classes were empty, the electrical organ in the ballroom was as yet untried, the equipment in the gymnasium remained untouched, no recumbent rug-wrapped figures nibbled biscuits on deck chairs, no honeymoon couple mooned about the bridal suite.

It struck Dudley Fitzpatrick Mott, as he bathed and put on a clean shirt, that nothing showed up the distinctness of the three main departments of the ship more than a voyage like this. It was almost as if the deck and the engine room and the whole apparatus for the reception and care of passengers were each in watertight compartments and had separate, unconnected existences. In so short a time, he thought wryly, how different it would be.

Once *Leviathan* had gone into service there would be none of this casual, carefree wandering about the ship poking his nose in here, surprising someone there. Once the fare-paying passengers had invaded *Leviathan*, he would be imprisoned again in routine. Even now, with so much of the "bigwiggery" aboard, he was not as free as he would have liked. Even now, as a good purser must, he was playing around with combinations of people, remembering that the lady superintendent wanted to meet the Managing Director of the Shipyard, that the Head of the Passenger Department's second wife was a cousin of the Ship Estimator, and that Captain Masterton invariably drank pink Plymouth Gin with never a touch of ice.

He was just lighting a cigarette and enjoying the comparative peace of it all when Charles Beecher put his perky head round the door and said:

"Hallo, Motty, I hope you don't mind but I've asked a popsy to your party tonight."

"I didn't know we had any aboard. Where are they stored?"

"You know this one all right. This is *the* popsy. I snitched her out of Sir J.'s pocket when no one was looking. *You* know, Motty, Miss Snub-nose of 1938."

"Good Heavens!" Mott said, for a moment really surprised, then, recovering, he went on: "*You* haven't changed much from the *Pluto*. Little Susan Spicer, eh? You didn't waste much time, I must say. But hasn't she got to dance attendance up in the Captain's cabin? That's where Sir J. and the V.I.P.s are gathering."

"No, she hasn't been asked."

"Nevertheless I expect that's where she'll be."

But Mott was proved wrong. In another twenty minutes Susan was standing in the Purser's guest cabin in her tightest black dress, a martini in her hand, listening on the one side to Dr. Kelly's views on last season's Rugby football, and on the other to the Second Engineer's technical and incomprehensible explanation of why differently pitched propellers would probably be fitted when the ship docked at Southampton.

Across the room conveniently near the drink table she watched First Officer Beecher talking to his cousin, the naval architect. Farther round the Chief Steward was demonstrating something with his hands to Mr. Fox, the Chief Catering Superintendent, and Leonard Quilly, who "had just looked in, Mr. Purser, on my way up topsides," was engaged in probing the designer who had done most of the hard work on the decorating contract, which meant the public rooms and the more important first class suites and staterooms. Over these and the eight or nine other people present Dudley Fitzpatrick Mott maintained a well-mannered and professional watch, making sure that everyone was properly introduced, that the drinks flowed as they should, and that no exclusive cliques marred the fair countenance of the party.

A gathering such as this was child's play to Mott. He had once had the notion of calculating how many such parties he had organized or attended in his twenty years' service to the company, but as this amounted very nearly to the number of days he had spent at sea, he found the statistics frightening and soon abandoned the idea; luckily he liked and respected people. Indeed, without that quality he could scarcely have dealt with the job as he did, and he would almost certainly not have reached the top of the tree at such a comparatively young age. The purser in the *Juno*, for instance, was sixty-three, and the other runners-up for the job in *Leviathan* were all seven or eight years older than himself.

Now, as he moved among the guests at his first cocktail party in this new, astonishing ship, his thoughts ranged back over his busy life while his imagination flickered toward the future, so that in some mysterious way it became all one fabric, the present merely being one particular spot in that fabric where he and his attention happened to be. He found he could do this with increasing skill these days, keeping a practiced eye on the machinery of outer circumstance while he himself, the real Dudley Fitzpatrick Mott, dodged about elsewhere, invisible and free.

He smiled at Susan and received a little half-smile in return. What would happen to her? She was trying — and trying so hard not to show it — to be the sophisticated girl taking all this in her stride. Mott knew she was "thrilled to bits" and was no more blasé about *Leviathan* than he had been on joining his own first ship as a spotty cadet of eighteen. What would happen to her? No wonder Charley Beecher could not let her alone for five minutes, making her meet the other deck officers who were there but not leaving her with them for long, declaring even at this early stage a proprietary interest in the girl.

Well — that was the way it went. The early stages were always the best. The excitement of like meeting like, of getting to know each other, of being brought alive by the presence — and in some cases even the remembered presence — of the newly loved. It was only as the thing matured that troubles came. The repetition of old routines, the love-making that no longer thrilled, the onset of marriage, children, and responsibilities that never seemed fair. Would that have been his fate had he married Julia, who had preferred a not very successful career on the stage to married life in the mid-twenties, but about whom, of them all, he still felt more deeply than he cared to admit. Or, with him away at sea and Julia perhaps touring, would marriage have had any meaning? Would it have worked? He shook the thought away from his mind.

That girl being fussed over by Charley Beecher reminded him a little of Julia ten years ago. She had the same independent stance, the same, quick, innocent smile. More boyish, perhaps, in shape, she did not have Julia's big bosom of which she had been so ashamed in those skinny, bedraggled twenties. The legs were good, too, with nice slender ankles and that trim little bottom shown off to such excellent advantage by the cut of the dress she wore. Hey! hey! hey! this would never do. Deftly lifting a martini from a passing tray, he addressed himself to Mr. Frederick Fox, the Company's Head Purveyor and Victualler, who must now be stopped talking shop to *Leviathan*'s Chief Steward. "Come and say a few kind words to the Chairman's new Publicity Assistant," he murmured as he drew Fox to one side. "I should think she's just your cup of tea, Mr. Fox."

Up in the Captain's day cabin, about half an hour later, was gathered the handful of men, the paramount ranking chieftains of yard and steamship companies, upon whom *Leviathan*'s fate depended, and through whose effort and experience the ship had come into being. Quilly and Peter Beecher went up together from the Purser's party and slipped in almost unobserved except for a brief handshake from Commodore Sir Norman Coxley, D.S.O., R.N.R.

Here the atmosphere was quite unlike that in the Purser's cabin. This was a gathering of Tsars. This was the sort of occasion to which Peter Beecher was totally indifferent and which Quilly relished with a kind of fascination. Though possibly more aware than anyone else of the hard process by which these talents and forces had struggled and fought with each other in giving birth to the ship, Quilly was still privately awed by the close presence in one room of the Managing Director, the Shipbuilding Director, and the Engineering Director of the Yard, the two Chief Architects concerned (though individually Quilly considered both of them ordinary in the extreme), the almost mythical Josiah Flint, the distinguished-looking Commodore of the most famous line of ships in the world, and his staff Captain, the Chief Engineering Superintendent of the Company, and the ship's own Chief Engineer who would soon be taking responsibility for *Leviathan*'s vast engines on himself, the Director of the Bank of England and the Lloyd's Underwriter, upon whose joint efforts the financing and insuring of the ship had proceeded so successfully in the face of what seemed at times to be paralyzing difficulties, the Company's Marine Superintendent, and the two heads of the Passenger and Freight Departments. Such were the distinguished guests at the Commodore's cocktail party.

No one else from the company was there, except Quilly. Mitchell had left the ship at Greenock and had returned to his London desk. Laban was *en route* from New York. Other lesser lights in the hierarchy, who happened to be aboard, had been tactfully invited to the Purser's cabin or elsewhere. Here gathered together as they might never be again were the men who comprised the brain-box of it all.

"Well, Captain, are you pleased with the ship?" Flint coughed, twitched his lips, and adjusted his pince-nez which was his way of showing that he had just made a frivolous remark. Quilly wondered what the effect would be if the Commodore said bluntly NO, he thought the great crate a useless collection of rivets. It would have been as good as a Bateman drawing. But Sir Norman Coxley, with his square, weather-beaten face was not given to experimenting in humor. He was a straight-forward, old-fashioned man of the sea, trained in sail and with forty years' service to the company behind him.

"She's a capital ship. Capital. The finest to handle I've ever been in."

"Will she get the Blue Riband away from the French?" the Bank Director asked, an innocent enough remark and one which merely repeated popular speculation, but which to Flint was like lighting a cigarette in a gunpowder factory.

"We are not giddy racing enthusiasts, Lord Lynton," he said, a cutting edge to his voice. "With this company safety always has been and always will be our first concern. Any fool can go after a record."

"I dare say you'd have no objection, though, if *Leviathan* does prove to be the fastest ship afloat. It can't do us any harm."

"This ship is designed to provide a certain service at a certain speed. If she does that," Flint glared at the distinguished Engineers then present as though he rather doubted their ability to handle a clockwork train, "if she does that," he repeated, "then she'll be doing her job and we shall all be satisfied. The question of being the fastest ship in the world has no importance at all — none whatever."

"Except to forty million British," Lord Lynton tersely remarked, "and to the French, German, and Italian nations." He had an acute distaste for little Flint and his dogmatic ideas. The fact that Flint was basically right only made it worse. Any time now he'd mention the *Titanic*. It was his permanent resort in this particular matter. Indeed no sooner had the thought entered his head than Flint went on:

"The *Titanic* was a lesson to us all." Flint glowered at his Lordship's involuntary smile. "The sea doesn't change in a quarter of a century — the North Atlantic still remains the most treacherous, dangerous ocean in the world. We all know the beating of any record means at some stage or other the taking of unjustifiable risks. That is something this company will not do." In his excitement Flint beat his knee with his clenched fist. Any suggestion of speeding invariably produced a reaction like this. Quilly had once heard it irreverently said that the Chairman's mother must have been frightened by a tortoise. But Sir J. was only repeating with quite unnecessary force the guiding principle behind the company's successful century in the North Atlantic, an altogether exceptional care for the safety of the passengers they carried. This in the long run was a far greater dividend-maker than any ephemeral question of speed.

"No one can accuse Sir Josiah Flint of being a road hog," Lord Lynton turned the argument with a smile. He had had no wish to excite the old man in this way.

"Thank you," said Flint with a glance at the gentlemen from Lloyd's. "Road hogs get unpleasant questions from their Insurance companies, I understand, and *Leviathan* certainly doesn't wish to invite that sort of thing."

"I hope we won't be penalized for being ahead of schedule on this voyage," the Commodore said. "We'll be anchoring at Cowes about breakfast time tomorrow, and going up with the midday tide. I hear there's quite a reception awaiting the ship."

Fabian Mitchell drove down to Southampton the next morning with his wife and daughter, Joan. As he had feared, Susan's escapade was disturbing both Joan and Alan, now back at Oxford for the last term of his second year. They were restless enough as it was. Last year he had had to use all the parental authority he possessed to prevent Alan capering off to Barcelona to fight for the Reds. Joan was more placid, it was true, but even she was sulky and dissatisfied these days.

What was wrong with them all? he asked. What was happening to England these days? It was no consolation that other young people seemed exactly the same. There was too much crackbrained pacifism about. We are all going soft, Fabian maintained; we kowtowed to Hitler, Mussolini, and Co., with scarcely a flutter of that fearlessness, pride, and independence which had made the country and the British Empire what it was.

Compromise — everything was compromise these days. Life was a damn sight too comfortable for the young, he thought, swinging the Humber round corners as if he were wielding a battle-ax. They all needed toughening up. Fabian took a cold bath every morning of his life; it spruced him up, as he put it, and in addition rendered him impervious to the archaic hot water system in the house. A cold bath and a brisk rubdown put him in the right condition to face any disasters the day might bring — but could he induce his own stripling of a son to follow his example? Not on your life. If he didn't himself march into the boy's room and yank the bedclothes off him, the brat would quite cheerfully sleep on till noon.

Just before reaching the docks they were overtaken with a toot of the horn and a wave of the hand by the Spicers' Rolls-Royce, driven just as aggressively as the Mitchells' car. "Uncle Harry's swanking again," Joan commented. "I bet he gets stopped at the gate all the same." Indeed this proved to be the case. By the time the Mitchells arrived Sir Henry Spicer, M.P., who never bothered with passes and suchlike tripe, was out of his car, shouting abuse at the docks police. These, who had had to deal in their time with more dangerous men than irate Tory M.P.s, explained that orders were orders and in the meantime blandly let in car after car ahead of the Spicers. It was nearly one o'clock before Fabian had sorted out the trouble, the cars had been properly parked and the joint party was in its privileged position by the graving dock.

Looking down the long vista of Southampton Water for a first sight of the incoming liner, Joan Mitchell slipped her arm through her mother's and surrendered herself to the thrill of it all. The family bicker and the absurd fuss Uncle Henry had made were done with and over. Now, as part of a swarming crowd which seemed to have got itself wedged into every possible viewpoint, a growing excitement took hold of her heart, bringing a surge of that same irresistible emotion the Coronation had induced in her the year before.

There was a moderate westerly wind and a gray patchwork

sky. After about ten minutes, mist clouds followed by rain rapidly dimmed and then blotted out the masts and hulks of other ships lining the route, each one of which was dressed overall in honor of the occasion. For a time it looked as if *Leviathan* would creep up on them almost unobserved. Then gradually the rain stopped and the mist lifted enough for a quick glimpse of *Leviathan* as a faint shape in the distance. A murmur went through the crowd and then once more the ship vanished in the haze.

But this veiled approach was not to last long. A convoy of small steamers, crowded with visitors, hove into sight unofficially escorting the giant, which now appeared trailing slight wisps of smoke. At the same time the deep reverberating note of her siren reached the dock as if a one-note fanfare was being sounded. In another two or three minutes the shape had taken on color. The black hull still merged into the sea, but the white upperworks and the curved distinctive bridge could both be seen underlining the dramatic gray and vermilion funnels. All around her tugs fussed and moved to the accompaniment of little white puffs of steam from their sirens, the notes of which reached the spectators some seconds later. Vanishing and reappearing through the swirling mist, *Leviathan* approached the dock with a slow majesty all her own.

White clouds and patches of light blue sky now began to appear. The weather was progressively clearing and there was even a hint of sunlight to come. Though still three miles away, *Leviathan* and her entourage dominated the horizon. Her upperworks changed from white to gray and back to white again as she passed through patches of sunlit water. The gay colored bunting and the dappled, sparkling sea gave the whole scene a kind of dancing lightness as if each inanimate detail was being moved by an invisible hand according to some sort of pattern and in order to emphasize the jauntiness of the great ship's first Southampton arrival.

Two small tugs, the *William Poulsom* and the *Wellington*, were leading her in with the rest close under her flanks, and as she passed in front of the lilac-gray *Winchester Castle*, the twenty-thousand-ton liner suffered a total eclipse. A large

R.N.R. Blue Ensign dwarfed the other flags *Leviathan* was flying, and as she neared the dock, the tall letters of her name painted in white on the bows seemed to overshadow the human beings clustered along her decks and looking down on the watchers ashore.

Among those people would be her friend Susan, and all the time, as the ship came nearer, Joan thought of her with a growing envy. Why, of the three of them, had Susan alone had the courage of her convictions? Why was Susan the one to astonish them all? Why was she in *Leviathan*, actually on board the ship, whereas Joan remained a mere spectator? Of course she'd been phenomenally lucky, but then luck came to those, etc., etc., etc. She bit her lip and tried once more to see things as they were. Was it only Susan's tomboy daring she lacked? Or was her father right after all? Were Alan and she a little soft inside? She sighed and instinctively squeezed her mother's arm, making some commonplace remark, then shot a glance at her father stiff and straight as the ramrod he was always talking about, watching the great ship coming closer and closer, absorbed in the scene and full of pride. He was set and sure. He really believed in those "right ideas" he held. Why was there such an enormous gap between that blind assurance and her own muddled uncertainty?

By now *Leviathan*, still using her own engines, was positioning herself for the move into the dock itself. The two leading tugs were now pulling at right angles on her starboard bow and the ship herself changed from a sharp silhouette into a perspective of towering lines, the overwhelming impression being one of immensity expressed in a complex of gracefulness.

The steel caisson had been opened in readiness and a few moments later *Leviathan* was straight in line with the mouth of the dock. The tug *Wellington* slid skillfully along the outer wall of the dock, the *William Poulsom* holding on a little longer; then, with another tug as buttress on the starboard side, *Leviathan*'s nose entered the dock. As she did so, heavy hawsers fell in pairs from the fo'c'sle to the quay. Scores of men caught each hawser and secured it over a bollard, so that yard by yard the ship could warp herself in.

In another half-hour *Leviathan* was poised with her keel exactly over a straight row of hundreds of blocks high enough to allow men to work under her. The caisson was closed and the emptying of the dock had begun. Workmen in punts scrubbed down the underwater parts of the ship as the level fell in the dock. A ten-ton crane alongside picked up a gangway and in another few minutes the distinguished visitors aboard were making their way ashore. One of the first to do this was Sir Josiah Flint, leaning rather more heavily than he wished on the arm of Susan Spicer.

Susan never forgot that week-end. Indeed if Joan Mitchell had not been accessible next door, she would never have lasted it out. To begin with there had been the embarrassment of meeting her parents while still on the Chairman's arm, and of her father's blustering remark, "Hallo, Flint, I see you've abducted my daughter"; to which Flint had testily replied, "I'm afraid the boot's on the other foot. She's a very forward young lady." The awkwardness had somehow or other passed off in a clatter of clumsy jokes, with her father condescending to them all in his jolliest Westminster manner, with her mother as usual scared even to open her mouth, with Uncle Fab at his "pomposiest" and Aunt Barbara somehow bringing Ascot into the conversation, which was a feat in itself.

Only Joan understood, exchanging a wink and a shy smile as Uncle Fab and Sir J. moved away toward the car for a private talk. Susan did all she could to avoid showing the rest of them round the ship but capitulated before very long. Then came the unending tour of inspection, getting in the way of stewards sorting out dirty linen, and of stores and equipment being moved into and out of the ship.

Her father was insatiable, demanding to see the engine room, into which they were forbidden entry, the kitchens, which they were asked to leave, and the bridge, where, in any case, visitors were never allowed. In any part of the ship where work was going on they received those searing looks of politely veiled contempt which men with a job to do reserve for unwanted and supposedly important visitors who ask inane patronizing questions, who hold things up, and who invariably get in the way. Susan by this time had acquired various nicknames in the ship and it encouraged her not at all to overhear one steward whispering to another, "That's the old geezer's moll showing us all off to the Duke, 'er Dad."

At last she managed to get them away and they had driven back to Dorking with her father alternately laying down the law and asking incessant questions, and with her mother sniffing into her handkerchief on being told that her one observation was "pretty dotty and dim-witted." Susan could never understand why her mother and father could not talk ten minutes together without bickering. She had discussed it very often with Joan, whose parents behaved in much the same way though never in public and "never," as they fondly imagined, "in front of the children."

"If that's marriage," Joan said as they sat curled up on the floor of the den, coaxing a smoky fire into life, "then it's spinsterhood for little me. Or I might be a nun; or a very high-class *cocotte* with a ravishing Mayfair flat. I've been seriously thinking of dashing up to London as you did and — well, experimenting a bit. You could always give it up. I bet all sorts of girls make a bit extra on the side without any one knowing. I know it's immoral but think how exciting it would be. All sorts of gorgeous men — instead of the same old face every day the rest of your life."

"And clients like Sir J.," Susan commented. "You'd have a terribly jolly time."

"He isn't like *that*, is he?" Joan asked, her sophistication blown away in a sentence. "I mean does an old man like that still — well, you know what I mean."

"No, he's too mean, I think," Susan said briskly. "He always wants something for nothing if he can get it."

"But do you mean to say there are women who'd . . . who'd do it with an old man like that?"

"I don't know," Susan said. "I suppose once you've taken the plunge, you'd do anything for money."

It had been on the tip of her tongue to tell Joan of the drab little pass Flint had once made at her but something caused her to keep silent, as though for some reason it wasn't fair to give the old man away. In any case it was scarcely worth remembering. She had gone round to the side of his desk to put a letter for signature in front of him and had found his hand stroking her bottom. Her first reaction was astonished curiosity. Then she'd caught sight of the sad, almost pleading look in his eyes. That really was a shock, and it opened up all sorts of new and unpleasant ideas. She put all of them out of her mind, smiled unhappily at Sir J. and moved herself just out of range, knowing that if he wished to pursue it further he would have to put his proposition into words or start chasing her round the room, neither of which she guessed he would do.

So the incident had come and gone. Neither of them had ever mentioned it since, but from that moment on Susan had understood the Chairman, the job, and herself in a different and more realistic way. Dismay had been followed by pity. She suddenly saw herself through the old man's eyes, and realized with a wave of compassion that he must at one time have been a determined and lusty young man. How would I be, she wondered, if my body grew crinkly and old but the same restless urge remained? That moment in the somber Liverpool office became a notch in her life. From then on she could never talk about sex in the old childish innocent way, the way Joan still carried on, protected by the dreams and illusions playing around in her mind.

"You could never be a prostitute, Joan," she suddenly said with a harshness which surprised her.

"I shouldn't want to be a 'professional,' Sue. Anyway, it's such a horrid word."

"Exactly. That's what I mean. You dress everything up in pink ribbons. You talk about *demi-mondaines* and ladies of easy virtue. The truth is a tart is a tart, whether she hangs around a street corner or has herself swished about in a large Rolls-Royce."

Joan sat up in surprise.

"What are you getting at? Why are you talking like this?"

"Because you and I think we see through marriage, because our respective parents sham all the time, because we're both

76

determined not to be caught like that. But you swing to the other extreme: you think there's something romantic in a long succession of different men provided they're nice and clean and decent. You see them all as Clark Gables or Errol Flynns. But I don't think it's like that at all. Once you do anything for money, you've got to take what comes your way, and that's more likely to be rich and disgusting old men than that dark-haired Adonis on the front of that magazine you just threw on the chair."

"But, Sue, I was only joking just now. You didn't seriously think I was going to run off to town and set up shop as — well, you know what."

"I don't know," Susan said, giving her a thoughtful stare, "I don't know at all. You can't just sit around in this day and age waiting for a husband to turn up. I've always thought you might do something crazy to get away . . . only in your case, Joany, I don't think it would work. You're much too kind-hearted and nice."

"But what can I *do*, Sue?" Joan wailed. "I'm absolutely fed up with all this. Each 'dainty afternoon tea' I go to with Mummy in nice comfortable houses like ours, I feel I'm going to suffocate to death."

"You could nurse. You've always said you'd like to do that."

"There'd have to be a war."

"There's probably going to be a war," Susan said grimly, "but why — before you can nurse, I mean?"

"Because Daddy says nice girls of our class became V.A.D.s in a war, but otherwise there are no openings for us. Then he makes some silly joke about little Miss Ashton, our district nurse, on her bicycle with her chilblains and her running nose, and asks if that's how I want to end up. If I suggest going to sea as a nurse, Daddy almost chokes himself with rage. He seems to think seagoing nurses do nothing but get off with the doctors. It's not like that in *Leviathan*, is it, Sue?"

"I don't know," Susan said. "I'll ask Dr. Kelly about it."

The week-end remained in Susan's memory for other reasons than this conversation with Joan. There was also a critical meeting with her father. In a sense this was inevitable and long overdue. Both of them knew this, but both of them had put off something which might turn out to be final. In the event both of them were unusually calm and self-controlled.

"I'm afraid you upset your Uncle Fabian," her father began at supper time on Sunday, "by not taking him into your confidence. After all he is number two in the whole Transoceanic setup. He'll be taking over when Flint kicks the bucket. If you want a job at sea he's the natural one to go and ask. I send dozens of people to him every year. However, you dashed off on a crackbrained scheme of your own."

"Which happened to come off, Father."

"As you say, it came off. Nevertheless if it hadn't and you'd got into trouble I've no doubt you'd have gone running to him to put it right." He paused, expecting Susan to argue back as she always did. This time, though, she held her peace. There were not going to be lost tempers if she could help it. "Your mother and I salute your independence" — a faint sniff from Lady Spicer provoked one of his "hot" looks in her direction — "however neither of us profess to understand the first thing about it. Perhaps you'd care to enlighten us."

"What do you want me to say?"

"I don't *want* you to say anything. Your mother and I would just like to know where we've failed you, that's all. Haven't we given you a good enough home?"

"Father, you know it isn't that."

"What is it then? Aren't the Mitchells and the other friends you grew up with good enough any more?"

"I want to do something with my life — while there's still a chance. As I'm a girl it isn't so easy."

"I suppose I'm just an old fogy, out of touch with everything going on in the world. I don't understand you young people any more — the boys at the universities don't want to fight and the girls all want to be boys. I don't understand — I just don't understand."

All right, thought Susan, you don't understand. And who does? It was the willingness to try that mattered. After a pause spent looking into the fire she went on:

"It isn't that I just want to get away from home, you must

know that. And I *am* very grateful to both of you. After all, I'm not a monster of ingratitude, am I?" She looked appealingly from one to the other. "Is it *such* a crime to want to be independent?"

"But don't you want to get married, dear?" her mother asked with a timid look at her father.

"I don't know," Susan said doubtfully, and then more independently, "in any case I don't see what that's got to do with it."

"Well, dear, you're not very likely to meet someone suitable on board ship. I mean, the merchant service isn't — well it's not exactly a gentleman's profession is it?" Her mother quavered and then faltered to a stop. "What I mean is, it's not like the Royal Navy, is it, Henry?"

"Oh! really, Mummy, that's just about the most snobbish thing I've ever heard you say."

"It happens to be true, though," her father chipped in. "The merchant service may be the salt of the earth. I'm not saying anything against it at all. Your mother means that by and large they're not our sort of people. And she's right. Your merchant service officer may be all very well on the bridge of a liner — he doesn't cut much of a figure in a Mayfair drawing room. Of course, that's a snobbish observation to make, but I'm sorry to say that's how life is in this day and age. And you know that as well as I do."

"Yes," Susan said coolly, "I do — but it doesn't worry me so much. The time may come when there aren't any Mayfair drawing rooms any more."

"Oh! well, if that's the case, then there's nothing further to discuss."

The discussion did, in fact, come to an end at that moment, as Susan was called to the telephone. She walked out of the room shaking inside both at her father's arrogance, and also because she knew he was perfectly right by his lights and was only trying to do the best thing possible for his daughter. She picked up the telephone in the hall and heard a familiar, yet unplaceable voice at the other end of the line.

"Miss Spicer? Miss Susannah Spicer?"

"Yes, it's Susan speaking."

"You sound very grand," the voice said, "almost as grand as your butler, or was that the under-footman twice removed who answered the phone?"

"Who is this?" Susan said impatiently.

"All right, all right, don't bite my head off. It's not old crabber-nose speaking, it's — "

"Good Lord, you!" Susan said, the tension expiring out of her as a thrill of pleasure swept in. "What are you doing, ringing me up at home at this time of night?"

"I'm lonely," Charles Beecher's cheerful voice came across. "*Leviathan* is definitely not the same without you. It is not the same. In fact she's just a dirty great hulk in a concrete dock."

"Those are treasonable words, Mr. Beecher. The company's latest ninety-thousand-ton —"

"Oh! don't give me that line of bull, Miss Spicer. I know it by heart. Why not catch the next train down to Southampton and cheer up a poor lonely sailorman? I know a club where we can drink all night if we want to — as a matter of fact that's where I am at this moment."

"Sorry. I'm going to Liverpool tomorrow."

A mock wail of fury banged its way into her ear.

"Have you no sense of adventure, Miss S? Pinch that elegant Rolls-Royce I saw you poshing off in yesterday and we'll drive till the dawn. I tell you I miss that neat little figure with the short blond hair disappearing round the corner of A deck square, leaving just the faint trace of Chanel Number Five."

"It's Arpège, as a matter of fact, and I think you're a bit plastered."

"I certainly shall be," said Charles. "I don't enjoy missing you at all. I'd like to be dancing in your arms all night and not only dancing, if it comes to that, I'd like . . . Oh, damn! there are the pips, and this is a call box. Hey! Sue, sweet Sue, I love you, Sue."

"Nonsense," said Susan. "I'm the Chairman's moll, didn't you know?"

But the line went dead with a click and a buzz.

⚓⚓⚓⚓⚓ IV ⚓⚓⚓⚓⚓

Leviathan was just over a week in dock. During that time her bottom was cleaned and painted, she was equipped with four new propellers of slightly different pitch and her more permanent stores and fittings were all put aboard. By this time, also, most of the crew had been signed on, except for a proportion of the stewards, and were acclimatizing themselves to the ship and their duties. The next event in her life was to be the journey back to the Clyde for her acceptance trials. With these satisfactorily completed, she would then be turned over to the Transoceanic Company for her maiden voyage to New York.

All berths for this voyage had now been fully booked. Indeed, unless anything was to happen during the trials to hold her up, *Leviathan* was already set for a busy season. In this the company was undoubtedly lucky. It had a new and magnificent ship to bring into service at a time when the activities of that gruesome quartet, Hitler, Mussolini, Stalin, and Franco, were seriously disrupting the pattern of transatlantic tourism. Many Americans in the habit of making an annual summer visit to the old world were not doing so this year. Hitler's annexation of Austria in April, Franco's continued progress in Spain, and the ever present Danzig Corridor and Sudetenland problems certainly constituted no open invitation to a peaceful and carefree Europe. Such, at any rate, became the picture painted in Max Laban's opening remarks at the various travel agency conferences he attended.

Ethel and he were now established at the Savoy after one of the best trips across they had ever had. The *Juno* was among the largest and most famous liners in the company's fleet. Though thirty thousand tons smaller than *Leviathan*, she was spacious and comfortable according to the ample ideas of 1911 when her keel had been laid. Her four raked funnels and her overhanging counter stern were known all over the world since not only was she for a time the Company's crack ship on the North Atlantic, but she had also proved herself one of the most popular cruise liners there had ever been. Old-fashioned in looks and with a speed of only twenty-three knots, she was now rapidly going out of date but what she lacked in nattiness was made up for by exceptional service, based in turn on the disciplined bravura which Captain Basil Bellerophon Banks seemed to achieve in any ship he commanded.

Indeed, Banks's ideas and the force with which he applied them permeated the ship. He was strict. He demanded a little extra effort, a little more than the best out of every single member of the crew; but he was fair, he was understanding in the way he applied the rules, and above all everyone on board from the oldest quartermaster to the youngest bellboy knew there was a captain in command of the ship.

Ethel, who was coming to relish the man's gusto and eccentricities as she got to know him better, had tried to sound him out on the way it was done. But Banks was not as simple as she thought.

"What makes a good captain, madam? Why God of course," he had startled her by saying. They were up in his cabin after dinner one night, a time Banks usually kept to himself. But on this trip they were overloaded with celebrities and Banks had scarcely seen anything of his two good American friends. Now they were comfortably seated in his day cabin, Banks in the great oak chair he had had made for use at his desk, Max and Ethel on a more conventional settee. In front of the captain next to his calendar stood Eliza's celluloid text.

"They say responsibility is a gift of heaven," Banks went on. "They say it distinguishes man from the animals. Well, madam, as you can guess, responsibility is any captain's long suit."

"All right," said Ethel, "so God makes a good captain. How does He set about the process?"

"*Aha!*" Banks exclaimed as though she had made some very clever move in a game of chess. "If that was to be compressed and put in a capsule, do you think it would do anyone any good?"

"Well, that's not what I'm asking. But I don't want you to

82

give away trade secrets, Captain, at least not in front of my husband."

"Perhaps your husband can answer that better than I can, madam," Banks said with a twinkle. "I'm only a simple seaman. You pose me a management problem."

She could never get a direct answer out of him, and later that night Max had said it was tactless of her to ask.

"Why?" she retorted. "I'm only trying to find out what makes the man tick."

"If you go to Buckingham Palace," Max said, "you don't ask the King of England what makes a good King."

"The King of England didn't fight his way up to command of a transatlantic liner."

But it was never any good trying to make Banks explain himself or the way he did things. He would simply twitch his beard and say it was all in the book of the rules. People who scarcely knew him assumed this to be the company regulations. A good deal of it certainly was in the company manual but any officer who joined a ship under Banks's command knew better than that. On first meeting one of his officers, Banks kept introductions short and to the point. After he had learned the officer's name, rank, and duty, he would present the newcomer with a copy of the Bible.

"Here is the Book of Rules, sir. In it you will find directions for known or unknown emergencies of any kind. I commend it to you and you to it. May God bless the voyage we are about to undertake."

Then with a brisk handshake and a cool nod, the officer would be sent to get on with his job without further ceremony or fuss. Names were rarely used; men were addressed as "sir" and women as "madam" and woe betide the junior officer who thought it funny to be called "sir" by his captain. He was likely to find the next watch he kept a nightmare he would never forget the rest of his life.

As soon as the *Juno* passengers had been cleared at Southampton, Banks had gone over to look at *Leviathan* in the graving dock. He was in a contented mood. That evening he would be digging in the garden of his Sussex cottage with over a fortnight's leave to enjoy. Everyone on the New York run was rested for one voyage in six and this particular relief came at a time when the garden needed his maximum attention. But first of all he wanted to see what sort of ship *Leviathan* had turned out to be.

He walked on board and asked for the Commodore but Sir Norman Coxley and the Staff Captain were both ashore. However, the Chief Officer, who had been with him in *Pluto*, welcomed him warmly and told him of the voyage down the Clyde and from the Clyde to Southampton, showing him the bridge and the captain's quarters, and giving him freedom of the ship. No one could serve under Banks without coming to know the range of his idiosyncracies, one of which was to wander about the ship by himself in an apparently aimless fashion. This was disconcerting and sometimes embarrassing but Banks never took advantage. There are times for a captain to inspect a ship and there are times to keep out of the way. If on these private prowls Banks came on something he should not have seen, he simply ignored it. At first the crew were suspicious and resentful, but soon they came to accept it as an unwritten rule, tested on several occasions when a particular misdemeanor Banks had stumbled across had subsequently come up before him, through the normal channels, and had been dealt with as if it were the first that he had ever heard of the matter.

Banks himself used these haphazard walks as a kind of communion with the ship itself and with the invisible principalities and powers which controlled its destiny. This was an instinctive action, a kind of inner alertness which Banks never bothered to formulate in words, because he had long believed that there were other ways of knowing than through the five senses and a slow classification in the brain.

A ship was alive — not in the doggy-woggy sentimental sense of possessing a subhuman personality — but as an organized functional thing. If you rode a horse you could, if you wished, talk to it in words but you could also know about that horse and control it without any language at all. A ship was not quite the same but it acted as a kind of prism for some of the forces bearing down both on it and on humanity. If you know how to watch and how to listen, you could apprehend a great deal about that ship and how she would behave. This particular ability was well developed in Banks, and even in dry dock a short prowl round the echoing, empty newness of *Leviathan* seemed to add to the mood of contentment which already possessed him. She would probably be a happy ship, he decided, and God willing he would command her before he was through with the sea.

He was examining the detail of one of the huge glass panels in the main restaurant when a girl's voice behind him said "Captain Banks, sir?" He turned to find a smallish, blond-haired girl looking up at him with lively questioning eyes. He did not immediately answer but looked her up and down. This close aggressive attention usually aroused, in the object of the attention, an aggressive wish to retort, thereby losing the battle of wills, so to speak, almost before it had started. This girl, however, seemed to be quite undisturbed by his gaze. In fact she was even daring to smile.

"That is my name, madam."

"The Purser's compliments, sir, and will you go and have a drink with him in his cabin?"

Banks stared at her thoughtfully a moment or two longer.

"Thank you. What is your name, may I ask?"

"Susan Spicer . . . sir."

"And what do you do?"

"I'm a purserette, or I hope to be very soon."

"A what?"

"A Lady Assistant Purser, I believe is what I'll eventually be called."

"Hm!" said Banks. "A new feminine invasion, is it? And what are your duties to be?"

"Give the Purser clerical assistance, help entertain the passengers, be a sort of Press agent for the ship, and perhaps one day type out *your* reports and letters, sir." Then before he had time to reply she turned and led the way to the door.

"If you follow me, sir, I'll show you the way to the Purser's cabin."

Up in Liverpool Flint was already missing his "girl mascot" more than he cared to admit. And this emptiness was the worse because he could quite well have kept her up there in the office on some pretext. He could have continued to enjoy her company, or have taken her on as a companion-secretary, which at one time he had been strongly tempted to do. He was a rich, autocratic old man, and possibly Susan would have stuck by him for a time. He had let her go south, though, and join *Leviathan* for a number of minor reasons and one big one, against which he did not choose to fight.

The smaller reasons concerned the Lady Superintendent and the Marine Superintendent, who were respectively for and against the idea of introducing purserettes but were unanimous that the sooner they were put into uniform and under discipline the better. In this they were joined by Fabian Mitchell and by Mason, the publicity man, who had been instinctively against Susan and any sort of competition in his job right from the start. None of these heads of departments would tolerate courtiers — one Quilly was enough in a company like Transoceanic — and for a girl such as Susan to walk in and gain what might soon become a powerful and private access to the Chairman was in their minds offensive and nearly scandalous. The company's higher command was a delicately balanced machine where each cog had its own specific function to carry out. An amateur, however good-hearted and charming, could not be accepted for long — and certainly not when she had the Chairman's ear as Susan seemed to have. So, feeling old and tired, Flint bent to the wind. He would not provoke his subordinates beyond a certain point.

Such then were the small reasons for Susan's departure south. The big one was Susan herself, who had made it crystal clear that if she did not go to sea in *Leviathan* she would remove herself and do something else. The girl had a will of her own and Flint knew she would do as she said. It had been a bad mistake to show her, even for a moment, that she meant something more to him than just another clerical employee. One little gesture had lost him any hold he had over the girl. Alone in his office he sighed to himself. You had to pay for everything in this world, but not always, alas, with money.

Thus Susan had become one of three girls who were to initiate the Lady Purser scheme — one being sent to *Leviathan*
and one to each of the other ships on the express New York
run. It had originally been intended to give them a course of
instruction ashore but the scheme had blown hot and cold for
so long that there was now no time for this, and so individual
pursers were given the job of training their purserines or
purserettes in the way they thought best, it being understood
that if the girls were not satisfactory the scheme would be
dropped for good and all.

"So you see, you and your opposite numbers in other ships
are on trial," Dudley Fitzpatrick Mott had told her when
she reported for duty, "without any of us quite knowing what
the rules of the game are going to be. One thing's certain —
you won't have much time to yourself once we get going, so
you'd better be prepared to turn your hand to anything in
emergency. As I see it, you'll mostly be secretary to the Staff
Captain and to me — and that's a very agreeable prospect for
me, I may say. But you'll also be learning about manifests and
bills of lading, so that you can be of some practical use when
you lend a hand in the office."

The day *Leviathan* came out of dock Susan got her neat
blue uniform with its Transoceanic buttons and its single
white stripe round the sleeves showing that she had the equivalent rank of cadet. She was pleased with that uniform and the
way it suited her. Earlier, she had suggested to the Lady
Superintendent that she might be allowed to wear trousers
as her working rig during the day but this had been received
in painful silence.

"We've never had a request of this nature before," the
Lady Superintendent had said. She looked on Susan with
cautious dislike in view of her arrival via the Chairman's
office.

"I understand you've never had girl pursers up till now,"
Susan said. "I merely thought trousers would be warmer and
more practical for working that's all."

"You happen to have a figure which can no doubt look reasonable in trousers," the Lady Superintendent went on. "I'm happy to say our stewardesses are somewhat plumper in build. Neither they nor the nurses nor the shop assistants have ever shown the slightest wish to ape the men they work with to the extent of wearing their clothes. And what do you imagine the passengers would think? This is the Transoceanic Steamship Company, not the *Folies Bergères*."

There were other snags to the job. She was sharing a cabin on B deck with three other girls, a very different state of affairs from the first class single cabin she had enjoyed on the trip south when Flint had been aboard. Four women in one cabin was not Susan's idea of luxury and she set herself the aim there and then of getting a cabin to herself, or at any rate of sharing it with only one other person. The tiny rest room, too, was not designed to encourage anyone to relax too much and Susan quickly saw that her life would be spent either in the Purser's office where she worked, or in the cabin class restaurant where it had been decided she would take her meals, or in the cramped inside cabin where she would sleep. The twelve-day round trip across the Atlantic was going to be no pleasure cruise for those who worked the ship — yet provided she could learn to adapt, it would become an adventure once more, spiced with a new determination to see how comfortable she could make the conditions she found herself in.

Moreover, she liked the first sight she had had of the other three girls in the cabin. They were an assorted collection. None had graced a girls' public school as Susan had done, and none of them was likely to be presented at Court. The upper berth over Susan's bunk was taken by a girl called Veronique Anderson, half-French, half-Scottish, who was to run the perfume and gift shop aboard; on the other side was Pamela Davies, a rather severe-looking nurse; and above her Gloria Dowkins from Barrow-in-Furness, who would be the principal assistant in the Beauty Parlor and Ladies' Hairdressing Saloon. Susan smiled to herself as she visualized her parents' horror were she to bring them all home in a bunch. All of them were older than Susan. Pamela Davies was around thirty,

Veronique about twenty-seven, and Gloria Dowkins a sharp and attractive twenty-four.

And there was friction from the moment they came together in the cabin. Pamela Davies who neither drank nor smoked objected to Gloria Dowkins who did both, and whose first action on waking up in the morning was to light a cigarette. Veronique was especially neat and well made-up, which entailed an undue use of the only good mirror in the cabin. Susan, accustomed up to now to unlimited space, tended to strew her bits and pieces all over the place. Pamela Davies, in the opinion of the others, washed far too much and too frequently. They would need a lot of tact with each other in settling down. Yet since they were all of them there of their own free wills, and since they were living not only for themselves but to provide part of the service in the greatest ship in the world, they each managed to keep their petty selfishness within bounds.

"And if it does become too much of a wasps' nest," Charley Beecher said after listening to Susan's descriptions, "you can always move in with me. Just say the word and I'll fix the whole thing with Motty."

"You don't think the Captain would have anything to say?"

"Good heavens no. The old man just wants all his little boys and girls to be happy. Let them have what they want, he says — it's the company motto. And if the Germans can sport their 'strength through joy' whoopee ships, is Great Britain to lag so far behind? I should think not. In any case, *Leviathan*'s soon going to have so much sex aboard it won't know what to do with itself."

"Don't you ever think about anything else?" Susan asked primly.

"*Is* there anything else?" Junior First Officer Beecher inquired. "I thought that was all agreed a long time ago. No one at sea ever thinks of anything else. Why should they? That's why girls were put into the world. And very nice it is too."

So *Leviathan* sailed away again to the north. This time only experts were aboard. This time she took nearly three days for the trip carrying out her forty-eight hours continuous steaming test *en route,* and her fuel consumption and engine capacity tests. The brake horsepower of each of her sixteen turbines was established. Boiler pressures were plotted and she completed some two dozen runs over the measured mile, followed by lengthy turning trials.

Day after weary day the tests went on, the figures being checked and analyzed and argued about. Her full speed proved to be nearly thirty-one knots, though this figure was kept the most secret of all. Lifeboats and life-saving equipment were tested, in fact every machine or device installed on board for a particular purpose was put through its paces, examined, checked, and rechecked in the cold critical light which plays on any ship about to leave her builder's hands for good and all and go into service.

Meanwhile she was watched by experts all over the world. While Flint, in the Liverpool office, drummed his fingers on his desk and mentally walked round every new figure and fact as if it were a move in chess, naval architects and engine designers, shipbuilders and ship owners, Navies and Governments in Germany, Italy, France, Holland, America, and Japan used such information as was published together with the gleanings of their considerable intelligence services to determine what effect the ship would have on their respective mercantile marines. *Leviathan* and her progress had become a world news item.

Rumors inevitably started. Any pause, any slight change of plan, any mishap however trivial was seized upon and magnified, in some cases to the point of disaster. A delay in weighing the anchor could mean a weakness in the capstan engine, delays in the operation of water-tight doors and fire-resisting roller shutters encouraged the raising of doubts about safety factors, though the company's record in this respect was perhaps the best in the world. Indeed, the rejection of any piece of equipment which failed under test (and there were few enough of those) was eagerly devoured abroad by the forces of envy and jealousy which *Leviathan* had already aroused. Any vast enterprise involving incompletely known risks which shows every sign of becoming an established success inevitably attracts a morbid desire in certain quarters for catastrophe to strike.

But such unexpressed wishes and doubts all came to nought. Indeed the only accident of note, when the blades in one of the four turbogenerator sets were partially stripped through too eager a start, never reached the outside world, but was the subject of an acrimonious and private inquiry by the Chief Engineering Superintendent.

As the main body of the trials came to an end, the Managing Director of the Shipyard issued a statement to the Press which wrapped up and tidied away the whole long process of *Leviathan*'s design and construction. "The Directors and Staff," it said, "wish to inform their workers at Clydebank, Sheffield, and other places where the hull, machinery, and fittings of R.M.S. *Leviathan* have been made, and also their neighbors on Clydeside and their friends elsewhere who have shown such extraordinary interest, encouragement, and support during the building of the vessel, that the speed and trials of *Leviathan*, ending today, have been in every way successful, and that the performance of the ship has more than fulfilled their expectations."

A few hours afterward, *Leviathan* was formally handed over to her ship's officers, the directors, and officials, the technicians and the experts clambered down into the waiting tender for the last time, the builders' house flag was hauled down, and the Transoceanic Company's flag was hoisted at the main truck in its place. Final expressions of good will and good luck were exchanged and then, without further ado, the great ship sailed away from her birthplace to begin the life and the service for which she had been built.

Both Max and Ethel Laban were enjoying their annual few weeks in London which, this year, would culminate in *Leviathan*'s maiden voyage to New York. They had a host of friends: Mitchell put a Company car at their disposal, Quilly got them the best seats at the most popular shows, and they even went down to Sussex and spent a night with Captain

Banks, who met them at the door of his cottage looking like a bearded bull in his gumboots and gardening togs.

At first sight there seemed to be rather more of Captain Banks than of the thatched cottage he lived in. This notion grew in Ethel's head as he introduced them to his diminutive, bird-like sister who kept house for him, obviously worshipped the ground he walked on, and happened to be the only relative he had left in the world. The Labans were shown to their room under the eaves, banging their heads five times in three minutes on unexpected fifteenth-century beams. There was no running water and the privy was a good fifty yards from the house near a clump of trees at the bottom of the garden.

The cottage had been acquired by Banks's father, himself a sea captain of some character and renown. Captain Morgan Banks, in addition to being Welsh and to having spent nine-tenths of his life in sail, had also been of a highly religious turn of mind — a lay reader, and much addicted to the more martial hymns such as "Onward, Christian Soldiers," which he would often bellow lustily on his morning visits to the little house in the trees. It was from their father that Banks got his early grounding in the Bible, just as it was from the gentle submissive mother that Hilda Banks got her endurance and the sense of humor on which it relied.

"Actually my name's Brynhild," she told Ethel while her brother was taking Max for a tour of the garden, "which was due to our father's passion for Wagner. But it's such a mouthful it had to be shortened, of course, and anyway Mother could never stand anything German at all. Is Mr. Laban interested in horticulture?"

"Oh! so-so, you know," Ethel answered vaguely. Max's interest in flowers was in fact limited to a charge account at the next door florist. "We grow geraniums on our penthouse terrace."

"Oh! do you?" said Hilda Banks, her eyes bright with interest. "I've never been to New York. The Captain's always going to take me 'one of these days' just as Father was always going to take my mother round the world, but it never came off — and anyway someone has to stay behind and look after the home."

"You must insist that he does," Ethel said, who had taken instantly to the tiny Brynhild, "you must come and stay with us. I'd adore to show you New York."

"Well, we'll have to wait and see, won't we?" said Miss Banks, unconsciously repeating the phrase with which her mother had met the surprises and disappointments of her life, with its long periods of loneliness and its sudden eruptive activity when Captain Morgan Banks was home from the sea.

"I'm afraid you'll find it a little primitive here," she went on. "I do keep on at the Captain to have the water and electricity put in — they're in the village, you know, but I'm afraid he won't hear of it as our father wouldn't before him. Our father hated machines. He said the more we relied on mechanical contrivances the more we put ourselves in the power of the Chief Engineer of them all. He was referring to Satan, of course. Funny, isn't it, when you reflect that his son has command of one of the biggest 'mechanical contrivances' that ever put to sea." Miss Banks poked the fire and then gave her habitual look through the window at the oak tree by the front door. "The *Juno* was always a particular *bête noire* of our father's. He predicted a terrible fate for the ship and, indeed, for the entire Transoceanic fleet. I think it would have shocked him to death to know that his son had now ended up in charge of her. And what he would have said about this new monster they're all talking about I shudder to think."

"We're going back to New York on *Leviathan*'s maiden voyage," Ethel said, "so we don't want any curses or spells on that ship, thank you very much."

"Oh! you won't get them from me," Miss Banks hastened to say. "I'm very much to the opposite point of view. If I had my way I'd fill the house with electricity. I'd wallow in luxury and comfort from morning to night — but you mustn't give me away to the Captain, and of course you mustn't think your beds haven't been aired, there's been a hot water bottle in them since yesterday morning."

That evening with the Banks was something the Labans never forgot. For months afterward Ethel would wake up in the middle of the night and find herself laughing at the memory of Captain Banks, his paunch and his beard monolithically framed in an old hooded leather chair, exchanging opinions with her husband, while Brynhild flitted in and out, plying them all with coffee and brandy after one of the best duck dinners Ethel had ever tasted, all of which had been cooked on a small and ancient iron stove with the improbable name of "The Permeator."

Having entertained him in New York, having watched him as Captain of his ship on board the *Pluto* and the *Juno*, it now seemed incongruous, somehow, to find him playing a civilian role unconnected with ships and the sea. Nor was it merely a spare-time hobby. Basil Bellerophon Banks was a Church Warden, as his father had been before him, to the discomfiture of the Vicar, a determined gardener, President of the local youth club, and one of the village's three Liberal voters. He was an intermittent but sizeable nuisance to the Rural District Council, a ferocious shove ha'penny and darts player at the Swan, an enthusiast of opera and the possessor of a 1927 Arrol-Johnson cabriolet, which was almost his only concession to the mechanical age he lived in.

"You certainly have the best of both worlds, Captain," Laban had said at one stage of the evening. "This and the *Juno* and New York — they make a nice contrast with each other."

"Well — I'm not a millionaire," Banks retorted, "but then I never intended to be." He shot the American director a penetrating look. "It depends on the God you serve."

"We both serve the Transoceanic Steamship Company," Laban said drily.

"Would you continue serving the company if it paid you what it pays its sea-going officers? I'm not insulting you, sir, but I know damned well you wouldn't. This company may get the pick of the bunch — but it gets them for a song. Yet boys keep on going to sea and they keep on becoming captains of ships. Why is that? Because there are still people around who prefer to sacrifice their lives to the idea of service rather than

94

to buy and sell. That's what I mean by the God you serve. And make no mistake — it's a sacrifice all right. There are always far better jobs ashore."

"I don't think the company's unduly mean. It always has put quality first, and quality costs money."

"Well, sir," Banks went on with a twinkle, "I'm not conducting a union meeting with the pair of you guests in my house; I'll reserve that for Captain Masterton and the Chairman. I'm just pointing out that there must still be something very powerful at work in this country to make men like myself choose service at sea instead of the pursuit of a fortune." He poured out more brandy for them all. "As a matter of fact that's part of the secret — the little we do get paid. It's a test of motive. Like becoming a priest. You've got to want to be a sailor one hell of a lot. Now you know as well as I do that if this was an American company I'd be getting three to four times my present salary — yet Americans still can't run their ships as ships have to be run. And why is that? Too much money, too much phony democracy — you'll pardon my vehemence, madam — no acceptance of the idea of discipline let alone discipline itself, no discomfort, no sacrifice, and no *esprit de corps*. How can you have *esprit de corps* if you only go to sea for the cash?"

Miss Banks coughed nervously and shot little glances at Ethel.

"Right," said Laban in no way taking offense. "America's a continent, not a tight little island. We don't go to sea, we go west. And as far as *esprit de corps* is concerned, there was plenty of that when we broke away from the British."

"*Aha!*" Banks said beating his knee with his fist. "You're proving what I say — of course there was — you were all serving the *idea* of freedom. You were sacrificing your immediate self-interest for a bigger *idea*. Ideas run the world — to serve God by serving other people is a bigger idea than the amassing of wealth."

"Though one sometimes leads to the other," Laban remarked, "as in fact it has with this company. And personally I don't see why service shouldn't be based on hard cash and good profits. It's a question of value for money. We provide a service no other company can rival — and after all these years I'm still not sure I know why. Of course, Captain, I'm only a salesman — almost an untouchable by your standards."

"Oh dear!" Ethel said, winking at Miss Banks who seemed to have shrunk into a sort of pixie ball. "I'm quite sure this discussion isn't wise. We ought to lead the talk into calmer places, don't you agree, Miss Banks? The trouble is I'm always fascinated when anyone starts arguing with Maxie. I just have to sit and take it at home."

"You were the one, Ethel, who wanted to know what made a good captain of a ship," Laban remarked easily. He enjoyed prodding Banks into action — not that much prodding was needed. "A few more evenings like this and you'll very soon know."

"It's quite simple," Banks went on, "service depends on discipline — and discipline on the will to serve. British seamen have a tradition based on the intelligent acceptance of discipline. Not blind abject slavery such as the Germans admire, but discipline for a purpose — thought out, questioned at times, but in the end freely accepted. It's a splendid tradition — salted with humor — but of course, madam, when it comes to the point, discipline is nothing but the obeying of orders given by someone you may not especially like."

"I'd say discipline bases itself on fear," Laban said. "It certainly does in Germany."

"Of course it does. We're all afraid of something — it's a condition of life. But nowadays no one bothers to *define* what we fear — not in ordinary life. Were we not told to fear God, sir? That was the old idea — and God is what we serve. Or we used to. But of course, nowadays people are much too clever for that. Life's too comfortable, too cushioned, too easy for an old-fashioned God to be any sort of terror today. People are under the dangerous illusion that Nature has been or will soon be mastered. Why serve God when Nature is there to serve us? Why bother with God? So we allow ourselves to be carried along by life, drowsy and half asleep, as long as the carrying is smooth and easy enough. But put to sea in a storm, madam, and people's ideas very rapidly change. Our mastery of Nature doesn't seem quite so sure. Well — at least there's a doubt. So then they see a need for a captain and a hierarchy. Then men do as they're told because they don't want to drown. And since it's still comparatively easy to drown if you challenge the North Atlantic in winter — the question of discipline on board ship really settles itself. Fear God and obey the captain — or else! Thus, Q.E.D. Discipline is based on fear. Another brandy, sir?"

"You must admit, Captain," Ethel remarked after this outburst had subsided a little, "that it's easier for the British. You naturally respect authority — you don't mind being told to do things — but Americans won't have that at all. All men are equal and all men are free."

"That, madam, is the biggest fallacy in this preposterous, socialistic, ant-heap age."

"Yes — well I should never try and put it over on *you*, Captain, but it was the idea behind the French and American revolutions. And I don't think we've done so badly when it comes to the point."

"When it comes to the point, madam, Americans will discipline themselves in the same way as anyone else. The trouble is they may do it too late. I dislike to remind you, but 1917 was three years after the war began."

"I thought the war would come into this. That was not our war, Captain, and it need never have been."

"The next one will be. Or is Hitler none of your business over in the States?"

Feeling in the room had suddenly mounted and a silence fell. Ethel's early dislike of this domineering outspoken bully flooded back. What he said may no doubt have been logically right. She didn't care. She was not going to be patronized or put in her place. She and Maxie, as Jews, regarded Hitler as very much a part of their business. But there was not going to be a war — that was definite. And America was not going to be trapped once more into rushing to the support of an arrogant, out of date colonialism based on this sainted hierarchy and discipline which this great ugly bear had been arguing. She felt like bringing in Palestine . . . but checked herself. After all Max was a director of Transoceanic, and this barrel of pomposity merely one of his employees. The evening suddenly seemed spoiled and she set her mouth in a hard, determined line. No — there was not going to be a war, Hitler or no Hitler. She shook her head firmly and said it aloud.

"There's not going to be a war, Captain Banks. There *can't* be another war."

But Banks, too, had become aware of the feeling in the room and did not reply. He felt a little guilty at putting on this display, as he called it to himself. It wasn't really fair. He liked the Labans and they were guests in his house. He decided that he'd made a mistake and, that decision made, that it must be corrected at once.

"I must beg your pardon, madam," he said, "for talking as I have done tonight. It was my fault — a mistake. I apologize. These things are better not discussed — nowadays."

"Nonsense," Laban said briskly. "If British and Americans can't say what they think to each other when there's a difference of opinion, then there's no hope at all. In fact we *should* have it out. One thing, though, I can assure you, Captain Banks, and that is that Hitler is very much America's business — just as Palestine is. But in both cases we happen to differ about what should be done."

"You can't appease a dictator." The twinkle had come back into Banks's eyes. "I ought to know — I'm a bit of a dictator myself. We should have nipped off the buds a long time ago. Now he's well rooted and almost in flower. He's marched into Austria, and the Lord knows which of us is next on his list."

"Then how would you stop him, Captain?"

"Drop a bomb on his head when he isn't expecting it. Grasp the initiative. In fact," Banks said, sitting up and giving both his guests a hard look, "go to war before he does with us."

"No!" said Ethel. "It — it doesn't bear thinking about."

"That's exactly the trouble. It doesn't bear thinking about, so let's bury our heads in the sand and hope for the best. I can assure you, madam, that Hitler is thinking of *us*. And they're not very nice thoughts from our point of view. He'd like his old colonies back, he'd like the gold in the Bank of England, and I've no doubt he's got his eyes on *Leviathan*. It's just about his size for a yacht, don't you think?"

Almost as if the name *Leviathan* had some magic effect, there was a knock at the front door and a moment or so later Miss Banks returned to say it was Barker, the village policeman, with a message for the Captain, a message he had to deliver personally. Banks impelled his amorphous mass out of the chair and into movement with a surprising speed, as though a steel spring lay concealed in the jelly, and while he was out of the room Brynhild explained that as they had no telephone, if any important messages came through, the village policeman was always got out of his bed. Usually it was something to do with the ship, but as the Captain was only halfway through his leave and the *Juno* nearing New York, it could scarcely be that, Miss Banks went on, and then quickly added to Ethel:

"You mustn't be upset by the way the Captain carries on about war. It's his time in the R.N.R., you know. He has such very pronounced opinions, just as our father did — which, of course, not *all* of us agree with — and he does love to throw them about." Her shy smile and little fluttering movements gave Ethel a deeper insight into her life than words could ever do.

"Oh! that's all right," Ethel said, "it's all part of our education."

"But I don't think guests should come to this house and be 'educated,'" Brynhild went on anxiously. "I *do* know the Captain likes you both very much — in fact he told me I was to be on my best behavior, and whenever he does that, I know we've got very special guests! — so you mustn't take offense."

"Personally," Max was saying, "I always prefer a man to say what he thinks."

"You must certainly come to New York," Ethel found herself adding with a smile, "and be a very special guest in our home for a change!"

Then Captain Banks came back into the room carrying a piece of paper in his hand. His whole demeanor had changed. The ebullience, the aggressive cockiness of manner had vanished. Instead a gravity and a stillness appeared to possess him. Lost in his thoughts, he seemed scarcely to notice the others in the room, and it was a moment or so before he spoke.

"I'm afraid there's been a tragedy in *Leviathan*," he said at last. "The Commodore had a heart attack on the bridge as the ship was entering Southampton this evening. He died ten minutes later." Banks stared into the fire as the others thought over the implications of this sudden news out of the blue. "And I've been appointed Captain in his place as from two hours ago." Banks went on, almost to himself, "May the Good Lord preserve my soul!"

⚓⚓⚓⚓⚓ V ⚓⚓⚓⚓⚓

Aboard *Leviathan* the death of Sir Norman Coxley had been a piece of high drama. The ship had made good time on her passage down from the Clyde but the weather had steadily worsened as they came up Channel. This did not affect *Leviathan* in any noticeable way. In point of fact, they wanted a bit of weather, "to shake the ship together" as the Commodore put it, but a strong westerly wind in Southampton harbor made the problem of bringing her alongside the ocean berth exceedingly tricky. Charles Beecher, whose job as a junior first officer included the charge of all navigational appliances such as chronometers, compasses, charts, sounding appliances, flags, and signal controls, was on the bridge which was his station for entering or leaving harbor. Also on the bridge was the junior third officer, the Chief Officer, the Commodore himself, and the pilot.

Shortly after the pilot had come aboard, the Commodore had retired to his cabin for nearly ten minutes. This in itself was odd, and when he reappeared on the bridge his weather-beaten face seemed unusually pale and drawn. But though the others remarked on this to themselves nothing was said aloud. Polite inquiries about the Captain's health as a ninety-thousand-ton liner comes into port in a high wind are not generally encouraged, and in any case his behavior appeared perfectly normal, except that he was continually searching for something in his pockets. At last on one of his perambulations across the bridge he murmured to Charles:

"Can't find my jumbo, must have dropped it somewhere. I suppose you haven't seen it anywhere, have you?"

"No, sir, I haven't. I'll have a look for it if you like."

"No, no, not now. It doesn't matter." And then with a sigh he had continued across the bridge. Charles looked over to the Chief Officer, who had overheard this conversation, and they raised their eyebrows at each other before continuing with their jobs. The Commodore's "jumbo" was known throughout the fleet, being a tiny elephant carved in white ivory which he used to hold in his left hand as a mascot whenever there was a tricky problem to face. It was supposed to have been given to him by a Maharajah for successfully navigating a typhoon in the Indian Ocean, but there was also a rumor that it had been pinched off the mantelpiece of a Bombay brothel in a typhoon of a different kind. Whatever its origin, Sir Norman Coxley's jumbo had been with him on over seven hundred Atlantic crossings, all of them completed without mishap.

Six tugs were being used to berth *Leviathan* and as the ship turned beam on to the wind, two of them parted their lines. Such a moment is highly charged with anxiety for any captain, since, although the berthing is carried out according to the pilot's instructions and advice, the captain remains fully in charge and responsible in every respect for the safety of the ship. Should an emergency arise requiring, in his judgment, a different course of action, he should and would override the pilot and bring the ship in himself. But in this case, *Leviathan* continued to maneuver according to plan and at that moment the Commodore caught sight of his jumbo lodged in one of the gyro compass leads. He bent down to pick it up but his hand never reached it. Instead, clutching his head, he collapsed on

101

the deck with a hoarse cry. Instantly taking over command, the Chief Officer had the Commodore carried to his cabin by the Third Officer and one of the seamen. Ten minutes later the ship was alongside. By this time both *Leviathan*'s doctors had been summoned but there was nothing they could do. Unable to speak and, indeed, without regaining consciousness the Commodore had died. *Leviathan* had claimed her second life.

The news was headlined in every major newspaper in the world, one of the more sensational ones expanding it into a breathless second by second drama in which the gigantic vessel bore down remorselessly on the jetty bent on self-destruction with the Captain slumped over the engine room controls, the ship drifting nearer and nearer the quayside driven to within an inch of disaster by the gale, howling in the rigging. Yet in the nick of time the marine monster was saved by the lightning decision of the Chief Officer, who seized the engine room telegraph and rang down full speed astern at the same time declaring, "The Captain's ill; I take over command." Other papers imagined the tense scene in the engine room, "where by some sixth sense the Chief Engineer knew the man-made behemoth was in peril, and sweeping aside his less experienced subordinates himself took control of the million eager horses confined in the ship's vast turbines." In one account stewards fell on their knees in the Garden Lounge and prayed for the safety of the ship — "About as likely a sight," Charles commented to Susan, "as if you'd dashed up on the bridge in your scanties and taken control yourself."

"I might do it yet," Susan retorted. "Now I'm aboard *Leviathan* there's no holding me back."

"You'll find our new Captain will have something to say about that. He doesn't approve of women — at any rate not at sea. You'd better watch your step. Old Belly Banks is pretty hot stuff when it comes to making people do what he wants — or so the Chief Officer and Motty say. They're both old ships of his."

"I've already met him," Susan replied. "I don't really believe he's the holy terror he thinks he is — it's mostly beard and hot air."

"Hm!" said Charles. "We'll see what you say about that in six months' time."

It was three days later. The ship was once more in dock at Southampton and Charles had at last succeeded in getting Susan to come on a "run ashore." While this was a step in the right direction, from his point of view, each was wary and nervous of the other. They were having drinks at a little country pub near Botley, having driven there on a fine May evening in Charles's M.G. Midget. She had looked exceptionally attractive, he thought, with a red scarf tied round her head, and he had enjoyed the occasional envious looks he had received on the way. He wondered how long it would take him to make her, and what she would be like. The spirited ones were always better value, he considered, than the wide-eyed clinging types, who in any case were apt to cling a little too long. But there was friction between them right from the start.

"I hope you like beer," he said, "like a proper sailor."

"I'd rather have a tomato juice, if it's all the same to you."

"We aren't going to get very far on *that*."

"You've no idea how far I go on any kind of drink," Susan retorted, "and please don't bully me to have things I don't want. It just makes me shut up like a clam."

Not a girl for the pub-crawl, he thought ruefully, as he ordered a tomato juice and a pint of beer — and came back to find her looking at him with a disconcerting little smile.

"Do you try and take all your girls by storm?" she asked. "Don't you like getting to know us first?"

"I can always be civilized by a pretty girl," he answered glibly, raising his glass, "and here's to the prettiest and most attractive one I've met in years."

"Thank you, Mr. Beecher, for that gracious and obviously well practiced compliment. What was the next move my predecessors made? Throw themselves into your arms?"

"What have I done to deserve this attack? I haven't even made a proper pass at you yet. And if this is going to turn into a taming of the shrew, I warn you, my little lady, I lose interest in double quick time."

103

But Susan seemed to be unruffled by the violence in his voice, and he felt, angrily, that he was getting hot under the collar to no effect. He liked to run things himself, not to be told where he got off by a girl.

"You're nice," he heard her saying, "when you're hot and indignant, only I was wondering why you had to show off all the time, or is that just a part of the technique?"

He pursed his lips and looked at her for a moment or so in silence.

"You know, I believe you could be a bossy little thing if you didn't have a firm hand kept on you — once you were married, I mean."

"You certainly don't waste time, do you? How many similar conclusions have you jumped to with how many similar girls?"

"There hasn't been a similar girl. You're unique."

"But I thought all deck officers with Master's tickets were fully experienced?"

"You can be fully experienced, Miss Spicer, and still have moments of frustration. Even junior officers in *Leviathan* don't have it all their own way all of the time. My God! They don't!"

"Tell me about some of the previous girls in your life."

"Certainly not. I'd rather talk about you."

"There have been oodles of them, haven't there?"

"No," said Charles with a dead straight face. "I grew up very late. Women have always been a mystery to me. As a matter of fact I'm practically a virgin."

"But you're always eager to learn?"

"Oh, yes, honey child, how did you guess? Shall we go somewhere else — and you could give me a lesson on the way?"

During the course of that evening a few of the rougher corners were rounded off, but he still seemed to Susan a rather shallow and frustrated man. She liked him and he frequently made her laugh. He had a quick wit, spiced with malice. He could mimic a person's chief characteristic with pointed accuracy, he was hot tempered, inclined to be arrogant, and talked so incessantly about sexual prowess that Susan began to believe him impotent; yet there was no doubt he was physically attractive, and on the long journey home she had a continuous struggle to keep him at bay with an occasional brushed away kiss. After each failure he would tear the guts out of the little sports car, skidding it round corners and shaving through traffic lights, taking it out of the car and doing his best to frighten her at the same time. She did not enjoy that part of the evening. He had to have his way quickly and if denied it became abrupt and petulant.

"I believe you're a prude," he said after the fifth attempt to kiss her on the mouth and do something alarming with his right hand, "and if there's one thing I detest it's a tease."

"When you only have one idea in your head," Susan retorted, "it gets a bit boring after a time."

"Oh! well, of course if you're bored we might as well pack it up straight away. There's nothing like telling a chap he's wasting his time."

She leaned over and kissed his left ear.

"Don't be such an eager beaver," she said, "give it a little time. You're like a schoolboy, not a responsible officer of thirty-one."

"Thanks very much," he said bitterly as the tires screamed and the little car bumped and banged its way into motion again. "I've had my full whack of 'giving it a little time.' When you're at sea there never is time. A few hours at home, a few hours in port — what chance does that give a chap of getting anywhere with a girl? You spend your life at sea dreaming about someone you love and then being thwarted the few hours you do happen to have with her. No wonder every waterfront in every port in the world is lit up with juicy red lights. Can you blame a sailor for not behaving like a poshed up little gent when he gets into port?"

"I suppose you don't have to go to sea," Susan remarked coolly; "there are other jobs if it matters as much as all that."

"Not go to sea? It's unthinkable."

"Then it's probably a good thing there *are* a few tarts about in the world, if that's all it means."

"Don't be so damnably smug."

"I'm sorry. I'm just trying to see it your way."

"You know perfectly well how to see it my way," Charles snapped back, "without reading me lectures."

They relapsed into silence for a while, each following his and her own train of thought.

"What's it like in a brothel?" Susan asked eventually as they raced along the streets to the dock gates.

"I shan't answer that question — and you can draw any conclusion you damned well please."

"Don't be cross with me, Charles. Try and see how it is for me, too. I do like you very much." He looked at her out of the corner of his eye. "Really you're dreamy — sometimes — when you don't keep butting your head against the wall."

"Well," he said after a tussle with his feelings, "you're a pretty nice wall if it comes to that."

They parked the car near the ship and she helped him put up the hood. As they screwed down the butterfly nuts on the top of the windshield, their heads came close together and he again became aware, as he had done countless times that evening, of her freshness and the scent of her hair. There was a little dimple to the right of her mouth and her skin seemed to radiate a cool lusciousness like ripening fruit. He wanted her so badly at that moment that his whole body trembled.

"Sorry, Charles," she said softly. "I've been a beast the whole evening. You've been very sweet and I've enjoyed myself very much."

Then she kissed him gently and lingeringly on the mouth, her lips soft and parted, so that a kind of peace suffused them both. Then she suddenly giggled.

"Now what's the joke?" he asked, but without the irritation and testiness which had gripped him before.

"Just us," Susan said, "with out bottoms stuck out either side of the car. It's so fearfully romantic, isn't it?"

"The posture is always ridiculous," Charles said as he slammed the door, "but after all we're only poor bloody human beings. We have to take what we're given and to hell with the looks."

"That's what I mean," Susan murmured as they walked over to the ship looming out of the darkness like a Goya giant. "If only you'd give things a little more time."

"I'll try," he said, still calm and happy, "but don't be too harsh with the rationing. Time's shorter than you think."

The following week-end the Labans were invited down to Fabian Mitchell's home near Dorking. To Fabian this was a duty he did not greatly enjoy, and to the Labans, in marked contrast to the previous week-end, it was much the same mixture of business and pleasure that made up their life in and out of New York.

It seemed to Ethel at times that her existence lately had been nothing but a long week-end party. The backgrounds changed, it was dandy weather or it rained, the men talked business and played golf, the women showed off their homes, and by Monday night the week-end had become just another faint notch in the memory. New York, Connecticut, London, Surrey — it was the same meaningless repetition of the same clichés, with the same polite smiles, the same assumed interest in other people's lives, the same martinis before dinner and the same letters of thanks to tidy it all away.

But Max loved it, and for his sake Ethel threw herself into it without ever raising a fuss — to him it was always as if there had never been a week-end before, to Ethel as though she was continually being sentenced to short terms of prison for some unspecified offense she was unaware of committing.

This week-end, coming as it did after the death of the Commodore and before *Leviathan*'s maiden voyage, was to be the Labans' last one in England this trip — and, with the darkening international scene, perhaps for some time. Though Fabian looked on Max Laban as an aggressive little Jew, he was under no illusions about his value to the company. Like it or not, eighty per cent of the transatlantic passenger business consisted of Americans these days. Max Laban's drive and his wife's sharp wits may have had little direct connection with the lion's share of the bookings which the company got. It could be argued that having been the premier organization for nearly a century and spending the money they did on American advertising, the yearly rise in business was almost automatic and unconnected with personalities — but Fabian knew otherwise. So did Flint, who was also staying the week-end, and so did their by no means unobservant competitors in the Atlantic passenger war.

With *Leviathan*'s departure the following week-end, it would have been strange if the ship had not taken up most of their thoughts. The Labans described their night with the Banks and Ethel asked why, if Captain Banks had been given command of *Leviathan*, he did not automatically become Commodore of the Line.

"Because he's not the most senior captain afloat," Flint explained. "It should by rights be Anderson of the *Orpheus* but Anderson won't accept *Leviathan*. He's within a year of retiring and so is MacDonald, the next on the list, so that's how Banks came into the picture."

"But why should Captain Anderson turn down *Leviathan?* It's the plum job of all, isn't it?" Ethel asked. They knew Captain Anderson and liked him very much, as they had known Sir Norman Coxley. He was a white-haired old man with a gentle personality.

"He told Masterton he was scared of the ship. Said she was too big and he was too old for the job. He's not, of course, or we'd have retired him before, but there's a lot of superstition about. He said, 'She's killed off one Captain and she's not going to do the same to me.' Once a seaman gets that sort of idea in his head, there's no shaking it out. Captain Banks has his eccentricities — and his enemies — but I think he'll measure up to the job."

"I'm not altogether happy about some of the publicity we're getting," Fabian remarked. "Poor Coxley's death has touched it all off again — you know what I mean — 'The Legend and the Myth' stuff about *Leviathan*, and all that astrology bilge. I see one of those bright boys worked out a horoscope for the ship showing she's especially prone to fire. I had Paxton on the phone from Lloyd's almost before I could reach my desk — did I want a cut-price Householder's Comprehensive policy on

Leviathan including fire and theft? They thought the risk of theft slight enough to make up for the ship's dubious stars."

"And we can't be so sure about theft," Flint commented drily, "there's one notorious robber known to have his eyes on *Leviathan* — Herr Schicklgruber from Germany — and we can't insure against that."

"That sort of publicity doesn't do us any harm," Laban remarked, "until we do have a fire, of course. So far as I'm concerned in New York, every time *Leviathan*'s name appears in the Press, the selling job becomes easier. She's a glamour ship and glamour has to stay in the headlines."

How lucky he is, Ethel thought of her husband, to be so absorbed in his work. With an attitude like that every single incident connected with the sea could be turned to account. It was food for his highly developed commercial instincts — those abilities of which he could still feel slightly ashamed in an elegant country house such as this.

She looked across at her host, stiff and erect by the fire, and at his quiet, cold-looking wife. What was it about the English that made them so alien and difficult to understand? They took so much for granted that now, in other parts of the world, had come violently into question. They did not think of themselves as the salt of the earth, they simply knew that they were. It was true you could admire and respect them, but to like them — that was another matter entirely.

And yet again, she thought, as the men continued with their endless "Leviathanitis," the moment you started to generalize, the theory fell in a heap. She looked across at the daughter sitting so subdued in the corner, so pudding-like, so inhibited — and yet, if you found the right key, so ready to come alive and flower as the woman she was intended to be. That was one of the troubles with the British, she thought, they didn't want their girls to grow up into full blooded women. This Joan or Jane, or whatever her name was, already at nineteen showed all the traces of a masculine education followed by masculine neglect. Why didn't the women fight back? Ethel could sense a great deal of femininity bulging unsuitably out of her tweeds and her sensible shoes. The girl was quick to react and, if in any way surprised or embarrassed, revealed a most likeable charm. Her figure needed taking in hand, those pearls could be thrown out of the window and a few pints of cosmetic in quite unladylike colors splashed about to advantage. Most of all, however, she needed attention — plain sexual attention from the men, young and old, in the room. An American girl would have had them all milling around; a French girl would have — well, there was no point in thinking about that — but here was this diffident, shy little rose waiting to be mated to some gauche, bowler-hatted replica of her father, tongue-tied, nice, conventional; and in the meantime dying of boredom with no one sparing her a glance.

Then Ethel said something which was, in fact, to change Joan Mitchell's entire life. She said it almost without thinking as the end product of her reflections about nicely brought up English girls and their usual fate.

"You should come on over to New York," she said to Joan Mitchell; "get your father to bring you along on one of his trips and then stay with us."

The girl's eye lit up at once but her first reaction was a dutiful glance at her father and mother.

"Do you really mean it? I'd love to."

"Why, of course, I do. Why don't you come on *Leviathan* this next week-end?"

"Oh! no, I'm sure that's quite out of the question. Isn't it, Daddy?"

"What's this subversive idea you're putting into my daughter's head, Mrs. Laban?" Fabian asked, interrupting a discussion on the Atlantic conference. "I've enough trouble keeping her in order as it is."

This reaction, in every way typical, clinched it for Ethel. She determined there and then that she would get the girl on to *Leviathan*'s maiden voyage if it was the last thing she did.

"But surely every inch of space is booked up, isn't it, Daddy?" Joan asked. "I mean — the first trip is really something exceptional, isn't it?"

Ethel frowned. All that would have to be changed — the girl was beaten before she'd even tried.

"Of course it is," her father snapped; "you might just as well try and gate-crash the Royal enclosure at Ascot. I'm sorry — it's a nice idea but quite impracticable."

"I'm sure you could put an extra bed in your stateroom," Ethel went on.

"I dare say I could, Mrs. Laban," Fabian said with a rather condescending smile, "but I can assure you I won't."

"Well, we can — can't we, Max?"

"Sure," Laban said, half mocking, half serious, not yet seeing her purpose, "or I could sleep in the bath. I've done that before now. Who's joining us this time?"

"Why, Joan here, of course."

Fabian decided that this sort of nonsense must be nipped at its root.

"It's very kind of you to make these suggestions and to ask Joan to stay in New York — but I'm afraid it will have to wait till some other time."

"But you *could* come, dear, couldn't you? If we could find you a berth," Ethel persisted. "I mean you aren't tied up in a job or anything like that over here?"

"Good Lord, no, I'd come like a shot. Perhaps I could share Susan's bunk. I'll ask her in a moment or so when the Spicers come in for drinks."

"You certainly will not," her father said severely, and then explaining to Flint, "I hope you don't mind — I've asked one of our female employees in for drinks this evening together with her parents. The Purser of *Leviathan* has apparently let her home for a week-end."

Flint grunted noncommittally. He had been enjoying the battle of wits between Mrs. Laban and Mitchell. He wished Quilly had been on hand. He would have relished the initial exchange of grape shot, and there might well be a need for his diplomatic powers later on. Flint was not in the slightest degree interested in seeing Miss Mitchell take passage to New York in *Leviathan* but he laid a private bet with himself that somehow or other she would be catching the ship. Susan will arrange it all, he found himself very nearly murmuring aloud, an almost illicit pleasure coursing through his old veins because she would soon be here in the room. As a result of Susan's brief career as his special self-imposed assistant, he had rediscovered the pleasures of being unpredictable and naughty. After all, he was an old man of some considerable power, he told himself, and old men had special privileges. Moreover, an unexpected freakishness on the part of the boss helped to keep subordinates on their toes — and even though he would eventually take over the company, Mr. Mitchell was still subordinate to himself. An occasional reminder of this did no harm.

Fabian himself was seething with inner fury at Mrs. Laban's suggestion. To begin with, he and his wife had been on the point of sending both their children across to the States — Alan to an American university — if an arrangement could be made with Oxford — and Joan to stay with friends in Washington, D. C. But this would happen in its own good time. He was not going to be jockeyed into it over a week-end. He had no intention of becoming a victim of American hustle and he could think of many more suitable families for Joan to go and stay with than little Maxie Laban and his pushing wife.

It would certainly have been fun for Joan to have come with them on this trip — had he been Chairman himself, perhaps he might even have stretched a point and got her in somewhere, but as number two he did not care to ask for such a favor, and he did not consider it wise from the company point of view to set an example which might well lead to requests for other concessions in other directions.

He glared angrily at Ethel's back as he replenished her glass. Damn her interference! Typical, he thought sourly, of all the sides of America he most disliked, and equally typical, he felt, of both his children who, for reasons he did not understand, seemed far more drawn to the brash vulgarity of America than they were to the sober good breeding of their own country. He'd have a word with Joan later that night — or her mother would. There was no need whatever for her to have responded so eagerly to Mrs. Laban's impossible suggestion — especially since she was well aware of her parents' views.

At that moment the Spicers arrived, Sir Henry as usual seizing the limelight with his wife cowering away at his side. Then behind them, radiant and smiling, came Susan looking unusually chic and self-possessed in her black dress with its tiny waist. Ethel, who had never met her before, took to her at once. Max had told her the story of *Leviathan*'s purserette and now that the girl had arrived in this room full of conflicting emotions, ideas, ages, and personalities, she saw her quality at once. She knew she was Joan Mitchell's best friend and she could well see what a disturbance her adventurous outlook had caused. Indeed, the moment Susan arrived, Ethel noticed how Joan Mitchell had suddenly come alive as though her voltage had been stepped up in some way. She also intercepted an incautious and totally revealing smile from Flint, which he at once suppressed and tried to cover up with a coughing fit. She saw Mrs. Mitchell's cold disdain as Susan walked over and kissed her "Uncle" Fab on the check. She realized that by English standards Susan had well overdone the perfume; she took in the father's blustering schoolboy personality and the mother's utter negativeness; she saw Flint regain his protective scowl, and her own husband, bless him, react to a pretty pair of legs as he always did. A breath of life blew through the room and Ethel felt herself tingling with pleasure as she had not done since landing in England.

Susan herself got the atmosphere in the room the moment she entered. With a wink at Joan, she walked over to where Flint was sitting and immediately began talking about *Leviathan*. Until she could find out why Uncle Fab was so ruffled, she realized that it didn't much matter what she said. She knew Flint wanted her beside him and she gave him the full dazzle, at the same time taking in the rest of the room without apparently doing so, much as a cat will alert its senses as it stands up, yawns, and stretches itself.

"I'm surprised you can tear yourself away from *Leviathan* at a time like this," Flint remarked. "You can't have enough to do. I shall have to check up with Purser Mott."

"If you could see how your employees are expected to live," Susan retorted, "you'd double our salaries at once."

"Now what's wrong with the living conditions? Are the plush seats in the ladies' lavatories not to your liking?"

You disgusting old reprobate, Susan thought, you'll pay for that later on. Aloud she said:

"With four hard-working girls cooped up in a cabin the size of a matchbox, I'm surprised you get anyone to work for you at all."

"Well, Miss Spicer, I've no doubt you won't be long in *Leviathan* before wangling a cabin to yourself. Where would you like one built — up on the sun deck? Perhaps the Chief Engineer would turn out of his."

Susan laughed.

"The engineers *have* got just about the best accommodation in the ship," she said, "and of course they're only responsible for getting us from A to B; whereas the Purser's department, as we all know"— she raised her voice slightly and pulled a face at Fabian —"the Purser's department can make or break the ship's reputation. Though, of course, I don't suppose that matters very much, sir, does it?"

A few moments later Susan had the Labans, Joan, and Flint as a kind of private audience within the cocktail party, listening to some of her day-to-day experiences in *Leviathan*. With her base secure, so to speak, on Flint, she talked for the benefit of Max Laban whom she clearly enchanted, and obliquely for Ethel whose reactions were far more subtle. She very soon became aware of the repressed antipathy Fabian had for the American Director and she also appreciated, without making any attempt at the kind of internal political maneuvers in which Quilly specialized, that Laban was of more value to Flint than Fabian would ever be, while not losing sight of the fact that at any moment Fabian might become Chairman of the company himself. She realized that Ethel understood these different relationships unintellectually and instinctively as she did herself. She observed the delicate balance between dangerously powerful personalities which it would be disastrous to upset and she tried to become as little involved in it all as she could while continuing to be the focus of their attention. Towards the end of the evening Ethel put her at ease in one direction by saying briskly:

"You and I will be seeing a whole lot more of each other,

honey, now that you're going to be a frequent visitor to New York," and this was then capped by Flint who remarked as the Spicers were taking their leave:

"Since you've clearly assumed the functions of Staff Captain and Purser, Miss Spicer, no doubt you'll have little difficulty in finding a berth of some kind for this young lady here on *Leviathan*'s maiden crossing." He jerked his pince-nez in the direction of Joan Mitchell.

"Is that a Chairman's instruction, sir?" Susan asked with a quick glance at Fabian who had overheard the remark.

"It is *not*," the old man replied with a wily twitch of the lips. "I gave up instructing young ladies a long time ago."

"I'll speak to the Purser about it," Susan said, wondering if there would be an explosion from Fabian who was ruffling up like a badger at bay.

"You may speak to the King of Siam," the Chairman said, leaving her neatly out on the limb and half sawing away the branch, "but you'll do so on no one's authority but your own. We don't want to upset the passenger department, do we, Mr. Mitchell? Not when they've had as tricky a time fitting everyone in as they have over this maiden voyage of *Leviathan*'s. However," he concluded, dismissing Susan with a curt nod, "the Transoceanic Company has always specialized in achieving the impossible. It's a fine, healthy tradition to have."

There was certainly no week-end or night off for either the Purser, the Chief Steward, or the Chef of *Leviathan* during that critical period before she sailed on her first scheduled trip. All three were harassed, overworked, and sleepless. At this time with a profusion of stores of all kinds coming aboard, with the London and Liverpool offices continually making last-minute changes in passenger accommodation, with the menus for three classes for the round trip to be worked out so that, among other things, rough replenishment calculations could be got ready for New York, with new equipment to run in, with a staff, though far from inexperienced, not yet working together as a team, with visitors wanted and unwanted, necessary and frivolous, all pouring in and out of the ship, with boat and fire drills interrupting the most intricate jobs and with sailing day and the arrival of over two thousand passengers approaching day by day, hour by hour and sometimes as it seemed to Mott minute by minute — there was no time for anything but the most intense concentration. War could have broken out and Mott would scarcely have noticed, George Stone's mother-in-law could have died without the Chief Steward raising more than a smile, the Maginot Line could have melted away and the Chef, Monsieur Jacques Bonachard, *ancien combattant* and fanatic Boche-hater, would not have given it more than a passing "*Quoi donc, mon petit, on est foutu.*"

Although *Leviathan* was the newest and by far the biggest, she was not, of course, the first express liner the Company had put into service. Previous experience over the past ninety years had been sifted and refined into an ordered program on a few sheets of paper. All of them knew what had to be done. It was simply a question of doing it and of adapting to any new conditions which 1938 and this particular ship might impose.

"Which is a damn sight easier to say than to do," Mott said to his number two, as they had a nightcap together after one particularly strenuous session. "On days like this I end up feeling like a vigilante. And I'll probably be trouble-shooting all through the night."

"I'd like to shoot that 'distinguished foreign journalist' the London office saw fit to wish on us today," Kennicote said. "Three and a half hours I had of repeating figures and facts that are all on the handout, each one questioned and checked in some extraordinary middle European accent —'seexty towersand ex, ees it? for fun foyage, und fife hundert braces of pffeasants? Ach! und twenty fife tunss potatoes — ees enough for Noah mit his Ark — yes?' "

"Noah mit his Ark — more likely Adolf mit his spy," Mott commented, "though what possible interest a list of bacon and eggs can be to the *Fuehrer*, I can't imagine. But I've always found people are easily dazed by size and quantity — reel off seventy-five prize oxen, twelve hundred lobsters, ten thousand oysters and a bemused expression comes into their eyes; chuck in eighteen hundred pounds of sausages, twenty thousand pounds of fresh fish, and three hundred assorted bottles of sauces and it begins to loom as vast and remote as the National Debt — and sometimes I wish it was."

But the program was met dead on time, and a good two days before *Leviathan* was due to sail she was fully stocked. Linen and library books, coffee and cough drops, potted palms and picture postcards were all in their proper places. Butchers and bakers, doctors, musicians, and hairdressers were all aboard. The lifts operated, there was steam heat in the calidarium of the Turkish bath and over two dozen different blends of Scotch whisky were available in the semicircular bar of the observation lounge. French scent, German cigarette lighters, West of England cloth, and Italian silk scarves were on sale in the *Boutique;* British projectors were all set to run previews of the latest Hollywood films. Shuffleboard and deck tennis nets together with tombola tickets and the gaily painted wooden horses for the evening races were ready to be used. The "Orpheusotone" organ had been tested in the main lounge, the most-up-to-date printing press stood poised to produce it's first *Leviathan* edition of the Transoceanic *Daily News;* bainmaries and electric salamanders were in working order in the kitchens; thermotank ventilation blew hot air into passenger cabins; and elegant Regency writing tables in the first class drawing room awaited the pressure of feminine elbows and the scratching of pens.

By this time a tremendous air of expectancy could be felt all over the ship. *Leviathan* now possessed every essential and most of the luxuries appropriate to the greatest ship in the world. She was spick and span, fresh paint gleamed everywhere, any metal which could be polished shone, lights blazed and sparkled, and the huge expanses of promenade deck had been scrubbed and holystoned until they were glowing. In every part of the ship, stewards in their white gloves and black bow ties dodged along alleyways and into cabins. The confectioner had made a table-sized model of the ship in icing sugar which was on display in the main restaurant. Mail, telegrams, and bouquets of flowers had started to pour on board, and passengers' advance luggage had already been stowed under the supervision of the sharp-eyed Baggage Mister.

By now Captain Basil Bellerophon Banks had presented his last Bible to each and every officer serving under his command for the first time. The ninety-six Engineer officers, the three doctors and the seven hundred and sixty-five stewards and stewardesses were all aboard. The ship had been blessed by a Bishop, officially visited by the Mayor and Corporation of Southampton, adopted by a grammar school in Norfolk, and privately inspected by the King and Queen who had presented her with a Royal Standard in token of this special interest and attention.

The name of *Leviathan* together with innumerable photographs and descriptions made daily appearances in the Press of almost every country of the world. Unknown to the authorities, a black kitten had been smuggled aboard, the gift of a blind grandmother from Tunbridge Wells. Lifeboats and crew had been inspected and passed by the Board of Trade, tugs had been ordered, good weather prayed for and her first Bill of Health prepared. Now only the passengers remained to join. *Leviathan* was ready.

So at last the great day arrived. It dawned fine and calm with almost no wind at all — ideal sailing weather, in fact — and for this Captain Banks offered up a little prayer of thanksgiving more fervent than usual. Then at eight o'clock came the key inspection of the crew by the Board of Trade surveyor. Mustered at their boat stations in life jackets, this was no perfunctory ceremony — but was more vigorously carried out than it ever had been before. Although the name was never mentioned, those responsible for passing the ship remembered back just over a quarter of a century to the day the *Titanic* sailed; this added bite to the rigorous practice of boat, fire and bulkhead-door drills.

Then in the time-honored way the crew filed past the doctor — no replacements being found necessary — "Survey 22," which was Board of Trade clearance for any ship carrying over fifty third-class passengers to a port outside the United

Kingdom, was prepared — the ordinary Board of Trade clearance — the American Bill of Health from the United States Consul, French clearance for Cherbourg and the British Bill of Health were obtained. This latter in its archaic form, going back over the centuries, always gave Banks a subtle pleasure and during the morning he stole a few minutes to relish its wording again. "To all to whom these presents shall come. I, the undersigned Officer of His Majesty King George in the port of Southampton send greeting. Whereas the vessel called the *Leviathan* of Southampton, whose Master is Captain Basil Bellerophon Banks, D.S.C., R.N.R., is about to sail from the said port of Southampton on this seventeenth day of May in the year of our Lord nineteen thirty-eight, and from thence for New York and other places beyond the seas with 3,295 persons on Board including the said Master. Now, know ye that I, the said Officer, do hereby make it known to all men and pledge my faith thereunto, that at the time of granting these presents no plague, epidemic cholera nor any dangerous or contagious disorder exists in the above Port or Neighbourhood, etc., etc., etc." The ship's Articles and official Log Book, the ship's register, and the complete crew list visaed by the American Consul were also put aboard and thus paper-wise and formally *Leviathan* was clear to sail.

Meanwhile from about nine o'clock in the morning the passengers had begun to arrive. Cars and taxis delivered individual parties to the Ocean Berth and the first of the London boat trains drew in alongside the ship shortly after ten. Long lines of white-coated stewards eroded mountainous conglomerations of luggage rather as an army of ants will eat into cake. There was no fuss and a kind of silkiness in the movement of all this baggage, which was a pleasure to watch. The welcoming of passengers was a process the company had perfected over the years. Even here the discipline for which Transoceanic was renowned showed effect. The welcome was very important. First appearances often make the deepest impression and a steward with a heavy suitcase can, if he wishes, give a mutinous aspect to a ship in a matter of seconds.

Even before *Leviathan* sailed, however, it began to be apparent to Mott and his assistants that there were not enough hands for the job. Admittedly the circumstances were exceptional. Before any sailing the tension either keys people up or puts them on edge in a negative way. There are always people who lose things, ask inane questions and wish immediately to change their cabins. Celebrities must have special treatment, which all takes time and attention — and on this trip there was no shortage of star personalities from every profession. Mott was prepared for all this and had schooled his staff, so far as he could, to sort things out as quickly, politely, and intently as possible, but by the time the last boat train was disgorging its first class contents, Mott's sixth sense told him that the situation was temporarily out of hand.

In addition to the flood of passengers, the world's Press, photographers by the dozen, and the newsreel companies were there in strength. Despite the necessity of having passes, a really enormous crowd of friends and sightseers infested the ship and the quayside. Half the nurseries of southern England had evidently been pillaged to provide bouquets of flowers which there was neither time nor labor to sort and which began to pile up in a kind of floral slagheap on the promenade deck. Though duty-free supplies to the bars would not be released by Customs till the ship was outside territorial waters, almost every first class cabin seemed to sprout bottles of champagne which were drunk, because of a shortage of glasses, in tooth-mugs and, in some cases, in the as yet unused soap containers.

By noon all hope of sorting out the greetings telegrams pouring into the ship had vanished; these began to accumulate in one corner of the Purser's office as if some vast tree had suddenly shed its leaves. Seven different people felt seasick, although the ship was still firmly secured to the jetty, and four of them actually were sick in different parts of the ship. One child got its fingers stuck in a grating and another half-strangled itself in a life jacket. Two undergraduates who tried to climb the rigging of the foremast were brought before Banks and berated with such force and violence that one of them tripped over a table and cut open his head. An Irishman of no fixed address was caught clambering into one of the lifeboats and an excitable lady dropped her handbag containing twenty pounds into Southampton harbor.

Meanwhile Sir Josiah Flint was established in his stateroom on the sun deck, having been photographed and interviewed to the limit of his endurance. A junior Cabinet Minister, four American, three British, and two French film stars were studded about the ship. A posse of international bankers mingled with British and American industrialists and their wives. The B.B.C. was broadcasting a running commentary to the world. In every cabin the passenger list in its gold-leafed cover was being studied for friends and acquaintances. An antiquarian bookseller and an Armenian oil millionaire were already haggling in a corner of the smoking room, one of the richest Dukes in Great Britain had complained that he could not buy a packet of Woodbines in the Observation Bar. A well known London hostess had staggered aboard in a state of chronic inebriation, six thousand postcards of the ship had been given away before the ship sailed, the Labans, the Mitchells, and Joan were aboard, an extra bed having been put in Fabian's stateroom. Quilly was threading his way round a theatrical impresario's party on A deck. Half a dozen foxhounds being exported to an American hunt were baying in the kennels up on the sun deck. Monsieur Bonachard was threatening to drown one of the younger sauce chefs in his own "abominable concoction." A popular bachelor journalist with his arm round the waist of a fair-haired Scandinavian boy was giggling at one of the murals in the Veranda Grill. Susan had walked approximately ten miles since breakfast and had not sat down once. People were laughing and people were crying, and now stewards were walking round every deck beating gongs and calling on all visitors to leave the ship. Down in the boiler room the furnaces roared, and up on the bridge flags were being prepared for hoisting. "All visitors ashore please. All visitors ashore."

Alone in his cabin, a few minutes before the last gangway was hoisted out, Banks prayed to his Maker for a successful voyage for the ship and for the reserve of strength he felt he would need to be *Leviathan*'s Captain. At last it was time. The deep, deep note of the siren sounded, the last hawser was let go and to frantic cheering and waving both aboard and ashore, *Leviathan* began slowly to move away from the jetty. Her maiden voyage had begun.

⚓⚓⚓⚓⚓ VI ⚓⚓⚓⚓⚓

THE next morning George Stone, *Leviathan*'s chief steward, had himself called as usual at seven o'clock. A cup of tea, a digestive biscuit, and a copy of edition No. 1 of *Leviathan*'s *Daily News* were put beside his bunk and he began the familiar execution of another day. Stone was a great believer in routine. In a ship the size of *Leviathan* almost any hour of any day could be relied on to produce crises of one kind or another which had, as their object, the disruption or embarrassment of the catering department. This was the great daily challenge, and as Stone took out from beneath his pillow the handkerchief in which he wrapped his teeth every night (always keep things handy, boy, he'd been told when a youngster), as he sipped his tea and read his paper, he anticipated almost with relish what this first day at sea would bring in the way of unexpected attempts to knock them all off balance. He glanced out of his porthole, giving the gray Atlantic his morning glare. Whatever the events ahead, there would be very few the routine could not take care of provided it was strictly observed. He got up, squared his shoulders and prepared to ensure that it was.

By eight-thirty sharp, he was next door in the catering office reading and initialing the night log books for the previous night. There had been dancing in the Veranda Grill till nearly four A.M. A Mrs. Carlton South had sent for the doctor in the middle of the night and had been given a sedative. There was a leaky steam gland in one of the pantries on B deck. Nothing exceptional there. No births, no deaths, and no marriages.

He walked along forward to the tourist section, invariably the first port of call on this morning prowl. The ship's movement could scarcely be felt, but none the less there were the usual pale, worried, despondent groups sitting listlessly in the lounge and smoking rooms. Stone could never decide why third class passengers always looked so ill at ease and afraid. There were very few emigrants on this trip and during his long lifetime afloat, Stone had seen a steady improvement in conditions. The humiliations of steerage were largely a thing of the past. Nevertheless, the lower in the social scale — that scale of which all stewards in liners are acutely aware — the less easily people adapted. No doubt these working class people were overawed by the ship, Stone reassured himself comfortably. His own mother had slaved in a Nottingham laundry, but Mr. Stone had long ago put that fact out of his mind. Mr. Stone did not regard himself as a snob, but had he been called one to his face he would not have taken it as an insult. Life was what you made it. The best would always come to the top — the dross would always sink to the bottom.

With a brief lecture to the tourist Chief Steward on the sloppy appearance of three of his men, Stone proceeded to make a few civil inquiries of the tourist Chef, over whom he had far less control and in whose hands, to a certain degree, his reputation lay. Then he proceeded aft to the cabin class where he repeated the dose. In both these classes breakfast was almost over, whereas in the first class it had hardly begun, and in any case the majority of first class passengers breakfasted in their cabins.

By nine-thirty Stone was himself eating in lonely state in one of the first class private dining rooms. During this time no one at all was permitted to approach him, except for the young steward who brought his food. This was a rigid rule he had made in order to secure at least half an hour in each busy day to himself. He also ate lunch and dinner by himself, but at these meals there were always people to see him, reports to be received or other interruptions he had perforce to accept. These he could do nothing about, but Mr. Stone's kipper was invariably sacrosanct.

At ten o'clock on the dot he was back in his cabin to receive the daily reports of his principal heads of departments. Every day these experts saw him in the same order which, roughly speaking, was one of ascending importance in Mr. Stone's system of valuation. First came the linen steward reporting usages of sheets, towels, cloths, and napkins. Next came the confectioner to be given orders, among other things, for three birthday cakes, and some special buns for a children's party. After him came the Chief Butcher, the Chief Barman, and the Storeman, all with their demands in triplicate, working three days ahead, which Mr. Stone would pass after a cautionary use of the blue pencil — and then finally Monsieur Bonachard, the Chef, with a whole string of "impossibilities" and complaints.

But these were to be expected. This was routine. Both Bonachard and Stone knew that if anything was seriously wrong there would be special visits and different tactics on either side. This was merely the blowing through of the daily accumulation of minor dirt, much as the pneumatic soot-removal equipment in the boiler rooms kept important working surfaces clean. In any event, all of them were the slaves of time with nearly ten thousand meals to be prepared each twenty-four hours for well over three thousand souls. Time was certainly the master on board *Leviathan*, and with a brief exchange of civilities, the Chef returned to his kitchens while Stone spruced himself up, brushed a speck of fluff from his uniform, glanced at the watch presented to him by a Texan millionaire and clicked his false teeth. It was ten-thirty, and time for the Captain's rounds.

For the first two days Joan Mitchell scarcely saw Susan for more than five minutes at a time. She had not expected her friend to be so continuously caught up in the job and she badly wanted someone other than Ethel Laban to whom she could let off steam. This was no criticism of Ethel but simply a kind of puppy-wish to play. To Joan this trip was a fairytale she had never even dreamed could happen to her. Every moment sparkled in her mind: each hour had the possibility of a new adventure, deadened only by her mother's well-bred boredom and the opaque way her father's acquaintances seemed to take it all for granted.

Indeed, her parents' outlook was something Joan had never understood since she could reason. Now more than ever she found it irritating and alien. In private they ran down the Labans' "facile adolescent enthusiasm" as "so typically American." It was "not done" to be too eager about anything. It was "common" to gush. Life became nothing but a question of manners. For instance, at meals both her mother and father had been brought up always to leave part of any course uneaten — it was vulgar to finish whatever was on your plate, and to mop up any spare gravy or a particularly delicious sauce with a bit of bread was decidedly "lower middle class."

Then again Joan, like Susan, had a natural curiosity in the way things worked. To her mother this was unfeminine. It verged almost on the bluestocking approach which had "never done any girl a scrap of good — as a woman that is." Her father had the outlook of a 1914-18 "officer and gentleman." It was the sergeant major or, in her father's case, the petty officer's job to know how things worked, his function was to retain ownership and control. "Simple couldn't tell you, old chap," she had heard her father so often say either to Alan or to one of his friends. "I'd have to get hold of one of those technical johnnies to explain it all. We're all in the hands of the experts nowadays, don't you know." It was as though there was a mystique in not being aware of the detail of anything, much as royalty never handles money, and at times she wondered if her father had some picture of himself as a bewigged and beruffed aristocrat in modern disguise.

Or was it all simply a mask? When she listened to her father talk shipping, she got the impression that he always knew more than he said. She was sure, on the other hand, that Mr. Laban said everything he knew, but with her father there always seemed to be something in reserve. This could be bluff — the diabolical cunning of perfidious Albion — or it could simply be that he did know his subject so well that only certain aspects of it were worth discussing.

After breakfast each day, which she took independently in the main restaurant, her mother having hers in the stateroom, and her father only appearing after he'd walked ten times round the sun deck and had a cold bath, there was a delicious period of being on her own. This was when she most wanted to have a gossip with Susan, and on the first two days she had hung about the Purser's office on A deck square, hoping that Susan would be able to leave her little desk for a cigarette and a chatter. But Susan was always being given things to do.

"We're getting so far behind, I doubt we'll catch up before we arrive in New York," Susan explained. "The mail isn't even sorted yet that came aboard at Southampton. We're all flat out all of the time. Mr. Kennicote, the number two purser, was up till five o'clock this morning keeping an eye on the gambling in the smoking room and the dancing in the Veranda Grill. The manifests *have* to be ready . . ."

"But surely you don't do *everything*, Sue, do you?"

"No but I get all the odd typing jobs thrown at me — just because I'm quick — and then Sir J. likes to have me hanging around whenever there's the faintest excuse. I had to play chess with him all yesterday afternoon — and you can imagine how popular that made me down here. Look — the Press are being taken round the engine room at eleven. Would you like to be included?"

"Yes, please, count me in on any Cook's tours you can."

So in the intervals of being shown the kitchens, the store rooms, the boiler and engine rooms, Joan took to mooching about the ship on her own. Her curiosity, at home inhibited, now led her to explore any part of the ship to which her fancy took her, from the radio office to the tourist class children's playroom. No one seemed to mind. Although it was company practice to impose a strict segregation of the classes once their ships were at sea, Joan quickly discovered that the stewards and stewardesses had much too much to do for them to worry about one stray girl, and on the only occasion when she had bumped into the Master-at-Arms while actually climbing over a barrier, she had explained with a furious blush that she was only visiting a friend, whereupon a side door was unlocked and she was ushered through with a smile and a wink.

In fact, although time seemed to have different proportions at sea, she soon found these solitary mornings all too short.

Soon it was "snifta time" as her father put it, time to go along to the Observation Bar for the prelunch tomato juice cocktail with her parents while her father took his regulation quota of pink Plymouth gin and entertained a new collection of Very Important Passengers, and her mother looked her dull, elegant, disinterested self.

One of the people it was impossible to panic no matter what pressure was applied was Jimmy Johnson, the senior barkeeper in the Observation Lounge. "Lounge," in fact, was something of a misnomer, since the semicircular forward segment of the promenade deck was as tightly packed with small black-topped tables and tubular chromium chairs as its designer, and the determination of the public to compress itself into one place so long as that place was fashionable, would allow. Jimmy Johnson was the number two barman in *Leviathan* — the senior one being in the main dispense bar of the first class restaurant — and he was one of the liveliest men in the North Atlantic. In fact, Jimmy Johnson, at forty-five, was at the top of his form, and that meant at the top of any running his competitors might make. There are three main qualities a first-class barman must always possess. He must have an exact memory for people and mixtures, he must be deft, and he must command a first-rate team of subordinates. Jimmy Johnson had all these abilities to a marked degree. He had sharp eyes, a sense of humor, and would stand no nonsense whatever, either from his staff or from those of his customers who thought they could catch him out in any of the dozen ways in which a barman is vulnerable.

Jimmy had been twenty-five years with the company, and in each ship which he had operated for any length of time there had been record profits for the company, a steady accumulation of wealth in his own bank accounts in New York and London, a growing reputation, and a waiting-list of stewards who wanted to become a part of his team. Through all this, and perhaps because of it, he was a happily married man, with four children, who thoroughly enjoyed his life. There were some evenings when his legs were so tired they would scarcely carry him back to his tiny cabin, but the bar was always left immaculate and the next morning he would be there crisply attentive, that slightly sardonic smile round the corners of his mouth, waiting for the first of his customers to try and put a fast one over on him.

The Purser and he were old shipmates and friends. It had long been a custom of Mott's in any ship he was in with Jimmy to take the first drink of the evening with him across his bar. This was before the evening round of cocktail parties began, and since Mott never touched alcohol during the day but enjoyed his first Scotch as much as Jimmy did himself, it was always a pleasant few minutes of relaxation for them both.

On the third evening out from Southampton Mott took Susan up with him for the first time. They had just managed to survive the most grueling day any of them had experienced. Ahead of them that night lay the gala dinner and dance with its balloons, paper hats, and enforced jollity. This was the one part of his job Mott really detested, and into which, therefore, he put more effort and attention than anything else. Indeed, he was always the life and soul of the party, keeping his real feelings not only hidden but as much out of his consciousness as he could until the ghastly festivity had been successfully completed. Because success was the key to it all. There could be nothing half-hearted about any of the entertainments offered aboard *Leviathan*. It was an understood thing from Sir Josiah Flint to the youngest commis steward that nothing was good enough for *Leviathan* but the biggest, brightest, and best.

Even as they were being introduced, Susan recognized a potential friend and a tower of strength in Jimmy Johnson. She could see that Motty and he got on together as two independent men can respect and like one another despite the uncrossable gap of job and status. The Purser took his first pull at the whisky and seemed to brighten visibly.

"Have I been looking forward to that!" he said beaming with enjoyment.

"How's it been today, sir?" the barman was asking.

"Worse than ever," Mott remarked. "Miss Spicer, here, is talking of resigning in New York . . ."

"Never," Susan put in.

"We still haven't sorted the mail, sixteen thousand postcards of the ship have gone so far, and we're right out of stamps. I think that's all they do — sit around writing picture postcards."

"They're up to one or two other things as well, sir," Jimmy said with a smile at Susan. As he talked he filled an order for two martinis, a John Collins, a daiquiri, and a Scotch, apparently without effort, neatly put away the steward's order slip in a wine glass and wiped his bar clean. Each movement was sharp and distinct, yet made with the minimum expenditure of energy. He was a pleasure to watch.

Mott glanced at his young assistant. He had taken a great liking to her. He did what he could to keep this under control and hidden, but he had to admit that she brought him alive and stimulated his senses, so that standing beside her now to one side of this flashy bar, which Mott privately thought in atrocious taste, her youth and her freshness seemed to vibrate all along his tired nerves, feeding and restoring him in a subtle, invisible way.

As he formulated this thought, he gave her another glance and found himself looking straight into her cool green eyes. Neither of them said a word, yet Mott had the impression that his inner ideas and feelings were known to her. He looked quickly away, got out his cigarettes and, offering her one, took another himself. This wouldn't do at all. He was twenty years older than she was, the top man in his particular line of country, subjected almost every Atlantic crossing to sexual approaches of one kind or another from lonely widows or wealthy dissatisfied wives, all of which he took in his stride without being affected inside at all; now here was this girl, the youngest and most junior member of his staff, appointed to *Leviathan* as an experiment, nothing but an experiment, and in some extraordinary way, without saying a word, she had managed to show that she knew perfectly well what had begun to ferment in his feelings, that she did not find it in any way extraordinary or repellent — in fact that she understood. It was something of a shock. Abruptly he finished his drink.

"Well, I must go and change," he said, "so I'll leave you in Jimmy's tender clutches. She can have another glass of sherry if she behaves herself, Jimmy, but after that my responsibility ends. See you in the morning, Susan."

"I'm afraid you'll see me before then," Susan answered. "I've been asked up top by the quality tonight. The Labans have made up a party. We're having dinner in the Veranda Grill and then getting down to some solid dancing."

"Who's we?" Mott asked, pausing as he went.

"His theatrical Lordship, Joan Mitchell, Blossom — and myself," Susan said, again wriggling herself into a more comfortable position.

"Well, you oughtn't to be in any danger there," Mott remarked, a slight note of sarcasm in his voice. "Hope you enjoy it."

"Thank you, sir, I'll do my very best. I'd curtsy if it didn't mean getting down off this stool."

"You can save that for the office tomorrow. See you later, my lady."

Mott gave her a smile and left. Susan turned to find Jimmy looking at her shrewdly over his rimless glasses as he sliced the peel off a lemon and tossed a bottle of gin in the air.

"Settling down all right, miss, are you?" he asked, a glint of amusement in his eyes.

"Yes, thank you, Jimmy. Everything's fine."

And so it was except for the physical exhaustion she felt. She determined somehow or other to get a cabin to herself. As the voyage progressed, the bickering among the four of them in the hen coop had steadily increased. This had centered on the feud between Pamela Davies, the nurse, and Gloria Dowkins, the hairdresser, over smoking in the cabin. Gloria Dowkins did exactly as she pleased and to hell with the others — an attitude she expressed in good Barrow-in-Furness shipyard language. Pamela Davies glowered and muttered and behind her back had complained to the Surgeon who had passed it on the Purser's department, with the result that the humorless and dictatorial crew purser had threatened to haul them all up in front of the Staff Captain if he had one more peep of unnecessary trouble.

Veronique and Susan kept well out of it but the atmosphere was far from pleasant and as they grew progressively more overworked and tired, so did their patience and good humor shorten. "Lancashire slut" Miss Davies would mutter, and "Mean S.O.S." Miss Dowkins would comment as she lit another cigarette and blew down a cloud of smoke on the bunk below. "S.O.S." in this instance standing for sexless old sourpuss.

But there were always compensations, Susan discovered, if she kept alert for them and did not have preconceived ideas as to where they should come from. For instance the bathing situation was chronic and Susan hated making-do with a shower, but just when she was beginning to think she would rather have a long hot bath than a diamond necklace, Ethel Laban had suggested that she could drop in to their stateroom and have a bath whenever she liked. It was only a temporary expedient but that didn't worry her at all. A bath was a bath. In fact that was what she'd do now, if she wasn't going to be in their way. She slipped off her stool, thanked Jimmy and made her way down to the Labans' cabin on the main deck.

Later that evening as Ethel did her second duty tango with Lord Harborough, or "his theatrical Lordship" as Susan had called him, she began thinking about her two "adopted daughters," and the curious pattern fate could make of people's lives. Already both Joan and Susan had become her firm friends. Despite the difference in age, they got on together in a way neither of the girls' parents could possibly understand. In fact, understanding was perhaps the key to it all, the blending force that cut across age and experience and nationality.

She looked over at Susan dancing with young Mr. Blauerson, the real brains and drive behind this new London management which had had six successes in a row, one of which was to open in her brother's biggest Broadway theatre in a few weeks' time. Susan was drawing him out or he was drawing out Susan, she couldn't decide, but one way or another they seemed to be deeply involved with each other. Lord Harborough, himself, who was nearer her own age, and was unashamedly the money in the setup, must have been following an almost parallel train of thought to Ethel's, since he suddenly said:

"You know, Ethel, if it hadn't been for meeting your father on a transatlantic crossing twenty years ago, I'd never have got myself interested in the theatre at all. We met in the bar on board the old *Pluto*, I think it was, and he started a long panegyric about the magic of the theatre and the excitement of putting on plays, then suddenly turned to me and said he was a thousand short for his next London production, and how was I fixed? I was so hypnotized by his enthusiasm I remember going down to my cabin and writing him a check then and there."

"And I remember him coming back to us and saying, 'I've got me another sucker to put money into *The Dilemma of Dr. Fong*,' or whatever it was called."

"That's right, it *was* a Chinese thriller," Lord Harborough said, "and I don't think your father thought it had much of a chance. Of course he made that clear from the start. He said that was what made it exciting."

"I wouldn't know about that," Ethel replied, "but Father *always* expected the unexpected. He was a great improviser. He could act on an idea quicker than anyone I ever knew."

"I made nearly nine thousand pounds out of that one play alone. Then I lost it all and about ten thousand more of my own discovering that the theatre isn't as simple as it looks, nor as honest as your father happened to be. Then I met Terry Feinmeister, and we started quite a lucrative partnership as you know. It was Terry who discovered Blossom a short time before he died. So here we all are."

"And now Blossom seems to be discovering Susan," Ethel remarked as the tango came to an end and they returned to their table.

"Hm!" said Lord Harborough with a dry smile. "I rather wonder about that."

Elsewhere in the main lounge, which had tonight become the largest ballroom afloat in the world, Mott and Captain Banks watched the first gala dance as it went on its way. This was a rare appearance for Captain Banks, who spent as little time as possible away from his bridge. The company provided him with a Staff Captain for this sort of thing and he privately disliked its inanity and artificiality as much as Mott did. The sight of a lot of aging men and women self-consciously trying to be funny in paper hats made him think of Babylon, Sodom, and Gomorrah. It was a terrible insight into the vacuity of people's lives, especially those of the rich and the great such as were now foxtrotting on the ballroom floor. He preferred the less inhibited vulgarity of the tourist class where people did things for their own pleasure and enjoyment rather than to be seen by others. These high and mighty, solid, un-happy-looking first class passengers condescended to "join in the fun" because they thought it was the thing to do and because of the utter boredom of their private lives. A couple of world cruises on a millionaire basis had shown both Banks and his Purser some of the inner misery in high places, the violence, jealousy, and hatred which lurked so near the fine outer graces of the rich. Well . . . let them patronize as much as they wished — they were paying for it.

Captain Banks took good care to keep such ideas entirely to himself. He was a captain of a ship not an arbiter of morals. Not even Mott suspected his Captain's feelings as he watched him now, a bearded mammoth of a man, standing on the dais and dwarfing the band as he bluffly presented the prizes for the Fancy Head-dress Parade.

Nor did Mott really think in the same way himself. While detesting this sort of hothouse jollity except, say, at Christmas time, Mott was none the less much more interested in people than his Captain was. During his long years at sea he had been made aware by experience of almost the whole range of human weakness and hypocrisy; but his innate sympathy and respect for the other man's life, however warped, violent, or explosive it might be, had given him a humility which was in no way servile but which helped him to keep his own selfishness in the background and to look out at the world from time to time from inside another man's head. People were his business and he liked them as they came, young and old, pretty and plain, gentlemen, bounders, and out and out rogues. At one time or another they had all been through his hands and in their very different ways he relished them all.

By now it was one o'clock in the morning and the crowd of dancers had begun to thin out. Captain Banks had returned to the bridge, older passengers were going to bed, one or two younger couples were exploring the more shadowy parts of the boat deck, Ethel Laban's girdle was hurting, and nightcaps were being ordered in the recesses of smoking room and lounge. The great ship tore west through the night at over thirty miles an hour. They were now more than half-way across.

In spite of the growing excitement of the daily run figures, Flint continued to protest that *Leviathan* was not and would never be out for a record. No one, however, believed him. Every day he found himself defending this point of view against the Pressmen on board, giving B.B.C. interviews, and answering the same old questions from London and New York on the radiotelephone. Though each day so far the ship had bettered the *Normandie*'s time, Flint obstinately refused to speculate or in any way be budged from the position he and his predecessors had adopted.

"The company's proudest possession," he said in his crisp Scottish voice, "is its unique record in the North Atlantic. We shall always put that first — we shall never jeopardize it however tempting the circumstances may happen to be." His reporters and interviewers privately thought this unctuous poppycock.

"Then can we say you're not interested in speed?" one of the correspondents said in exasperation at the end of a briefing about the ship's New York arrangements. "If *Leviathan* does break the record, you can imagine what's going to happen when she gets to New York."

"We're interested in providing a service," Flint tried turning the question as he always did. "A service is something you rely on. We've our hands quite full enough doing what we say we'll do without worrying about speed records, and such-like trivia."

"Unfortunately suchlike trivia is what the public wants," the reporter said drily, "and they're certainly watching *Leviathan* for the Blue Riband."

When Laban heard of this brush with the Press, he charged up to the Chairman's cabin and remonstrated as forcefully as he dared.

"Records are things all shipping companies are proud of — and why not? What's wrong with doing things better or faster than anyone else?"

"Faster isn't necessarily better, Mr. Laban," Flint retorted.

"Any record in the Atlantic Ocean costs a tremendous amount of energy, endurance, and courage," Laban went on, "to say nothing of time and thought before beginning the attempt. We've all put in the time and the thought — we're well heeled with energy, courage, and endurance. Then why *don't* we cash in on the results? This company and Great Britain have both been proud as all hell over past records and achievements. So what's wrong with *Leviathan* adding another? You yourself keep saying that this ship is the realization of national hope and pride and the advent of a new epoch in mercantile shipping . . ."

"Are you criticizing me, Mr. Laban?" Flint asked, quietly furious.

"I'm stating the thing as I see it from the American point of view."

"Well, then, kindly desist. It's a matter of the greatest regret that a silver cup should have been donated for something essentially invisible like the Atlantic Blue Riband."

"Suppose we win it anyway?"

"We shall not accept it."

"That's a fine piece of lousy publicity, I must say," Laban said, as angry as Flint was. "That's carrying British understatement to ludicrous extremes."

"We shall still have the honor of being the fastest ship in

the Atlantic without engaging in a competition for a silly little prize, Mr. Laban," Flint remarked, indicating that the interview was at an end.

"If we sweep the board, I still think we ought to do some shouting about it."

"Do you, Mr. Laban? Let us first see if *Leviathan*'s going to sweep the board before talking like that."

This exchange took place in *Leviathan*'s fourth evening at sea, when supposedly there was only just over twenty-four hours to go, and it was symptomatic of the tension which gripped officers, crew, and company officials. By this time most of the passengers had got over their liver attacks and any queasiness caused by the sea and were becoming bored and critical.

It was now quite evident that Mr. Fox had been right and the Chairman wrong over the steward complement of the ship. All the stewards in all three classes were being badly overworked and as always happens when undue pressure is put on a team, the few that chucked in their hands, working as sulkily to rule as they could, threw an even greater strain on the rest. Complaints to the Purser trebled on the fourth day out and in some cases it took all Mott's tact and good humor to mollify passengers with real or alleged grievances.

Behind all this, too, so far as the ship's staff was concerned, lay the vaguely defined threat of New York with its hordes of visitors, its receptions and dazzle to be added to the ordinary work, already intense, of cleaning and restocking the ship in a matter of hours for her return voyage.

Then on the evening of that day they ran into fog. Charles Beecher was on watch when the Captain decided to reduce speed to fifteen knots, and they were down to twelve when he came on again at four the next morning. Any hope of a record run had thus vanished in less than ten hours and in a short time it would become a question of whether their scheduled arrival in New York would have to be postponed.

Charles was not, of course, aware of the argument in high places over record-breaking runs. In company with the rest of the crew, he naturally hoped *Leviathan* would walk away with it as a fitting climax to her maiden voyage; but as the deep note of the siren continued to reverberate through the mist, the old, old, wisdom of putting safety before everything else struck him forcibly now as it had never struck him to such a degree in any ship he had ever served in before. There must be something about size, he thought, which stepped up an experience of fog, frightening enough in any liner, to really terrifying proportions when seen from *Leviathan*'s bridge.

The invention of radar still lay in the future and a desperate responsibility now rested on the lookouts at the stem head, crow's nest, and the wings of the bridge as it also lay on the officers and quartermasters on watch. There were no ships known to be in their path and no icebergs had been reported but both were possible. They were much nearer their journey's end than the *Titanic* had been but, though no one mentioned the name, a similar disaster could occur so instantly that it did not bear thinking about.

From time to time Charles studied his Captain as he stumped belligerently from one side of the bridge to the other. No one spoke, and a deathly, clammy silence enveloped them all. At twelve knots the ship had no perceptible vibration or movement and except for a very occasional two or three degree roll, they might have been stopped in some misty lagoon.

As an antidote to the fear and anxiety they all had to endure, Charles thought about Susan, a habit which had never left him since the first time they had kissed. Susan, in fact, was now firmly established in his heart and he had only to think of her somewhere far far below in her little bunk for a pounding and a suffusion of longing to be released into his bloodstream. In common with all lonely sailors in the long night watches, Charles let his erotic imagination have its full play. Depending upon his mood, such dreams were either a means of escape or the ultimate frustration in a life at sea. The real thing was so rare — indeed, opportunities for it were so spaced out in the monastic life of any sailor aboard ship — that Charles had no guilty conscience at all in slowly undressing Susan, kissing the little nipples of her small thrusting breasts, and then carrying her in his arms, naked and softly protesting, to some vast canopied bed — as the siren sounded monotonously and all of them stared unseeing into the fog. Dreams such as that were not especially satisfying — the more so since Charles was an active and hot blooded man — but at least they helped. Imagination, feeding as it normally does on letters and photographs, seemed to Charles to be a dangerously self-perpetuating thing. It so nearly gave you everything you needed and it left no untidy aftermath such as usually happened in real life. Though it worried him a great deal and would not leave him alone, Charles had not thought very deeply about sex. He vaguely understood that all men were differently sexed — or possessed this power in different degrees, and this was certainly true of the women he had so far experienced . . . but he was not naturally an introvert. He did not examine his urges clinically, he simply took them for granted.

The trouble with dreams and imagination, he decided, was that they were an effective substitute but they left a sour taste in the mouth. Even masturbation, that universal habit which everyone indulged in but no one admitted or discussed, was not adequate relief — even in the woman-starved conditions of life at sea. It was simply not good enough. But it was one thing to reach such a conclusion, Charles thought wryly, quite another to start putting it right. Soon they would be running a two-weekly round-trip schedule to New York and back. Out of those fourteen days not more than four would be in harbor. What chance did that give a man?

Dawn brought an appreciable thinning of the fog. By the time the forenoon watchkeepers had taken over, Captain Banks had increased speed to twenty knots. He had not been to bed all night, but the reserves of strength in his great carcass were such that he scarcely felt himself tired. No sexual dreams disturbed his consciousness. He walked up and down the wide curving bridge, praying silently as he often did, without words but trying with his heart to offer up a trust and a faith in the God whom he felt at times to be both father and friend.

The fog had made him vigilant but his trust in God had

neutralized that corrosive anxiety which would normally have been generated by the enormous responsibility he bore. He glared out at the fog, knowing that the key to it all was to have faith and to be increasingly alert. "And He said unto them, It is not for you to know the times or the seasons, which the Father has put in his own power. But ye shall receive power after that the Holy Ghost is come upon you. . . ." Hm! thought Banks, giving the officer of the watch a ferocious look, we shall see about that. We shall see.

By now the fog had all but dispersed. Aft and below in the hotel section of the ship another day had begun, breakfasts were being served, night log books were being initialed and read, hangovers about to be cured. To those in the ship who almost never even saw the sea it made no difference that a handful of men on the bridge and up in the crow's nest should have had a disquieting night. *Leviathan*'s first experience of fog left them unmoved except for a universal disappointment that there was now no chance of beating the record. Captain Banks increased speed to thirty knots, took a last look round the bridge and went down to his cabin for breakfast. With no other incidents to interrupt them he reckoned they could still make the Ambrose Light within a couple of hours of their scheduled arrival and with luck even on time.

So *Leviathan* arrived for the first time in the staggering port of New York. An idea of the interest the ship had aroused and, to those with previous experience of New York, a suggestion of the reception awaiting them could be gleaned from the newspapers which came aboard with the immigration officials and the pilot. Pictures and every known detail of the ship were splashed across front pages and in special supplements. The Mayor would be giving a civic reception at City Hall, and even as these papers were being consumed on board, aircraft were buzzing the ship, filled with commentators, photographers and sightseers.

Joan Mitchell, joined at intervals by Susan, spent as much time as possible on the promenade deck gazing at the ever changing skyline in an almost hypnotized way. It was very hot. In fact *Leviathan* and the first heat wave of summer arrived simultaneously in New York. Steaming past the Statue of Liberty with the slow majesty of her ninety thousand tons, *Leviathan* not only provided the crowds on shore with a unique spectacle, but also gave her passengers on board a series of New York panoramas of rare brilliance and impact.

Even Fabian, who was a regular visitor to New York, admitted that each time he arrived it was as though he had never seen it before. One's sense of time slows down at sea and although a mere five days had passed since they had left Southampton, it had seemed to them all like a much longer voyage. Now at last they were nearing their journey's end, the gulls wheeling and mewing in the hard, clear sunlight, the skyscrapers of downtown Manhattan standing out in depth as if part of some towering confection created in ferroconcrete instead of the icing sugar it resembled.

Now as *Leviathan* came abreast of Battery Park at the tip of Manhattan, a prodigious crescendo of sirens and horns became audible, together with the wail of fireboat whistles. From the decks of a stubby looking pleasure steamer representatives of the British colony, including a party of unidentifiable but obviously important personages, cheered *Leviathan* lustily from beneath a cluster of British and American flags. "God Save the King" was played on long silver trumpets by fifteen girls dressed in white trousers and black hussar hats. To this hotchpotch of noise was added the occasional sad keening of some exiled bagpipes. The cheering and the shouting blared into an unending level of noise which continued without interruption as though everything had saved its breath for this one great occasion.

Many buildings in the city sported both Union Jacks and the Stars and Stripes and every vantage point on the river front from the Battery to 50th Street was crammed full of spectators, as was every window and roof within sight of the Hudson. Some buildings as far as a mile inshore were crowded with people waving handkerchiefs, throwing confetti and ticker tape out of the windows, and dancing and clapping with tireless energy as bells rang and hooters blew off steam. It was difficult to believe how the welcome could have been more ecstatic even had *Leviathan* shattered every record on her maiden voyage. It was a fantastic experience, almost a royal occasion both to those on board and, as shown by their actions, to the thousands upon thousands of people ashore who watched the giant liner's slow progress up river to her terminal berth at the Transoceanic Pier. The maiden voyage was over. *Leviathan* had arrived on time.

⚓⚓⚓⚓⚓ VII ⚓⚓⚓⚓⚓

DURING the summer and autumn of 1938, *Leviathan* established herself as Queen of the North Atlantic. In July she broke the record for the west-bound crossing and in August she did the double journey in better time than the *Normandie* and thus became the possessor of the coveted Blue Riband. Flint, except for one much quoted public speech, relapsed into a somewhat pawky acceptance of this fact, while the rest of the company and the country itself felt prouder than ever of the great ship. Indeed, *Leviathan* had already become a national asset, symbolizing the might of the whole British Mercantile Marine which still carried nearly a third of the world's seaborne trade. She was thought of first as British and then only afterwards as the crack ship of the Transoceanic Fleet.

Not only was she a symbol, she had also begun to prove herself commercially. She was economical, fast, and had at once become a favorite in the keenly competitive North Atlantic passenger trade. She made her voyages consistently full. She was coining money and coining it fast, the only drag in this direction being the absence of a consort, since the *Juno* and the *Ceres* took a full day longer for the voyage and thus slowed down the combined schedule.

In all sorts of ways by the time "Munich" came about, *Leviathan* had shaken down into an expertly operated, fast-moving, luxury hotel. The steward complement of the ship had been increased by nearly a hundred but not before there had been a strike on the quayside at Southampton in which a hundred and fifty men walked off the ship with their kit-bags a few minutes before sailing time. Such an event had never occurred before in the history of Transoceanic and the effect was immediate. Flint had been consulted at once on the telephone by the Marine Superintendent at Southampton. His first reaction was bluster and abuse. He threatened to have someone's head for this disgraceful slur on the company's name, and that someone, he opined, would be the Marine Superintendent at Southampton who had signed on the men.

But when briskly informed that he could and would have the Marine Superintendent's resignation there and then if the men's case was not fully investigated as had been promised, he capitulated and gruffly agreed to put things right. So the strikers went back on board and the ship sailed an hour late.

Then Flint began to hedge, blaming both the Chief Marine Superintendent and the Chief Catering Superintendent. Aided by Quilly he began once again playing them off against each other and once he had them simmering, he quietly disappeared, as he had done very often before in times of crisis, for a few days' holiday in Scotland. But on this occasion such tactics merely resulted in a united front among his subordinates. He returned to find that Fabian had authorized the increase in steward personnel in his absence and when he lost his temper and accused his deputy of selling the pass, Fabian produced a handful of resignations which would take instant effect if the Chairman did not see reason. From then on Flint ceased to interfere and the good labor relations the company had spent so long in building up were restored in a new balance of power.

"Balance of power" on another scale was, perhaps, the keynote of that last full year of uneasy peace. 1938 saw the final believably serious attempt by England and France to adjust themselves politically to a Germany about to burst out of the Versailles eggshell. It saw a strengthening of the Rome–Berlin axis. It saw Franco on the home straight in a ravaged desolate Spain. It saw the seizing of Austria in the spring and the dismemberment of Czechoslovakia in the autumn. It saw the utter spiritual lunacy of Munich. From then on, to anyone who could understand, it was only a matter of time before another great war would break out.

To the Transoceanic Company, and especially to Flint and Fabian, it meant a number of ominous conferences with Ministry of Transport, Admiralty, and Government officials. It meant a complete disruption of their schedules when the Fleet mobilized on 28th September; it meant an immense increase in uninsurable risks; it meant planning in a vacuum and the almost certain disappearance of any calculable margin of profit; it meant the placing of the contract for *Leviathan*'s sister ship in a cloud of uncertainty; and finally it very nearly caused the cancellation of the world cruise intended for *Leviathan* during the first four months of 1939.

Right through the Munich crisis, this pet project of Laban's hung by a thread and, even after the false optimism of Chamberlain's "peace in our time," the decision to go ahead with the cruise was only taken because of the hard dollar advance paid by a galaxy of American millionaires and the personal desire of Flint to participate in this cruise himself, the first really big luxury he would have allowed himself in the whole of his seventy-three years' life.

By the time the autumn crisis was upon them Susan felt almost a veteran at her job. She was also the only survivor of the three purserettes who had pioneered the scheme, the girl in the *Juno* being unable to stand the pace and the one in the *Ceres* having got married to a radio officer in the same ship. Both girls had been replaced, although powerful voices at Head Office had urged the abandonment of the scheme, especially after the marriage. The Lady Purser Brigade in fact was only kept in being because of Susan's continuing hard work — and perhaps with a weather eye cocked on the Chairman.

Susan herself was quite unaware of this responsibility she carried. She simply went on doing the job. Her enthusiasm for the sea had by this time been somewhat tempered by her first dozen crossings of the Atlantic. Though progressively exhausted, she managed somehow or other to remain active and cheerful. On each voyage she proved once again an ability to tackle more work than she thought possible. This endeared her to all the pursers and especially to Dudley Fitzpatrick Mott, but the job was coming to be regarded in her own eyes as a self-created millstone round the neck.

Yet she was still enjoying herself. After much lobbying and one big explosive row, the hen coop had been broken up and she now shared a much smaller cabin with Gloria Dowkins, the chain-smoking hairdresser. There were two reasons for this. One was that neither the nurse nor the shop assistant could stand Gloria's "brash vulgarity" any more — and the other was that Gloria and she had taken a liking to each other. It was an improbable combination at first sight but with characteristic frankness Gloria had analyzed it the first night they moved into their new cabin together.

"You're all right," she had said, as she lay on the top bunk smoking her first "uncriticized" cigarette. "You don't mind me carrying on like I do and you can say what you like to me. I don't care. But there's nowt you can do with a dry old virgin like Pamela Davies. The trouble is she's 'dainty' in the way she goes on about things in herself and hard as old grit on the outside. She'll never marry. Who wants a sort of medical Sergeant Major chasing you about the house, washing her smalls every time the bell rings? And as for Miss Vera Knickers" (Gloria's anglicization of Veronique or of anything foreign always made Susan laugh, although it had very soon ceased to be funny in the hen coop), "that one's simply a stuck-up little snob. Being half French, she's just so much better than anyone else, I don't think. But behind it all she *is* still a woman. She'll get a man all right."

Most of Gloria's waking thoughts seemed to center on men.

"What about me? Will I get a man?" Susan asked.

"You can have a parcel of mine," Miss Dowkins replied tartly, "in fact you can have the lot of them. I'm fed up with the whole flaming breed. Take 'em, they're yours."

This was usually her attitude, Susan discovered, about a day out of New York or Southampton. Then there was nothing good in any sort of male creature at all. The next day open criticism would cease and from then on till they arrived in port she would be brooding and full of dark thoughts. Susan did not know who her men were, nor indeed whether she had a single steady or a selection of them in both terminal ports. But as soon as the gangways were out Gloria was ashore with her little handbag and a kind of half-proud, half-restless look in the eyes, which usually occasioned a remark from Nurse Davies on the lines of "Well, we all know what *she's* gone off to do," followed by a sniff and, "Frankly, if you ask me, I think it's disgusting. Of course it's typical of a girl from that sort of background. What can you expect?"

As Susan came to know her better, she secretly envied "the Lancashire slut." She was sexy and voluptuous in an un-abashed way. Full-bosomed, full-bottomed, full-lipped Gloria Dowkins was only superficially pretty, and most of that was the product of her own beauty parlor. But she was alive with a kind of animal vitality. She was likeable and fresh, despite the endless cigarettes and the obvious overindulgence in drink and, Susan presumed, sexual activities of the more earthy kind. There was nothing dainty about Gloria, but heads turned as she passed and her progress along the ship's working alleyway was marked by a chorus of whistles from the stewards which in no way disturbed her and which would never have been aroused by Nurse Davies in a month of Sundays. Moreover Gloria Dowkins seemed to like her.

Despite the gap in upbringing, job, and personal tastes, they had something for each other without intruding or wishing to interfere in the other's preserve. It seemed odd to Susan, when she at last decided what it was, but they trusted each other. She would have felt perfectly safe on one of Gloria's wilder parties as long as Gloria herself was there. She had a control over men and a warm-hearted understanding of their needs and behavior which was a kind of invisible armor. She was generous yet calculating, hopelessly sentimental yet full of a practical common sense. She knew what men wanted and it neither appalled her nor in any way spoilt her enjoyment of the preliminaries which she insisted on extracting. "You can tease men as much as you like," she once remarked, lying on her bunk staring at the deckhead, "so long as you aren't really a tease — if you see what I mean. Everything has to be paid for one way or another. That's rule number one in the game. Once that's understood on both sides, you can have yourself a whale of a time. But it's better if you pay in advance — then you can really let yourself go."

Susan never knew quite what she meant and it was never any use trying to pin it down in words. She didn't think Gloria operated for money, in fact she was sure she didn't; but the further reaches of her philosophy were accessible only to someone of equal experience and Susan, who was still a virgin, could not be admitted. "That's what I mean — you haven't paid," Gloria said cryptically when they had once come near to discussing it. "Once a thing's paid for, it's yours. But I shouldn't let it worry you. It's coming your way all right. You're no prissy little prude."

This might be so, but it didn't seem to help Susan very much when it came to dealing with someone like Charles Beecher. She had asked him to give it time, but time only seemed to increase the pressure, making it worse. By now he was head over heels in love with her. Sometimes this made him one of the best companions she'd ever had, at other times, it seemed to imprison him in a pit of gloomy despair.

Although he had never asked her, she guessed he wanted to marry her but as that situation was, at any rate for the moment, hopeless, she never let him reach a "position of no retreat." Perhaps this was being a tease or having something on the hire purchase. She didn't know. Undoubtedly Gloria Dowkins would have said, had she ever been asked, "Give the lad his onions and be done with it; there'll be another one along in a minute," but to Susan this was by no means the answer she sought.

She liked Charles, in fact she liked him a lot. She enjoyed his love-making and at times she wanted him very much indeed. But, on the few occasions when they could have "gone the whole hog" as he put it, something made her pause and draw back. She was not yet ready, she told him and herself, but she was by no means certain that that was the real reason. She was simply not sure.

146

Intermittently through the summer and autumn Ethel Laban had watched the progress of her two chickens, as she sometimes regarded them. There was always a bed for Susan each time *Leviathan* docked at New York, and Ethel felt happy that the girl had now lost her initial diffidence in accepting American hospitality and in taking the Laban penthouse overlooking the Hudson as her home from home. These fortnightly visits pleased Ethel as they delighted Annie and Eliza, and they also kept Joan Mitchell's conscience at ease over the length of her own New York visit.

There had been strong pressure from both parents for Joan to return to England before the real summer heat of New York but she was having the time of her life, and Ethel had discovered that an occasional transatlantic telephone call was enough to set everyone's mind at rest. Moreover, as New York got really hot, the week-ends spent by the sea up at Westport tended to lengthen so that Ethel and her protégée would only drive into Manhattan if there was a definite reason or some function they had to attend.

Occasionally Ethel asked herself why she bothered and what she was doing it for. Was it only to make up for not having a family herself? She could never be entirely sure. Of the two girls Susan was unquestionably the livelier and the one she was more naturally interested in. But there was a sweetness and a sensitivity in Joan Mitchell which Ethel found very appealing. The girl was opening out in the American sunlight and Ethel found this process very agreeable to watch.

Now that she realized her life would always have other people's children dotted about in it rather than any of her own flesh and blood, Ethel concluded that she might as well derive vicariously as much pleasure from this state of affairs as she could make it yield. She enjoyed her brother Oliver's brood of five, but she had known them from birth. They were part of a familiar landscape. These two shyer and more reserved English girls, however, were to be enjoyed in a different, rather more adult way. She had to help interpret America to them, and see that the process was not overdone; indeed, she felt an almost parental responsibility for both of them, with the added freedom of knowing that if she so wished she could pack them both off in a matter of days.

But this she had no wish or intention of doing. When Susan became due for her one-voyage-in-six stand-off, Ethel had suggested that she take it in New York and for some reason had been pleased out of all proportion when Susan had accepted the invitation. She had given the girl a fortnight she would never forget.

This had taken place in early September when only a few of the theatres were running in New York. They had made Westport their headquarters. All Ethel's friends were roped in to help, and while Europe worked up to the grim realities of Munich, Susan and Joan spent the time bathing, playing tennis, and going to cocktail parties. They danced through the night and went to Sunday barbecues in a carefree holiday atmosphere which put the crisis at the end of the month into even greater contrast than it would naturally have been and which, in any case, removed *Leviathan* and her job completely out of mind.

Yet Ethel saw that even while Susan was enjoying this break, the girl realized that she was really only doing so because it *was* a break, a welcome break from a job to which she must very soon return. Ethel in no way fought this state of affairs. She appreciated not only that it had to be that way, but also that Joan Mitchell envied her friend for the lack of aimlessness which was now beginning to gnaw at herself and her enjoyment of life.

"So why don't you get a job here in New York?" Ethel had suggested to her one day when she was down in the dumps, and although Joan automatically replied that she would have to ask her parents, the seed was planted and a week later Ethel wrote a long letter to Fabian telling him all about his daughter and suggesting, in view of the European crisis, that she be allowed to stay on in America and take a temporary job.

She thought there would be opposition to this, and indeed Fabian's first reaction on reading the letter was a wave of frustration and anger. Here was Europe teetering on the edge of war and there was his son preaching pacifism at Oxford and his daughter gallivanting away in New York, her mind on transatlantic frivolities, merely wanting the excuse of a job not to come back.

Then, as the September crisis deepened and it began to be apparent to millions of ordinary people that there really was going to be a war, Fabian had second thoughts. It was kind of the Labans. If the bombs fell on England, and fall they soon would, then at least Joan would be three thousand miles away in safety. It was a disappointment to his wife. She had plans for the autumn, and after Christmas they might all have gone skiing in Switzerland. But with Hitler throwing his weight about like this, by Christmas, perhaps, there wouldn't be a Switzerland.

So he wrote an equally long and courteous reply thanking Ethel and giving his permission. Already it seemed an age since that first voyage of *Leviathan* and the subsequent fortnight he and Flint had spent in New York. In June, with the 1938 season well under way, neither he nor Flint had imagined that not later than the end of September the fleet would have been mobilized and liner schedules disrupted or canceled. Perhaps, after all, this was it, the holocaust, the last Armageddon our civilization would see. Now they were digging trenches in Hyde Park, air raid wardens went about wearing gasmasks and tin helmets and evacuation plans were being prepared for all the big cities.

It was true that his friend, Spicer, had become a Chamberlain man and therefore held that appeasement and the time it bought would solve most of their problems; but Fabian had begun to know in his brain what he had known a long time in his marrow — that a war was inevitable, that no compromise would save civilization from a madman like Hitler, and that they were all for it as they had been in 1914 but that this time it would be a thousand times worse.

Fabian's letter pleased Ethel and it also represented an unexpected way of escape for Joan, though Ethel took good care to talk about "chances and opportunities" rather than "ways of escape." She had no wish to estrange the girl from her home. The idea of America had to be accepted on one's own free will or not at all. It certainly appealed to the young and active, yet there must be some good reason why year by year the British immigration quota was never filled.

Ethel knew that this recurring fact with its superficial explanations always made Maxie sad. He was such an idealist, such a blender, and when two peoples, both of whom he admired far, far more than any other nationalities in the world, refused obstinately to blend except at the level of the cocktail party he felt it personally. He had grown up as do most Americans with the idea of success as part of his second nature. Success in business, success in marriage, and success with people was not only possible but was also the normal transatlantic order of things.

So, although Maxie said very little, Ethel knew how important it was to him that young Miss Mitchell should like and approve of America without any obvious pressure being brought to bear on her. About Susan she worried far less. She lit up, showed her enthusiasm and reacted energetically much as an American girl would have done. She had personality and charm. But Joan was quieter, shyer, and more reserved. Even Maxie said she was "far more English" than Susan. For this one really to take to America, and for America to find a right niche for her, became one of the undiscussed, apparently accidental achievements Ethel had determined upon which, without in any way taking credit herself, she would present to her idealistic husband.

Leviathan was approaching Southampton when the fleet mobilized and she was due for a turnround of five days. Instead, on direct Cabinet orders, she was oiled, restocked with food and sent to sea once more in just over twenty-four hours. Moreover she was filled to capacity with passengers despite the putting forward of her sailing date by nearly four days.

This was a foretaste of the many wartime emergencies she would undergo, and a useful exercise in flexibility. Because of her size and value, *Leviathan* was one of the most inviting single targets open to the German air force, and in the event of war it was policy to get her away from the United Kingdom and keep her safely out of range until she could be properly protected.

During that twenty-four hours the passenger departments in London, Liverpool, and Southampton, and the Purser's department on board *Leviathan* worked flat out round the clock. Mott, in fact, never even stepped ashore. Americans due to return to the United States in other Transoceanic ships were switched where possible to *Leviathan* and numbers of them, booked by other lines and on other dates, made their way to Southampton on the chance. Most of them were fitted in aboard *Leviathan,* and those that were not found berths in the *Pluto* whose Montreal sailing was changed to New York.

The German Government, in earnest of the situation, took the *Bremen* out of service and all her Southampton passengers were thus thrown on the market as well. Naturally their place was at the bottom of the queue and Mott had pleasure in refusing fifteen separate bribes, offered in different ways, to induce him to alter his list; in one instance he had a particularly determined American of German extraction, a thwarted Bremenite, removed from the ship by force, his protests, expressed in a guttural Middle Western accent, being blandly ignored by the two Masters-at-Arms concerned, as they frog-marched him into police care on the jetty.

"You didn't ought to have booked on a German ship, now, should you?" one of the Master-at-Arms replied to an especially violent threat from this gentleman *en route,* "not when it's little Adolf who's making us all this fuss and bother in the first place, and I don't care if you *can* buy up Buckingham Palace, King and all. You don't sail in *Leviathan* and that's that."

As it was, the Board of Trade regulations were tacitly ignored on both sides and *Leviathan* left Southampton with over a hundred passengers above her legal maximum, beds in the hospital and settees in the Garden Lounge both being pressed into emergency service. The smoothness with which this was effected and the co-operation Mott managed tactfully to extract from passengers whose comfort was thus eroded earned him another star report from Banks.

Indeed now that Mott had his staff working together as a team experienced in this particular ship, now that George Stone had more or less the number of stewards he wanted, and had them, too, working as a team, the entire hotel department managed to keep a little ahead of events and thus more in control of them instead of tagging along behind and always trying to catch up as had happened on the maiden voyage. Mott, in fact, welcomed Munich as an exercise in adaption. Let 'em all come; the more the merrier.

"If there's going to be a war," he told Susan as they took their "sundowner" one evening in the Observation Bar, "you can expect a lot more of this and on a much more intense scale. In any case, being on your toes may well be the difference between life and death."

"I believe you enjoy it," Susan said, looking at him.

"Yes I do. Don't you?"

"The people side of it — yes. The paperwork — no. How much longer do I have to go on bashing a typewriter?"

Mott shrugged his shoulders.

"You might as well ask how much longer Jimmy Johnson here is going to measure out gin or how many times I'll be asked how much Mrs. Fliegelstein ought to tip her stewardess. It's just part of the job. Someone has to do it."

"Can I put in for a typing assistant?"

"You cannot. You'll give the Board of Directors a heart attack. They think you're a pretty good luxury as it is."

"Huh! I'd like to see them shift a voyage report as quickly as I can *and* interpret the Purser's scrawly handwriting."

"You'll get your chance if ever this famous cruise comes off. You'll be so sick of 'people' by the time that's over you'll just want to settle back into a little simple typing as soon as you can."

"I doubt it," said Susan and smiled at him suddenly, "but then you're the boss. You ought to know."

She would not have dared to talk in this way in the earlier days and she took good care never to do so now in front of his staff. As between themselves, however, the relationship had changed. She knew now that Mott was interested in her as a woman. She knew also that he took pains to keep this hidden as much as possible from herself and certainly from anyone else on board. There were a number of reasons for this, some of them obvious, others, like Mott himself, more complicated and involved.

To begin with there was the difference in their ages, then Mott was head of the department in which she worked, and was clearly aware of the dangers attendant on playing around with anyone to whom he must give orders in the ordinary course of duty. Susan understood that he was as vulnerable as any master of a household would be who finds a good-looking servant dodging about his domain and then makes a pass at her one day when she happened to be cleaning his study. There is nothing visible to stop him, but from then on the relationship would have changed, there would be a different connecting force between them, and for any advantage taken there would probably be consequences of one kind or another.

Perhaps this was what Gloria Dowkins meant when she talked about "payment." At all events Susan saw and respected the position. Mott was vulnerable simply because of his apparent freedom and power. *Vis-à-vis* herself, the Purser was placed quite differently from First Officer Beecher. Charles, too, was under strict discipline, and had he been caught in his cabin making love to her, would have received a good sound "bottle" from the Chief Officer or the Staff Captain. This might go into his record but it would not affect his abilities as a deck officer navigating the ship. Were Mott, though, to lapse in that way it might well cost him his job.

Then again, whereas she knew Charles as someone quick to react and resent, but basically light-hearted, casual, and perhaps rather shallow, she knew the other far less well. Dudley Fitzpatrick Mott appeared bland, diplomatic and easy on the surface, but below that acquired and practiced urbanity she sensed a deeply glowing temper and a passionate nature. Susan had never seen him really angry but he had come near enough to it, even over some of her own idiotic mistakes, for her to realize what fire could blaze out of those smiling eyes once he had really been roused. He had a temper and he did not suffer fools gladly, not at any rate when they were members of his staff.

But now that she was settled in the job, she almost never fell foul of him through inattention or carelessness. And the personal relationship remained sealed away on its own little shelf. Both of them were aware of it but neither of them put it into words. Yet like a seed in the dark earth, it had germinated and begun to grow, hidden away and out of mind.

As *Leviathan* sped away from England and the Munich crisis, Captain Banks put his thoughts in order and tried to see as far into the future as he could. He was angry at the way things had happened, angry at not being able to leave the ship during the twenty-four-hour turnround at Southampton and angry at the national and chronic unpreparedness in which the British were always caught when a major crisis broke over their heads. And it was not as though they lacked warning. There had been a plethora of warnings. The rumblings from Germany had gone on for years. Anyone of the slightest intelligence knew what was inevitably going to happen. With the Socialists niggling away at rearmament like a lot of old spinsters dishonestly and giddily avoiding any single one of the hard facts of life, with half the Tories sold on appeasement and the other half brandishing a nonexistent big stick, with what was left of the Liberals about as effective as a puff of wind in a colander, with a Prime Minister looking like and about as imposing as a toothbrush in a wing collar, there seemed to be no hope at all.

For long hours Banks glowered at the gray rolling Atlantic Ocean, and at times gave up to despair. There was not the smallest pinpoint of light in a steadily darkening scene. Then, when everything was blackest, the religious habits of a lifetime came to his rescue. One or other of the great regenerating ideas in the Bible would present itself to his mind and as he began to meditate on its meaning, the love he felt in his heart toward his shining celestial Maker began its familiar alchemy.

Outwardly there was no recognizable change. Charles, or any of the other officers of the watch, the quartermasters, and the various messengers who came and went, continued to see their irascible, fiery Captain slogging up and down, occasionally fixing one or other of them with his penetrating gaze, crisply demanding an exact answer to an exact question and somehow or other bringing an archaic old-man-of-the-sea quality to the bridge of this vast modern ship. They did not know, nor could they ever know, that in his heart he was standing in quite another place — up a high mountain in the hot sunlight with the fair wind of heaven on his face in simple communion with his Father to whom all the dire deeds on this dark miserable planet are as so many children's games.

By this time Banks and *Leviathan* were well acquainted with one another. Every part of the ship, except the engine and boiler rooms saw an inspection by the Captain one day in six. In the beginning this had been a nightmare added to the other rigors of an overworked crew, but now, although the order of rounds was never the same two weeks running, the internal cleanliness and state of *Leviathan* was such that the inspection party which mustered daily at ten-thirty A.M. on A deck square found less and less to excite adverse comment as the heads of departments followed their great bear of a Captain on his perambulations.

Had he so wished Banks could have delegated this responsibility in great measure to his Staff Captain, indeed the idea of having a Staff Captain was to relieve the Captain himself of the bulk of routine. But Banks did not relish a spare dinner hanging around, as he put it to himself. He preferred to see everything for himself, and despite an occasional suggestion from old Popeye Masterton that it would be to everyone's advantage if he did delegate his powers a little more, Banks made it abundantly clear day by day that there was only one Captain aboard *Leviathan* and that was himself. Delegation of responsibility was not his strongest feature. Indeed in the four months he had had command of the ship no fewer than three Staff Captains had come and gone.

Despite obvious faults, Banks was the dominant personality

Leviathan needed. He was fully aware of his authority and he used it. Yet it was the man himself whose strength and character permeated the ship. *Leviathan*'s officers soon discovered, in dealing with defaulters, that the threat of being hauled up in front of Captain Banks was far more effective than the company regulations they were supposed to administer. After the first voyage there had been wholesale resignations and changes in the crew but thereafter things had settled down and except for the one-in-six relief system, *Leviathan* sailed with much the same personnel every voyage.

And the thirteen hundred officers and men who thus came to look on *Leviathan* as their second home, also came to accept and depend on their brawny captain with his old-fashioned conception of discipline, his high standards, and the well-worn Bible bulging in the left-hand pocket of his uniform reefer. They trusted him, they respected him, and some of them even liked "the big ape" or "the great bear," or whatever nickname it was they called him by. They felt nothing much could go wrong provided Banks was aboard. This reputation became greatly enhanced during a sudden strike of New York tugmen when Banks brought *Leviathan* alongside the pier in a high wind and, a couple of days later, took her out again without benefit of outside assistance.

Charles Beecher, who was on watch when these feats were performed had by this time become a Banks devotee. As he had every intention of getting command of his own ship as soon as he possibly could, Charles put himself in Banks's place whenever there was a problem of judgment to be solved, and tried to observe where he would have done one thing and his captain another.

But the handling of any ship is akin to diving — you can watch an expert as long as you like but you can only learn it by doing it yourself. The real feat, in Charles's opinion, was the intense calm and confidence which Banks generated in himself and in those close to him on the bridge. It was unthinkable, somehow, that things could go wrong in the presence of such positive assurance. That was the secret behind it — but he was no nearer to knowing how that assurance was acquired nor how it was imparted to others, as it so obviously was in *Leviathan*.

In fact Charles came to see, through watching his captain day by day and voyage by voyage, that there was a difference in kind between the knowledge a man had acquired and the being he possessed. In every man the blend was different but "being" was what primarily mattered; despite his Biblical reputation, Banks did not strike Charles as a particularly "good" man. However there was no doubt at all that he had exactly the right being for command of the greatest ship in the world. He was in every respect Master of *Leviathan*.

Charles, like his captain, felt raw and angry at the way things were going over the Munich crisis. Like his captain, and indeed in company with the great majority of Transoceanic officers, Charles belonged to the Royal Naval Reserve. If a war came, there would be an interruption to his normal career, but it would not necessarily be to his disadvantage. He had his Master's ticket. He held the rank of Lieutenant R.N.R., and he supposed he would soon be given command of a small warship such as a sloop or corvette in the inevitable expansion which would take place in the Navy.

Since to command was his main ambition in life, that was certainly one way of achieving it, and since all his competitors on the ladder of promotion would be similarly affected, his personal status was not likely to suffer.

But Munich made him furious in other ways. What was wrong with us all? What was all this half-hearted wavering about? Charles had no love for the Colonel Blimps and the many varieties of Empire-builders whose pride and rigidity had become music-hall jokes, but he was solidly, one hundred per cent, for the Empire itself and for the fact of it being the British Empire. His understanding of politics was instinctive and informed mostly by the news he read in the press. Like most of his contemporaries, he trusted neither the politicians nor the ambassadors, who seemed to flounder in exactly the same way whatever the country or the crisis in which they found themselves. He felt, without being able to quote examples or facts, that we were being let down in some diabolical way which would only come to light when it was all too late. England needed a great man — and where was he to be found? Nobody trusted Churchill, who was in any case a lone voice in the wilderness and not even in office. We had no single man in a position of power of the stature of Roosevelt. And even Roosevelt could not persuade half his countrymen to abandon their isolationist ideas.

Indeed, the isolationism of such large parts of America made Charles doubt whether the United States would even get into the war once it came. Looking at the European situation from the other side of the Atlantic, Charles decided that he would himself be an isolationist were he American. The country had been populated by people getting away from Europe who were basically anti-Empire in outlook. He did not blame them for this; indeed, he saw their point of view only too clearly, but it left England and France in a critical position so far as Hitler and Mussolini were concerned. Nothing seemed to add up. You read that Germany was desperately short of rubber and oil, and that without those two basic commodities a modern war must come to a halt in a matter of months. But was this so? It had stopped neither Mussolini in Abyssinia nor Franco in Spain. And Hitler was a hundred times more dangerous than either of his petty imitators.

The general malaise he felt bearing down on them all was reflected in his personal affairs. He was getting nowhere with Susan. He loved her and wanted her more than he had ever loved or wanted any girl in his life. But she only responded up to a point. She would neither go to bed with him nor would she marry him. True, he hadn't yet asked her to do either but he sensed what she would say if he did.

Moreover, he was not even sure he wanted to be married at this stage of his life. He looked round at his brother officers, most of them with dull little wives in dull little semi-detached villas they would eventually acquire from the Building Societies. Home meant high tea and diapers on the line, it meant presents for the wives whose enlarged snapshots in calamitous bathing dresses adorned each cabin wall, it meant an over-anticipated coming together on return from the sea, followed by an excess of indulgence in food, drink, and the bed, followed by the bored remorse of two mutually incompatible lives, followed by remorse at such remorse, and ended by the sailor's return to his ship and the beginning of the process all over again.

Charles realized, when he thought like this, that such an attitude in a Merchant Service officer like himself was quite indefensible. His own father was a tramp captain and two of his brothers were also officers in cargo liners with young families of their own. He loved his home and its contented atmosphere. But this was because his mother was a placid and contented woman who adored his father and accepted the situation in which she found herself. So did his brothers and their wives. If they were ambitious it did not seem to worry them much. Money was short but there was at least a security which was missing from the lives of many of their civilian friends. Moreover his sisters-in-law came from much the same background as themselves.

Susan was a different kettle of fish. She was no snob, he knew that, but you couldn't alter her family, her background, or any of the facts. She would never fit herself into a Wallasey or a Southampton suburb, and that or its equivalent was probably all Charles would ever be able to afford. Some mornings he looked at his freckled face in the mirror as he shaved and wished to high heaven he'd never met Susan at all. Then quickly he took that back. He would rather have known her intimately and suffer hell than merely admire her from a distance. She was exciting, stimulating, wonderful. Even if he never possessed her, he was the richer for having entered her orbit.

And he knew she was at least fond of him. He could make her laugh and she enjoyed his company. He was iconoclastic over the sea and the ship, he could scoff at Belly Banks and the sacred Chairman of the sacred Transoceanic Line, at a number of the things of which she was still a little in awe. But when it came to that Rolls-Royce of her parents, to that country-house background in England and to dinner parties with the Labans in New York or barbecues in Connecticut with the rich and classy, as his mother would have put it, he was not so sure of his ground. Being insecure, he tended to boast and be something of an aggressive know-all, and a young British know-all to boot, which, even as he did it, he knew was a mistake and only distressed Susan and her sort of people.

On such occasions he hated himself but felt there was no way of putting it right. He was trapped. It was almost as if another Charles Beecher had taken possession of him and was saying all sorts of things through his mouth of which he did not approve. The more he tried to stop this interloper the worse it became, so that not only did he make a fool of himself in front of Susan but he ended up in a shambles with himself in the bargain. As he usually combined this process with having far too much to drink, the penitence of the following day was a recurring and gruesome experience.

But although he could see no solution, he was never going to give up. Something would happen. To know what you wanted, to be determined to get it, to keep an eye open for the unexpected chance in a different direction, these were the precepts his father had dinned into their heads ever since Charles could remember. And if that outlook was suited to the sea — a woman if ever there was one — then it could certainly be made to apply to a snub-nosed, green-eyed young girl.

⚓⚓⚓⚓⚓ VIII ⚓⚓⚓⚓⚓

THE day before they got into New York the First Lord of the Admiralty resigned in protest against the Government's handling of the Munich affair. Appeasement had won the day. But no feeling of relief seemed to be present in *Leviathan*. Instead, a sense of dismal disaster lay over them all as they entered New York. By the time their passengers disembarked, German troops had moved in and taken possession of the

Sudetenland, thus putting the Czechoslovakian situation beyond any further negotiation, beyond intervention, and beyond any hope of remedy by statesmen or politicians.

Now that the ship was empty of passengers and safe in New York with a week to go before her next eastbound trip, assuming that "peace in our time" meant she would pick up her original schedule, an enveloping anticlimax settled over their everyday chores and activities. Perhaps with an understanding of this — perhaps accidentally — the Labans came to the rescue, inviting Captain Banks and the Purser out to Westport for a few days' relaxation and leaving the New York apartment in the charge of Joan and Susan. Annie went with them out to Westport and Eliza was left to look after the two girls in New York.

"And my instructions is to see you really done make this your home," she said as she brought Susan her breakfast in bed. "Nobody here gonna tell tales on any activity in this apartment while Mrs. Laban away, so you doing just exactly as you feel in the mood." Which Susan took to be an open invitation to abandonment, especially as Eliza inquired as she drew the curtains, "Don't you have no special boy friend in that old *Leviathan* you gonna bring home? Honey, if I was in your shoes . . ." a remark which was finished off without words, but with one of Eliza's most enchanting smiles and a kind of wriggle of the hips which she did whenever she felt good and happy. And perhaps she was right, Susan told herself as she luxuriated in a long hot bath, perhaps one ought simply to seize the opportunities which dropped so unexpectedly out of the blue, seize them and exploit them for all they're worth. Perhaps that was where Gloria Dowkins scored and she and Joan so lamentably failed.

She was not left long in peace. Later that morning the telephone rang and a familiar voice said:

"Umbrella here. How appeased can I make you today? The Foreign Office suggests a little light lunch at the Plaza followed by discussions in Central Park or a mooch round the Metropolitan, followed by cocktails at that place on 48th

Street, followed by two stalls at *I Married an Angel,* if you like Mr. Rodgers's music, followed by a little dinner and dancing at Rico's, followed by — well, what do you say?"

"It sounds ravishing," Susan said, "but miles too posh and expensive. I don't think you should spend all that money on me. I'm an Automat and subway girl."

"Listen, sweety, I've taken advice. The Automat doesn't serve caviar and the subway's only for getting to Coney Island and back."

"I'm mad about Coney Island."

"Right, we'll go there tomorrow. This is today and today spells a meeting up in the Oak Room — no, better make it in the hall among all those overdressed women. Be there at noon on the dot. Is it a date?"

"Thank you very much. Oh! Charles, there's Joan to consider — I did say I'd . . ."

"Hasn't she got a boy friend yet?"

"As a matter of fact she's got several — and there's a cocktail party we're being taken to tonight. Shall I ask if I could bring you along?"

She could imagine the petulant frown chasing across his face. There was a pause.

"Well, I'm all for free drinks," Charles said dubiously in the end, "but I did rather want you all to myself."

"We could just look in for a moment. I'd like to, for Joan's sake."

"All right, but you're to be nice *only* to me — is that understood? I'm not going to stand by while some well-heeled Yank snatches you away from under my nose, just because he happens to have a million dollars. The purser department still takes its orders from the deck, Miss Spicer, and don't you forget it."

She knew as she put down the telephone that one day his envy and jealousy would make things impossible between them. She was a little afraid of his violence. She had never seen it properly in action but she knew it was there. The sarcasm and the cynicism which were on the dark side of that open freckled face were at present kept in the background by a kind of impatient good sense. That and the discipline he had to accept as a first officer of *Leviathan* kept his temper under control most of the time, but Susan suspected that one day there would be a terrible explosion. He was exciting to be with, provided you kept yourself tuned to the same wavelength, but there was none of the ease and security, for instance, that seemed to shine out of Purser Mott. With him she felt warm and happy and safe; with Charles Beecher she felt as wary as if she'd been keeping company with a tiger.

Luckily Joan now had a job and was out during the daytime or Susan would have felt guilty for not seeing as much of her friend as possible during this unexpected break in New York. But Joan was becoming far more independent than Susan would ever have believed possible. She had a job in a travel agency on Madison Avenue and a growing rota of boy friends dating her under Ethel's apparently casual eye. Physically she was thinning out and losing her "rosy dumpling" appearance. She was also much more sure of herself and no longer so girlishly enthralled by Susan and her glamorous job — or so it seemed to Susan, who was delighted to find her more and more lively each time *Leviathan* came in to New York. There was now little trace of the inhibited, hero-worshipping adolescent she had been back home a few short months ago. But Charles could not stand her. He refused to see any change in the awkward, sexless, snobbish, and dull young daughter of the company's General Manager.

"Nor can she ever be anything else," he griped to Susan over lunch. "What you see in her now is the thinnest veneer. Crack it and out will pop the good old English suet pudding just as it was before."

"I don't see why you resent her so much. What has she done to put your back up like this?"

"Nothing consciously. Superficially we're the best of friends. Haven't you noticed our studious politeness to each other? After all, Daddy's the Boss, isn't he? She simply happens to be typical of everything I most abhor. I like people who do things — make their own way in life — not just sit on their fannies taking it all for granted because they happen to be their father's sons — or daughters. That's what's wrong with the Navy. It's so damn 'Royal' — such a 'gentleman's service' — there's no room for plain honest seamanship without any frills."

"In the first place," Susan said, a feeling of anger rising in her throat, "I don't agree with what you say about the Navy for a moment — "

"Now that's interesting."

"Charles, don't talk like that to me or I'll get up and leave you straight away. I hate the way you poke fun at everything you don't like or agree with."

"I'm sorry, Susan, but you can't really know about the Navy unless you've been in it."

"Both my cousins are Lieutenants R.N.," Susan said, "and Joan's father was in the R.N.V.R. through the war. He's seen a good deal more of the Navy than you have."

"They're such goddam fearful snobs. They think all Merchant Service officers muck about in coasters and can't speak the King's English. As though that had any importance at all."

"Then I don't see what you're doing in *Leviathan*, you talk like a disillusioned officer from some broken down tramp."

"A fat lot you know about that. My father's been in tramps all his life. He's not disillusioned."

"Then why are you so bitter about it all?"

"I don't know," he said unhappily staring at his plate. "I suppose it's something I've always felt and it's sort of come to the top over Munich. I don't think much of the 'ladies and gentlemen' who run things in England. They're so damned proud of God making them 'the ruling class' and they go on making such a monumental hash of it all. Just wait till we have a bit of real Socialism about the place. Then you'll see a difference."

"Ramsay MacDonald didn't do so well in 1931, did he?"

"You just don't know what you're talking about."

"All right," Susan said, "I don't know anything about it. My father happens to be an M.P., that's all. I've only had politics rammed down my throat since I was a child."

"A Tory M.P. — and a Chamberlain man at that. Anyway,

I thought you didn't like your father or his politics. I thought that's why you ran away from home."

She really didn't know how to deal with him when he was like this. She agreed with a great many of his views but for different reasons. The governing class *were* making a hash of things. She disliked snobs just as much as he did, and she'd had more than her fill of arguing about it at home. But none the less, instinctively she was on the other side of the fence. She couldn't intellectualize about Socialism and she had no arguments she could put up against him but there was something about it she neither trusted nor liked.

"I thought we were supposed to be enjoying ourselves," she said. "If you're going to go on complaining all the time, I'd rather we called the whole thing off."

He looked so crestfallen she immediately felt sorry.

"I can't help it, Sue; I feel a rotten old sod talking like this. I do love you enormously and there seems to be nothing I can do about it. I'd ask you to marry me if I thought it would help, but it wouldn't, and anyway I don't suppose you'd even look at a chap like me. Would you?"

She put her hand over his and looked him in the eyes.

"I wouldn't be sitting here now, Charles, if I didn't like you very much."

"There's a difference between liking and loving. *Would* you marry me, Sue?"

"I don't know. You'd have to ask me properly. I don't know. If I did I couldn't remain in *Leviathan* and . . . well, I suppose it's not all that important, but I really am beginning to enjoy it a lot."

"We could do it secretly and no one need ever know. Let's do it this afternoon."

She was privately thrilled and flattered even though the suggestion was quite absurd.

"No, sweety, that's not a very good idea. You *must* dash off and do everything straight away, mustn't you?"

He shrugged his shoulders and the corners of his mouth turned down.

"There you are, you see, I knew it wouldn't work out."

But he was so mercurial a person that in another hour's time, while they were looking at the Impressionists in the Metropolitan Museum, he had forgotten all about his lunchtime "hate" and even went so far as to say that no one but an utter fool would ever get married at a time like this, that a man's personal freedom was his most priceless possession, and that any girl worth her salt felt exactly the same.

"Ninety-nine people out of a hundred get married simply and solely because of a sudden sexual urge," he declared rather too confidently as they examined a Van Gogh. "Once that's run its course there's nothing to hold any two people together — apart from children and all that. Find a way round sex — as these boys did — and marriage simply hasn't any meaning or point. You should never get married, Susan, you're much too independent."

"I don't know that these boys did so well in the love line," Susan remarked. "They had a pretty rough time, what with cutting off ears and dying of gruesome diseases in the Pacific."

"Well, that's how it is," Charles said vaguely, as if that settled it all and there was nothing further to discuss. Indeed, during the afternoon it *did* seem to be settled between them in some mysterious way, as if it were a waste of time to argue any more; Charles regained his sunny mood, Susan let his attraction for her pour over and refresh her as they walked across Central Park, back to the apartment so that Susan could change in time for the cocktail party. He even made a special effort to be nice to Joan when she came in from her travel bureau a few minutes later accompanied by Jackson Levine, her immediate boss and the man who was taking them all on to the party.

"Gonna be a lot of shipping and agency people there tonight," Levine remarked as they got into the Buick and headed for the East Seventies where the party was being given. "The guys whose hard selling keeps you at sea and us in our jobs. Ever met any really determined salesmen before?" The others shook their heads. "Well, hang on to your hats, that's all I say, and to other essential pieces of clothing."

Jack Levine was one of those sharp, dark-haired, dark-eyed young men who seemed to be, if anyone was, typical of New

York. Susan watched him and Joan in the front seat of the car surprised at the attraction Joan obviously had for such a man.

At first sight it was an unlikely combination, at least it would have been very improbable in England. Joan was neither flashy nor obviously sexy and Levine was both. He was energetic, almost glistening and sleek like a cat, yet with none of that smarmy self-consciousness which educated English Jews seemed to adopt as a protective skin. Uncle Fab would have been horrified to see his daughter so obviously enjoying the company of this "smart alec," as he would have been labeled in Dorking. And not only enjoying it but succeeding herself in a feminine way astonishing to Susan, who had grown up with her. Joan made no effort to compete with the stream of gags, wisecracks, and stories coming from Jack Levine, yet she was no longer the dull pudding she had been in England.

She was obviously mad about him as a man and he knew it; but she did not simply sit and goof at him as she would once have done, but instead allowed herself to be the butt of some of his sharper remarks, particularly the anti-British ones, without becoming affected emotionally and, indeed, in some cases turning them back on Levine himself. To Susan, Levine was a sort of American Charles. Indeed Charles, she noticed, had now become strangely subdued. It was remarkable what a little competition would do. She leaned over suddenly and kissed him on the ear for no reason at all except that at that moment she thought him a poppet.

At the party itself there were the usual very dry martinis and trays of Scotch and Bourbon whisky. Almost everyone there seemed to have something to do with travel and there were buyers and bookers and ad-men with their wives, secretaries, and unclassified girl friends. The Lap o' Luxury Travel Organization Inc., shortened to Lapolux for everyday use, was strictly a first class affair specializing in making exceptional arrangements for very rich clients to whom price was unimportant but quality and speed of the essence.

It was a small setup in personnel, run, and indeed, thought

up by a Bostonian called Hamilton Codde whose Harvard career had been brought to an abrupt end when his father had thrown himself out of a thirty-story skyscraper in 1929, revealing the complete disappearance of the family fortune, and leaving a widow and her son to carry on in penury as best they might. The result of this disaster was to provoke an idea which had developed into a howling success.

Lapolux gave personal service and restricted its list of clients, though not racially as did some of its competitors. It charged very highly in some instances and not at all in others. It could always get you what you wanted, often at a few minutes' notice, and this was achieved by an understanding which Hamilton Codde personally renewed once a year with every really first-rate European hotel, by much use of the transatlantic telephone, and by the free play of percentages, bribes, honoraria, and sweeteners. Jackson Levine was the shipping expert in all this and was some sort of distant relation of Laban's as well as being his blue-eyed boy. Lapolux could always get anything they wanted from Transoceanic and the business done by both parties was prodigious and, at the same time, a closely guarded secret.

Once the initial introductions were made and the opening drinks consumed, Charles saw his worst fears realized. Susan was neatly removed when his back was turned by the pliable Mr. Levine and presented first to Hamilton Codde and then to other high-powered personalities as a sort of star guest, since she was a good-looking girl in a unique position in the world's largest ship and one in which a fair number of Lapolux clients would be embarked for the forthcoming world cruise.

At that moment Munich and the clouds of war seemed a very long way away, and at the same time, to Charles, almost unbearably present. What did all these wealthy, successful Americans imagine? That Europe could go up in flames while they bargained and bought and sold? Here everything was humming and bright. The depression had been licked and prosperity was flooding back. People talked about money most of the time and "things" for the remainder. They were uninhibited, noisy, and apparently happy.

Yet across the Atlantic was brewing up a cataclysm of terror — cold, vicious and depressing — which must sooner or later involve them all. He leaned against the wall, drinking far too much Scotch far too quickly, watching Susan being smiled at, made much of and flattered on the other side of the room. He had seldom felt in a more alien atmosphere, and he hated it all.

"You and I are going to see a lot of each other," Jack Levine whispered in Susan's ear as he slipped his hand in the crook of her elbow and led her away to another introduction. "Let me tell you something, honey, you're just about the hottest thing in this hothouse of a room. You're just naturally luscious."

"Well, thank you," said Susan. "I thought Joan was your guest."

"That's only because I hadn't met you, you great big eatable doll."

"Joan happens to be my best friend."

"And why not, honey? A girl should have friends. It takes all sorts to make a jungle."

Susan found that when she called herself a purserette it produced a look of puzzled inquiry on people's faces, but when Levine, on his own initiative, explained that she was really the ship's host*ess*, which she certainly wasn't, everything seemed to fall into place and be understood. The transatlantic function of a hostess was, indeed, a much more open and positive thing than it would have been in Europe.

"For instance," Levine told her when she asked, "every big Bermuda hotel has hostesses who find out the tastes of individual guests and bring people together. They're blenders."

"I don't think that would do a girl's reputation much good in England," Susan said.

"Yes, well you're in America now," Levine retorted, "where you can be a hostess on a salaried basis without necessarily going to bed with the clients. Not that I'm against that in any way, you understand. It's a free country. You know, I'm really mad about that blonde hair of yours."

"I'd just like to point out my boy friend standing over there by the door — you know, the one who sat next to me in your car."

"Oh him!" said Levine, catching hold of Hamilton Codde's third wife as she passed in order to introduce Susan. "What's a boy friend among friends? Send him back to his ship."

"I'll certainly do no such thing," Susan said sharply as she found herself being artificially gushed over once again, while the third Mrs. Codde's cold eyes made their expert appraisal. Mrs. Codde had first arrived in Lapolux herself as secretary to Jack Levine. She knew what it was all about.

Later in the evening when she succeeded in getting back to Charles she found him alcoholically philosophic, talking to Joan of all unlikely people.

"Ah! little Miss Party-Girl-of-the-Year is back in the slum area again," he greeted her. "Are you going to devote a little of your valuable time to us poor white trash — us poor British white trash, if I may say so, and I think I did say so with re-markable clarity considering the state of my glass. Are you aware," he went on without giving Susan a chance to retort, "that we have a date at the theatre in half an hour's time? Such being the case, the position, to wit the state of affairs, let us get the hell out of here at our best possible speed. I'm indebted to you, Miss Mitchell," and he bowed very low, spilling his drink while Joan looked at Susan with a hopeless little shrug, "for the pleasure of your absolutely spiffing com-pany while Miss P.G. of the Y. was doing her stuff with the quality and I do sincerely trust that . . ."

He was interrupted by a hand reaching out over Susan's shoulder and a very familiar Lancashire voice saying:

"Hallo, Charley-boy, fancy you being here and . . . why hallo, Susan!"

Susan turned to find herself looking straight into Gloria Dowkins's cleavage, framed as it was in an arresting red dress. She seemed to be squired by a bald-headed American of obvious wealth and popularity who had already abandoned her on a "Hiya Ham! Hiya Jack!" tour of the room.

"Why, Gloria!" Susan said quickly. "We might be back in *Leviathan* again!"

"We might not," Gloria retorted, "but we're going to be. Mr. Saxburger's coming on our world whatnot and so we're doing a little preliminary Manhattan cruise of our own. He's only got ten million dollars. Isn't that awful?"

Gloria's arrival sobered up Charles like a bucket of cold water straight in the face.

"What on earth are you doing here?" he asked.

"Oh! I get around, Mr. Beecher," Gloria said throwing her head back with a sniff. "I could ask the same thing of you if I chose — but I don't," she finished off with a wink at Susan. "Well, mustn't leave Art too long on his own."

"Leave who?"

"Art. Arthur Saxburger. He's in the brassière business."

"And I suppose he wants you to do some modeling for him," Charles said with a rather too knowing smile.

"Oh that!" Gloria said scornfully. "That's old stuff. That went out with the flood. No — it's 'Old Europe and its Culture' today. Art and culture, you know, they always go together — and you'd be surprised at some of the European culture I've had to wise up on in the last twenty-four hours. So long, Sue; you want to watch this wolf. He's got nasty fangs. See you back in the crate."

"Well, 'Charley-boy,'" Susan said as the taxi drove down Fifth Avenue towards the theatre district, "that was unexpected. I didn't know you and my cabin mate were buddies."

"We're not," Charles said defensively, "I hardly know her at all."

But that was certainly not Susan's impression. She enjoyed his awkward floundering, and in any case, she told herself, she'd find out the facts sooner or later from Gloria.

"She's a brash, cheeky young woman — never been known to call any officer 'sir' unless she could help it," Charles went on after a pause, as though it worried him in some way. "She's really nothing but a tart, when it comes to the point."

"When it comes to what point?"

"Oh! for heaven's sake don't let's waste time talking about Gloria Dowkins. She can look after herself all right — that's one thing she's certainly learned to do since she joined *Leviathan*."

"You were shipmates before then, were you?"

"Oh yes! Gloria's been around. You'd never think so now, but she used to be a fresh innocent little thing full of Lancashire nonsense — and very attractive."

"I think she still is."

"Not for my money. Now she's just out for everything she can get."

"We're all like that," Susan said, "however much we disguise it — so are men, only they're far, far worse because it's really your world and you can usually buy what you want."

He was always much nicer, she decided, when his nose was slightly out of joint, when he wasn't quite sure of his ground, when he felt he ought to be making a rather special effort. Perhaps because of this slightly guilty anxiety, the theater was a great success. By the time they reached Rico's for supper and dancing, Charles was once more at the top of his form.

"The thing is," he said as they danced, "I really do think you're exciting and wonderful and I suppose I like showing you off. I'm proud of you. I like it when men turn round and look at you in the street."

"Oh! that's just the peacock in you. You'd lose interest quickly enough, just as you did over Gloria."

"I would not," Charles said hotly, thus tacitly admitting what Susan wanted to find out. "There's far more to you than just sex. In fact that side mightn't work out at all."

Susan looked at him in surprise, wondering privately how he would be.

"Do you think so? Why do you say that?"

"Because it's the one thing you never can know till you try it. The most glamorous puss is very often about as alive as a piece of old rope. It's all gone in the looks."

"Like me?"

"Oh! you're not especially pretty. You're simply arresting, that's all. Anyway, we dance together very well and that's always a good sign."

"You sound as though you're blasé with experience. How many girls have you been in love with before?"

But he only hugged her more closely and smiled his private smile.

"I just read a lot of books," he murmured. "How about going over to my place for a nightcap?"

"To *your* place?" Now she was really astonished.

"Oh yes!" he said blandly as they walked back to the table and he settled the bill, "other people besides little purserettes have friends in New York who loan them apartments when they happen to be away on trips. We don't all have to stay with tycoons."

Now she was intrigued. Perhaps he wasn't quite as simple as he looked, and he knew how to keep a surprise. They took a taxi and Charles gave an address downtown, somewhere on East 10th Street she thought it was. The sense of adventure he had initially given her came back and tingled her nerves. He was confident, now, and strong, and the long passionate kiss in the taxi set her afire. She wanted him very fiercely and suddenly, and knew it was not something to be thought about, not something, indeed, which would bear thinking about, and that perhaps gave it an added tang.

They climbed the stairs of an old brownstone house to the top landing and after fumbling about with an unfamiliar key found themselves in a studio apartment with Mexican rugs and blankets on the divan and some surrealist-style paintings on the walls. Charles raided the icebox in the diminutive kitchen for soda and poured out two good stiff Scotches. He also turned on an electric fire, explaining that this was a "cold water walk-up" apartment without central heating owned by an actor he knew who was on the road with a play.

"Very primitive by New York standards and pretty old-fashioned, but very nice and convenient for us," he went on and then kissed her again. Now she could almost watch her resistance becoming merely a token flutter as his fingers found and pulled down the zip at the back of her dress and then almost before she was aware of what was happening he was fiercely kissing her breasts so that then she knew she was lost, and he took her in a blindly exultant wave, took her through a mounting ecstasy she had never known before in her life, a tempestuous writhing wonder of two naked entwined bodies, exploring the ancient wonderful gasping approaches to a climax for which there were no words except for the desperate calling of his name in the darkness till the passion was spent and they lay in each other's arms enveloped in an unworldly bliss, a soft velvety peace as she stroked his strong back, and her whole being seemed to sigh with pleasure.

"So that's what it is," she thought as she kissed his neck and shoulders and watched the reflection of a neon sign down the street blinking on and off like the beating of some other heart, remote, yet somehow similar to the one which now beat so close to her own. In a little while she felt him stirring again, and in a futile, instinctive search for her battered resistance she called out, "No, Charles, no, I can't bear it," but found herself stopped by his lips and the repetition, unending and deeper still as it seemed, of that total abandonment into which she had tumbled. "How simple and wonderful it is," she reflected, as the timelessness of the experience and its strength shone like a blazing light in her consciousness. Here for a little while she lay possessed of peace. A peace so powerful that it drove back into the shadows, like the filthy dark creatures they were, all the creeping remorse, doubts, and regrets which had plagued her before and which perhaps would return to the attack with the coming day. The neon light blinked the hours away, the fire glowed and the early morning noises of New York filtered in through the crooked window as the first man to whom she had ever given herself lay gently asleep in her arms.

As autumn finished and winter began, *Leviathan* continued her planned schedule and just before Christmas docked at Southampton for a bottom scrape and the final preparations for her world cruise. This had been organized because until her consort came into service she was uneconomic on the Atlantic run during the winter off-season, because a round-the-world cruise by the largest ship afloat was an excellent advertisement both for *Leviathan* and for the company, because she had been booked up beyond her "break-even" figure within a month of the announcement of the cruise, and finally because Sir Josiah Flint had decided he wanted a holiday in grand style to mark his semi-retirement from the Board of Transoceanic in January 1939.

On the first day of the new year Fabian would take over as Chairman and Flint, while remaining a Director, would give up his day-to-day hold on the company's affairs. To be elsewhere than in Liverpool yet still very much within the company's orbit during Fabian's first three months in control, struck both of them as a happy arrangement. Moreover it would cost Flint nothing, and this gave the old man real pleasure, since at a meeting held without his knowledge the Board of Directors had decided to present him with this ticket, worth over a thousand pounds, as first of the many tokens of appreciation which would shower on his head when his retirement took effect.

The cruise brought problems galore to be solved. First of these was the fact that *Leviathan* was too big to go through either the Panama or Suez canals, and if she were to round the South American continent by way of the Strait of Magellan she must do so before too much of the southern hemisphere summer had gone. The original idea of using Jules Verne's title and encircling the globe in eighty days had to be abandoned as it would have been too much of a rush. Instead the "Hundred-Day Cruise" became the slogan, and this would get them back to New York by mid-April if they left on 5th January.

After much fundamental arguing, most of which had taken place before *Leviathan* had even been completed, the cruise was set up on a two class basis, a good deal of the cabin accommodation being up-graded to first, the rest of it being merged with the better tourist cabins into a "super Second" class, no cabins of which would contain more than two people. Although the bulk of the passenger list was American, some three hundred British had also booked on this fantastic "essay in escapism" as one writer had it, some of them no doubt sensing, as both Flint and Fabian did, that this would be the last of such cruises for some time to come.

So Christmas 1938 saw *Leviathan* in the graving dock, Captain Banks in his Sussex cottage, Mott with his aged mother in Bournemouth, Susan at Dorking, Charles with his family in Wallasey, Joan in New York, and Alan skiing in Austria. Fabian had suggested half-heartedly that his children might care to spend Christmas at home and had even offered to pay for his daughter's passage, which in any case he could get at a nominal "company rate." But Joan had begged almost too eagerly to be allowed to remain in New York. She told him Ethel had laid on an extensive program of parties, and in any case she was now able to claim that Lapolux needed her and that this would be to the benefit of Transoceanic — even though Lapolux clients had long ago been booked in the best *Leviathan* suites. Fabian did not understand it, but he accepted the situation. So instead he asked Flint to spend Christmas with him and his wife before repairing on board *Leviathan* on 29th December for her voyage to New York. It would all fit very well and he would drive Flint and Susan down to the ship the morning she sailed.

By Christmas Susan had made another eight crossings of the Atlantic, bringing her score up to twenty. She had long been looking forward to the world cruise as a unique adventure, but the nearer it drew the more apprehensive she felt. This uneasiness, illogical and hard to pin down, was partly worry over her relationship with Charles, partly the growing attention Mott was paying her, and partly the prospect of being a long way from home while the war clouds gathered and perhaps the war itself broke out.

"My dear girl, you're in a perfect position at a time like this. Millions of people in this country would give their eyes to get away as you're doing," her father said when they discussed war and its likelihood. "To get away from it all, that's all the electorate thinks about now."

"That's just what I *don't* feel," Susan said. "If there's going to be a war, I'd like to be right in it doing something useful, not pandering to a lot of wealthy dumbbells with no idea in their heads other than their own pleasure. There's an awful sameness about very rich people — at least there is when you see them at close quarters week after week as I do. They're so — ordinary, so selfish about little things, and so dull and bored with themselves. Motty says American widows are the worst of all on a cruise, and I believe we've got over six hundred of them on this trip."

"You're always quoting Motty — Motty says this — Motty says that," her father said, looking at her in the aggressive way he kept for the opposition front bench. "What's so extraordinary about this purser?"

"Well, he's my immediate boss, Father," Susan answered, surprised both at the question and at herself for having provoked it. Her father was not blessed with great insight and if he had been impelled to ask such a question simply because Motty kept entering the conversation, then her feelings must be far more transparent than she thought. Thank heavens, she'd made no mention of Charles to her parents.

"Your mother and I have grave doubts about letting you go on this cruise," her father continued, a remark so disturbing in its context that for a moment or so she was nonplussed. She felt like pointing out that her father could scarcely stop her at this stage of things. Certainly there would be the row to end all rows if he did. "I hope you realize how broadminded we've been about this whole escapade," he went on. "Your mother hasn't been well and the normal thing would be for you to stay at home and look after her. However, you prefer to go gallivanting about the world," he shrugged his shoulders and raised his eyebrows, "enjoying yourself and having a good time —"

"I do work, you know, Father. I don't sit around just 'enjoying myself and having a good time.' "

"There's work and there's work," Sir Henry said as though he'd made the most profound observation. "I've no doubt you have the illusion of effort — I don't doubt your honesty and intentions — but I'm told that the whole purserette scheme

177

is not looked on with favor in high quarters. It certainly won't be extended and it may well be abandoned. That would scarcely be so if there was a real job to be done."

Susan stared at the fire and tried to marshal her feelings and thoughts into some kind of coherence. She'd made an aim not to fall out with her parents, not to fly off the handle during these last few days she was spending at home over Christmas. And here she was seething all over again.

"Men are extraordinary," she said eventually. "They simply don't want a woman to succeed. They pretend they're giving encouragement but all the time you get treated like a child, as though you're incapable of any sort of responsibility, as though you're only interested in a job as a way of getting someone to make love to you."

"I don't know what you mean," her father said huffily. "I never said anything at all about that sort of thing. Of course it's perfectly true, now you mention it. Women in business and women in politics — they're both equally disastrous."

"Why *can't* you give us a chance? We've got just as much to contribute as men, but anyone alive needs just a glimmer of encouragement and hope."

Later that evening when the Mitchells and Flint had come in for drinks, she seized the occasion for a counterattack.

"I hear the purserette scheme's a flop, and we're all to be paid off," she said to Fabian in Flint's hearing. "Is that going to be your first action as the new Chairman?"

She saw Flint wince slightly, and Fabian was clearly embarrassed at what he obviously thought a cool piece of cheek.

"I don't know what you're talking about, Susan."

"That's what Father claims, and he must have got it from somewhere. But I'd like to know *where* we've all failed. What's wrong with us all?"

"This is a highly improper approach," Fabian said, shooting Flint a glance from under his eyebrows, "at a highly improper time."

"Well you don't get anywhere if you don't take a risk, Uncle Fab — and I was only asking because it doesn't seem fair.

I mean, if we're not to be given a real chance just because of prejudice."

"You're an incorrigible girl," Fabian said with a slight smile. "It's true we haven't had many bad reports from *Leviathan* but I suppose you know that anyway."

"No," said Susan, telling a direct lie with a look of the sweetest innocence on her face. Unknown even to Mott, she was fully aware of each report that had been made on her service so far, but this was her own private secret, the value of which lay in its never being used for any personal purpose. "No — I just think it's nice to give people an occasional pat on the back. Or is it policy to keep company servants seething with discontent?"

"Transoceanic personnel are not 'seething with discontent,'" Fabian said firmly, "and this discussion is to stop forthwith."

"Wait till I get on the Board of Directors," Susan said, unmoved by his anger, "then the sparks really will begin flying. Sorry if I've dropped any bricks, but it's high time a woman's voice got just the breath of a hearing."

She moved off to get them more drinks, making a mental note that Flint had not said a word in all this but had, as usual, remained very quiet and very, very observant.

Dudley Fitzpatrick Mott usually spent his leaves in London or, occasionally, in Paris. This was because he was a dedicated theatre-goer in both capitals, as he also was in New York. He enjoyed the company of actors and theater people. A few of his friends were West End stars, others were on the way up and one or two were alcoholically on the way down, but all of them gave Motty a genuinely warm welcome when he breezed in from the sea.

This Christmas of 1938, however, having spent two days with his mother and sister in Bournemouth he only had twenty-four hours left in which to get up to London, see a matinee and an evening show and return to the ship. He could have done with a much longer break. He was finding *Levia-*

than far more exacting than any other ship he'd been in, and the prospect of the Hundred Days' Hard Labor ahead depressed him, which was in itself unusual.

"I don't know why I'm so low, but I feel I could do with six months in a sanatorium," he remarked as he said good-by to his mother, while she was feeding her cats and budgerigars. But Mother would have none of it.

"Nonsense," she replied in her businesslike way, giving her cheek to be pecked. "You know you really enjoy every minute of it. So would I, if I'd been a man. I wish I was in your shoes."

"You'd better come on the cruise next year, Mother, and see for yourself."

"Oh yes? And what would I use for money? Off you go and don't get into mischief. Send me a postcard from Hong Kong. Your cousin Willy always said it was the one posting he ever really enjoyed — and don't forget to look up the Burtons in Bombay. Anyway, you've got it all in your little book, haven't you?"

"Yes, Mother, it's all written down."

"Writing it down" was one of the sprightly old lady's precepts for the avoidance of muddle, a precept instilled into her in turn by her Victorian father. Mott always felt a strange sense of continuity when he remembered his mother had been born in the Crimean War and his grandfather the year after Waterloo. In those days they had lived their lives in accordance with certain principles, one of which was that the men of the family went out into the world and did things, while the women ran their homes against the day of their return. Mrs. Mott did this not in a soppy dutiful way, but with pride and intelligence and pleasure in a domain entirely her own.

Nowadays among Mott's married friends the edges always seemed to be blurred. There was more freedom and less distinction between the sexes. People thought it was cosier, but when Mott reflected on his mother's life he became very dubious of progress. He knew his mother missed him very much, and would have been greatly pleased to have had him closer at hand. But the tradition of independence ran strongly in their family, and their partings were brisk and unsentimental. Each got on with his own life, and at the next coming together, there was a wealth of digested experience to be shared.

His own life was as full as any man's could be, but he was always surprised at the interest and vitality his mother extracted from the day to day adventure, as she made it appear, of living the life of an eighty-two-year-old lady in Bournemouth. Even a visit to the greengrocer yielded as much human interest to her as a trip across the Atlantic did to him. This ability was no accident but a careful practiced art. The old lady could meet any stranger from any walk of life and after a few minutes' conversation see into and almost be a part of his life. It was from her that Mott got his own flexibility with strangers of every kind.

But on this Boxing Day trip to London, Mott found himself uneasy and restless for a reason he did his best not to acknowledge but which seemed to have got steadily worse over the last few months. This reason was quite simply Susan. He could not get her out of his mind. He did not like it, he did not want it that way, but that was the way it was. He no longer tried to argue himself out of it, to dragoon his thoughts and his feelings. He had come to realize angrily that none of this was of any use. He was driven by it as a machine is by a belt. He was hopelessly fascinated by her and he could not put her out of his thoughts. Like a scent, she was everywhere and nowhere all at once.

For a time he had forced himself to see her as little as he could, making her work under Kennicote, and no longer inviting her up for that first drink of the evening with Jimmy Johnson in the Observation Bar. This had only made it a hundred times worse. And there was no one in *Leviathan* to whom he could talk about it, no one who would understand, except perhaps Jimmy Johnson, and with him it would never be put into words.

Mott had been in love a number of times before. He knew the process, the stages it usually went through, the signs that appeared. He was a man of forty-one and he had enjoyed a full and varied, if somewhat unorthodox, sexual life. Yet this thing was gnawing at him as if he were a moonstruck adolescent. It was ridiculous and humiliating — at least such was his own opinion, so what it would be in anyone else's he did not dare to imagine.

He went to his matinee, thought it banal and desperately unfunny, did not go round afterward as he would normally have done to see the friend who was in it, but instead repaired to a hideous little drinking club in a back street near the Charing Cross Road. Here in the orange light and the pathetic paper decorations were gathered those lost souls who had no family to be concerned with over Christmas, the blowsy amateur tarts, and the second-hand car salesmen, whose restless trivial lives brought them together at the Mandarin Club with expressions of artificial Yuletide jollity and good will to drink round the electric fire with its glowing plastic coal because there was nowhere else to go.

Normally Mott enjoyed dropping in for a drink when the pubs were shut, he enjoyed being the welcome stranger in other people's lives while not being involved himself, but today he felt unbearably depressed. By the end of the week he would be *en route* for New York and a week after that *Leviathan* would be headed south for Trinidad and Rio full of people as aimless and escapist as the clientele of the Mandarin Club, but with very much more money to disguise it from themselves. Once again Mott would be at the controls of the hotel and entertainment machine. No one would see him ruffled, angry, or depressed. The wheels would spin, the passengers would feel seasick, recover, spend money, and drink too much. They would wear paper hats at gala dinners and buy useless souvenirs in foreign ports. There would be the usual petulant complaints, the usual gushing praise, and what would it all amount to? Nothing. There was no meaning in any of it. It would all go on in exactly the same way whether Mott was there or not. Someone would take his place, just as there would always be a Mandarin Club with people such as these trying to escape from themselves without ever admitting it. He suddenly saw himself as he was — a polished, successful, middle-aged man with no one to live for and no point whatever in life.

He had just decided he could not stand the Mandarin Club a moment longer when to his surprise Charles Beecher walked in with a girl whose face was very familiar but whom he could not immediately place. The little club was a favorite place for unattached Transoceanic officers and it crossed Mott's mind that he must have sponsored Charles Beecher for it on a previous London run. It also struck him that Charles's first reaction at finding him there was a quickly covered up embarrassment. He wondered why, and then as Charles introduced him to the girl he suddenly saw the reason and understood.

"Fancy running into you here on a night like this," Charles was saying. "What's it going to be, Gloria, another light or are you switching to shorts? What about you, Motty?"

"I've got a theater, I'm afraid, I'm just on my way."

"Have one for the road. Come on — it's Boxing Day and you've plenty of time."

So he allowed himself to be plied with another watered Scotch and then in turn stood a round while he listened to Charles describing the boisterousness of his family Christmas at Wallasey. As he talked Gloria slashed another layer of scarlet on to her full luscious lips, interpolating an odd remark or two about her own hectic Christmas at Barrow-in-Furness and letting it be known in her private feminine way that while she was glad to be on the tiles with young Charley Beecher she could also become very interested indeed in Dudley Fitzpatrick Mott. This she did with a single lingering look over the top of her compact as Charles bought some cigarettes at the bar and a subsequent remark about Christmas being all right if you liked kids' parties, but how her own preferences always ran to things rather more mature.

The obvious unspoken invitation made Mott want to laugh out loud. He wondered if Charles was aware of the girl's instant infidelity — or whether perhaps it was what he enjoyed. There was certainly something appealing and light-hearted about Gloria. Yet if he was swept up with her then what were his feelings for Susan? He had been so hotly enthusiastic when Susan had first joined *Leviathan*, talking his head off about her each time he had run into Mott, and then one day he had shut up like a clam as a man will once a woman becomes something serious in his heart. Mott had taken this to mean that Charles was really in love with Susan, though he had no idea of her reaction to it nor of Charles's success or failure with her — and here he was, the cunning bastard, playing it on the side with her cabinmate, with *Leviathan*'s notorious good-time girl with her roving eyes and her volcanic sex. Well, good luck to him, he thought. No one kept company with Gloria Dowkins for long without having their eyes well and truly opened. He only hoped that Susan was not involved in any way in which she could be hurt.

"Are you looking forward to the cruise?" Gloria was asking, by way of conversation — a question which luckily she answered herself. "It's going to make a change from the five-day New York run, isn't it? I hear we're going to be rotten with millionaires."

"Gloria's got a pet one of her own coming on the cruise," Charles put in. "A Mr. Saxburger, Potentate of the Bust Bodice and Brassière Business. The only snag is Mrs. Saxburger's coming too. But that's one for the Purser department, isn't it, Motty?"

"I wish all our problems were as simple as that," Mott said, tactfully deflecting the question. "I must be on my way. See you on board."

"Now there's a real man," Gloria remarked following his departure with her number two soulful expression, "manners and all. He's got such lovely eyes — why isn't he married?"

"He's been waiting for you to come along and take a hold of his life," Charles answered tartly, cupping her breast with one hand as he lit her cigarette with the other.

"I'll bet he respects a woman he's out with," Gloria said indignantly, smacking down his hand, "and I'll also bet he's got more than just one grubby little idea in his head."

The unexpected encounter with Charles and Gloria had

cheered Mott up considerably. By the time he took his seat in the second theater he had visited that day, his depression had been driven back into the shadows, as it always was when other people began absorbing his interest. It was only at times like Christmas, when he stood back from his life and made up accounts, that he felt pointless and adrift. Now, once again, on this one night in London before the world cruise began, the pleasure and enjoyment he habitually extracted from people and the passing scene returned and with it his sense of humor and his taste for the folly of human nature in general and his own share of it in particular. Life had a way of upsetting the most careful plans and just as Charles had obviously not expected to find anyone from *Leviathan* at the Mandarin Club on Boxing Night, which had added piquancy to the meeting, so now Mott was totally unprepared as he got up to go to the bar in the interval to find Susan, her mother, and her father sitting two rows behind.

"Well, well, well," he said as they wedged themselves into a corner of the bar while Sir Henry tried unsuccessfully to bluster his way to the top of the queue. "If things go in threes I wonder what the third surprise of the night will be? I've just met . . . an old friend I didn't expect to see in London and now here's the prop and mainstay of the Purser department in *Leviathan* — you must be jealous of your daughter going on this fabulous cruise, Lady Spicer," he went on, sensing that if he waited for Susan's mother to start a conversation he would wait all night. But Susan herself jumped into it by saying, "There's an empty seat next to us — or there has been the first act — why don't you come and sit with us — sir?"

"All right, madam, thank you I will."

Sir Henry appeared with their drinks, his red face two shades deeper after another of his usual encounters.

"Of course if you will ask for some exotic drink like Dubonnet," he said with a short laugh at his wife, "it's small wonder we have to wait all night. I hope the service is a bit better than this in *Leviathan*," he continued, glaring aggressively at Mott as if he expected him to deny it. "It could scarcely be worse."

"I've asked Mr. Mott to sit with us, Father," Susan said, and then turning to Mott on a sudden impulse, "If you're not doing anything afterwards why don't you come and have supper? Father's good for a bottle of champagne, aren't you, Father?"

"Well, I don't know," said Sir Henry, privately enjoying the way his daughter was taking charge. "If she's anything like this when she's aboard *Leviathan*, I wonder you haven't wrung her neck. She was always a bossy little girl. Be delighted if you'd join us, of course."

So it had gone that way. Mott had taken them round to meet his friends in the show and then, cheerfully abandoning the idea of two parties to which he'd been invited, went to the Ritz with the Spicers for supper and some mild dancing. The Ritz was a favorite of Sir Henry's and Mott was grateful to be spared the fiercer Boxing Night entertainment they would have had at some of the other West End hotels. He had over three months of that sort of thing immediately ahead. It was also the first time he had ever danced with Susan. This gave him so much pleasure he could have swept her up in his arms and carried her off as if he had been some medieval knight, and indeed, disguise it as he would, the excitement he felt communicated itself to Susan. On their third dance together, she arched back from him and looked him in the face:

"You dance beautifully," she said. "Why are you so scared of me?"

"Now what on earth put that idea in your head?"

"But you are, aren't you?" He found the steady green eyes very disconcerting. "I know you're the big white chief, and I'm only a sprat on board. I'm not talking about that."

They continued to dance looking at each other, trying to explore each other's thoughts without committing themselves to words.

"I think you're a very attractive and lovable girl," he said eventually, picking his words with care, "but I'm forty-one and you're twenty. I don't see a way round a gap like that."

"You don't look or behave like forty-one and I feel much older than twenty. Anyway, why bother so much about physical age? I don't. I don't care what age anyone is if I like him — and I do like you."

Mott laughed.

"You'll have a splendid opportunity of seeing why people do bother about physical age when this cruise gets under way," he said sardonically; "then you'll see what it's like to be a widow of fifty with no prospect of another man in your life except one you can buy. It isn't pretty. I suppose I'm cautious about you, Susan — because of this gap between us, I mean — it seems silly to get hurt or hurt other people if you can avoid it by taking a little thought."

"Is that why you've never been married? Have you always 'thought' it out of your system?"

"Good heavens, you do ask the most direct and aggressive questions," Mott said with a smile. "No — that is *not* why I've never been married. You've seen enough of life at sea even in six months to know why people either do or don't get married. I'm afraid you can't bully me into giving you the answers you want, Susan, though I salute the attempt."

A sudden intense curiosity to know how she would make love invaded him. There was a kind of wild willful devil-may-care streak in her which he had a longing to master.

"Am I allowed to ask questions myself? Or must I always be on the receiving end?" he inquired and felt himself hugged closer.

"Sir — you really are rather a poppet," Susan said. "Ask any question you like. I love inventing the answers I think people want to hear — it's the purser in me."

"I thought you were all caught up with Charley Beecher a short time ago. Is that a thing of the past?"

"Caught up with?" Susan countered quickly. "What extraordinary phrases you gentlemen use! It makes it sound as if dear Charley's going about *Leviathan* with a vacuum cleaner . . ."

"I thought you wouldn't answer that one," Mott said with a smile.

"Oh! Am I being evasive? Yes, I suppose I am."

"What — being evasive or still bespoke?"

"I think you'll have to work that out for yourself," Susan said lightly, "if you're interested enough, that is."

"In that case, you may be surprised one of these days."

"I adore surprises," Susan said softly, and held him close to her body for a moment or so. "Let's go back to the table, shall we? I'm tired of dancing."

⚓⚓⚓⚓⚓ IX ⚓⚓⚓⚓⚓

JANUARY 1939 was not an auspicious time to be setting off on a cruise round the world, in Captain Banks's opinion. Moreover, in his safe lay a large envelope covered with Admiralty seals. This, he had been told, contained code books and secret orders to be opened on receipt of an emergency signal, a silent reminder of the real world they were leaving behind as they sailed south from New York while bathing dresses and tropical clothes were unpacked and Veronique's stock of sun tan lotion began to be sold.

"However," Banks continued, having relieved himself of his own views on the international situation at the first conference of the voyage, "the Lord's wrath is the Lord's own affair. Our job is to ensure that this cruise is a flat-out thundering success. We've all done this before in other ships, though not on such a scale. We shall have trouble of one kind or another, and the way with trouble is to face it and do something about it before it can come to a head. I understand," he went on with a glance at Mott, "that we have four advanced alcoholics, two known homosexuals and a cohort of ladies whose interest in this cruise is not only connected with travel. So be it. My job is to command this ship, not reform the passengers' morals. But I do not intend Babylon to get out of hand. And while, for purposes of this cruise, *Leviathan* may well be the largest millionaires' yacht in the world, I want my officers to remember that in another few months we shall be back on our normal transatlantic service, I trust with an enhanced reputation and no casualties chargeable to Mammon."

They had embarked their passengers in New York without incident, and their first port of call would be Trinidad, in the British West Indies. Here for the first time they would come up against *Leviathan*'s one big snag as a cruise liner — they would be forced to lie two or three miles out, since there was not enough water inshore for a ship of *Leviathan*'s size.

But Laban and Lapolux in New York and Purser Mott on board had contrived to turn this to the ship's advantage by claiming that passengers were thus guaranteed exclusiveness — the trip in a tender to Port of Spain would be an adventure, and in any case it was healthier in tropical climates not to lie too close inshore, on account of the mosquitoes and flies. Selling *Leviathan*, in fact, was an example of how it was possible to have things both ways by taking a little thought.

In any case they would only be in Trinidad a day — sufficient time for those passengers who wished, to take a drive round the Savannah, sufficient for the purchase of sharkskin walking sticks and other curios, sufficient for grapefruits and mangoes to be laid in stock and for the ship to be bunkered with cheap oil at its source. Then it would be southeast round the Bulge of Brazil across the Equator and down to Rio.

At least it made a change, Banks conceded, and he was grateful for it in his fashion as he watched a shoal of flying fish skimming the surface of the Caribbean. He did not consider the average North Atlantic voyage to be dull or unexciting, but there were times when the five days across from Southampton to New York seemed to be too hurried, too restless, too business-like and bustling. Now with the sun beating down on them more strongly each day, with the ship to be kept humming but not at the pressure inevitable for a scheduled transatlantic service, even Banks himself began to enjoy the relaxed holiday atmosphere *Leviathan* exuded, although he did so warily and with a slight feeling of guilt.

Had the decision been his, *Leviathan* would not have been sent careering round the world at a time like this, but since that choice had been taken by others, and since he remained her Master, he was able to lull his Puritan conscience by telling himself that he was only doing a job of work. "Take counsel," Isaiah had said, "execute judgment; make thy shadow as the night in the midst of the noonday; hide the outcasts; betray not him that wandereth." And what were these rich pleasure-seekers, Banks thought as he stared at the blue ocean, but spiritual outcasts and wanderers? What was any of them, if it came to that, but a child playing in the path of a gathering storm?

The war — another war — he brooded, was all but upon them, this "burden of the desert of the sea. As the whirlwinds in the south pass through, so it cometh from the desert, from a terrible land. For thus hath the Lord said unto me — Go, set a watchman, let him declare what he seeth for Babylon is fallen, is fallen and all the graven images of her gods he hath broken unto the ground."

Yet Babylon was beneath him, quivering south at twenty-five knots, unaware of the coming crash in its sleep of the soul, its inhabitants, the great walking dead of the earth, eating their smoked salmon and caviar, drinking their instincts into a stupor, dancing and fornicating through the night while *Leviathan,* their smooth gracious prison, conveyed them at enormous expense and speed on their thirty-five-thousand-mile journey of escape.

Well . . . he was trapped in it all like the rest of them. "For the idols have spoken vanity," said Zachariah, "and the diviners have seen a lie and have told false dreams, they comfort in vain: therefore they went their way as a flock, they were troubled, because there was no shepherd." Squaring his shoulders and slipping the Book of Rules back into his left-hand pocket, Captain Basil Bellerophon Banks strode off the bridge, down six decks, and along to Babylon's main restaurant for an underdone fillet steak. The next morning they would anchor off Port of Spain — the first leg of their voyage completed.

Flint had, of course, started the cruise at the Captain's table but by the time the ship reached Rio he was heartily sick of his table companions. Luckily Mott had devised a means by which people were moved between Captain's, Staff Captain's, Chief Engineer's, Purser's, and Doctor's tables on a weekly change-about system which operated unobtrusively and to no rigid timetable, so that no one could feel slighted or take offense if he found new faces at his side. Moreover, he could always have his meals served in his stateroom or book a table in the Veranda Grill when he did not feel sociable — which was a large part of the time.

He was finding his retirement far more difficult to bear than he had imagined. Although every comfort was provided and every whim obeyed, he could not rid himself of a feeling of utter emptiness, as if he had got into a nightmare and was continuously falling from a high building, vividly conscious of the void rushing past him and fearfully awaiting the crack of destruction when the ground would spring up to meet him. After breakfast each day, his fingers itched for the nonexistent morning mail. No telephone buzzed, no secretary stood at the door. At Trinidad there had been an airmail letter from Mitchell mentioning the cargo situation in the Mediterranean and the appointment of a new Agent in Los Angeles, but worded as if it were a summary to a shareholder rather than the old question and answer, hammer and anvil, discussion between busy executives. It was in many ways as if he had ceased to exist.

Susan alone, on board, understood what the old man was enduring and made an intelligent attempt to comfort him. She played chess with him at all hours when she would dearly have liked to be resting herself, she saw to it that he was continuously supplied with the thrillers he consumed at a furious rate, and she popped up to see how he was getting on at odd moments, rather as if he had been a patient convalescing from a serious illness. But his depression seemed only to get worse.

"You know you can't fight it by just resenting it," she said one evening as he reluctantly ordered her a glass of sherry. Even though it was costing him little or nothing, he could not cure himself of the habits of a lifetime, and he hated inviting anyone to drink with him unless there was a business deal on the end of it.

"Can't fight what? I don't know what you're talking about," he snapped, fiddling with his pince-nez. They had crossed the line the previous day and Flint was now in his tropical rig, which consisted of old-fashioned white flannel trousers and a short sleeved blue checked shirt which seemed somehow grotesque on him. It suddenly occurred to Susan that the missing spats would have added the final touch, and it was all she could do not to burst out laughing at the thought.

"Your state of retirement," she said. "It's happened, Sir J., you've done it of your own free will, you might just as well enjoy the leisure you've earned. You've worked hard enough for it all your life."

"It all seems pointless . . . pointless," he muttered and Susan was distressed to see that his eyes were watering with tears. "It was a great mistake to come on this cruise. I don't fit in — how can I fit in with all these idle nincompoops who've never done a hand's turn their whole lives? I've *worked* all my life and that's what I understand and enjoy."

"But they aren't *all* idle nincompoops," Susan protested; "there's Mr. Saxburger, for instance, who's worked just as hard as you have. There's that oil man Reissen, Sanderson the meat packer, Phillips from Du Pont — there are at least a dozen self-made men aboard."

"A dozen!" Flint retorted, "as compared with the hundreds who can scarcely add up a bill — men like D'Arcy Payne, women like Mrs. Bayern-Schultz and Mrs. Statson, and decayed old deadbeats like Lord Passington and Sir Eustace ffender. What have they ever done with their lives, except pile dividends on wealth they inherited and snobbery on baseless arrogance. What a way to end a busy life!" He blew his nose and glared out at the tropical sea. Without thinking, but impelled by a wave of pity she put an arm round his shoulders and kissed the top of his bony head.

"It's not as bad as you think," she said as if speaking to a child that had fallen down and hurt itself. "You could enjoy it all if you gave it a chance."

He gripped her hand, and for a moment or so was silent.

"It's much worse than *you* think, my dear child," he said, "when you reach my time of life and nothing tastes good any more."

"But you've got what you wanted, you've made a success of your life."

"Hm! A fat lot of good it's done me. Haven't even got a son to follow me on."

"Oh! don't worry," Susan said lightly, "you can always leave your Management Shares to me. It's high time there was a woman on the Board."

"What do you know about Management Shares?" Flint asked, for a moment or two astonished at the girl.

"A darn sight more than you'd think," Susan said, a faraway smile in her eyes. "I'd love to give Uncle Fabian something to think about — well, make a little of the running."

"You're a girl with some extraordinary ideas in your head," Flint said gruffly. "It's a pity you're so frivolous about them."

"Oh! I mean everything I say," Susan said lightly; "the trouble is nobody ever believes me. Now it's time you went and changed. You've cocktails with the Chief Engineer before dinner and I've to help out the Purser with some of your decayed old deadbeats, as you call them."

She left him, as she always did, in a far better state of mind, and this continued through the inanities of the rest of the evening. But as he climbed into bed that night the depression began seeping back, that sour flat aimlessness which now seemed to be the real companion of his lonely old age. Why had he never bothered with a family? Why had he devoted his life to emptiness and wind? Taking one of the sleeping pills the doctors had urged on him, he dropped down into a depth of uneasy sleep wishing never to wake up, unwilling to resign himself to what he knew was the truth.

Rio de Janeiro gave *Leviathan* a welcome in keeping with the spectacular nature of the place. They sailed into the huge, beautifully proportioned bay early one morning, and from then on, under the aegis of the British and American Embassies, an almost continuous program of functions and private hospitality began to take place ashore, the reverse side of which was a flood of visitors of all classes and colors eager to explore and, if possible, remove souvenirs from the largest ship in the world. This threw a strain on the Master-at-Arms and the stewards on duty far in excess of what had been expected, and the rumble of discontent reaching the Staff Captain via the Chief Steward and the Purser turned into an almost mutinous roar.

Indeed there were disciplinary undertones from the steward department which were making both Stone and Mott raise their eyebrows and privately worry far more than they should. Two of the pantry hands and four bedroom stewards had been repeatedly drunk since leaving New York, and one of them had taken hold of Mrs. Klopatsky in her own stateroom and shaken her till her toupee had been dislodged. It was true that Mrs. Klopatsky had been in an advanced state of intoxication herself at the time and had rung all the bells in her stateroom merely in order to find out the time; but this was scandalous behavior and Mrs. Klopatsky intended making the most of it.

This steward, and another one who had sped Mrs. Marvin-Dakers on her way with a good sound slap on her ample behind, would be put ashore at Buenos Aires and, it was hoped, replaced by two Royal Mail Line stewards who had been in the hospital there; but in the meantime they had to be employed out of direct contact with the passengers and the fact that these incidents could take place at all was a straw in the wind to which neither George Stone nor the Purser could turn a blind eye. What was it that was going wrong?

Stone with his comprehensive experience of the behavior and mentality of stewards did not think it was because of money. The money was flowing all right. There was no trunk system aboard *Leviathan* except in the Veranda Grill, but there were complicated and traditional arrangements by which, for instance, a smoked-salmon sandwich, asked for by a deck steward because of one of his passengers' whims, would be "paid for" all the way back to the storekeepers although, of course, there was no charge to the passenger. This "seeing" of Bill and Charley and Mick, etc., ensured that those who worked in the background such as pantrymen and chefs got their fair share of the tips.

"I wouldn't be surprised if we had one or two amateur politicians aboard," Stone remarked when he and Mott were discussing yet another complaint about overtime and rules. "It all has a Communistic ring about it to me — and that's borne out by some of the skits on the passengers that have come to light in the 'Pig' lately."

"Skits? What sort of skits?"

"Well, there's one steward I have my eye on who can mimic Lady Passington as well as a music-hall comedian — and then there's another who produces this sort of thing." He held up an expert and cruel caricature of Mrs. Jefferson Tring, one of the widows, in an imaginary crossing-the-line ceremony. Curvaceously naked, essential portions of the lady's anatomy were covered with the diamond plaques she habitually wore and she was apparently asking King Neptune to show her his toasting fork, the caption being, "I'll make it worth your while."

"I don't see anything very wrong in that," Mott answered; "at least it lets off a little steam."

"Quite, quite," said Stone, clicking his dentures, "unfortunately someone else has written on the back: 'Mrs. Jefferson Tring inherited three million dollars from her stockbroker husband. Current unemployed U.S.A. six million,' which puts another aspect on it quite apart from the inaccuracy of the figures."

"Oh yes," Mott added ironically, "it was ten million she inherited, wasn't it? I don't think that's especially significant. I feel rather bolshie myself when I see all this fabulous wealth being chucked about or drunk down the drain — and let's face it, there's nothing new in this sort of thing," he pointed at the cartoon, "so long as it doesn't get out of hand."

"Would you consider it out of hand if a cartoon like this was then pushed under the lady's stateroom door in the middle of the night and only retrieved in the nick of time by the lady's own stewardess?"

"Well," said Mott, "I can't say I'd encourage the practice — you've no idea who it might be?"

"It might be one of about fifteen stewards," Stone answered, "or it may not be a steward at all."

"Except that the drawing was done in the steward's 'Pig.' "

"It wasn't done there, it was found there."

Apart from discussions with the Master-at-Arms and other of the ship's police, apart from warning the Staff Captain and the Captain that there was an unidentified troublemaker aboard, nothing could be done about it except to watch and keep doubly alert. In any event the raw material available to an agitator aboard *Leviathan* with a pair of sharp eyes in his head was so rich and variable that in many cases it almost caricatured itself.

There was, for instance, Mr. Grüssli from Minnesota, who was a health faddist with a penchant for raw snails, which Monsieur Bonachard angrily refused to supply, who wore shorts so brief and so tight that they left nothing to the imagination, and whose evening attire was a self-designed Roman toga which "allowed the body full play within its ample folds" but which, alas, on first being worn in the main restaurant, caught in a trolley of hors d'œuvres and was torn away like a banner with a great rending sound and an agonized cry from the ladies then at the same table.

Mr. Grüssli believed that one of the main factors in a continuous supply of health to the body lay in keeping one's feet higher than one's head, and at all times of the day he could be surprised in extraordinary quasi-indecent postures "ensuring his flow of nourishing health." He had also brought a consignment of expensively canned grass which he chopped and showered over his salad, thus further embarrassing the ladies at his table.

Then there was Whitaker Hornbeam, who came to Mott as the ship reached the River Plate estuary and required him to land and return to his home in Pittsburgh three trunks full of clothes.

"You're not leaving us, I hope," Mott probed anxiously, at a loss to know what was behind this extraordinary request.

"Certainly not, sir," Whitaker Hornbeam declared, "but I wish to feel free to leave at any moment I choose, and freedom, sir, is a matter of not being encumbered with material possessions. Moreover, by sending all my clothes except two suits ahead of my arrival I shall have something to get back to if you comprehend my principle, sir. So be kind enough to do as I say."

"Nothing easier, sir," Mott agreed, feeling himself in the presence of a madman and subsequently warning the surgeon to keep an eye on this eccentric passenger.

As the cruise continued the problems which Mott had to cope with seemed to multiply instead of decreasing, and by the time *Leviathan* had passed through the Strait of Magellan and was headed for Valparaiso, Juan Fernandez, Lima, and then on to Honolulu, there were nightmare days when he wondered what else could possibly happen.

"The disposal of clothing," he remarked to Susan one evening, as they once more had their first sundowners together, "either by the entire wardrobe or in job lots seems to be a feature of this cruise."

"You mean Mrs. Makarides and Dempster?"

"Oh! you've heard about it, have you?"

"The whole ship's shaking with laughter," Susan said, "the dear boy hasn't moved from his cabin all day."

"Well, jealousy's a dangerous thing — especially in the very rich. I hope we don't have any serious repercussions."

Mrs. Makarides whose immigrant Greek husband had left her an income of two hundred thousand dollars a year, was an old hand at cruising. With an eminently practical eye to her well-being, she had brought along Dempster, her current boy friend, a Nordic number with a shock of blond wavy hair, a splendid physique, and a private interest in one of the tourist class stewards which he fondly imagined a secret. Mrs. Makarides had equipped Dempster with a magnificent wardrobe of fifteen suits. But she also observed the proprieties and though their cabins were adjacent, they were apparently traveling separately. It was altogether a dignified and highly proper arrangement. In any case, the private affairs of the passengers were none of the company's business.

Unfortunately, human nature being what it is, by the time *Leviathan* had reached Rio a rival of Mrs. Makarides had shown an intense and growing interest in Mr. Dempster, and by Lima they had declared their intention of getting married. This understandably incensed Mrs. Makarides to a series of violent rows which she conducted in public both with Dempster and her rival, and the battle of insults raged at different times in every bar and lounge in the ship. Mott, in fact, became accustomed to Kennicote or another of his staff poking his head round his cabin door and saying, "They're at it again. Garden Lounge. Score forty-fifteen."

Then, halfway across the Pacific to Honolulu, it reached a climax one night while Dempster and his new lady were dancing in the Starlight Roof Club, which was what the Veranda Grill turned into after midnight. Well primed on Bourbon and resentment Mrs. Makarides proceeded unobserved to her ex-paramour's cabin and in the space of ten minutes had thrown every single one of the fifteen suits into the sea. This left Dempster with nothing but his underwear and the tropical dinner jacket suit he happened to be wearing.

"I'm fixing the gentleman up with some emergency clothing," Mott reported to the Captain the next day, "but I may ask you to see the two ladies concerned, to stop the vendetta growing any further."

"I'd like to award them a few days' hard labor," Banks said, "but I suppose Head Office wouldn't approve."

"I think we'll be losing Dempster and her rival at Honolulu, so Mrs. Makarides can have the rest of her cruise in peace."

"Peace is evidently the last thing she came on the cruise for. Warn her that if I have any more trouble of that kind she'll be landing at Honolulu herself."

"Aye aye, sir," said Mott. It was the tactful conveyance of such an order that made a Purser's life so exhausting and difficult. But remorse had set in and Mrs. Makarides surprisingly apologized and promised from then on to be good.

By the time the ship reached Hong Kong Susan was heartily sick of the cruise. At least on the Atlantic run there had been the prospect of a day in New York or a couple of days at home to look forward to after the strain of the voyage. Now the weeks went past in a tired haze of work, with the end of April still a peak in the distance of time and no let up or days off, no real Sundays being possible because of the nature of their work. Moreover the emotional pull of Charles, counterpointed by Motty, drew on even more of her energy without giving her much in return. Indeed, in low moments resting in the cabin, with Gloria on the top bunk smoking away and staring unseeing at the deck-head, she felt her life to be in a thoroughly tatty mess.

In the four months which had passed since she had first been to bed with Charles, she seemed in her own eyes to have grown up in a number of different ways, not all of them good ones. She was no longer a girl either in outlook or experience. She had long ago lost her adolescent illusions about virginity. Even before that shattering night in New York, when she had begun to find out for herself what it was all about, she had known that the world was not at all like the stereotype she had been given at school.

In the first place none of her mistresses at that establishment seemed to know anything alive and practical about men. The fetid Lesbianism of her English public school with its outward emphasis on games and sensible physical activities had long struck her as a totally inadequate way of preparing young girls for the realities of life. Sex, that richly potential garden a woman must cultivate with intensity if she is to fulfill her nature, was the one subject left clouded in illusion and awkwardness at school and never, under any circumstances, mentioned at home.

Yet every biography of every woman who had made her mark showed Susan that an understanding of sex was the one master key which would open every lock in a woman's life. In England this was distorted or disguised or simply ignored. She had once discussed it with Veronique, whose mother was French, and had been astonished to realize that by the time Veronique had reached ten years of age she had known everything one can know about sex short of experience and that, within the framework of devout Catholicism, her mother had actively encouraged and emboldened that side of her being.

Encouragement in sexual matters was inconceivable in an English girl's upbringing. It wasn't nice; it wasn't the sort of thing one ever discussed. Listening to Veronique's description of her home and then comparing it with her own and Joan's made her seethe inside. Her fiery rebellious spirit made her want to go back to that school and tell them they had taken hundreds of pounds from her father under false pretenses. Veronique, who was of a much more placid and quiet nature, could not understand her anger; but then no more could she understand the inert ignorant smugness of the well-bred English girls who visited her shop. Veronique had disdained the vulgarity of Gloria "but she is feminine. Her taste . . . well . . ." and she would give that deprecating French shrug of the shoulders and sideways look which conveyed the essence of her snobbism, "but at least she does not think there is anything disgusting in having a man on top of her in bed. She does not giggle, that one, and she is not an *allumeuse* in a twin set with her rope of pearls."

The aftermath to that unplanned, unexpected giving of herself to Charles had not been at all what she had imagined. From her reading of romantic short stories she had expected that after the "conquest" he would lose interest and she would be "bound in a lingering slavery" to an emotion which would be the price of her immoral behavior.

In fact she had never felt better nor freer in her life and it was Charles who had mooned about awkward and embarrassed and guilty, feeling that he had wrecked her for life and destroyed their own relationship in the bargain. She was surprised both at how little it mattered to her and at Charles's essentially *bourgeois* outlook for all his pretended Don Juan hatred of suburban domesticity. She suddenly saw that he really did want to make a "little woman" of her, shutting her away in a villa to bear his children and darn his socks. He scorned his brother officers who married and did exactly that to their wives, yet in essence this was what he wanted himself. It was then that she realized she would never, could never marry him. They were basically and completely dissimilar.

They had never repeated the experiment of sleeping together, although Susan, in the early days, would have welcomed it had it happened or had Charles contrived it as accidentally as the first time. But Charles was now quite certain he wanted to marry her. In consequence he had begun to revere her. He had put her on an idealistic pedestal, profoundly regretting his lapse, looking up to her and honoring her when all she wanted was to be loved and taken to bed without discussion or analysis, self-depreciation or spurious feelings of guilt. The light-heartedness had gone out of it. Now whenever they did a run ashore together, he was anxious and solicitous, serious and rather ponderously dull.

During the first month he worried himself silly that she might be pregnant and each time they met he would ask her about it. He never mentioned the word "pregnant," always putting it in a round about way which irritated her more than anything else. "Everything — er — as it should be — er — calendarwise?" "No unexpected hold-ups on the line?" as if she had been a factory or a railway system instead of a girl worried she might be having a baby.

She could, in fact, have achieved a fine state of anxiety herself had she been that sort of person since there had been quite a "hold-up on the line," but Susan had always felt that of all the worries besetting a girl that was the silliest and falsest of them all. If she was going to have a baby, she was going to have a baby and the world could think what it liked. It wouldn't be the first time such a thing had happened in the history of mankind and it certainly wouldn't be the last. She neither wanted it nor felt it would be anything but a ghastly nuisance, but if that was how it was to be then she would accept it and get on with her life.

Charles could not understand this attitude at all. To him she would be "ruined" and it would all be his fault. He thought her casual, callous, and almost revolutionary in her contempt for convention. He resented her lack of worry and he did not take well to her retort that after all she was the one who would have all the fuss and bother. He was having a good deal of fuss and bother himself and did not care to be reminded that it was all self-created.

"You're a damned sight too headstrong," he complained when the panic was over and Susan still refused to come round to his point of view.

"It was very sweet of you to buy a bottle of champagne," she replied, "but I'm not 'enjoying total relief' as you put it. I really do feel you've got it miles out of proportion — the whole dreary business. I simply don't think like that, Charles, and I'd much rather you didn't talk about it again."

"Oh very well," he said huffily, "if that's all it means to you. I'm sorry if my consideration for you is a bore."

"Not at all," she answered coolly. "I'm very touched you should feel as you did. I mean it — I really was touched. It just wouldn't have been the total tragedy you wanted to make it, that's all."

But the truth was that he had become a teeny bit of a bore. The fun had vanished from their relationship and she tended to avoid him and make excuses not to be with him. For all his bravura, he divided women into the old Victorian categories of "good" ones who didn't play around and whom you enshrined, and the rest with whom everything was permitted if you could get it and to whom no responsibility was due. And this had accidentally led to confirmation that he was conducting an intermittent affair with Gloria on the side. She had always suspected this but had only known it for certain when one day, to illustrate what she felt was false in his outlook, she had said almost at random:

"You know you wouldn't go on like this if I'd been Gloria."

"What do you mean? What do you know about that?"

"Suppose Gloria came to you one day and said she was going to have a baby. You wouldn't make all this song and dance over her, would you?"

"In the first place I'd never be sure it was mine. In the second Gloria's the sort of girl who deserves everything that comes her way. She's no innocent chicken."

"But you don't mind going to bed with her — if she'll have you."

"Why should I? She wants it just as much as I do."

"The risk is exactly the same for her as it is for me or for any other woman."

"Gloria can look after herself. It's quite different. You don't understand."

A little later on, he had followed this up by saying resentfully, "It's a great mistake you sharing a cabin with Gloria. I can just imagine you two pulling me to pieces and cooking things up."

"You flatter yourself. Gloria's never mentioned you once and I wouldn't dream of discussing you with her. Why do you say that? Have you told her about me, then?"

"No, of course not, but she's got eyes in her head. She can guess. She doesn't have to be told."

She knew then from his indignant tone of voice that he was lying and that Gloria must in fact be aware of it all. This notion at first made her very angry, but then when she realized that Gloria had never even hinted at it by so much as a look, she came to respect and appreciate her cabinmate more than ever.

Gloria, in fact, would gossip about anything except her own or Susan's personal affairs. Her zest for living and her capacity for enjoyment continually astonished Susan as, indeed, did her lack of envy or jealousy either of Susan or of the wealthy clients whose faces and figures she worked on at all hours. Indeed, if anything, Susan envied her. She seemed to radiate a kind of animal health and goodness. The widows all loved her and she was coining money. Certainly her morals were deplorable and her language when any of the stewards cheeked her was worthy of the Barrow-in-Furness shipyard where she had learned it. But paradoxically she shone with goodness and, except with someone like Pamela Davies, she was generous in her thoughts and warm-hearted in her understanding of motive and foible. Quite simply she enjoyed her life and when one day Susan remarked on this she said:

"Well, I've been lucky. I got away."

"Don't you want to settle down somewhere and raise a family?"

"It won't be in Barrow-in-Furness, I can tell you that. Yes,

I'd like half a dozen nippers. The trouble is I'd get bored silly with just one man about the house. I've got too much of the alley cat in me for that. Variety is the spice of life. But the men don't like it, that's where it all goes wrong. They want you all to themselves, the vain cocky bastards they are — and anyway it's always one rule for you and another for them. Can't get on without 'em, though, can we?"

Very little escaped Gloria when it was to do with people on board. Indeed on one of the rare occasions when the conversation turned personal Susan got a real shock. Gloria had been discussing one of her clients, a rich widow called Mrs. Nash.

"She's in a dreadul state. She's fallen like a ton of bricks — and with those hips she *is* like a ton of bricks — for the Purser. But she can't get to first base with him however hard she tries. He's polite but he won't take any of her bait — not even a nibble. Of course he's mad about you, isn't he?"

"I . . . how on earth did you guess?" Susan asked astonished.

"Saw him look at you once. Of course, you mustn't think I'm prying; I'm not. But you can't help seeing things, can you?"

"He's never made a proper pass at me — never put it into words."

"Don't worry, ducky, he will. Anyway, you ought to be tickled pink. I would be. I think he's a gorgeous man. He'd do you a fair treat. He's a real man."

"Have you . . . no, I'd better not ask that one," Susan said.

"I shouldn't answer it if you did. It wouldn't be fair on any of us."

"Good heavens, Gloria, is there any man aboard *Leviathan* you haven't had at one time or another?"

"Yes," she answered blandly, "there's the Captain. He'd be far too much of a handful with all that quotating he does from the Bible. Then there's a greaser from Liverpool . . . I mean a girl's got to be selective, hasn't she?" She winked to show Susan that although she was sending her up, there was no malice in it. Indeed she was as fond of her as Susan was of Gloria. "The old ones are best," she concluded. "Take it from Momma. Even when they get to be like Arty Saxburger. It's maturity that matters in a man. He's another one wants to marry me — I suppose I ought to be flattered."

"Where does the present Mrs. Saxburger fit into that?"

"She doesn't. She's just waiting for a chance to do him for the alimony. He's paying out two lots already. He gripes about it all the time but I think somehow or other he gets it off the tax. He's nice. He just likes to drink and have a good time."

"Why don't you take him up on his offer?"

"I don't know: I suppose I might one of these days. Only if I do stop larking about I'd want a family and all that — and I'm not sure Arty Saxburger is really the man for that. Then if you have a family, it means a home and a home means only one man — so we're back where we started. It's hell being a woman, isn't it?"

Meanwhile *Leviathan*'s progress round the world received almost more publicity than even Laban desired, some of it concerning her passengers, some simply for the ship herself, some good, some which would have been much better suppressed. At Honolulu one distinguished passenger, an ex-President of an American steel corporation, had finally given in to pressure from Washington and had abandoned the cruise in answer to a personal request from President Roosevelt to take charge of a Government productivity project. At Yokohama Mrs. Romaro had died of an apoplectic fit, and between Nagasaki and Hong Kong, Neils Jörgenson, an ex-world tennis champion and present playboy, had committed suicide by jumping overboard in shark-infested waters.

No one had yet been born on board but this had only been avoided at Hong Kong by rushing ashore a visiting Chinese lady with unseemly speed, the baby actually being born in one of the tenders. It was at Hong Kong, also, that *Leviathan* received special attention from the Royal Navy's China Squadron, being escorted in by the Twenty-first Destroyer Flotilla and sped on her way by the Commander-in-Chief himself, in the cruiser *Kent* with other ships of the Fifth Cruiser Squadron.

This attention from the Royal Navy on the far side of the

world gave Captain Banks and his officers a warm feeling of being looked after, almost of being at home after the emptiness of the Pacific and the alien insecurity of South America. In spite of the Sino-Japanese war and its international repercussions, Hong Kong to the passengers was just another port where silk should be bought and rickshaw drivers haggled with. To the officers it was a British Colony where law and order and an established civilization operated, of which they were a part, on which they could rely and which was backed up by the visible power of the Royal Navy.

Leviathan herself continued to live up to her expectations. She caused her engineers less concern than any other big ship they had served in, and she continued to behave herself beautifully in any weather they encountered. Wherever they went, her size was still the one single factor that seemed most to astonish, and in the Press-cutting books, which were kept up to date both on board and back home in Liverpool, apocryphal anecdotes and comments continued to accumulate. It had been said that two Great Danes, seen on the eighty-foot promenade for dogs, had been mistaken for mice, and that the main restaurant was so vast that the stewards did not come back for their tips but left their addresses. These and other "Texan-type" stories about the ship were a small indication that *Leviathan* was far from being the gauche, unwanted monster which her critics and competitors would like to have dubbed her. She was popular and successful and the pride taken in her by the company was, so far as the world could see, completely justified.

By now it was early March 1939, and Fabian had been sitting at Flint's desk in the old Liverpool office for two full months. During this time he had been responsible for only one casualty on the staff and that was Quilly. Quilly had foreseen this as soon as it became certain that Flint was retiring. Indeed Quilly had all but decided to quit himself when his job disappeared in the first reorganization which Fabian instituted on gaining control. Flint, who had guessed this would happen, had made sure that his henchman would receive adequate compensation, and he had been offered a directorship in a big London travel agency. Flint had recommended Fabian to let bygones be bygones and to keep Quilly somewhere in the organization but Fabian would have none of it, and by the middle of February, the late Chairman's spy — and Laban's most valuable contact in the London office — had gone on his way, bitterly and privately planning revenge, but for the moment impotent.

Meanwhile travel agents all over the world were booking up berths for another transatlantic season, but the tone was faltering and when Germany suddenly invaded and annexed the whole of Czechoslovakia in the middle of March, the prospects for a healthy summer tourist season dwindled away in a cloud of despondency.

In every office, in every club, in every home the possibility of war found its way into everyday talk. Franco had won in Spain and had been recognized, the I.R.A. was exploding bombs in telephone kiosks and railway left luggage offices, Mosley and his Fascists made piffling disturbances in the East End of London and a new wave of undergraduate pacifism swept through Oxford and Cambridge.

The merry men of Munich still argued that it would never be in the *Fuehrer's* interests to go to war, and the King and Queen paid a state visit to the French President. But the feeling of bemused unreality seeped more and more into ordinary day-to-day life. There was a helplessness about this drift into war which saddened the old and disgusted the young.

How pleasant it must be, Fabian considered, when he thought about the international situation, to sail round the world in *Leviathan* at a time like this. Certainly to be away from Europe, where the tension was steadily mounting, and to have no responsibilities any more like Flint, struck Fabian as an almost blissful state of affairs. He did not understand the depressed tone of his predecessor's letters, full of pawky unwanted advice, and when Susan commented in one of hers that she thought the old man was dying of a broken heart it puzzled him even more.

What on earth was there to break his heart about at that time of life? Flint had achieved all — in fact almost more than he had set out to do. He had made a pile of money, had run the biggest steamship company in the world like the autocrat he was, and if he had no wife or family to mourn him when he died, well, when Fabian thought about his own wife and his son and daughter, perhaps Flint was not suffering the tragedy he thought he was.

After what amounted to a blunt order, Joan had returned from New York to nurse her mother through an attack of pneumonia but she was no sooner installed at home than she began pining for New York and not a day passed without pressure from her of some kind to be allowed to return. Alan, his son, had joined the Oxford University Socialist Party and was active in every pacifist organization he could join, tramping through the rain on rallies and protest marches and making Fabian glower with shame whenever he thought about it.

Moreover, now that he was Chairman and had perforce to spend most of his working life in Liverpool, he had begun to consider selling his Dorking house and moving north. His wife was strongly against it, and he was no lover of Liverpool and its environs himself. The net effect on his personal life, therefore, was to make it more lonely and frustrated than ever, and he tended, as indeed had Flint before him, to live more and more in the business he ran, sometimes even remaining at Liverpool over the week-end and snatching a Sunday game of golf before plunging that same evening into what he called some "pre-effort for the week's work."

Fabian was much more of a plodder than Flint. He relied far less on instinct and far more on the accumulated, crystallized experience of a century now embodied in the company lore. Whereas Flint's reaction to any problem was to sit quietly suspecting every motive until a solution — and preferably an unorthodox one — suddenly whispered itself in his ear, Fabian would call for the considered opinion of the experts, summarize and weigh it up as if some higher authority would one day call him to account and then pronounce a decision at length and on paper. He called this "making it watertight" but to his subordinates it just seemed a long-winded waste of time.

It was small wonder, Captain Masterton remarked one day

to the Chief Engineering Superintendent, that Fabian had wanted his son to go into the Civil Service. He would turn Transoceanic into an unofficial government department before he was through. No one had ever known quite where he stood with Flint, but with Fabian they knew only too well and once a decision was taken there was almost no chance whatever of it being changed.

⚓⚓⚓⚓⚓ X ⚓⚓⚓⚓⚓

THE suicide of Neils Jörgenson had caused repercussions in *Leviathan* which took some little time to work out, and which disturbed both Mott and Stone far more than either was prepared to admit, while so many of the real facts remained hidden. The immediate and outward reaction was what it would have been in any first-rate hotel — a deliberate playing down of the event so far as the passengers were concerned, a ban on publicity of any kind and subtly increased pressure to distract attention by stepping up organized entertainment.

Luckily a day later the ship had reached Hong Kong where perhaps the maximum distraction was available to the passengers, and which allowed Captain Banks and the Colonial authorities to hold their inquiries in what they imagined to be secrecy. The next day, however, the full story had in some mysterious manner found its way into the hands of the Press. No suicide is simple or easily explicable, and since this had taken place at night after a forty-eight hours' almost continuous drinking bout, the possibility of its being either an accident or murder could not be ruled out. But Jörgenson had tried it about six months previously with sleeping pills, and had declared his intention then of not botching it again. The Surgeon had been duly warned, but since Jörgenson had never any intention nor occasion of calling for his services, there was nothing he could have done.

Indeed there was nothing anyone could have done, since Jörgenson, who was free and of considerable wealth, could not be forced to stay alive if he chose not to do so. He was a man in his waning fifties and had come on this cruise accompanied by a young man he referred to as his business manager and secretary, though what exactly was the business he managed was never made clear. This young man, whose name was Terence de Voss, was much in demand among various of the widows' cliques since he seemed to remind so many of them of the sons they had never had. Socially both he and Jörgenson were assets and added to the gaiety of the cruise. They were gay and trivial and they made people laugh.

Young Mr. de Voss was naturally shattered by the news, and since he was Jörgenson's heir, the Hong Kong Police, who investigated the suicide, immediately suspected they might have a case of murder on their hands. Reluctantly, however, de Voss revealed an impeccable alibi. In direct contravention of a number of the ship's rules, he had been attending an impromptu concert in the stewards' "Pig and Whistle," as the guest of the same tourist class steward in whom the suit-losing Mr. Dempster had shown such an interest earlier in the cruise. Not only had he been where he should not have been, but he had gone there in "drag," taking part in the concert arrayed in one of Mrs. Klopatsky's more daring dresses which had been borrowed for the occasion without her consent. This let him out of any complicity in Jörgenson's death but it left Mott and Stone with the honey of a mess to clear up.

"And of course it would be Mrs. Klopatsky," Mott said ruefully when reporting it all to the Captain, "who can't really be enjoying much of a cruise having been assaulted by her steward before we reached Rio and now having her hideous dress borrowed for this disgraceful performance."

Banks's first action on having all this brought up before him was to close down the stewards' "Pig" for the remainder of the cruise. He did not enjoy doing this, since thereby he was punishing hundreds of innocent, over-worked stewards who, in any case, had firmly disapproved of the concert in the first place. But he was determined upon setting an example and maintaining discipline, actions which have never made any captain popular. He then had the steward up in front of him, blasted him verbally in Biblical language for twenty hot minutes and dismissed him from the ship there and then. He also warned Mr. de Voss in a way the young man had not been spoken to since his nursery days that any more misdemeanors of this kind would result in his own summary dumping at the next available port. After this statement, and in any case chastened by the death of his friend and patron, de Voss gave no further trouble from then on.

At this point it would have been reasonable to suppose the incident over but it was precisely then, when the hue and cry had died away, that Mott became certain they really had troublemakers aboard. Anonymous insults were found in his office and his cabin, complaints about conditions of service jumped to a new record, breakages of crockery and disappearances of silver both showed a bad increase, and a kind of sullen atmosphere seemed to settle over the steward department. Stone clicked his teeth in despair and Mott warned the Captain that any more repressive or punitive measures that might be necessary could well produce a mutiny of some kind. Most of the passengers were not affected except for a general slowing down of the service but those who ran the ship realized they had an explosive situation aboard which might well result in violence, or at least in the paralyzing of *Leviathan*'s internal services and the disrupting of the cruise.

It is perhaps more difficult to keep a thing secret in a ship than almost anywhere in the world. This is especially so when whatever is to be kept secret involves the corruption of men dedicated to jobs they like and are doing of their own free will. That was why Rees Llewellyn, the steward in charge of the first class library and the prime organizer of trouble on board *Leviathan*, could feel a justifiable pride in the subversive work he had so far achieved.

Except for the individual leaders of the different cells he was creating aboard — none of whom knew any of the others — his activities were unobserved, his aims unknown, his potentiality unassessed, except by the mild, rather likeable solicitor to whom he reported on his leaves in Cardiff. This solicitor, who also did a number of jobs on the side for the German

Consul General, was also unknown to and unsuspected by the British security services, since outwardly he was ordinary and respectable with a practice consisting mostly of small tradesmen, garages, and light engineering works of which all but one were entirely innocent and unremarkable.

Yet this man, with the unexciting name of Sidney Johns, hidden away in a Cardiff suburb, was later proved to be a key agent in the sabotage and destruction of the British Mercantile Marine in the coming war and its disruption beforehand in peace. Neither a Communist nor a Nazi, he was a strict professional in the direct pay of the Soviet Embassy — a fact the Germans knew nothing about. He also had at his disposal considerable sums of money from German sources, about which the Russians knew nothing. His main job was to recruit and place agents where they could remain hidden until there was a specific job for them to do, and to find a man like Rees Llewellyn, and to place him in a ship such as *Leviathan*, was an achievement he felt very pleased about indeed.

Llewellyn himself was an active Communist, although in his present capacity he had been ordered to sever his previous connections with the Party. His father was a poor Swansea schoolmaster and he had fed off Karl Marx from an early age. Unlike his father, however, who was an intellectual bigot, Rees Llewellyn was sly and shrewd enough to prefer exploiting revolutionary fervor in others rather than be consumed by it himself, as his father had been.

As a result he had turned himself into a first-rate steward who knew about books and had made it clear that he preferred the quiet job of looking after the library to the hurly-burly of the ordinary stewards' life where the chances of picking up fat tips were considerably greater. Rees Llewellyn was polite and efficient. His manner with wealthy old ladies in search of a sentimental story was impeccable and had Stone or Mott been asked for a list of sea-lawyers and troublemakers in the ship, Llewellyn would have been the last candidate of all. Johns had instilled in him the one golden rule for an effective agent, which might be formulated as an ability never to become involved in an argument or indeed in any sort of project which had not been carefully thought out and planned beforehand, however tempting the opportunity for a "kill." As a result, the fomenting of discontent was done by other stewards, one or two of whom he betrayed himself in all apparent innocence to the authorities. A pawn or two was always expendable if this resulted in a better position for the queen, and though the pawns might not like it much they never found out how nor by whom they had been given away.

Before coming on the cruise, Llewellyn had been told that as the main target, which was the total destruction of *Leviathan*, could not be effectively planned for the present, he should concentrate on the disrupting of arrangements whenever possible, on the subtle and continuous besmirching of the company's name and on a general breakdown resulting, if this could be brought about, in the abandonment of the cruise. It was a formidable task to be given, and to begin with it did not seem to Llewellyn as if he would have the slightest success.

But Marxism taught that the capitalist way of life, and therefore the behavior of capitalists, contained in itself the seeds of its own destruction. One or two of those seeds had germinated already in outbursts of jealous violence among the widows, and in Jörgenson's suicide after some tawdry blackmail by one of Llewellyn's trustier assistants which never came to light at the inquest.

Then Mr. Grüssli, the health faddist, had conceived a notion that the ship's ventilation was inadequate for the Tropics and that it was to the interest of the ship's doctors to suppress this fact. He began a campaign for the improvement of crew living conditions which was certainly none of his business but which resulted in a long meandering report of the kind that got easily and damagingly misquoted. This report was secretly "leaked" by Llewellyn to local papers at the ports they visited and eventually at home became the subject of a correspondence in *The Times*, to the annoyance of Fabian Mitchell and other company officials.

The fostering of rumors of all kinds was another of Llewellyn's specialities. There were rumors about the safety of the ship, its apparent fire risk — there had been three minor fires by the time *Leviathan* reached Bombay — and the possible inadequacy of the lifeboats in emergency. There were rumors of delays in the cruise program, of mysterious infectious diseases reputedly suffered by some of the crew, of the misrouting of mail, of the magnificent target *Leviathan* would make for a U-boat should war break out while they were still on the cruise. There was a rumor that *Leviathan* would break her back in a certain kind of sea. There were rumors of every distressing kind, most of them wild and completely unsubstantiated, but most of them also leaving behind a slight trace, the merest element of doubt, on which insecurity and anxiety might feed — and all of them having been started or sped on their way with a dividend by Llewellyn and his invisibly growing team. This, then, was the agency behind the "sullen and explosive atmosphere" which the Chief Steward and the Purser had perforce to take note of and report to the Captain in the course of their duty.

The great majority of the stewards and stewardesses in *Leviathan* were loyal, hard working, and reasonably contented. A number of them had been with the company most of their working lives. Some of them had wives or husbands in other ships of the Transoceanic fleet. It was a "family" company. Moreover, the acceptance of discipline was ingrained in any steward or seaman who had been more than a few months at sea in one of the company ships. To organize a mutiny, therefore, would be both extremely difficult and extremely damaging, if Llewellyn could bring it off.

On the other hand *Leviathan* had not been designed as a cruise liner. Her normal life was one in which it was almost impossible to work up anything like a full-scale strike or a mutiny. But on the long hundred days' cruise, much of it in tropical heat, at close quarters with the acute selfishness and self-indulgence of the very rich, with the news from home and the outside world consistently running downhill, so to speak, and now finally with the enforced closing of their only "club" because of the misdemeanors of a few of them — the loyalty and good will of the majority were not far from the breaking point. Llewellyn knew this at Bombay, as he also knew that he must catch the time at its right moment or never at all. Most of the stewards aboard would never lend their active support to a mutiny — but, if only a passive refusal to work could be guaranteed even for a time then Llewellyn knew that a most interesting situation could be created and exploited.

The organization for which the mild Mr. Johns of Cardiff was working had managed to include in *Leviathan* four of its most experienced agitators. These men were quite unknown to the ships' authorities, they had never fallen foul of any officers, their records were unblemished and they were expendable in emergency as Llewellyn was not. Throughout the crisis, therefore, Llewellyn remained hidden and apparently uninvolved while these four men, and the fifteen or sixteen lieutenants they had managed to enroll since the voyage had begun, "carried" the mutiny, acted as ringleaders and spokesmen and eventually — when the mutiny was quelled — were disposed of ashore as had been foreseen.

Llewellyn gave the word as *Leviathan* sped southwest from Bombay toward the Equator and Madagascar. An ultimatum on working conditions, overtime pay, and the reopening of the stewards' "Pig" was presented to the Chief Steward and when this was rejected out of hand, the "planned chaos" began. Breakers in the electric galleys were pulled so that no meals could be cooked. The bakery came to a halt. Monsieur Bonachard's peremptory orders were no longer obeyed, and in the early stages he was locked fuming in his little office. Pickets were put on the various cold store rooms and the restaurants were paralyzed, no tables even being set for lunch. Meanwhile no work was done in the passengers' cabins, beds were left unmade, trays remained uncleared and the bell system was switched off. On the promenade decks no stewards appeared, no "elevenses" were served, the elevators stopped running and Jimmy Johnson was not allowed to prepare or open the Observation Bar.

As soon as Mott realized what was happening, he and Stone went to see for themselves and within a few minutes found themselves hustled into the salad and hors d'œuvre larder and deftly locked behind a wire screen where, without being able to see properly, they were forced to listen to a continuing tirade against conditions of service in *Leviathan*. Kennicote, who followed a few minutes later, was ambushed and similarly locked in the dry goods store off the working alleyway and the key officers and ratings who could have raised the alarm were immobilized and accounted for one by one. The ship's telephone exchange was silenced simply by cutting off the current and it was when the telephones went dead on the bridge that Banks and the Staff Captain first realized that something was very wrong in the ship.

Llewellyn had done his work well. He had insisted that there was to be no violence and no destruction of property. It was to be a trial of strength. There was to be no attempt to take over the ship, the navigating and engine room departments were not involved, and it was realized, of course, that the Captain would use force in order to re-establish control of the ship, force which was not to be resisted. Moreover the stoppage was only partial. Some stewards refused to co-operate and continued to work as usual, and indeed Llewellyn was one of these, only leaving the library and the issuing of books for an odd moment or two out of apparent curiosity to see what was going on.

But the chaos caused by the temporary disappearance of the Purser, the Chief Steward, the Chef, and their staff assistants, and the stopping of any normal routine soon made the "hotel" part of the ship look as if a disaster such as had struck Pompeii had befallen it. This was more remarkable in the passengers' accommodation than anywhere else, since under normal working conditions one bumped into a steward or a stewardess round almost every corner and now it was as if the ship had been abandoned. This would have been the time, Llewellyn saw clearly, to have set fire to the ship had he had the materials at hand. But an attempt at total destruction was not to come yet. This partial paralysis was enough shock for the present.

The mutiny, although played down as much as possible, could not be kept from the passengers. Susan and the two assistant pursers on duty in the office first began to suspect that something was wrong when the telephones went dead and passengers in ones and twos began to collect at the desk complaining that they could not get hold of their stewards. Then when first Mott and then Kennicote disappeared, to be followed by the two assistant pursers, Susan was left alone in the office, at first intrigued, then puzzled, and finally alarmed.

To begin with she had seen one of the stewards she most disliked run down the main staircase with a leer on his face. This was odd in itself since nobody ran in *Leviathan* unless something was wrong. Then Jimmy Johnson had beckoned to her from the side door and told her there was "a bit of trouble down below" and from then on reports of the disturbance began to multiply.

At one point over the heads of Mrs. Klopatsky, inevitably one of the first to complain, Mrs. Makarides, Mr. Grüssli, and Mr. de Voss, she caught sight of a stern-faced Charles Beecher followed by a Master-at-Arms but he did not spare her a look as he strode down the corridor, and it was from Gloria who came racing along from her beauty parlor that she learned most of the facts.

She would dearly have liked to pull down the shutters of the office and get into the fun herself but with most of the "difficult" passengers asking excited and inane questions outside she felt she ought to remain calmly assuring them that there was nothing to worry about at all. She was not helped in this task by Lord Passington, who declared that it was like 1917 in St. Petersburg and they could all expect to be herded in a cellar and shot, nor by Mr. Whitaker Hornbeam, who appeared first in one life-jacket and then subsequently in two so that it looked as if his head was sticking out of some sort of toffee apple.

Indeed, Susan did her best, as a good purser should, to minimize the trouble and pass it all off as "just one of those things." But she was far from feeling secure herself, and it was remarkable how instinctively people reacted the moment the surface of things was scratched. Though there had at no time been any suggestion of danger to the ship itself — nor anything on which a rumor could base itself — here was Mr. Whitaker Hornbeam acting as if the ship was on the point of being abandoned and three of the widows asking for their jewelry from the safe and going away with little bustling movements and worried, furtive looks to conceal this form of movable wealth about their persons.

That morning no daily sweepstake was organized on the ship's run. This was often a minor duty which fell on Susan and she began to get out the blackboard as usual, almost automatically inscribing Flint's standing order of one ticket on number seven. But by noon it was obvious that this was no day for sweepstakes. The routine was that promptly at noon the Purser's office shut for the lunch period. By an effort of will Susan kept going today until noon and then with what she imagined as a confident smile, she pulled down the shutters, locked the safe and afterward stood for a moment alone in the office wondering where she should go and what, if anything, she should do.

Then on a sudden impulse she decided to go down below and see what was happening for herself. Her heart beat wildly and for a second or so she was reminded of the first time she had ever stood on the high diving board at school, wondering how she could ever make herself plunge down into the water below. Her skin tingled and she knew she was deeply and physically afraid. She hesitated a moment longer and then, telling herself that logically there was nothing whatever to cause her alarm, she slammed the door of the office behind her, locked it carefully and then set off down the stairs with her head in the air. She might not be Joan of Arc, but there was no harm in pretending to a little of that really ridiculous courage.

A mass meeting of stewards and cooks had assembled in the main kitchens of *Leviathan* consisting of most of the hundred and sixty cooks and several hundreds of the stewards, packed tightly against the preparing tables and serving bays and overflowing through swing doors into the main restaurant, now kept open by the crush. By this time it was technically open mutiny since the meeting had long ago been ordered to break up by the Staff Captain, which order had not proved enforceable by *Leviathan's* police.

In actual fact a token break-up had been ordered by the strike leaders, the meeting re-forming ten minutes later more densely than before after a certain amount of scuffling and fighting between the militant strikers and the regulating staff, an attempt to arrest the ringleaders having failed. By this time Mott, Kennicote, Stone, Bonachard, and other important captives had all been collected and locked in the dry-goods store, the key being held by one of the four ringleaders. Two parleys had taken place between the Staff Captain and the mutineers. Specific demands had been made and rejected by both sides. The mutineers wanted new guaranteed overtime rates, a re-opening of their "Pig" and no victimization. The Staff Captain demanded an immediate dispersal, the release of all hostages and a return to work before any investigation whatever would take place.

So a deadlock had been reached, and as things at present stood the mutiny was effective and the mutineers were on top. Both sides, however, were aware that a situation of this kind could not remain static. One or the other must give — would have to yield — and indeed it was in the interests of neither side for the disorganization to drift on into a state of anarchy.

Susan had first approached the meeting through the working alleyway but although the stewards on the fringes had let her squirm in a certain distance, she had been blocked completely just beyond hearing range of the main haranguers and some greater distance from the door of the dry goods store where with many winks and nods she had been told the Purser and the others were incarcerated.

So she had slipped out again unobtrusively and made her way up a deck and into the main restaurant. Here again she was thwarted by the density of the crowd. None of the men she found herself crushed against had shown her any personal antagonism, and indeed most of them had been sheepishly apologetic. Just as she decided that the whole thing was a dead loss from the point of view of personal activity by herself, she caught sight of another of her *bêtes noires* among the stewards forcing his way in from the outside, whispering some sort of password to people in his way who then allowed him to pass. She saw that if she wriggled a little way to her left this new arrival would have to pass very close beside her, so she moved accordingly and heard him whisper, to a giant of a sweating pantryman who had refused to let her pass, "O.K. by Spencer," then almost at once found herself face to face with the man.

"You keep out of this," he snapped at her angrily, "we don't want any pussies around here — go on, beat it."

Susan flushed and for a moment thought of standing up to him but in a flash another and much better idea presented itself to her mind and with a hot angry look she did as he said and slipped out again at the back. Then, as casually as she could she extracted herself from the mob racing up the main staircase and along to the cubby hole behind the Observation Bar where by a stroke of luck she found Jimmy Johnson alone, smoking a cigarette with a wry smile on his thin face as though he was privately enjoying this unusual state of affairs.

"Well, Miss Spicer, have you been down to the bargain basement to see for yourself?"

"Yes, yes I have, Jimmy. I was told by that cabin steward Ford, or whatever his name is, to keep out of it, but I think I've discovered the password and I've found out, also, that Mr. Mott, Mr. Stone, and the others are all locked up in the dry goods store. I think we ought to go and get them out."

The smile left Jimmy Johnson's face.

"I shouldn't interfere if I were you, miss. There may be a bit of real trouble down there before we're through. You don't want to be involved in that. That's something for the Master-at-Arms. Anyway, I suppose Spencer has the key of the dry goods store and we certainly couldn't break down the door. Not as things are."

"Doesn't the Chief Steward have a spare set?"

"He carries them on him."

"Well, then, who else would have keys?"

"There'll be a set on the bridge, of course."

"Perhaps Mr. Stone didn't have his spare ones with him. Let's go and look in his cabin or his office. Come on, Jimmy, I need some support. I can't be Robin Hood all by myself."

"This isn't a game, miss," Jimmy said severely. "The Captain and the regulating staff will be doing something about all this. I don't think I'd get into it if I were you. It's none of your business."

"It's everyone's business. Come and help me look for the keys in the Chief Steward's cabin."

Reluctantly and with obvious misgiving Jimmy Johnson followed her down to the cabin, where to the surprise of both of them they found the bunch of keys in the top drawer of the desk, the first place they looked. Susan took them and then turned to Jimmy. By this time she had had second thoughts about involving him.

"Perhaps it *is* better if you don't come down," she said, "you're committed in a way I'm not — I know you don't really feel in sympathy with this sort of strike, Jimmy, but after all you haven't opened your bar, have you?"

"I can't open the bar because I haven't got any stock up, miss, and I can't get at the store."

"You don't want to be called a scab, Jimmy, do you? I suppose it really isn't any of your business."

She had intended to let him out of it casually, but instead she saw he was resenting her attitude as a piece of cheek and that she had needled him without really meaning to. It was the first time she had ever seen him ruffled.

"Come on then," he said sharply, "I doubt we'll get anywhere with it but we can try."

They set off down below and soon were threading their way along the working alleyway towards the dry goods store. It seemed as if the mutineers' "policemen" were all pantrymen, from one point of view the natural enemies of all stewards who actually served food to passengers, who ordinarily did an "in between" job, and who now seemed to have placed themselves between the leaders and the mass. But a judicious use of Spencer's name acted like magic, added to the normal respect in which Jimmy Johnson was held, and after about ten minutes of careful progress through the crowd they had reached the door of the dry goods store.

Here they came on the worst obstacle of all. The door was stolidly guarded by a giant of an assistant butcher who refused either to budge or to react to a mention of Spencer's name. It flashed through Susan's mind that he did in fact look like the traditional ogre of the fairy tale and only needed a knotted club at his side to make the picture complete.

"I don't think Mr. Spencer *has* sent you along," he said contemptuously looking at Susan, "so I'm afraid you're not going to get inside that door, Mr. Johnson. Not till we get this thing settled."

It was just as the barman had feared, and now that they'd come up against this opposition, the temper of the crowd turned quickly against them. "Go on, bugger off out of it," a voice said from the crowd, "you don't belong here." This was followed by some graphic references to Susan's anatomy which made her flush with anger. Then things began happening in a hurry. "Give her the bum's rush," someone yelled, and on a sudden instinct she gripped hold of Jimmy Johnson in a panic. But this was useless against the surging violence of the mob.

All at once everyone seemed to be fighting. Jimmy Johnson's steel-rimmed glasses were smashed off his face, tearing his cheek as they went, there was a kind of windmill effect of fists and grim faces and then before she could collect her wits, someone had picked her up by the neck of her jacket and a handful of her skirt and was hustling her out and back along the corridor. The fear and indignity seemed to give her a speed of perception which was like lightning and as she felt herself carried along by a wave of angry men, she suddenly realized what they were going to do. Also on C deck, along which the working alleyway ran fore and aft like the main bone of a spine, was the swimming pool, and as the shouting mob hustled her on she knew they were going to throw her in. Now she was really scared.

By this time she had lost touch with Jimmy Johnson but miraculously she still clutched in her hand the Chief Steward's set of keys, and on an impulse she twisted and swung them hard at her assailant's face. This was so surprising and so effective that she felt herself dropped and although the momentum of the crowd carried her on for a while, she knew she was free. She turned and saw that she had torn open the man's cheek; at the same moment there was a movement in the other direction from the crowd and to her astonishment and relief she found herself picked up by two familiar strong arms.

"Susan! You shouldn't be here. Are you all right?"

It was Charles Beecher flanked by the Master-at-Arms, two of the regulating staff, and behind them a squad of tough-looking seamen.

"Yes, I'm fine," she said breathlessly. Her jacket was torn and she was thoroughly tousled, but this was the end of violence. Even as they exchanged these sentences the crowd was scuffling away and in a moment or so the working alleyway was empty except for the overflow on the stairs aft leading up to the main kitchen.

"How do you come to be mixed up in this?"

"We were going to rescue the Purser and the others."

"You know where they are?"

"Yes, they've been locked in the dry goods store. I've got the Chief Steward's keys. Come on."

She knew he would try and stop her but before he could do so she was heading off down the corridor with that independent toss of the head. She had an account to settle with the giant. But by the time they reached the door, the ogre had disappeared with the rest of the mob and there was only a confused shouting from inside. In another moment or so Susan had opened the door and released a scowling Mott and the others. The local mutiny was over, the process of restoring law and order had swiftly and angrily begun.

Reactions to the mutiny were confused. Susan, suffering from shock but refusing to admit it, caught a chill, then a cold, then a mild attack of pneumonia. Flint simply did not believe it could happen, and when told that it had, snapped "Nonsense." Banks flung himself into a rage lasting five days, during which the bridge became unbearable and rounds a purgatory. In accordance with the regulations he was furious with Mott, Mott with Stone, and Stone with his own descending hierarchy. To all of them this would be a black mark on the record and, if there was other trouble to follow, it might well be fatal to their careers. It was little consolation to each that he was at the top of his profession; it only made the fall that much the harder. Most difficult of all in the days immediately following the mutiny was to exhibit that urbanity, nonchalance, and ease which the passengers had come to expect of the staff under almost any circumstances. The passengers were on the outer wheel of circumstance, they knew nothing and cared nothing about the internal flurrying and scurrying which in a sense kept the wheel turning.

That there had been trouble of some sort was obvious to all the passengers. No work had been done on their cabins, none of the bars had opened, and lunch had had to be served from the cold table since the disorganization in the kitchen was for the moment complete. But the ringleaders of the mutiny had all been arrested, discipline and routine had been immediately restored, and by the evening normality had returned. Like the storm they had had off Patagonia, it had come and gone without leaving a trace so far as the passengers were concerned, and in the evening Jimmy Johnson, with a piece of plaster over his cheek and his spare pair of glasses on his nose, did a record night's business in the bar.

Mr. Grüssli, of course, wanted to know the full story. He was for the men and against the officers even before he had found out what it was all about, then, quietly aided by Llewellyn in the library, he concocted another of his famous reports. He pestered the Staff Captain with fads and fetishes and eventually secured an interview with Banks himself. This proved to be an experience he was to regret as long as he lived, since he was scarcely in the Captain's cabin when Banks swung out of his big oak chair like a bull entering a ring and roared:

"Now, sir, I've sent for you" (this was news to Grüssli) "because I understand you've again been poking your nose into matters which are a long, long way from being any of your concern. Why?"

"Well," Mr. Grüssli faltered unnerved by the force of this attack, "it's occurred to me . . . well, I wanted to put the men's point of view to you over —"

"You're a passenger, sir," Banks interrupted, "and I should advise you to remember that fact. I am the Captain of this ship, and under God's good guidance and in accordance with the company rules I shall command and conduct matters as best I see fit. If you have any complaints over the service, the food, or the entertainment provided, you have a legitimate reason to see the Purser, and if you fail to get satisfaction there, to bring the matter to the Staff Captain or to me. The discipline and the conduct of the crew is solely to do with the Captain of the ship. I want no one-man political parties in *Leviathan*. I intend this ship to be run as I say. So understand this, sir. Just as I have power over the men under my command, so I have the power to put you ashore at our next port of call in the charge of your Consul as a vexatious and intractable passenger. And do not think for one single second that I shall hesitate to do so. You have a ticket for this cruise which is your contract with the company, but contracts can be brought to an end with due notice on either side. I give you this notice now, sir. One more piece of interference from you and you step ashore at Madagascar. Is that understood?"

"If you do that," Mr. Grüssli quavered, "I should . . . well, I should have to consider suing the Transoceanic Company for damages."

"You are naturally free to do as you please," Banks said, glowering into his beard, "once you leave this ship. But I should remember, sir, if I were you, that you are not the only person able to go to law. I have a record of eighty-seven complaints, interviews, and asinine suggestions you have made since this cruise began. That is an average of more than one a day. There is also the question of the inaccurate, uninformed, and damaging report on crew living conditions which you saw fit to concoct and issue to the Press at Hong Kong. For that, sir, and the malicious damage caused to the good name of *Leviathan* and the company, you would be liable in law."

"It's . . . it's a goddam outrage," Mr. Grüssli stamped his foot in annoyance. "I'll . . . I could make you pay for this."

"Don't be too sure about who's going to pay, when it comes to the point. 'Boast not thyself of tomorrow; for thou knowest not what a day may bring forth. Hell and destruction are never full, so are the eyes of man never satisfied.' I commend the twenty-seventh chapter of Proverbs to your attention, sir. The maxims it contains are very much to the point."

It was all very well, Mott reflected ruefully, when he heard a verbatim report of this interview from the Captain's "Tiger," it needed saying and it was high time Mr. Grüssli learned some of the facts of life, but it left on their hands — or to be more accurate on his hands — the weight of one dissatisfied passenger. Mr. Grüssli would go grizzling back to Minnesota and his diet of raw snails, and from then on would do his best to denigrate the Company whether in fact he found himself landed at Madagascar or not.

He thought about ordering a bottle of champagne and asking Mr. Grüssli along for a quiet chat but as Mr. Grüssli did not touch alcohol, that did not seem to be the solution. And there were so many other problems to be solved. So he ordered a bottle of champagne anyway, drank it himself, went down to the ship's hospital to see how Susan was getting on and then for the first time that cruise had a meal sent along to his cabin, together with another bottle of champagne, and thus, pleasantly and quite by himself, got comfortably pickled. Tomorrow was another day, and its problems could be dealt with when they arose.

By the time *Leviathan* reached Cape Town, the passengers, except for a subdued Mr. Grüssli, had forgotten all about the little trouble in the Indian Ocean. In any case, almost none of them had any idea of the extent of the mutiny and that word itself was never mentioned. It was simply a "bit of trouble due to the equatorial heat." *Leviathan*'s quiet, friendly service re-established the goodwill which the great majority of passengers had always felt toward the ship since coming aboard, the widows continued to vie with one another in the lavish cocktail parties they gave, Lord and Lady Passington continued to lead the English Old Guard, and the main problem of the day continued to be the curing of one hangover and the setting-up of another.

Behind the scenes, though, the effects of the mutiny went on being felt. Fabian was horrified at the airmail report he received from Madagascar, and at one time considered flying out to the Cape himself. It was shocking, and the only consolation he could find was that Flint was aboard and could not, therefore, blame him in any way.

As for the old man himself, it was in one sense as though the end of a world had come. That there should be a mutiny at all was bad enough, that it should take place in *Leviathan* on their first world cruise with himself aboard was calamitous. His pride had been dealt a bitter blow. He bore this in silence, but the hurt went very deep. These were dreadful times to live through, he thought somberly as he watched Table Mountain come into sight.

Things seemed to be getting worse every time he picked up a paper. Now there would surely be a war followed, perhaps, by anarchy and collapse, but somehow or other he had never associated such possibilities with the company. The company had survived other wars. In a sense — and quite illogically — he had always thought of the company as standing apart from and above such dire events. Naturally in another struggle, as in the Great War, the company would be involved, ships would be requisitioned, sunk, and replaced, but these things lay outside the life of the company itself.

A mutiny was something utterly different. Here anarchy and collapse for a few short hours had come within a microbe's crawl of the company's heart. Unquestioning discipline, an established order, and the routine which was its skin had for a century stood behind the single great idea of "service." This, in essence, was what the company had to sell, and had sold with success all these changing years. Now, when he thought of the scenes Mott and Susan had described, he would tap his gnarled old fingers on the edge of his chair and the tears would spring into his eyes. He was seventy-three years old, and everything that had given meaning to his life seemed to be slipping away out of reach. This whole cruise had been a mistake. His retirement was a mistake. He knew now as a fact something which before he had only suspected — he was finished with life, he wanted to die, but most of all he wanted to die in harness.

It took Susan ten days to recover, so that to her great annoyance she missed both Madagascar and Cape Town. At the start it frustrated her very much to be out of things at this most curious time in the ship's career, not only out of things but, because of the fever, scarcely even interested except in the small world of the sick bay and later on, the spare first class stateroom into which Mott had her moved. Here, while recuperating, she had a stream of visitors, of whom Flint, Mott, and Charles Beecher were the most frequent. Through them she kept in touch at second hand with the life of the ship. But it was as though she was out of gear. Their opinions and anecdotes were no substitute for her busy everyday life, her own impressions, and her own judgment.

A number of the widows showered her with presents — flowers, champagne, and books — so that at times she felt like royalty in the attention she received. She had not been ill enough to go to bed like this and surrender her life to a curriculum of drugs since school. At first she fretted both at being out of it all, and because other people were having to do her work. Then one day a pleasant calm settled upon her and she decided to enjoy this "time out" for all it was worth. Around her the hundreds of different activities which made up the ship's day were begun, developed, and ended. The daily newspaper was printed and distributed, meals were cooked and eaten, oil poured into the great furnaces, and the ship tore on, headed now back to New York. People woke up, read books, played games, went to the cinema, drank cocktails, made love, and went to bed again. Tickets were bought on sweepstakes, postcards written, cables and phone calls received, and none of it for the moment had anything to do with Susan as she lay in bed, drifting back and forth among the many colored memories of her life.

Once the fever was over, her body's weakness brought with it a clarity of mind, together with a depth and detachment she had rarely known before. It was like having trudged up a mountain in blinkers to find suddenly that she could see all round and that the body was no longer a drag. At times she felt she could almost float. She was on a different level of being in herself, comparable only with that relaxed state of love and happiness which had come upon her after she had first slept with Charles. She found things connecting up in her mind, the hurrying scurrying fragmentation of her daily life ceased for a while and she began to see things in relation to one another, and sometimes as a whole.

All these months she had still had a vague feeling of guilt at having left home. She thought that perhaps her mother had been secretly in sympathy with her, but her father had never understood this "thrust toward independence," as he called it. He thought it unfeminine, but he had long called her a tomboy, and to him femininity was synonymous with a compliant subservience. She supposed that was why he had married her mother, since she had never once, so far as Susan could remember, stood up against him or said him "No." Poor Mother! What a life she had had. Yet wasn't it really her fault? What would have happened if she had had even a peck of her daughter's rebellious spirit?

She thought of her large comfortable home with its procession of self-important political figures drinking her father's whisky. She thought of Tess, the black Labrador bitch, and of Cooper, the cat. She thought of the Mitchells next door down the road, both Joan and Alan rebels like herself but not so forthright about it; then she looked round this rather consciously luxurious stateroom she was in and wondered what, if anything, she had achieved by running away to sea.

At that moment Mott came into the cabin with a novel she had wanted to read in his hand. He walked straight over to the bed without saying a word, leaned down and kissed her on the mouth. She did not resist him. Indeed she put an arm round his neck and kissed him right back. The suddenness with which this had happened — and it was the first time he had kissed her — surprised them both and had a sort of freshening effect.

"I don't know why I did that," he said as he straightened up, "but it's something I've wanted to do a very long time."

"Oh! you're just exercising your usual *seigneurial* rights."

"I might do it again," he said, sitting on the bed and rather shyly caressing her breasts. "I've had a one hundred per cent louse of a day."

They smiled at each other with the understanding of two old friends.

"I always knew I represent simply a means of escape," she said, "Who is it now? Mrs. Klopatsky again?"

"No, it's Mrs. Ormsby and her love letters, Mrs. Patrickson and her 'private little drinkies in her private little cabin,' and Mrs. Nash more or less wheeling her bed into my day cabin, You know what I think? I think sex is disgusting."

"No, it isn't," Susan said, composed and enjoying herself. "It's a most remarkable invention." She opened her arms and again they kissed, both of them once more surprised at how natural and pleasant it seemed.

"I really believe I love you, Susan," he said. "I suppose that strikes you as very silly and senile."

"No," Susan answered, stopping his wandering hand from further exploration of her body. "It doesn't strike me in that way at all."

"As I shall probably be sacked because of the mutiny, I wondered if you'd care to marry me and share my rather inadequate pension. I've been working it out. We could always open a guest house in Bognor Regis."

"It's very sweet of you," Susan said gently, "but I'm always being told that tomboys are not the marrying type."

"Do you know something, Susan?" Mott cut in abruptly. "I believe you're the most wonderful, ravishing, radiant woman I've met in my whole life. My heart turns over each time I see you. I think I could eat you, I want you so much."

She reached over and touched his hand, moved by the intensity of his feeling.

"You're very sweet, Motty, you really are. I'm very fond of you, too."

He got up rather jerkily and walked over to the porthole, staring at the sea.

"Well, there it is. Mustn't get too serious about it, I suppose. God knows I'm not the answer to a maiden's prayer."

She snuggled comfortably back against the pillows, smiling to herself.

"It's certainly what my parents would say," she agreed, "but after all it's *my* life, isn't it?"

"Yes, Susan, it's your life and that's what makes me hesitate. I know you seem much older than you are but you're still really so very young."

"Oh! fooph! That sort of age doesn't matter."

"I'm rather afraid it does," Mott said sadly, "and there's no way round it."

On an impulse she clambered out of bed, went across in her flame-colored pajamas, turned him round and took him in her arms. Where did you draw the line between fondness and love? He excited her — perhaps not quite in the torrential way Charles had done — but none the less she wanted him as a man, she admired and respected him as a man, and the fact that he was forty-one and she not yet twenty-one struck her as supremely unimportant.

"You shouldn't be out of bed," Mott said, "you'll catch your death of something or other."

"You, probably," Susan said, "and I might rather like it."

There was a click as the door opened and Flint stumped in, stopping abruptly and adjusting his pince-nez at the extraordinary sight which greeted his eyes. There was a momentary pause full of hideous potentiality, then Susan decided that attack was the best form of defense and said sharply:

"It's usual to knock before you enter a lady's bedchamber, so don't look so shocked, Sir J.; we were only kissing each other."

"Hm! Well . . . hm!"

This slight indecision was fatal to any attitude of shocked disapproval Flint might have intended to adopt, because the next moment Susan had come over and taken him by his thin bony shoulders, implanting a kiss on each of his crinkly cheeks.

"Now you're not to be shocked. We were only kissing each other because we're rather in love. We weren't misbehaving, you know. So don't you be nasty about it, will you?"

Flint cleared his throat nervously as he found himself looking down straight at her firm little bosom under the open v-neck of her pajamas. With Susan it was one shock after another. But she had the initiative and kept up the attack.

"And you needn't think we make a habit of this either," she went on, smiling at him with a kind of innocent poise. "That was the first time we've ever kissed. I know it's not very proper but it was all my fault. I got out of bed and kissed Motty — and that's all there is to it. Now I'm going back to bed and you're going to sit down and be nice to me while I get you a drink. Come on."

Taking him by the hand she led him to the chair by her bedside and sat him down as she climbed back into bed, arranged herself and rang the bell for the steward.

"I beg your pardon, sir," Mott said, for the first time in years a little awkward and hesitant. "I'm sorry about the lapse."

"Lapse?" Flint said gruffly, again adjusting his pince-nez on his thin angular nose. "I don't know what you're making all the fuss about. I saw nothing improper going on."

"Thank you, Sir J.," Susan said beaming and giving him another kiss on his cheek. "You're a poppet and I love you, too."

"Hm!" said the old man with the glint of a smile at the Purser. "I don't know so much about that."

⚓⚓⚓⚓⚓ XI ⚓⚓⚓⚓⚓

AFTER a brief day at Tristan da Cunha *Leviathan* set off for Bermuda and New York on the last leg of the cruise. By now it was April 1939 and in another few weeks the ship would be back on her normal transatlantic schedule, the cruise nothing but a memory and a report on an office desk, the widows disposed of, the feuds and the fighting forgotten.

Banks had prepared the greater part of his cruise report by the time the ship was within a couple of days of Bermuda. The mutiny had, of course, been separately investigated. After a due period of penitence the stewards' "Pig" had been re-opened and the overtime rates which had actually triggered off the trouble provisionally increased. The company did not like it, especially as the increase had been obtained under duress, but it would not be out of pocket since the crew-wages formula was based, as it was in many other companies, on bar profits from the sale of drink and cigarettes. So automatically prices went up, and in one sense those members of the crew who drank a lot of beer were no better off.

The four ringleaders of "the trouble" were landed at Cape Town under arrest and the majority of the steward personnel, with an underlying feeling of guilt at the way things had happened, returned to their work with relief and the prospect of the big tipping spree with which it was hoped the cruise would end. Llewellyn, writing a highly secret report of his own, was well satisfied with the way "the trouble" had gone. He had lost four good henchmen but they would merely have their names and papers changed and would then proceed to other jobs in other ships. He himself, as far as he knew, remained unde-tected and unsuspected.

This was true as to Llewellyn's actual identity, but Mott, the Staff Captain, and Banks knew there had been and possibly still was a silent enemy in their midst. None of them discussed it very much because, as things were, they had no positive evi-dence of any kind to go on but all of them brooded about it as they went about their daily work. Banks, in particular, made himself more remote than ever. The idea of hierarchy was an essential part of his philosophy, and since he stood at the top of *Leviathan*'s own tree of command, he was able to give this idea full rein.

In the beginning he had come down from the mountain peak to give an impulse to the cruise. He had done this with private reluctance because it was part of his duty — but once the machinery was turning he had progressively withdrawn.

With the exception of Flint, he saw as little of the passengers as possible and each time he found Flint on the bridge, the freedom of which had been given him as a very special favor, he resented the little man.

Occasionally as he paced up and down his day cabin, meditating on the chapter of the Bible he happened to be reading, he would pause and wonder why he felt as he did. Perhaps it was the ancient reserve a Master has always felt toward an owner, however cordial the outward relationship may be, the hidden disdain of the man who faces the hazards of the sea, who takes the risk with his life, for the exploiter who makes the profits over a city desk. Perhaps it was that *Leviathan* was personal to both of them, a possession given into their hands in trust which in some way possessed them in return.

Certainly both of them looked on the great monster as "my ship" despite the obvious background of the company and the rest of the fleet without which *Leviathan* could neither have been built nor operated. Thus there was an instinctive jealousy which both would have discounted with their minds but which dodged in and out under cover of the pride they both felt in the ship. At all events Banks acknowledged he would be pleased and relieved when Sir J. was landed at New York.

There was little doubt that the cruise had been a success. This could have been claimed had there been no other indication than the large number of passengers wishing to book their same cabins for the same cruise the following year. Three stewards had been offered positions in private houses on the Eastern Seaboard. A trip across the States in a Cadillac was being arranged for two of the assistant pursers by Mrs. Ormsby and, of course, Mott had received an open invitation to stay as long as he liked in Mrs. Nash's Newport mansion. A weekend's racing in Virginia was being laid on for George Stone and Jimmy Johnson. The Chief Engineer, the Doctor, and the Staff Captain were all bidden to a Texas ranch, and Gloria Dowkins had agreed to become the fourth Mrs. Saxburger, a piece of news which saddened Susan a great deal, both because she would thus be losing a cabinmate she had become very fond of, and because it was obviously a decision about which Gloria herself was far from sure.

"Art's a bit worried, too," Gloria confided to Susan, as the ship neared Bermuda. "It's all been so goddam amicable, he says, what with me and him whooping it up some nights in their cabin while she and Curly were up to no good elsewhere in the ship — with all of us knowing what was going on all of the time." Curly was a very good looking Radio Officer who had fallen in love with the third Mrs. Saxburger early in the cruise and had thus relieved the ebullient Art of his most difficult problem. "You see I know it's all very naughty and wrong," she went on with a giggle, "but there can't be any blackmail over the alimony as both sides have surprised the other in turn, if you see what I mean and really it's all been a bit of luck. Last time Art and I were making love to each other she walked right into the middle of it, rootled around for a sweater, patted him on the head and walked out again. I mean what can you *do* with a woman like that?"

"But does he love you and would he look after you?"

"He'll look after me as long as we get along all right in bed and, speaking frankly, at his age that isn't a problem. He just loves a good time, which he never had when he was young or with either of his first two wives, and he is so filthy rich."

But there was a wistful look in Gloria's eyes. She did not seem to be aware of this herself. She did not pity herself. She took things much as they came. She knew there was a price on everything you wanted and she had never expected something for nothing. But Susan felt that Arthur Saxburger, for all his good heart and his generous ways, was scarcely the man for Gloria. You could not forget his bald head and his paunch. She could surely do better than that.

"If you could choose anyone you liked . . ." Susan began.

"You're just a romantic," Gloria said with sudden force, as if Susan had really touched a sore spot. "I'd marry Charley Beecher if I thought it would do either of us the slightest good — but it wouldn't. With Artie at least we won't have to skimp."

The sudden introduction of Charles into the conversation brought Susan up all standing. She had had no idea they were on anything like such intimate terms.

"Has he asked you to marry him?"

"Of course he has. He asks everyone he goes soft on sooner or later. He's got a sort of obsession about it. But I'm too much of a tart for his liking. Can't think what he means — can you? God! I don't know what they expect, these men. Park Lane and all the trimmings on a junior first officer's salary. And if he had it, he wouldn't know what to do with it."

"I . . . I didn't know you and Charley had reached quite that . . . state of affairs," Susan faltered.

Gloria gave her a sharp penetrating look.

"Oh! he still raves about you, of course, but you'd be totally unsuitable too. Let's face it, honey, for quite different reasons you and I are neither of us made for a neat semi-detached residence in a quiet suburb. It just wouldn't work."

But to Susan it was still a shock. She, too, had long known she would never marry Charles Beecher but somehow she hadn't expected him to swing straight from her to Gloria Dowkins. It upset her vanity. Worse — it made her acknowledge with a stab of dismay that she was just as much of a snob as anyone else. Something in her said, "I don't understand how he could want to marry me one moment and then Gloria the next," but she did not voice her thoughts and a moment or so later she found the next Mrs. Saxburger studying her again.

"My guess is you'll marry Motty before you're through with *Leviathan*," she said. "You could do a whole lot worse. Of course you could probably also do a whole lot better."

"I'm not in such a panic to get myself married," Susan said coolly, "after all I'm not yet twenty-one."

"Then there's always old Flinty-boy," Gloria went on with a rare touch of malice, "the old ones are quite often the best."

"You should know about that," Susan said tartly, but Gloria had the last word as she usually did.

"You could make us a lot of money by suddenly opting for Flint," she said. "The odds against your marrying our beloved ex-Chairman have more than doubled since the cruise began.

I could get about fifty to one if I tried. Don't let it worry you, honey," she went on seeing Susan's angry look, "there's nothing much secret in a ship — not even in one this size, and no one ever believed in all that chess — not for a single moment."

"Good heavens above, if they're making a book on it — what sort of person do they think I am?"

"A woman," Gloria said with a laugh, "just the same as anyone else."

When Joan Mitchell had returned to England to nurse her mother, she took with her a new determination acquired in New York. Susan had seen this developing over the months but it had been a shock to her parents. The girl had grown up a lot. To Fabian it was all part of the "ununderstandability" of the younger generation, but as her mother's convalescence continued, Joan began to sense that her mother was more on her side than she had been before.

Mrs. Mitchell in her cool, distant way had never been given the ability to communicate. Conversation in the Mitchell home consisted mostly in the exchange of battered but comfortable clichés. Joan had been brought up — expensively enough — to fit into the conventional background which both Fabian and his wife so greatly admired. It would probably be Sir Fabian and Lady Mitchell before very many years had elapsed, now that Fabian was head of Transoceanic. This was success and one of the rewards of acceptance, the logical rounding-off of a pattern.

Had Alan decided to follow in his father's footsteps, or indeed do any of the things considered suitable to a young man of his education and class, then Fabian would have been delighted. Had Joan, in turn, shown any interest or aptitude for London deb parties and the drift of pleasure into which girls who did not need to work so easily slipped, then again Fabian would have played the stern yet indulgent father and privately would have preened himself on the way his kids had turned out.

As it was he could do neither. Alan had become a Socialist and a pacifist, indeed, he was talking of going into politics on the Labor side. That was bad enough; but for Joan, then, to prefer the glitter of New York to the solidity and worth of English country life was incredible to Fabian and something for which he felt the Labans were largely to blame. Joan had been seduced by the glamour of New York and now her values had gone "off."

No sooner had he got her back to England on the excellent excuse of her mother's illness, than the girl was campaigning to return to New York. She had even had the impertinence to suggest that she had been "tricked" into coming back, that her mother was far from desperately ill, and that now she had probably lost her place and her chance in that travel agency with the ridiculous name. As if that sort of thing had the slightest importance in a girl's life when she could be comfortably at home looking around for a suitable husband among her own sort of people.

But Joan had learned a thing or two about quiet determination from Ethel Laban. She liked New York and she wanted to go back. Indeed, as soon as her mother's convalescence had progressed to the stage where she was up and about again, Joan intensified her campaign. Fabian tried to laugh her out of it, he jeered and he sneered, he tried grumpiness and an occasional outburst of temper; it was no good at all. He laid on theaters and dinner parties in London, he gave her presents, he sent her to an aunt at Cheltenham who took her racing, at Easter he even suggested they all go over to Paris. Except that he made his daughter feel miserable and "caddish," he had no success whatever.

On a sudden impulse and because Flint intended staying some months in the United States instead of returning to England in *Leviathan*, Fabian decided to meet the ship in New York and take his wife and daughter with him. They had a standing invitation to stay with some wealthy friends on Long Island, "the right sort of Americans," as Fabian described them, a phrase which made Joan see red. But at least it got her across the Atlantic again and once in New York she knew she could count on Ethel Laban's support in re-establishing herself, if not with Lapolux then in some other job which would give her an independence. That was, in fact, what she really wanted. An independence, a freedom to pick her own friends and live the life she herself had chosen of her own free will.

"You say you don't understand us, Daddy," she said one evening on the voyage across, "but what you really mean is that you don't agree. You're always saying the English quality is a flexible, self-respecting independence. You admire it in others but you don't like to see it at close quarters either in Alan or in me."

"Well, of course, if you're going to talk like that," Fabian said huffily, "there's no point in further discussion. It's a fine state of affairs. I must say, when my own daughter reads me a lecture."

"I'm not doing that, Daddy, I'm just trying to show you how *we* think, Alan and I."

"I blame all this on young Susan," Fabian cut in. "She put these scatterbrained ideas in your head."

"Even if she did," Joan said nervously, "at least she isn't trying to make us into something we're not." She was still frightened of her father's powerful personality and the rage he could bring to bear on her once he was roused.

"So that's all the thanks your mother and I get for giving you a good home and a first class education," Fabian began and then noticed she had begun to cry. "And it's no good getting out of it by sniveling."

"I don't like 'sniveling' as you call it. I don't *want* to snivel. It just isn't fair, that's all. We *are* grateful, but we want to be ourselves, that's all."

"And I suppose you think Susan's done well for herself — traipsing about *Leviathan* in a menial capacity when she could be —"

"'Sitting around at Dorking useless and idle, spending money other people have earned. Don't you see, Daddy, young people like us want to *do* things. The world's changing and we want to have something to do with the new things that are coming. Gosh! I almost wish there was a war; then we could do something useful for a change."

239

"And you think you'll find what you want in America?"

An almost passionate note crept into her voice.

"You can do anything you like in America. People take you for what you are — not for what your great-grandfather did. People give you a chance. There's life and ideas and excitement. You feel *alive*, Daddy, don't you see what it is?"

But Fabian never had and he never would. He relapsed back into his gloomy internal resentment, feeling somehow that both his children had let him down, through no fault of his own.

Bermuda saw *Leviathan*'s passengers indulging in the last great spending spree of the cruise. The three hundred and sixty-five coral islands which make up Bermuda have long been especially attractive to visiting Americans with a taste for quality and the money to indulge it, but the quantities of sweaters, Scotch whisky, and French perfume which came aboard during the forty-eight hours *Leviathan* spent in Hamilton Sound astonished even Mott.

The insulated life of the very rich always fascinated him. Occasionally it gave him twinges of envy; at other times it horrified him. To imagine it was one thing; to live in close daily contact with it and to have to minister to it another. Big money knew there was so little in the world that could not be bought either openly and directly or with the exercise of a little ingenuity. And money always got what it wanted. To go round the world as a kind of chaperon to such wealth was a test. He had done it before and survived, but not perhaps at such pressure as there had been in *Leviathan*.

Continually disillusioned, almost always amused and fascinated, Mott himself was in a unique position in *Leviathan*: he was the bridge, the balancing connection between positive and negative, between what was actively sought and what passively resisted the search. Like a bank manager, he had always to be trusted by the very rich and by those he brought into contact with the very rich. He had to sell to his clients and he had to persuade his own staff. Officially the "selling" had been done before the passenger came aboard, and the "persuasion" was unnecessary as he had the right to give orders — but Mott had never relied on the regulations. He had always favored the carrot instead of the whip. It was what a man really wanted inside himself that drove his individual machine.

To see the desire lurking behind the outward request or complaint, to spot the real motive, to appreciate that the private "I want" backed by a million dollars was the most powerful thing in the world he had to work in, to decorate and disguise the crude emotions and appetites of his "guests" into some sort of manageable civilized behavior, through it all to remain day by day and at all times urbane, easy, firm, reasonably cheerful, tolerant, and understanding was Mott's task, and also, he had discovered, his pleasure.

Mott, in fact, was the prism concentrating and refracting *Leviathan*'s life. Early in the cruise he had been nicknamed "Mr. Leviathan" and by the time the ship returned to New York, it had become common among the passengers to say, "Oh! I must ask Mr. Leviathan how many dollars I ought to pay," or "If Mr. Leviathan says it's O.K., then it's O.K. by me." Mott took it as a compliment, though one evening when he was so addressed in front of the Captain, he could see that Banks did not like it at all. If anyone was to be referred to as Mr. Leviathan, then in the Captain's opinion that man was himself. But nicknames happen and they stick. The passengers called him Mr. Leviathan and it was the passengers who mattered. They paid.

Mott's philosophy, indeed, was a much more subtle one than his Captain's. Whereas Banks could and did refer every question which came his way to the Bible using its authority to back up his own, Mott relied on the far more complex and powerful force of human understanding. He tried in every problem to relate the part to the whole. When someone was making trouble or had done something wrong, he tried to do that most difficult thing of all — to see it through the other person's eyes while at the same time remembering himself.

He had found long ago that this brought things mysteriously into proportion, he knew not how. He did not automatically react, and it was therefore as if there was a small cushion between any event and himself. He had discovered that although he was involved as Purser of *Leviathan*, or simply as a man in a particular fix, there could still be a tiny measure of detachment — an ability to stand back and see the thing dispassionately, and at times compassionately. He called this giving space to another in himself, and it worked, at times miraculously, taking the heat out of a row or preventing a quibble or a petulance from developing into a deep-seated resentment.

Banks, of course, was the ultimate authority on board, and there could be no argument with God. There was no doubt that Mott's responsibility was in no way comparable, that an error of judgment on his part would not result, as well it might on the Captain's, in a full scale disaster. But Mott was in far closer contact with the sole reason for the ship's existence — her fare-paying passengers. He was successful and popular, and it was Mr. Leviathan who would first spring to mind when afterward the passengers remembered their extraordinary trip round the world.

So, on 16th April 1939, *Leviathan* secured alongside the Transoceanic Pier in New York, her hundred days' journey completed, her arrival watched by a large crowd, among whom were the Labans and the Mitchells. The deep note of her siren sounded "familiar and friendly in the North River," as one reporter put it, "and reminded New Yorkers that once again the greatest ship in the world was back in port and would very shortly become a regular visitor now that we are once more at the start of another summer season." Unfortunately the optimism of the Press was not reflected in the advance booking figures over which Laban and Mitchell had been brooding the last couple of days.

A month previously Czechoslovakia had been annexed by Hitler and almost every day the drift of the news took the world nearer and nearer to war. Almost every day in Germany it seemed as if battleships were being launched, churches disestablished, and Jews persecuted. The arrogance of the dictators grew more marked, while in England the great majority of the Conservative Party then in power supported

Neville Chamberlain, the sixty-nine-year-old man who started "this business of man-to-man talks for peace." Winston Churchill was still regarded with the utmost suspicion.

Appeasement and the avoidance of hard facts made up the political climate in England; isolationist indignation and sententious appeals for peace to Hitler and Mussolini that of America. It was not going to be a year for taking pleasure trips to Europe and so far as fast transatlantic travel for the business man and politician was concerned, an event which was to make *Leviathan* rapidly obsolescent had taken place about two weeks previously.

On the 27th March the Pan-American *Yankee Clipper* had flown out of Baltimore for Lisbon with the first full complement of passengers aboard. Two months later the first regular transatlantic air service was inaugurated from New York. From that moment on the title of the fastest ship in the world lost a great deal of significance. *Leviathan,* in one sense, was already out of date.

"However that needn't distress us too much," Fabian remarked to the conference held at the Bowling Green offices the day after *Leviathan* arrived; "there'll always be people who prefer the safety and comfort of going by sea. And those people, I hope, will always feel attracted by the superior comfort and service our company is able to offer. You'll never get me to risk my neck thousands of feet up over three thousand miles of inhospitable sea. I doubt if this fancy new service is going to be really commercial for some years to come. We are still supreme on the sea and that's how I intend this company to continue."

Flint, who had taken a seat to one side, sniffed and began cleaning his pince-nez. He had always thought Fabian a smug pompous ass, and here, to his mind, was fresh proof after a gap of three months. It gave him almost a physical pain to realize that "his" company and "his" ships were now under Fabian's control. Once again he wished sincerely he could die quickly and suddenly, without knowing anything further of the downward stretch he saw only too clearly ahead. But Fabian was again addressing this conference of high company officials and travel agents, and to Flint's dismay he heard himself being dragged into it by name.

"We are still fortunate, indeed, to have available to us the experience of the man who for the last quarter of a century has made the Transoceanic Company what it is, and I'd like to ask Sir Josiah Flint's opinion on this new Atlantic air service which is stealing our thunder."

There was a silence as Flint felt the attention of everyone fastened on to him.

"I'm afraid I don't share your optimism," he said with a wry twisted smile. "I should recommend we buy as many Pan-American shares as we can lay hands on, and in the meantime go all out for freight."

Now there really was a silence. Flint could feel a wave of rage and frustration coming at him from Fabian Mitchell. Quietly and deliberately he proceeded to enjoy the discomfiture he had caused. That would spoil his successor's complacency for a while.

"I see we have a slight division of opinion," Fabian said blandly, after a pause. "We shall, of course, go 'all out for freight,' as indeed we do now. As to passenger traffic, only time, I suppose, will show which point of view is correct. I find it hard to believe, though, that *Leviathan* and her consort will be the last large liners we or our competitors will build. And I still think we have far more to offer than anyone else in the game. The airline companies have a long way to go. It's going to take more than a pretty hostess and a few bottles of free champagne to topple this company from the pre-eminent position it holds in the transatlantic passenger trade."

By the time the conference was over the buffers and disguises were all in place again and neither Flint nor Fabian revealed a trace of the deep animosity each felt for the other. Life, whether personal or corporate, still had to go on and with *Leviathan* due to sail for England in forty-eight hours the cruise post-mortem — or that part of it which affected New York — had to be conducted with all dispatch. Mr. Grüssli, for instance, had left in a flurry of anger to seek out his lawyer; the luggage Mr. Whitaker Hornbeam had dispatched from Buenos Aires had failed to arrive. Two of the widows left without either tipping or paying their doctor's bills, and the lavish expressions of praise from the majority which Mott and the Chief Steward had received inevitably possessed a reverse side, all the details of which would require meticulous investigation. The crew, from Banks to the youngest steward, felt exhausted and stale and badly in need of leave. Then, finally, there was "the trouble" and its aftermath.

Fabian, Flint, Banks, the Staff Captain, Mott, and George Stone went into what seemed to Mott an endless conference, while around them the great ship was restocked with food, water and fuel for the last leg of her journey back to Southampton. After the hundred days of never quite knowing what eccentricities, whims, and surprises his millionaire passengers would produce or require, Mott had hoped that the emptiness of the ship would be as refreshing as a run ashore.

For forty-eight hours no one was going to send for him and complain that the ship's course did not allow any sunlight to shine into cabin XYZ, or that there was too much sunlight, or that they'd missed taking a ticket on the daily sweepstake but hadn't heard the result so could they please buy one now even though it was half an hour late. For forty-eight hours there would be no wrestling with cocktail-party lists, no complaints from Mrs. Klopatsky and no little invitations to "drinkies" from Mrs. Nash. He would not have to warn Mr. de Voss to stay away from that tourist class steward with the blond hair, he would not have to sit up half the night investigating the reasons for Mr. Jörgenson's suicide, nor spend hours haggling with Hong Kong *entrepreneurs* over a misunderstanding in the contract for boat hire.

Instead, for forty-eight hours he found himself repeating for the benefit of Fabian and other company officials exactly what had happened that bad morning in the Indian Ocean when "the trouble" had come to a head and what he thought was behind it and just how sinister and serious it was. Indeed, long before *Leviathan* was due to sail, Mott had come almost to wish that the passengers with their variegated requests and foibles were back again on board in full strength, instead of this ceaseless going over of the same old ground in search of new clues. And it would all take place all over again once the ship got back to Southampton. He was thoroughly sick of it all.

On *Leviathan*'s last night in New York Mott had provisionally fixed up a run ashore with Susan. She was staying with the Labans as usual but they were all to meet at a cocktail party Fabian was giving in *Leviathan*'s Garden Lounge. Fabian had wanted to hold this party in his suite at the Plaza, where he and his family had established themselves in some considerable style awaiting *Leviathan*'s arrival. But he had abandoned this idea when Flint had remarked in passing, "I can see the Chairman's expenses will be climbing Mount Everest this year." The use of expensive non-company hotels for company personnel was, to Flint, a form of unnecessary showing off, but since he himself had just returned from a lavish world cruise with all expenses paid, he was in a poor position for imposing on his successor the Victorian parsimony he had so admired all his life.

It was a sizeable party and *Leviathan*'s gardener had provided a splendid display of spring flowers. Fabian himself was returning to England in the ship the next day and his wife and Joan would be staying out on Long Island with the family of a New York banker who was there that night. Hamilton Codde and the Lapolux people were there. Ethel Laban had brought along her brother, who in turn had asked Lord Harborough and Blossom, since once again their plays were filling his theaters; they too were returning to England the next day in the ship. Captain Banks stood monolithically in among the tubbed tulips, a stiff Scotch in his hand. Lord and Lady Passington, looking like the caricatures of themselves found in the stewards' "Pig," had been invited as *ex officio* leaders of the British community on board *Leviathan* during her cruise. The British Ambassador in Washington, who happened to be on a visit to New York, and the British Consul-General were both there, together with the heads of the British Information Service and the British Empire Chamber of Commerce. The Garden Lounge was packed. A whole clutch of stewards had

had to curtail their leave in order to see this party through, and since it was a company party there would not be many tips. If the guests, the majority of whom took their drinks and their canapés without even a look at the smiling stewards who served them, could have heard the grumbling and the griping which this extra party had occasioned down below, they might have paused and given a thought to some of the problems with which Mott and Stone had to live, and which, manipulated skillfully by someone such as the quiet Llewellyn, resulted in "the trouble" which had surprised them all in the Indian Ocean. But no one except Mott did give it a thought. This was April 1939. A steward was a steward and a job a job. People had other things on their minds.

"I thought we might slip ashore in about an hour," Mott whispered to Susan once the party was under way, "how are you fixed with the Labans?"

"They're taking Sir J. on to dinner with a friend of theirs in General Motors," Susan answered, "so that takes care of that. Could we ask Joan Mitchell and her boy friend to go with us? I've hardly seen anything of her at all."

"Whatever you like," Mott answered, secretly hating the idea. He wanted Susan to himself for just an hour or two, but he had no intention of showing his real feelings. In any case he had long realized that possessiveness over a girl like Susan would be fatal. She would give herself or she wouldn't, as and when she chose. He was happy it should be that way. He was in a blithe state of love for her which seemed to melt away the difficulties and obstructions of everyday life. So long as she was somewhere around and he could be with her from time to time that was all he asked for the present. In the event, however, neither of them was to go ashore that night.

The fire began after the party had been going on for about an hour, and it was caused by one of those freak chances in a millon that seamen dread, and which at sea can end in disaster. One of the guests, without thinking, threw the butt of his cigar over the side. This was still alight and the stiff breeze then blowing carried it down and, aided by a sudden gust, in through the porthole of an empty cabin four decks below. There it fell on the bed on which happened to be stacked a pile of folded blankets left there in readiness for the following day. The cabin was not in use at the time nor were the ones on either side, so that the fire had a chance of catching hold long before anything was suspected. The porthole should not have been open, but for some reason it was, and the wind blowing in gustily provided the draft the fire needed in its early stages and, once it had caught, the driving force to carry it on elsewhere. Nobody knew how long it had been blazing, in fact, when the smell of burning paint reached up into the Garden Lounge at about the same time as it was noticed elsewhere in the ship. By the time the alarm was raised, some six cabins were well ablaze and the fire had the initiative.

Up in the Garden Lounge, Banks noticed it first. To begin with he thought someone at the party must have dropped a cigarette in a corner where it was scorching the paint but when the faint odor continued to tickle his nostrils, he suddenly felt a shiver of uneasiness, between his shoulder-blades. He put down his drink, gruffly excused himself and walked out of the Garden Lounge forward toward the main staircase.

At this point he thought his senses must have tricked him. There was no trace of the fire either in smell or sound or activity. In fact the ship seemed exactly as she always had been in port, deserted, quietly lit, and faintly humming. Perhaps he'd made a mistake. The fire risk in a ship of *Leviathan*'s size was so terrifying that an occasional false alarm might be excused in the interests of vigilance. He paused, thinking that perhaps he ought to go back to the party or at least make his excuses, when once again the merest trace of an odor made its presence felt in his nose.

This premonition of danger flashed through his mind and electrified his senses. Gathering himself into motion — and it was surprising how quickly and lightly he could pad about once his awareness was working at full pressure — he strode over to the ship's side and looking down was appalled to see smoke pouring out of a couple of portholes somewhere aft down by C deck. He turned and ran to the bridge as fast as he could —

but by the time he reached it, the fire alarm was already sounding and the fight had begun. The duty officer was already down at the scene of the fire, the sprinkler system had come into play, and fire parties in smoke helmets and asbestos protective clothing were at work.

But fire is never an easy element to deal with, and in a ship honeycombed with ventilation ducts such as *Leviathan*, once a fire gets hold, its control is very far from being a simple matter of chucking on a few buckets of water, up-ending a few containers of foam, and hoping for the best. Fire creeps in a ship, feeding on paint and dust and stray scraps of material much as it will creep in forest undergrowth, only flaming up in odd bursts and unexpected places. It seems at times as if it has a will of its own, deliberately seeking out the food it needs, and it did not surprise Banks to learn that the paint shop on the next deck below and some further distance aft had already been totally gutted.

Meanwhile Fabian's party had come to an abrupt, hustled end. There was no panic but his guests were hurried off the ship at all possible speed, leaving behind odd gloves, hats, and handbags. Then with that strange compression of time which takes place in a crisis it seemed as if almost at once units of the New York fire department were tearing along to the ship and with them, of course, reporters and photographers and police.

Leviathan lay starboard side to the pier and the fire was raging on the port side, so that fireboats were needed to reach the ship from the basin. A gusty northwesterly wind was blowing down on the ship's port side, which added to the difficulties of maneuvering and tended to drive the fire further into the ship.

By now there was a full emergency on board *Leviathan*. Two of the fire party had succumbed to the fumes and were being treated in the ship's hospital. About thirty cabins, stores, and offices were blazing on three decks before at last the fire was sealed off and began gradually to be brought under control. During the whole of this time Flint and Fabian had paced, separately and together, along the promenade deck, Mott and Susan had collected the most important papers and money in the

Purser's office against a possible abandonment of the ship, Laban had made himself into a kind of one-man collection and distribution point for news on the pier and the great fire aboard *Leviathan* had already taken its place on the front page of the next day's New York and London papers.

By midnight, however, *Leviathan*'s life was out of danger, and though there was considerable damage where the fire had been the ship's seaworthiness was no longer in question. Preparations were therefore continued as before for the ship to sail the next day. At one time it was doubtful if she would get passenger clearance, and to have had to sail empty to England would, indeed, have been a sorry end to her cruise; but after meticulous and repeated examination by the New York harbor authorities throughout the night and the next forenoon, she got a modified clearance, and at two o'clock the next afternoon *Leviathan* sailed. As the last hawser was slipped and the ship began to ease out into the North River, a rather hollow-eyed Mott turned to Susan who was watching at his side and said:

"That was some run ashore we had last night. How do you feel?"

"Terrible, thank you very much," Susan replied, "but what a shame Mr. Grüssli and Madame Klopatsky weren't with us to share in the fun."

"Yes," said Mott, turning to go down below, "and I've no little drinkies with Mrs. Nash to look forward to, either. Grim, isn't it?"

But perhaps the angriest man aboard sat quietly counting his stock of stamps in the first class library and wondering to himself how he could possibly have been so unlucky as to be drinking schnapps with a German Vice-Consul at a club on 14th Street when what was potentially the worst disaster that had happened to *Leviathan* had come and gone without his being in any way responsible and, what was worse, without his being there to exploit it on the spot when it happened. Steward Llewellyn handed out a stamp for a postcard to an elderly lady passenger with his usual glistening smile. His time would come. Sometimes, though, it was very difficult to wait.

THROUGH the summer of 1939 *Leviathan* successfully forged the second uneasy season of her life. By now the novelty had worn off; now from the point of view of the transatlantic passenger trade she was just another liner on a fortnightly service to New York, by now familiar, by now taken for granted while her even bigger consort was being constructed with all possible speed.

To the Admiralty and the Government, however, *Leviathan* was a sizeable problem. Her ninety thousand tons made her a magnificent target. Certainly her speed was an asset. It would cause great difficulties for an attacking U-boat and, unless there were freak weather conditions, would make it unlikely she would be caught by the new German pocket battleships. But she would need cruiser protection, perhaps even battle-cruiser protection in certain circumstances, and that would be expensive and wasteful, especially as the Royal Navy only possessed three capital ships with the requisite speed. A suitable conversion, however, could enormously increase her carrying capacity, so that the pros and cons were about evenly balanced.

To those intimately concerned with *Leviathan* the last summer of the peace, indeed the last few months of a way of life which was never to return, took them all in different ways. Fabian, as head of Transoceanic, found himself co-opted into Ministry of Transport committees, planning the best use not only of his own but of other company ships. He enjoyed this sort of work a great deal. His secretary let it be known that he appreciated the use of his R.N.V.R. rank even though he was only a Commander. He was popular with the Admiralty officials and the naval staff officers he had to work with. He was jovial, if sometimes a little blustery. He was easy to get on with and he "talked the same language," which would certainly not have been the case if Flint had been doing the job. Although it was fashionable to jeer at the "bumbling tea drinkers," there was far more of the Civil Servant in Fabian than there was of the business man. Flint had detested the whole complacent tribe and had never minded saying so but Fabian secretly admired them, and since 1939 was in a sense the beginning of the Civil Service age, he was in his own eyes at least much more suitable for the job than his predecessor.

By midsummer Fabian had been Chairman of the company for six uninterrupted months. He was far more easy-going than Flint had been and, despite that fiction of the ever open door which the old man had propagated, more accessible and amenable. Yet Flint's shadow still fell over everything he did. Even though Flint had first of all gone on the world cruise and had then spent three months in America, the fact that he was still alive, still a director of the company, and still the repository of so much experience, to which Fabian felt he should and did refer in the constantly changing situations of that troubled summer, took away from the absolute authority he longed to possess. Had the roles been reversed there is no doubt that Flint would have gone his own sweet way — as he had done, indeed, when Fabian's father had died. But Fabian did not possess that dictatorial ruthlessness which had made the old man such a law unto himself. He was more of a committee-man, more the leader of a team, and this defect or quality in his nature made it impossible for him to enjoy being "Captain of his ship" as he had for so many years longed to be. The plain truth of the matter was that Fabian was essentially a number two; he never admitted this to himself and, indeed, he had the illusion of being much better at the job than Flint had ever been, but Flint had taken over in an era which was still basically one of cut-throat competition and he had the qualities that era demanded; Fabian was of an altogether gentler mold and he was lucky, in one sense, that the business world of which he was now a leader would soon have to play second fiddle to Government. What would have shown up as mediocrity twenty-five years before, was beginning to be looked on, even by his enemies, as a reasonableness and a willingness to compromise, which the coming war would in any case impose upon them all in the national interest.

Flint had remained in the United States after *Leviathan*'s cruise both because the Labans pressed him to stay, and because he had nothing to go back to England for. Indeed, the private emptiness of his life became publicly apparent during the summer, when he suffered a stroke. It was not a bad one, and the paralysis proved to be only temporary. What did emerge, however, was the utter negativeness of his personal life. Ethel, who looked after him, both when he went to hospital and later during his convalescence, was appalled by the bleakness surrounding the little man.

"I just can't realize he only has one relative in the whole wide world," she told Max after trying to discover if Flint wanted anyone informed of his illness. "His wife's sister, whom he hates and won't have anywhere near him, is the only family he's ever had apart from his wife, and from all accounts he gave her a fairly disagreeable time."

"He was born an orphan," Laban countered. "Maybe if that's how you start that's how you have to go on. I think with him it's always been pretty well deliberate. He never did *have* to be so mean and dried up. That's been his choice for as long as I've ever known him."

"Well I think it's just terribly sad to reach that age and not have anyone at all."

"It's lucky you don't do business with him," Laban remarked dryly, "or you'd find out what a strength it's given him. To be as deprived as he was and still survive — there's nothing much can beat you later on in life."

"What's the point of suceeding in business if you end up alone like that? You've always had a Hitler complex about business success. Thank God you had me to keep your sense of proportion."

"You shouldn't say things like that," Laban said. "I don't care to be compared with Hitler at a time like this."

This kind of exchange always made Ethel sad. She loved her energetic husband very dearly, but nowadays he seemed to be getting increasingly serious and preoccupied, so that at times they talked to each other almost as strangers. She knew, for instance, that his motive in having Flint to stay for so long was far more commercial than personal. He wanted to pick the little man's brains now that he was through with being the company's

Chairman. In fact to have Flint as a kind of captive in his sphere of influence enabled him to speak to the new Chairman with increased authority, and phrases such as "I was talking this over with Sir Josiah the other day," had begun to creep into his letters to Fabian. The departure of Quilly had been every bit as irritating as he had feared. He now had no spy in London or in the Head Office and his relationship with Fabian, who was privately and deeply anti-Semitic, was more remote and formal than with Flint, although the latter had always been a much less predictable person to have to deal with.

Susan, of course, saw Flint during *Leviathan's* visits to New York, first in the hospital and then at the Labans' while he was recuperating. What had begun as pity in her, had become transmuted into a kind of compassion and, as Ethel could see, there was now a genuine affection between them. In this Susan had become the dominating force. Ethel instinctively understood this power but it almost shocked her husband. Susan's candor, her refusal to be browbeaten, and the outspoken things they said to each other at first made Laban uneasy and then, since she seemed always to get away with it, bred in him a new respect for the girl.

To begin with he had thought it bravado, now he saw that it was a real, unbullyable independence. She related things to their proper place. She did not pretend to knowledge or experience which she did not have, and if Flint took advantage of this, she worried away at him until he had explained what was behind a particular problem in a manner she could understand. She seemed to be devoid of false pride. This put her in a strong position with someone like Flint and to a lesser extent Max Laban, one of whose weapons was to assume that a well-aimed jibe at ignorance would disconcert and thus bring an opponent under control. This worked with the faint-hearted, the fickle, and the diffident. It failed completely with Susan.

"I think the girl's so self-confident she's kind of smug," Laban remarked one night to Ethel after Flint had been throwing his weight about in a dictatorial manner which had only made him ridiculous. "I don't see how she dares stand up to him the way she does when she hasn't even been to bed with him. She was talking like she was his wife or his mistress tonight. I can't see why he tolerates it."

"They could both have a sense of humor," Ethel commented, "and anyway she doesn't have to go to bed with him to keep that kind of emotional hold. She's got him in a way he's never been got before."

"You think he's in love with her?"

"He's so mad about her I wouldn't be surprised if he left her all his money."

"I can't see him doing that."

"He has to leave it to someone."

"There's always the orphanage."

"There's always his sister-in-law, but I don't think she's going to be lucky. And she has two grown-up sons, I believe."

Whatever Flint really felt about Susan remained a secret between himself and her. As the summer wore on, though, Susan's own feelings towards her two "beaux" aboard *Leviathan* seemed to develop. At least they deepened towards Mott and they grew away from Charles Beecher, who in any case had now taken up with Veronique Anderson and was to be seen at all hours in her *boutique*, no doubt discussing, as Gloria had once remarked, the exact percentage of profit on a square inch of scarf. This scratchy attitude of Gloria's had stemmed from the very early days when Veronique had let it be known that she was not giving discounts and percentages to members of the crew, her *boutique* being for the passengers, etc., etc., etc.

"That's what a drop of money-grubbing French blood does to you," Gloria snifted. "Just let her come in one day for a facial and see what her bill is from me!"

Veronique had always kept to herself, and perhaps it was a trace in her of Susan's independence which had attracted Charles. At any rate he had begun to pursue Veronique, and at the same time Susan found herself reverting into being a friend. She accepted this at first with a slight twinge of resentment and later on with relief. Charles could keep nothing to himself once the heat was on. He made her his confidante and asked her advice. Occasionally he would be a little shame-faced about it, and once even went so far as to ask if she minded very much that he'd got caught up with another girl — but usually he was far too self-absorbed to bother with Susan's reactions. He took her friendship for granted and trusted her completely, but the candor with which he discussed Veronique and her reactions made Susan ask him one day:

"Did you ever talk like this about me? To anyone else, I mean."

"No, of course not. What an extraordinary question. There *was* no one like you to talk to."

"I'll bet you told someone though. Gloria, for instance."

"*She* knows everything, anyway, that one does," Charles said as though that was a puerile question. "You don't have to tell Gloria things, she just knows."

"You're always saying women are supposed to be the gossips. I think men are far worse."

"It's not the same thing. It doesn't mean anything to a man, I mean when he talks about the women he's slept with — oh! I know it sounds awful saying a thing like that to you, sweety, because in fact you *did* mean an awful lot. But a man will discuss the physical side of making love to different women quite happily over a glass of beer with another man. I don't think women do that among themselves — or at least if they do it's all indirect."

"No, you're right there," Susan said reflecting on this for a moment, "they'd rather show each other the things they've been given, that's their way of bragging, and let the implications remain unsaid. What man did you discuss *me* with over a glass of beer?"

"You're really incredibly persistent," Charles retorted with a touch of annoyance, "I don't know. Motty perhaps."

"Oh! *no*, Charles," Susan wailed, "you didn't talk to him of all people, did you?"

"Not in detail of course,' he said quickly. "It was only in passing. Anyway, he's mad about you, isn't he? He's not the jealous type or I'd never have mentioned a word. He's a good one, is Motty. You can trust him all right."

"You're the limit, Charles, you really are."

"Well, I'm sorry, but I don't see why. We're all friends, aren't we? And you must have — you must know all about him by now, don't you?"

"It's none of your business," Susan said hotly, "and I wouldn't dream of telling you anyway. Is that how you classify all the women you know?"

"Pretty well," Charles said cheerfully, "and it's not such a bad way at that"

"I think you're quite awful — it's just an obsession."

"If it is, sweety, it's a fairly normal and healthy one."

The thought of what he might have said to Motty sent shivers up and down her back. It was as though she'd been going about naked without knowing it, and for a while she felt intensely angry with him. Then one day she asked Motty:

"What did Charles say about me? When he told you about — about us."

"I can't remember," Motty said casually, lighting a cigarette while his brain raced. "He's always talking away about his fabulous conquests — I never listen properly. Most of it's made up anyway. He's a talker, and they aren't the really dangerous ones. You can talk anything into nonsense, if you try. It's the quiet ones you want to worry about."

She didn't believe him, but she felt a little relieved. She knew at any rate that he wouldn't brag or pass things on. Now that she'd been in the ship a year, she had come to admire him very much more. He was a sort of repository of secrets, a role he played without fuss or ostentation. People told him stories and gossip and there it stopped. Perhaps respect and admiration for both his moral courage and the way he bore up under the daily pinpricks of the job was behind her feeling for him as a man.

She liked him and trusted him a whole lot more than she ever had Charles. She enjoyed his being in love with her. It seemed to feed her instead of becoming something she had to resist. He made very few awkward demands and he applied a sense of humor to the situation, so that his feelings were never "a bore." With Charles the business of falling in love had seemed to swamp his whole life. It was either totally black or totally white. Electricity crackled in the air, occasionally making a splendid display but more often discharging itself in pointless storms.

With Motty there were rarely any storms and, although from one point of view, this might be considered a little dull, Susan preferred to have it that way. He was a busy, active, and intelligent man who loved her very much and of whom she was deeply fond, perhaps, even loved. He did not have Charles's explosive gaiety, but on the other hand he was always fun to be with. So as these relationships changed and deepened, the last summer of the peace went on its way.

Captain Banks watched the war coming nearer with a kind of grim restlessness which he found increasingly difficult to bear. The bridge of a ship gives plenty of opportunity for reflection, and with each voyage *Leviathan* completed, the contrast of the luxurious life the passengers led with the realities of the Atlantic Ocean as they were and as they would be in war grew more vivid, more pressing, more difficult to avoid.

He continued to carry out meticulously the passenger responsibilities which a liner captain normally has, but the careful seating of the Captain's table, the daily lunchtime and evening cocktail parties, the gala dinner-dances, the whole intricate apparatus of the entertaining of passengers seemed to Captain Banks, as September 1939 drew nearer, to become almost grotesque. As the caviar was ladled out (about five hundred pounds' worth of it was consumed each trip), as the champagne corks popped and the rich jewelry sparkled in the Starlight Grill, Banks thought not so much of Babylon and Pompeii but of England in 1917, when the U-boats had the country down to a week's stock of food, of the sinking of the *Lusitania,* that single act of brigandage on a defenseless ship full of women and children which more than anything else revealed the real nature of twentieth-century war and the total eclipse of chivalry.

If such Great War barbarities could shatter a century of peace in four short years as they had done, then what horrors could erupt into life in this coming war? How paper-thin was the veneer between civilization and savagery, he reflected, and what was it that separated those two opposite points on the swing of the pendulum? Here were his passengers dressing for dinner — and some of the women changed their dresses five times a day — eating, drinking, and playing like grown-up children day in and day out in their thousands as *Leviathan* wove to and fro across the great ocean — here, each trip, were the same people, it seemed to Banks, but with different faces — the same film star, the same Bishop, the same Yorkshire business man, the same Duchess — all of them dancing unconsciously to the same magician's tune, all of them in a waking sleep almost complacently unaware of the grim invisible powers which moved in their predetermined courses carrying humanity on a tide first one way and then another, each sheep in the magician's flock tricked into the idea that he had free will and was not in fact a sheep but a lion.

There were one or two lions about, one or two people just a little less asleep than the others and Banks watched them pass through *Leviathan* from time to time, always a little detached, a little more wary than the others. But in the end the same flood would engulf them all. He shrugged his shoulders and stared brooding at the vast gray expanse of this ocean which had been so much in his life.

Was this coming war the Flood itself, or merely a foretaste of worse things ahead? "And God said unto Noah, The end of all flesh is come before me for the earth is filled with violence through them; and behold I will destroy them with the earth. . . ." Banks found his thoughts returning time and again in the summer of 1939 to the story of Noah and the Ark. It had always been a favorite of his father's and one of his earliest memories was of the construction of an ark with the cubits reduced to inches and oak instead of gopher wood. He had been seven at the time, and he remembered his father telling him that when he was older he would understand the allegory in another sense, that it was the duty of each human being to construct an Ark in himself, an invisible vessel made of invisible materials, yet none the less more real and durable than gopher wood, into which all that was essential in a man could be put when the flood waters began to rise. But he was too young at seven, so his father said, to understand the great idea behind it; he would have to wait till he grew up. His father never did explain it later on because shortly afterward he died, and from then on Banks had had to think things out for himself.

In company with most men who carry high responsibility on their shoulders, Banks had a deep sense of fate and perhaps what could best be described as a preparedness for death which gave him considerable strength. The bearing of responsibility entails the limitation of what lesser men regard as freedom, but since Banks held strongly to the idea that humanity was as much chained in a cave in 1939 as it was in Plato's time, the *voluntary* acceptance of added burdens meant that in reality his spirit was just a little bit more free.

Since the one certain fact about life is that one dies, it had long seemed to Banks that one should be prepared for this event, and that the best method of doing this was contained in the Christian ideas so clearly set out yet so cleverly disguised in the Gospels. In fact, to learn to die to certain things in life which it lay in man's power to do meant, in Banks's philosophy, that one was taking such sensible steps as one might to survive the actual moment of death. With that in mind it did not seem to him in any way odd that life should be looked on as a re-hearsal for death. The more one could die to the obvious and powerful seduction of life, while still operating fully as a human being, the more watertight one made one's own Ark or soul — the only vessel which could ride out the waters of death.

And death, it seemed to Banks as the summer wore on, was hovering closer and closer over them all. Whether one thought of it romantically as a dark figure in a flowing cloak or arith-metically in terms of statistics, it looked as though death had digested its heavy meal from the 1914-18 war and was now hungry for more. But God had made a covenant with Noah, and the Ark had been saved. As Banks paced up and down *Leviathan's* bridge, he wondered in passing how much of an Ark this great ship would prove to be, and what sort of cove-nant, if any, could be made on her behalf.

The war, when it did eventually begin, changed *Leviathan's* life overnight. To begin with she was diverted to the Clyde, since Southampton was too vulnerable. The first "evacuees" came aboard and from that moment on the accommodation began to stretch. From then on the hedonistic character of the ship progressively disappeared for the duration, and she became what in essence she always had been, a very large, very fast maritime conveyance capable of transporting a whole army division in one single move. For this purpose, however, she would need to be stripped of the rich decorations, the deep armchairs, the thick carpets and the hundred and one other fittings which went to make up the over-all impression of luxury the Transoceanic Company had been at such pains to foster.

On Saturday, 2nd September 1939, though, *Leviathan* sailed in her original state but carrying approximately a thousand over her normal capacity, the majority of these being women and children. She was escorted by two cruisers of the Home Fleet for the first twenty-four hours, and escort was then taken over till mid-Atlantic by a battle-cruiser and her attendant destroyers. From then on *Leviathan* continued alone to New York without incident of any kind.

The day after she sailed England was at war, and that same day the *Athenia* was torpedoed without warning some hundred miles to the south, the first liner casualty of the war and an ominous repetition of German U-boat tactics of the first world war. Banks received this news in grim silence and although, for obvious reasons, he ordered the sinking to be kept secret, within a few hours it was known throughout the ship.

This first wartime trip was in many ways a caricature of *Leviathan's* previous sailings. Though overcrowded, the same high standard of service, the same range of entertainments, indeed even the same carefully prepared cocktail parties took place. But no one really gave it much thought any more. People's minds were on the war and the future, the new anxieties of the British passengers on board began to take over most of their waking thoughts and Americans were divided, as they long had been, between the merits of involvement and isolationism.

Meanwhile *Leviathan* sped west at an average of thirty knots, only a few determined first class passengers dressed for dinner, life boat drills were held twice daily, and everyone wore or carried with them their life-saving jackets at all times. There was an air of tremulous expectation throughout the ship, compounded half of a mental readiness for disaster and half of a feeling of anticlimax when nothing adventurous did in fact happen.

Back in the United Kingdom the expected all-out attack which one school of thought had imagined as Germany's first move did not materialize, and except for a few token air raids, the country got on with the mobilization of its armed forces, the issue of ration books, and its plans for the evacuation of children from the big cities. Over it all lay an air of dulled apprehension, of uncertainty, and of dubious leadership. The contrast with the beginning of the Kaiser's war could not have been greater. Uneasy apathy was the particular mark of the way the Second World War began in Great Britain, a shrug of the shoulders and an attitude of "so what?" being its outward and joyless symbol. The Great War had started as a romantic crusade; the Second as a kind of dazed, irritated duty which was not to blaze up into real fighting anger till the summer of 1940 when Churchill took over the leadership of the country at almost our blackest hour.

The Royal Navy, alone of the three services, had entered the war fully prepared. As early as the 15th June large numbers of reserve officers and men had been called to the colors. The Reserve Fleet, fully manned and exercised, had been inspected by the King on 9th August, and on the 24th of that month the Fleet had been ordered to its war stations, and indeed for some weeks before the actual declaration of war the Home Fleet had been based in all its strength at Scapa Flow. This "finest-tempered instrument of naval war in the world" needed one thing to make it invincible — a First Lord of the Admiralty who knew the service, who knew what he was talking about, and whose personal caliber and that of the eight-hundred-year old Royal Navy he would control would be equally matched. On the evening of Sunday, 3rd September, the first day of the war, it got what it needed expressed in a three-word signal to the Fleet from the Admiralty. This simply said, "Winston is back," and in ships all over the world, both men-of-war and the liners and tramps they were there to protect, hearts bounded and a new pride surged. Whatever else might be wrong, the Navy was ready and Churchill was back at the Admiralty.

Flint had returned to England late in June and had almost at once been asked if he would accept an appointment in the Sea Transport Division of what was to become the Ministry of War Transport. This suited him very well and only the aftermath of his stroke prevented him from taking up his new duties the very next day. The wiry, gnarled old body had a tenacious hold on life and a kind of peasant wisdom which enabled him to know when his doctors were telling him sense and when they were merely "tapping him for fees." He had no illusions about his stroke. He was seventy-three and he knew his days to be numbered, but he also knew that with care he was still capable of great effort and work. Six months' idleness had been more than enough. Now he was rearing to get back to the one thing he loved and upon which he had spent his life — the management of merchant ships belonging to the finest mercantile marine in the world.

Only now instead of merely having one company under his control, he was to have a considerable say in the operation of the twenty-one million tons of the Merchant Navy itself. In this appointment both sides were lucky and, though his character and Churchill's bore no resemblance to each other, his knowledge and expertness in Merchant Navy affairs would be a balancing factor to the new First Lord's control of the Navy. No signal saying "Josiah is at the helm" was made, but friends and competitors alike in British shipping circles and the City of London united in pleasure at his appointment and in certainty that he was the right man in the right job at the right time.

Almost the first thing he did was to have Quilly offered a position as his assistant, the second to try and get Susan appointed his secretary. In this, however, he ran into opposition, both from Fabian and from Susan herself. The former had taken offense at the way Flint had immediately chosen Quilly. Though nothing directly to do with the company, Quilly knew far too much about the way things were done at Transoceanic. He knew the personalities. He knew what was and was not possible. His presence took the edge off Fabian's own committee work at the Ministry, even though they rarely bumped into each other directly. Quilly had always been a dangerous little man, in Fabian's opinion, and he resented the way the same old cabal was being set up indirectly over his head. He did not want to see Susan on that side of the fence and neither he nor the company's Lady Superintendent co-operated when her release was asked for.

To begin with, too, Susan herself had reacted against the suggestion. It was true she was finding her life in *Leviathan* somehow more grueling now that she was into her second year at sea. During the summer she had at last got a little inside cabin to herself but she missed Gloria's rambunctious company, and although she was coming to be known as part of the land-scape among *Leviathan*'s regular passengers, she did not intend to remain a purserette all her life. If there should be a war, she had privately decided to join the Wrens, thus ensuring that if she could not actually go to sea in a warship, at least she would be doing the next best thing. Then out of the blue had come this offer to join Sir J. at the Ministry.

"Dear Susan," Flint had written in a letter she found await-ing her at Southampton early in August, "I have been offered the post of Director of Maritime Planning at the Ministry of Transport, and as such am directly responsible to the Minister who is in turn in the Cabinet. Thus while I have at last realized my ambition of becoming a Civil Servant, I have none of the tribe between me and the top, but shall instead have them under my orders. If war should break out, it will be a responsible, onerous job. I shall enjoy it, of course, but I need assistance. Quilly is joining me next week and I am writing now to offer you the position of personal secretary. The pay would be nomi-nal, since it has to come out of my own allowances and I should not want you to be under any control or supervision from the Civil Service. But I know you will put service to your country above financial considerations. The job will be interesting and in view of the political background in which you grew up, you could be of some help to me, so I trust you will visit me in London during this turn-round in order that we can discuss it further. We shall have to secure your release — or at any rate get you seconded from the company but I do not anticipate difficulties there. Yours, etc., Jos. Flint." He had then added as an afterthought, and Susan smiled at the strain he would have undergone in bringing himself to express such sentiments, "I need hardly remind you of the personal esteem in which I hold you, nor the pleasure it would give me to have you at my side."

She and Motty had planned a theater-going week-end in London together and she took an hour off from this to go and see the old man in the austere flat he had taken in Jermyn Street.

"It's very sweet of you to offer me this job but you know I'm quite happy in *Leviathan,* and if a war does come I'd be joining the Wrens."

"I thought you were fed up with wearing a uniform. This would be far more interesting work."

"It sounds to me as though I'd merely be typing letters all day — and no doubt playing chess all night. I really do hate typing, you know."

"I don't know what you think you'd be doing in the Wrens. Firing the guns? You've got a romantic idea of the Navy."

"I don't see myself as a Lady Admiral in charge of a fleet," Susan said, "but I would at least be a bit nearer the war."

"I thought you'd jump at the chance. Any girl would in your shoes."

"I'm not any girl," Susan said, "and anyway, why should I give up the sea for an office ashore when the pay's so rotten?"

"Well, of course, if you want to bleed me to death, I'll see if the money can be improved. That's not a promise, mind."

"It isn't really that, Sir J., and you know that, too. It's the job that matters. Now if it was some sort of executive job with more responsibility — then that might make a difference, of course."

"Hm," Flint grunted, "up to your old tricks again, aren't you? And what does a slip of a girl, who's been one year at sea in the Purser's department of a liner, think she can offer that's worth an executive job in the Mercantile Marine? I see you've still plenty of nerve, Miss Spicer."

"You don't get anywhere unless you have," Susan said cheerfully; "you said so yourself."

Motty had laughed when she told him of this interview.

"He's right, of course," he said. "I don't think you'll get very far on that tack."

"I wish I'd never touched a beastly typewriter — it's like a chain round my neck."

"It got you to sea in *Leviathan*. You can't have it all your own way."

"At least I can try," Susan said. "It's such a man's world anyway, a girl hasn't much of a chance."

So she stayed on in *Leviathan* to Flint's surprise. He had expected her to put up an initial resistance to the job, but he never doubted she would take it in the end. He'd raise the salary a shilling or two, give in on one or two minor points, but he'd get her in the end. So when the war did come, therefore, and Susan sailed in *Leviathan* to New York, Flint felt he had lost a battle. He did not care to admit — even to himself — that he was wrong but perhaps after all the girl meant what she said. Perhaps after all he would have to arrange a little executive responsibility for her and maybe an assistant to do the letters. On balance it would come to much the same thing, and his determination to get her remained, if anything, strengthened.

On the outbreak of war there were known to be in the United Kingdom some twenty thousand trained and organized Nazis. Neither Mr. Johns, the Cardiff solicitor, nor Steward Llewellyn of *Leviathan* figured on this list, perhaps because Johns had never been connected openly with either the Nazi or the Communist Parties, and Llewellyn had long since turned in his Party Card.

Neither of them, of course, had any idea whether one or the other or both might be on the security list or not. Both took the many careful precautions they had been trained to use, and assumed, until caught, that their interests and affairs remained unknown. Indeed if they were to be in any way effective no other procedure was possible. For a large part of the time Johns got on with the ordinary affairs of his business and Llewellyn continued to be a library steward in *Leviathan* for whom no passenger had anything but praise. During the summer they had had meetings in London and Birmingham and Bristol, never twice in the same place, often with the rendezvous changed at the last moment and with nothing to inquisitive eyes which could connect either with the law, the sea, or subversion. Indeed, people who brushed into them in the pubs and cafés where they met saw only two amateur gardeners, armed with catalogues and trade papers and little diagrams drawn on table tops of asparagus beds and, it might be, cantilevered greenhouses.

Between Johns and Llewellyn, however, there was a cold, disciplined jealousy, and nothing approaching a friendship. Both were at different places in the setup and both were in it for money, though behind Llewellyn's dark eyes there did lie the embers of an adolescent anger at "capitalist oppression." But the organization's money was good, and there was always the prospect of more, especially since the hierarchy had signified its pleasure at the troubles organized in *Leviathan* during the world cruise. The next objective, discussed in a Basingstoke café between Johns and Llewellyn a few days before war broke out, was the total destruction of the ship, preferably at sea so that there could be no question of salvage.

"Pest control takes a lot of money," Llewellyn remarked idly turning over the pages of *The Amateur Gardener*, "and total eradication calls for resources way beyond a gardener such as myself. It's usually necessary to get in a firm of consultants."

"The consultants you mean will be available as soon as the pest control campaign opens — though naturally the pest has to be found before any action can be taken. That and the speed of movement of the pest are the problems of outside control.

A good gardener like yourself would be far better advised to concentrate on attack from within. When rats eat phosphorous poison it burns their insides . . ." then since there was no more danger at the moment of being overheard, Johns dropped the cover talk and continued, "I've had a successful container made in the shape of a box — in fact there are six volumes of the *Encyclopedia of Gardening* which hold enough nitroglycerine to blow the bottom out of the ship. You can store them in that cupboard in the Library which you say is always locked, but the problem of course is the fusing and the placing. This could best be done in New York, but we consider it far more suitable if it takes place at sea. That is the present intention."

"So that I can perish with the ship, I suppose," Llewellyn commented bitterly. "Well you can count that out for a start."

"The fee is twenty thousand pounds in dollars or Swiss francs," Johns remarked tersely. "For money on that scale a certain risk must be taken. I need hardly remind you that in any case the ship is U-boat target number one, and therefore it is fully possible that the result desired may be achieved," he quietly dropped back into the cover story as the waitress brought them more coffee, "by outside pest control at no additional cost. Anyway, I'll be sending you the *Encyclopedia* the day after tomorrow — so at least you'll have it on hand."

Thus when *Leviathan* sailed on 2nd September 1939 she carried with her in a locked cupboard in the library enough high explosive to blow her to pieces, but as yet the method by which this objective was to be attained had not been worked out. Llewellyn continued to issue library books and sell stamps with his usual bland assurance, but inside himself he felt a fear and anxiety to a degree he had never before experienced. On no previous occasion had he ever been so desperately committed nor in such personal danger. He had frequently visualized a situation such as this in the past, imagining he would be able to take it in his stride. When it actually happened, however, he found his courage deserting him and the *Encyclopedia* in the bottom left-hand side of the cupboard becoming an obsession both in his waking thoughts and in his dreams.

So *Leviathan* duly reached New York, berthing as usual at the Transoceanic Pier after her first wartime crossing. For the moment she was safely out of range of enemy aircraft, mines, and U-boat torpedoes. She emptied herself of her passengers and for a while there was a pause. Her future had not been decided, and in the meantime intense activity took place at home as convoy plans and the whole apparatus of control of the Merchant Navy were put into force.

While the country mobilized and the Army and Air Force were brought up to fighting strength, while barrage balloons made their appearance over the great cities of England, while the British Expeditionary Force was being prepared to take its place on the Western Front, it was on the Royal Navy alone at this time that the burden of active fighting fell.

Overwhelmingly superior in strength and numbers to the German Navy with which Hitler started the war, with Italy and Japan still uneasily neutral, the Royal Navy's task was primarily to face "enormous and innumerable duties rather than an antagonist" as Churchill put it. From the first hour of the war the Admiralty became the active center of events.

Numbers of German U-boats had been in their prearranged positions on 3rd September and within the first four days had accounted for three important ships off the coast of Spain in addition to the liner *Athenia*. Outward-bound convoys were brought into force immediately and by 16th September the first homeward-bound convoys had sailed from Freetown and Nova Scotia. By the end of September convoys were in regular operation outward from the Thames and Liverpool and inward from Halifax, Freetown, and Gibraltar.

Nevertheless, by this time twenty-nine British and fifteen neutral and Allied Merchant ships of a total tonnage of 185,000 had been lost. Although these figures were considerably less than Hitler was entitled to expect, with suprise on his side, they were nevertheless enough to bring into acute focus the central problem the Royal Navy had to solve — the general continuance of Britain's world-wide trade without interruption or hindrance, and in particular the supply to the British Isles of the vast material needed to survive and later on to win the war. In this *Leviathan* was later on to play a considerable part. For the present, however, she was to be kept secure but idle alongside her pier in Manhattan. Her time was yet to come.

⚓⚓⚓⚓⚓ XIII ⚓⚓⚓⚓⚓

F ROM being perhaps the most publicized ship in the world, *Leviathan* became the most mysterious. As long as she remained at her pier in New York there could merely be speculation as to the changes being wrought inside her hull but every move she made into the stream was clouded in rumor, a good deal of it deliberately false.

This was a new and at first unnatural function for Laban but he was soon putting as much energy and enthusiasm into keeping her name out of the Press as previously he had put into the glamour buildup. Though *Leviathan* was a British ship in a neutral port, a benevolent wink from the authorities allowed the regulations to be read as leniently and as much in her favor as they could possibly be.

Indeed, *Leviathan*'s speed and capacity was later on to become a major asset in the Battle of the Atlantic. But before this came about the whole of her interior accommodation needed to be changed. An ability to carry over two thousand passengers on carefully scaled degrees of luxury, was modified to transport a possible fifteen thousand soldiers and their equipment in one lift.

Carpets, chairs, curtains, decorative panels, and show cases were all removed and carefully stored. Row after row of tiered bunks together with washing and toilet facilities were installed. The main restaurant was converted into a self-service cafeteria which would eventually serve two meals per person throughout the twenty-four hours.

In the initial stages, however, there was no question of transporting such vast numbers, for the simple reason that the carrying capacity of a ship is normally limited by the lifeboats and rafts on board; the very outside figure *Leviathan* could take was set at eight thousand. The other limiting factor which reduced this figure still further in the early days was the supply of fresh water on board. This is a problem in any ship though not so acute, perhaps, on a short Atlantic crossing as it is on longer tropical voyages. The War Office, however, had laid down a scale of eight gallons of fresh water per head per day for all troops embarked, and this resulted in less than four thousand being carried on any one trooping trip during the first eighteen months of the war.

Control of the great ship, of course, passed from the company to the Government, though she continued to be manned and administered by Transoceanic. During the twilight war, as it was called by some, or the "phony" war, as it was by others, *Leviathan* remained on the eastern seaboard of the United States.

Indeed there was considerable argument in the beginning against converting her at all, since the spirit of Munich died hard, and until the spring of 1940 there was still a body of opinion which fancied that a deal would be made with Hitler, and that German military efforts until then (including even the destruction of Poland) were more or less in the nature of a large scale bluff.

During this first winter of the struggle there were two factors in the war at sea which made it basically different from the 1914-18 war. One was aerial bombing and the other was the magnetic mine. Both these factors caught the British inadequately prepared, but the chance recovery in December 1939 of an unexploded magnetic mine enabled the "wiping" and "de-gaussing" of ships to be undertaken with a fair chance of protection. The "wiping" of a ship of *Leviathan*'s size was not practicable and so another modification that was installed during the first couple of months of 1940 was the thick electric girdle running round the inside of her hull which neutralized her magnetic field.

These first few months of the war saw many changes, also, among *Leviathan*'s officers and crew. It had always been company policy to encourage its personnel to join the Royal Naval Reserve, and as a result the greater part of its fleet was proudly entitled to fly the Blue Ensign. But almost at once the problem of dilution arose — trained officers were wanted for war ships of the Reserve Fleet coming into commission and at the same time the company's ships had to be able to go to sea.

Whereas under normal conditions sailing schedules had been known a year in advance, it was now quite possible that *Leviathan* might have to sail at a few hours' notice to the other side of the world with a half-trained crew. Until now the company had been in such a strong position that it could select and accept officers and men who had done their training elsewhere. Thus Transoceanic got the very top of the cream. Overnight this changed, and Banks realized that when they did next go to sea a greater strain than ever would fall on the experienced officers who remained.

For the moment though, the problem was principally one of boredom and frustration, a feeling that *Leviathan* was out of it all here in New York, that the war was being settled elsewhere — which was certainly true — and that because of her size the ship would never be risked in the way that other liners were — which was an assumption only partially true.

Charles had been appointed away before *Leviathan* had left England on the 2nd September, being now a watchkeeping officer in a County Class cruiser. Four other deck officers and seventeen engineer officers had also been snatched away by a rapacious Admiralty. Banks had been left, but his Staff Captain had gone. Mott was still there, but his second purser, Kennicote, and George Stone's second steward had both left the ship. Jimmy Johnson was still in the Observation Bar with no customers to serve. Llewellyn was still in the first class library with no passengers asking for books. Finally, by Christmas, Susan left to join the Women's Royal Naval Service, her departure seeming, at any rate to Mott, to set the seal on the end of the ship's "decorative" career. Mr. Leviathan's Luxury Floating Hotel was a thing of the past, the Giant High Speed Crate her new role for the duration.

Before Susan went, however, two developments took place which affected both her private and public lives. The first of these was that she met, fell badly in love with, and very nearly married a young Bostonian up at Oxford called Philip Storm, a cousin of Hamilton Codde, who had come back to the States on *Leviathan*'s last voyage because his father was dying but who was so pro-English that he had every intention of returning there as a volunteer. The second was the accidental unmasking of Llewellyn, and the discovery of the *Encyclopedia of Gardening*.

This took place after *Leviathan* had been nearly three weeks in New York and happened so casually that the effect on Susan, on Mott, and even on Banks was shattering, and from then on the incident and its possibilities made frequent unwelcome appearances in their dreams. To Banks, minded as he was, the discovery was a clear Act of God; to Susan and Mott, to Stone and the Master-at-Arms and, indeed, to the U.S. security forces, it was one of those million to one quirks of Fate which are inexplicable on logical grounds, yet which seem never to be far away from events on which history hinges.

After it was over Susan kept thinking that she must unconsciously have been suspicious of Steward Llewellyn all along, but she had honestly to admit that this was not so. The discovery of the *Encyclopedia*, therefore, was pure accident and came about because one forenoon she was combing through the library for a book she wanted and finding a cupboard locked, as indeed was normal practice, she turned to ask the steward to open it, finding she was alone in the place. Llewellyn, in fact, had been summoned to the Chief Steward's office on some routine query and had left his bunch of keys by the catalogue on his desk.

Susan waited a moment or so for him to return and then when he did not do so she impatiently opened the cupboard to get at the book she wanted. Curiosity then took her a stage further. One of the standing complaints in *Leviathan* was that new books for which there was a queue were always being hidden away and unfairly distributed. With this thought in mind, it occurred to Susan to have a quick look in another cupboard down by the Steward's desk to see which books were currently being held back from general circulation.

It took her a moment or so to find the right key and when she did open the cupboard she found only some *Encyclopedia of Gardening* stuffed away at the back, a tin cash box and the folder of stamps which Llewellyn habitually used. This was a disappointing return for such illicit curiosity and Susan began to feel a little guilty at prying as she had done. She locked the cupboard and was just returning the keys to the desk when Llewellyn returned, catching her in the act. The color seemed to drain from his face and he became suddenly and violently angry. In fact for a moment or so he lost control and accused Susan in raging terms of poking her snotty little nose in where it had no business to be.

Susan knew she was in the wrong but she was astonished and upset by the violence of this outburst and though Llewellyn apologized gruffly before she left the library, he had let himself go with such extraordinary force that Susan began to be suspicious. She turned it over in her mind for a few minutes on getting back to the office and was thinking about reporting it to Motty when the Purser came in himself, took one look at her and asked if she was feeling ill.

"You're as white as a dodo," he said briskly. For some reason dodos were always white in Mott's mythology, just as coots were always queer. "What's the matter? Been seeing a ghost?"

"No," Susan said a bit shakily, "and I don't suppose it's of the slightest importance, but I've just had a strip torn off me by Steward Llewellyn."

"Is that all?" Mott scoffed. "Well, well, well, I expect you can arrange a return match if you're feeling vindictive."

"It's not that," Susan said, "it's just that I don't understand why he should have got all at once into such a terrible rage. We've always been the best of good friends up to now."

"I should forget it," Mott said. "Everyone has a lapse or a liver attack from time to time. Unless you want to make it a matter of discipline, of course."

The trouble was she couldn't forget it. She brooded about it the rest of the morning, trying to find a reason for Llewellyn's extraordinary outburst. That was really what gnawed at her — there was no *reason* in it at all. Then suddenly it seemed odd

274

to her that there should be four volumes of a book of reference on gardening tucked away in that cupboard. Why gardening? What was that to do with the sea? And if that was supposed to be for the passengers' benefit why was it hidden away in a cupboard? She went along and confided her doubts to an unsympathetic Mott.

"Really, Susan, I don't know what's got in you, making this mountain out of a molehill. Leave it alone. Forget it, for heaven's sake, the poor chap probably got on the wrong side of George Stone, that's all — and you're not far off getting on the wrong side of me if it comes to that."

But the morning's event had begun a ferment in Llewellyn as well. The strain of knowing what he had brought on board, and of the fact that he could be hanged for doing so, apart from possibly blowing himself up in the process, had preyed deeper and deeper into his mind for the last three weeks. Despite all the self-control he could muster he was in a highly jumpy state, as unstable as the nitroglycerine in the cupboard which was causing him such concern.

He had never had to take on such a big assignment as this before. It terrified him. He could not sleep, he was off his food and his temper became so ragged, he knew, sooner or later, it would let him down. To leave his keys out of his possession for five minutes, even while he washed, was something he never did — never normally considered possible — and to have left them that morning as he had done and then to find that damned girl prying about in his cupboard was the last straw.

The plan had been to destroy *Leviathan* at sea but he had not been given the tiny detonators needed until the ship had arrived at New York. No one knew when and under what conditions they would next go to sea, and in any event Llewellyn preferred not to be aboard when the explosion took place.

He realized that Susan had been poking about in his cupboard, but he did not know how much she had seen nor what she suspected. The astonished look on her face, though, when he had blown his top was a warning to him that he had aroused a dangerous curiosity and a resentment, the settlement of which might lead straight to disaster.

Late in the morning, therefore, he decided to get out while the going was good. He fitted the pencil detonators, adjusted the fuse for twelve hours later, and then left *Leviathan* for ever. He carried with him his "escape" papers showing him to be a Canadian domiciled in Vancouver. Picking up a suitcase of clothes at an address in Greenwich Village he took a Greyhound bus headed west for St. Louis and California.

Meanwhile at the Transoceanic pier the safety of *Leviathan* hung on the thin thread of Susan's uneasy, unsatisfied curiosity. Mott had scoffed at her suspicions and there was no one else she felt like discussing it with; indeed, there was nothing to discuss, it was simply something she did not understand which made her restless and uneasy.

In a more general sense Susan had other things on her mind as well. The first and continuing problem was of getting back to England and into the Wrens. She had tackled the Consul-General about this one night at a cocktail party at the Labans, but there was very little he could do to help. She had to be released from company service and then somehow or other get back to England. Mott did not want to lose her for both personal and official reasons, but he passed on her request to the Captain, who gave it his blessing. So far as Banks was concerned the fewer women aboard his ship the better. She had also written to the Director of the Women's Royal Naval Service at the Admiralty but in those early disrupted weeks of the war, she did not really expect an answer and when one had eventually come, it had only confirmed what she already knew — that she must somehow or other get back to England and take it up there.

On top of all that there was this whirlwind affair which Philip Storm had occasioned. Mott sensed what had happened almost at once, and his efforts to keep out of the way and not interfere gave Susan more heartache than anything else. It was one of "those" situations, understood by all three of them, but none the less inevitably painful. In fact, Mott's acceptance of it made it in some ways more difficult to bear. "If only he'd get good and mad and take a poke at you," Susan told Philip one night, "it would clear the air a damn sight better — but it's just not in Motty's character to behave like that." "And if I could really hate the guy, that, too, would help," Philip had agreed, "but I can't. I like him enormously and I think he does me."

In the ordinary course of events Susan would have gone ashore in the afternoon of the day the bomb was discovered. But Philip was up in Boston with his father and she did not feel in the mood for another of Ethel Laban's parties. Joan Mitchell had gone to Canada *en route* to England and Susan had decided to have a cozy evening aboard, washing her hair and writing some letters. But the morning's episode would not leave her alone. So in the first dog watch she decided on impulse to go and see Steward Llewellyn and find out the truth for herself. But the library was locked and Llewellyn had gone ashore.

Had Susan been anyone but Susan she would simply have shrugged her shoulders and given it up. But the streak of dogged obstinacy in her drove her to discover that it was not Llewellyn's turn for shore leave and that he had left before lunch on the excuse of seeing a friend of his in the newspaper kiosk on the pier. This was technically improper, but since Steward Llewellyn was not on the list of ship "skates," he had been allowed ashore. As he hadn't returned, however, the Master-at-Arms had begun to be suspicious and by the time Susan came up with her inquiry, an investigation had already taken place and a report been made to the Chief Steward and the Chief Officer. He would certainly be "in the rattle" now when he returned.

The instinct which had driven Susan thus far now seemed in her own eyes fully justified and once again she braved an interview with Motty. This time she was not to be laughed or jeered out of it, and since she was not normally a person to panic, Mott bestirred himself, sent for Stone, checked up on the facts and at Susan's suggestion decided to have the cupboard in the library opened. Privately he still thought it a lot of fuss about nothing but when the cupboard was eventually opened and the bomb discovered, events happened so quickly there was scarcely time for surprise. There in front of their eyes lay a bomb with the detonator in place and the silent fuse, which was of the type where acid eats its way through a wire, already partially corroded. After a second's stunned silence, Mott ordered everyone out of the library, left the Master-at-Arms on guard and raced to the nearest telephone to inform the Captain.

Banks, who was in the process of changing into plain clothes to go ashore, was literally caught with his trousers down. Struggling back into them and snatching up his monkey jacket, he sped down to the library, crept in, took one look at the infernal machine and then slipping out as softly as he had entered, ordered *Leviathan* to emergency stations. With the library as the center of an ever widening circle everyone in the ship was ordered to evacuate to the pier, under the direction of the Chief Officer; meanwhile, Banks himself returned to the library.

Now there was a stillness and a quiet in the room which Banks, more alert and alive than he had ever been in his life, found miraculously matched in himself. He became like a huge silent cat moving almost weightlessly about the library for all his great girth, picking up an armchair as if it were made of matchwood so that he could lie on the deck and get to work dismantling a bomb he knew nothing about and which might at any moment explode in his face.

Now enclosed in a kind of breathless calm he felt the close presence of the Angel of Death, as he had done once before at Jutland. There was an immediacy here in this room, hovering, watching as Banks's huge hands and somewhat pudgy fingers felt their way round the *Encyclopedia of Gardening* easing it out of its shelf and then on to the deck, one sharp movement of any kind meaning the end of himself and the ship and perhaps of that part of New York.

By this time everyone aboard *Leviathan* except engine room, deck, and radio watchkeepers had been hustled ashore and moved off the pier. Very naturally the sudden exodus of hundreds of men, some of them half dressed, caused attention both by the police and a little later by the Press. Thus, while Banks was trying to work out whether the detonator unclipped or unscrewed, and having decided it screwed, was then discovering that it had been inserted at an angle and that the screws had been partially stripped, a general alarm was being raised on neighboring piers, traffic nearby was being diverted — and since it was the rush hour, the chaos was considerable. Meanwhile Susan had phoned Max Laban and soon the top brass in the police, the port, and the city of New York were all aware of *Leviathan*'s bomb.

It took Banks nearly an hour to ease the detonator out of the bomb and get the fuse into a bucket of water. By the time he had done this he was drenched in sweat, as if he had spent the time in a Turkish bath. Moreover there was no certainty that this was the only bomb on board. As soon as the immediate panic was over, therefore, Banks and the American security officials who had now arrived in strength instituted an intensive search throughout the ship, and in the meantime the F.B.I. broadcast Llewellyn's description throughout the United States, and the hunt was on. By midnight no other bomb had been discovered and *Leviathan* reverted to normal, at any rate in outward appearances. In reality, though, this had been the closest shave yet to those who knew the facts.

Philip Storm's father and grandfather had been lawyers, and this was what Philip himself intended to be. After Harvard and a couple of years at Oxford, Philip would normally have settled into the Boston office, as his father had done before him, marrying a suitable girl from a New England family and in turn producing a family.

But this was 1939 and all sorts of lives both in England and America were being disturbed. His first graduate year at Oxford had been far from tranquil, culminating as it had in the outbreak of the European war on one side of the Atlantic and his father's serious illness on the other. Then on the passage across Susan had entered his life, and from that moment he was decided upon two things — to marry Susan and to return to England and join the R.A.F. or the Navy.

But between a decision of that kind and its execution lay as many frustrations and difficulties as Susan herself was to undergo before finally becoming a Wren. If it was difficult for

Susan as a volunteer abroad to rally round the flag, it was considerably harder for Philip to do so round someone else's flag. But he had a strong sense of pattern. Once decided on what was right for himself, he was not to be thwarted. All the Storms had strong wills, but this will power, which in his ancestors had taken the family to its present prosperity, was in Philip's case a fledgling.

With his father dying and his mother firmly set against any of her children fighting in any war, let alone one that was no direct concern of America's, he had to be very careful in the way he went about putting such a decision into practice. Luckily he had a younger brother who had just entered the law firm, two sisters at home, and an uncle who was his father's partner and who could keep an eye on family affairs in Boston. He could be spared, and his mind was made up.

During the last three months of 1939, therefore, Philip became almost a commuter between Boston and New York where Susan was and between Boston and Montreal where the process of "fiddling" his way into the Royal Canadian Navy was taking place. On two of these trips Susan got leave and went with him, returning via Boston where she met his family. By this time he had asked her to marry him and she had accepted, but they had decided to keep this a secret for the present and defer it until there was at least a chance of being together.

Now that she had met someone she really did want to marry, it seemed somehow typical and familiar to Susan that it should be hedged around with difficulties. It was as if something inside her knew more or less what was to happen, as if her life at this time was a kind of maze through which she had to feel her way by trial and error. It seemed ironic to her as well that just as Charles had confided in her as a friend once the passion between them had gone and he was newly absorbed in Veronique, so now she should find herself behaving in the same way with Motty.

"Only Charles, of course, was hotheaded and jealous," she said, the night her release from Transoceanic came through and she was free to go back to England, "whereas you're a calm old bird I can say almost anything I like to without feeling I'll be breaking your heart."

"I don't think I've a heart left to be broken," Mott said, "and anyway you were always careful about other people's feelings."

"You've got a heart all right," Susan said; "the trouble is me. I really don't see myself settling down with the diapers; I enjoy this sort of life far too much, and I dote on my independence."

"You think you'll be able to keep it if you marry Mr. Storm?"

"Oh, sort of," Susan said. "I'd have kept it if I'd married you but I shouldn't have gone on in this job. With the war on, though, and Philip at sea as he probably will be, it's really a question which doesn't arise."

"If you think like that there's scarcely any point in getting married, is there? Not that I'm trying to put you off . . ."

"No," Susan said cheerfully, "when I think it out with my mind there doesn't seem to be any point in marriage at all — not as things are — but I expect we'll go ahead just the same."

"Then you must really love him, Susan," Mott said quietly.

"I think I do," she said, and then after a slight pause, "I wish it could have been you."

"So do I," he shrugged his shoulders. "But there it is. At my ripe old age you only survive if you don't fight about the things you know you can't have."

"Perhaps you'll have something else instead just as good. After all I wasn't the first girl in your life."

But Mott only smiled and poured out another drink.

"Well, anyway, Susan, *Leviathan* won't be the same without her one and only purserette, so you'd better come back as a Wren."

"I'll be back," Susan said, though without much conviction. "I don't know how or when, but come back I shall."

The Labans gave a cocktail party for Susan's departure, and here too there was an overlying air of change, of sadness, and of something having come to an end. All the old friends and acquaintances were there, from Jackson Levine to Blossom who was again in New York with Lord Harborough staging the inevitable success at one of Ethel's brother's theaters. Mrs. Klopatsky and two other prominent passengers from the world cruise showed up under Hamilton Codde's aegis, and the head of Lapolux, whose business was shrinking day by day, was nevertheless in his sunniest mood since it was through him that Susan had met Philip Storm.

Jimmy Johnson did the drinks, Laban made a speech recalling some of *Leviathan*'s big moments and linking Transoceanic's "star hostess" with them, Captain Banks wearing the ribbon of the D.S.O. on his uniform, newly awarded for the bomb episode, condescended to put in an appearance, and the Purser's department on board presented Susan with a naval brooch to which they had all subscribed. Even Mr. Saxburger and Gloria had been brought along, and it gave Susan quite a pang to see her old cabinmate now swathed in mink but otherwise unchanged, except for an inch or two on the waist and the trace of a transatlantic accent.

"You know something, honey," Gloria confided to her at a quiet moment in the party, "I envy you going home to England. In fact I've been on the point of packing it all in and doing the same myself. Can't sit around here in New York with all that lot going on back home, can you?" she asked rhetorically, fingering the diamond and ruby plaque hanging round her neck like a badge of office. "I mean a girl gets restless, doesn't she, when she has it too good for too long? The trouble is Art and I have gotten so goddamned fond of each other, I can't make the break. You see, he's never *not wanted* to get divorced for such a long time before and it worries him, if you see what I mean. He keeps saying he must be getting old — well, of course really he is, but he says he's never been so fond of any of his wives before and I suppose I feel the same. One of these days, though, I'll just up and go. Do you think I'd get into the Wrens? And what as, for heaven's sake — a beautician?"

Altogether it was a nostalgic evening. Special security dispensation had been given so that the party could be held on board in the "old" Observation Bar, nowadays deserted, through the windows of which West Side Manhattan could be seen. But already those square ports had wartime deadlight shutters on the outside, blackout material draped the doorways and the possible escape of any pinpoint of light at sea was, so far as Susan could make out, over prevented. Already the gay stools and tables had gone, the semicircular gallery being turned into a briefing and lecture room. The decorative panel behind the bar had been covered by a blackboard and rows of close-packed school-type benches suggested a mixture of station waiting-room and university lecture hall.

"It won't be the same without you, miss," Jimmy said during one of the lulls, and then with a deprecative gesture at his old bar, "well — it isn't exactly the same now, is it? And you've seen a few parties here in your time."

She had indeed, but now in the ship's new role, with the interior fittings gone and the outside already a naval gray, it needed an effort to remember those hot tropical evenings on the cruise, now nearly a year ago, with the shoals of flying fish leaping and darting over the waves, with Mr. Grüssli in his toga and the ill-fated Neils Jörgenson weaving his way among the widows, with Motty giving her a quick drink before she went up top for the evening game of chess with Sir J., with the strange chaos of "mutiny morning," and now so very recently the discovery of Llewellyn's bomb. Tomorrow she would be aboard the old *Pluto* bound for England, the war, and a new life. No one knew what would happen to *Leviathan*, where the great ship would go, nor what she would do, but the thought of saying good-by to her tomorrow, possibly for ever, gave Susan the sort of pang she had not felt since leaving home for her first days at a boarding school.

She looked across the room. Motty was talking to Philip, and idly she wondered what was going on in their minds, without feeling impelled to go across and find out. "Mr. Leviathan," alone of the people she had known connected with the ship, had grown in stature in her eyes. There was the Captain, of course, but in fairness Banks must be excluded from the field since, after all, no one knew Banks as a man — he was simply the remote and all-powerful Captain. All the others had shrunk somewhat on getting to know them better.

Everyone told her *Leviathan* would not be the same without her. But what did that mean, and who knew what anything was going to be like? Perhaps Ethel Laban, her original staunch friend and ally, intended it more sincerely than the others and catching her eye she went across to talk to her now.

"I should hope your ears are burning," Ethel said with a smile. "A whole heap of nice things have been said about you tonight."

"That's just because you're getting rid of me for good and all."

"Oh, you'll be back," Ethel shot her one of her sharp comprehensive looks. "I'm not mad about Boston in the ordinary run of events — neither is Max — but we both like your Philip Storm. I'm glad you'll be marrying an American."

"That's not on the schedule as things are at present. Not yet anyway."

"You were never a girl for the schedule," Ethel said with a laugh, "go ahead and marry him as soon as you can. That's Momma's advice. I had a letter from Joan this morning. She seems to enjoy being a Naval V.A.D., but says she's already homesick for New York. I miss her, too. She was kind of 'comfortable' to have around."

"I wonder how you'll classify me when I've gone."

"Well, certainly not as 'comfortable.' You brighten things up. Max is going to miss recommending you to passengers for 'the special treatment' — but then as there aren't any passengers any more . . ." she finished it off with a shrug and a sigh. "I wish we could all see more than two inches in front of our noses. Max says the U.S. is bound to get into the war but the climate isn't right as yet — whatever that means. I used to get good and mad about it all. Now I don't seem to care very much one way or the other. And that's bad, Susan, that's bad."

"In that case you must be a member of what my father calls 'the modern generation' — he's always saying the spirit of the age is 'couldn't care less' and it's the end of the Empire. But I think the poor old Empire has been coming to an end for so long, it isn't dying at all. In fact, just you wait and see how we all pull ourselves together when the crisis comes."

"What crisis? Your war's been running three months already and everyone seems to take it for granted — I mean the sort of stalemate it's in — like *Leviathan* being kept here idle in New York."

"Oh! I expect there'll be a crisis just as soon as I get into the Wrens," Susan said with a little smile, "anyway — as you say — who cares? I'll see what can be done to liven things up."

The next day at noon Susan sailed from New York in the *Pluto*. It was a bright, cold December day, and Manhattan seemed to sparkle in the crisp sunlight. All the good-bys now had been said and although she knew Philip was in the small crowd on the pier she could no longer see him, nor the figures on *Leviathan* across the basin, among whom no doubt would be a pensive Mott.

As the *Pluto* drew out stern first into the Hudson, turned and headed for the open sea, she took a last look at the great ship now oddly drab and forlorn in her gray paint. What a change was there from the smart spanking liner of only a few months ago — when the pressure of the schedule was on and every moment counted both at sea and in her harbor turn-rounds.

Now, somehow, she looked almost forgotten and neglected. She had been so brilliantly the center of gravity in the Western Ocean, which was itself the center of gravity of the liner trade of the world, that to see her lying there now in company with other giant liners, similarly idle, was to be vividly reminded that — for the present at any rate — the limelight was elsewhere, on Europe, on the war, on the submarine-infested Western Approaches to the British Isles.

The *Pluto*'s cargo holds were full but her passenger accommodation was almost empty. It was strange to be going to sea not in *Leviathan*, and strange, too, to be heading north for Nova Scotia where the ship was to pick up her convoy instructions. Mott had got her a splendid stateroom and she knew a number of the officers on board the old liner, but she still found it hard to realize that she had left *Leviathan*, perhaps for ever.

Even though sailing days, and the partings they entailed, had become a familiar event in her life she was always affected by them. Now as, mechanically and in a dream, she attended her lifeboat drill and settled down into being a passenger in another ship, her thoughts and feelings still revolved round *Leviathan*, and the sadness of saying good-by. "You'll be back," they had all continued to say right up till the end, and who knows? Perhaps she might. Even Banks had unbent a little when she went to take her leave of him and the ship.

"Well, madam," he'd said giving her hand the usual abrupt shake, "to begin with I viewed your presence in this ship with grave misgiving. I can only say, now, that you've done the job much better than I expected, very much better indeed. I'm sorry to see you go, madam, and I trust we shall have the opportunity of serving together again when the war is over. I wish you good luck in the Ladies' Navy."

Then, with a curt nod and a twinkle, she had been dismissed. She had smiled a little ruefully as she made her way down from the Captain's cabin. She might have a visible effect on men as different as Flint and Charles Beecher, she had never at any time made the slightest impression as a woman on Captain Banks. He had remained exactly as he had seemed when she had first approached him all that time ago while he was examining the dragon mural in the main restaurant.

Correct, detached, and fully aware in any situation at any moment of being a Captain in command of a ship, his inner thoughts remained inscrutable and hidden. Long ago Ethel Laban had recounted their visit to the Sussex cottage, and ever since she could visualize Brynhild and her flurrying and scurrying; but apart from that she had no more idea of Captain Banks's private life, now that she had left the ship, than when he had first come aboard and taken over command. Well . . . all that was now in the past. The old *Pluto* rolled and creaked her way north through the cold December sea so much slower and somehow fussier than *Leviathan* — and there she was being carried back to England, away from it all, and yet in a different sense back to it all, to start another cycle of experience.

Back on board *Leviathan* Mott threw himself with far more vigor than usual into the daily routine. Without Susan dodging about somewhere in the offing, the ship seemed emptier than ever before and this comparative idleness in which he was now a prisoner had a corrosive effect on his spirits. The Battle of the River Plate and the sinking of the *Graf Spee* earlier in December had sparked off in him a desire to get on with the job — any job so long as it was something to do with the war. That night he was asked to a cocktail party at the British Club and friends had invited him to stay the week-end at a village up the Hudson. He had accepted both invitations but he knew that neither would help him escape his heaviness of heart. Susan had gone. No longer would she be at her little desk looking up with a smile as he came into the office, nor would she be around for the odd drink or the unplanned run ashore. The first few days after she had gone were as depressed and tasteless as any he could remember. He felt old and wearied to his teeth with routine.

Six days later, as the so-called fast convoy in which R.M.S. *Pluto* was included approached the northern coast of Ireland, three ships were torpedoed, among which was the *Pluto* herself. This took place at five o'clock on a squally, black morning and within seconds of the explosion, the old ship had heeled over badly to port and was clearly sinking. Susan had been thrown out of bed but quickly scrambled into some trousers and a sweater and then, struggling into her life jacket, made her way as best she could to her boat station, which was on the starboard side. As she got out on deck it was obvious that the starboard lifeboats would never be launched and then, the order to abandon ship having been given, she found herself carried off down to the port side in what, in the darkness, seemed like near panic.

All the time the old liner was settling down in the water, as she did so heeling over more and more to port. The lifeboats on that side had all been got away and people were jumping in after them and scrambling down the falls. For a moment or so she thought this would be the end. It was so dark she could not even see how far below the sea might be but she knew she would have to jump for it.

She hesitated for a second or two and then found her mind made up for her by a greaser yelling at her in no uncertain terms to get on and jump or she'd go down with the ship. So, in the grip of a terror she never forgot the rest of her life, she leaped as hard as she could, bundled herself into a ball as she jumped and after a timeless drop hit the water with a paralyzing smack. The force of this impact carried her under the sea and in rising to the surface, she nearly choked. Moreover the panic was still there in the sea since she was only a few feet from the ship and unless she could get away, she would be sucked down as the ship sank.

All around her were men and women struggling as she was to get away from the ship's side in a sea which was not only rough but numbingly cold. She gasped and spluttered and at one stage felt she would have to give up, but the life jacket kept her afloat and after the early spasms of panic had passed a kind of inevitability possessed her which brought its own strength. If this was the end, then this was the end, and there was nothing she could do about it.

The picture of *Leviathan* set in clear sunlight against the New York skyscrapers suddenly came into her mind and its incongruity nearly forced her to laugh. She thought of the spacious settees, the potted palms in the Garden Lounge, the smooth-running elevators and the smart crowd in the Veranda Grill — and then of herself floundering in this icy sea. Those months in New York she had wanted to get into the war and do something useful were now being requited.

At that moment as the cold began chilling her bones, she was in the war all right, no doubt about that. How ironic it was and what a tiny gap lay between the warm comfortable routine of life on board a luxury liner and this . . . how Motty would smile, and Jimmy Johnson as he stirred the martinis in the Observation Bar, how easy it would be just to drop off and never wake up . . . but as this thought came into her mind, so also came a warning that this was one thing now she must fight; here, bobbing about in the sea, she must struggle against a drowsiness of mind, struggle somehow or other to keep awake, or perhaps she really might drop off for good.

This effort of will which she now called up in herself with so much difficulty produced an instant and almost miraculous result. Numbed dead in body her mind came alive with a detached intensity she had never experienced before. Suddenly she became aware of and at the same time seemed to dwell right inside the indestructible essence of herself. She was alive in her soul, her psyche, or that innermost seat of consciousness which in a timeless and wordless way she now knew survived the death of the physical body to which it was attached with no more permanence than that of a guest in some friendly house. Yet in an extraordinary way the guest was also master of the house as well, a state of affairs she had never before experienced in the conditions of her everyday life.

Thus it was that an hour later with just a flicker of warmth left in her body, she was hauled out of the sea by strong arms from the anti-submarine frigate detailed to pick up survivors. Her first ordeal by water was over.

⚓⚓⚓⚓⚓ XIV ⚓⚓⚓⚓⚓

LEVIATHAN came into her own as a war vessel in the summer and autumn of 1940. By this time doubts about whether it was worth while converting her had all been blown into dust by events, and she was now from truck to keel the largest and fastest troop transport in the world. During that fateful summer of 1940 the pattern of the war had abruptly changed and a completely new balance of power, at any rate in Europe, had been struck. With Norway, Denmark, Holland, Belgium, and France all occupied by German troops, and with Italy belatedly joining her unloved partner, the area of fighting rippled out in a few short weeks from the center to new perimeters, bringing with it complications both to the Axis and to the Allies. It was at this moment that the fighting in the North African deserts began.

The twilight war had gone for ever and now the full horrors of the night were upon us all. The western end of the Maginot Line, in which such trust had been placed, had been turned and reduced overnight into one of the world's costliest white elephants. The old Western Front had long disappeared. Dunkirk had come and gone, France had fallen, and the North Sea and English Channel were now the only barrier to invasion. With the shattering of his world Chamberlain, too, had resigned, broken and disillusioned, and Churchill at the eleventh hour was rallying the country for its lone stand, that siege and vigil which was to continue for eighteen months until Pearl Harbor brought the United States into the war and altered the balance of power yet again.

In September 1940, while the Battle of Britain raged in the air over Kentish fields and invasion was nightly expected in the quiet villages of southern England, *Leviathan* was employed ferrying troops from Australia to the Suez Canal, with intermittent trips up and down the east coast of Africa to Cape Town. British control of the sea continued to be nearly absolute despite the U-boat menace and an occasional flurry from a German raider. The Battle of the Atlantic had not reached anything like a danger point, and after the grim necessity of neutralizing the French fleet at Oran had been faced, the Mediterranean still remained more a British than an Italian lake.

Aboard *Leviathan*, however, the general progress of the war was a matter reserved for the daily news-sheet and the six o'clock B.B.C. news. *Leviathan*'s own life as a troop transport was in much closer focus, and each day brought old problems in new guises to Mott, to the Staff Captain, and to Banks himself. Always in the forefront of these came the relationship between the troops on board and the ship's personnel, the allotting of accommodation, the control of movement with its effect on the trim and stability of the ship, and the continuous feeding of thousands of men in varying climates and varying seas.

"You would certainly notice enormous changes in the great lady," Mott wrote to Susan almost a year after she had left the ship, "and there are days when I can scarcely believe we were once the smartest passenger liner in the world. This morning I told the Commanding General at the daily conference that a mile and a quarter of sausages had been consumed by the troops at breakfast, which seemed to tickle his imagination. Veronique's shop at 'Piccadilly Circus' has become a sort of 'ready-use' jail for transient defaulters and there are drills of one sort or another in progress in different parts of the ship at almost any hour of the day. My personal war against souvenir-hunters continues, you'll be amused to hear, though there's very little left to be pinched which doesn't require dockyard tools and a gang of men. Someone on this last trip, however, effectively stopped the seven hundred electric clocks aboard by purloining the gilt and onyx one in the smoking room and busting the circuit in process. The Aussies are a pretty tough lot, and the discipline is apt to be down-to-earth and severe, with none of the frills of the gentler English, but their hearts are in the right place and I've yet to meet the cobbler who isn't a good scout once you stand up to him in the way he expects. The heat in the Red Sea is more even than Mr. Grüssli in his toga could have borne, and the return trips, when we carry a sizable quota of prisoners-of-war, keep the bo's'n and the deck storekeeper pretty busy with one burial at sea after another — at times it's like a sort of assembly line. This sounds callous, I know, but nowadays I seem to deal only in numbers, ranks, and categories — the individual attention we used to give our passengers is something I look back on almost incredulously, as if it were part of another life. I need hardly tell you that the Captain, of course, conducts each and every burial service himself with his usual flourishing and style and, I fancy, much private gusto. No matter how many padres we may happen to be carrying, it is still my job to keep any priest from going anywhere near him. So you see, *that* hasn't changed, and we all fear competition in our different spheres. As always I think about you a great deal and wonder when we shall meet again and if you will ever come back to the ship."

There had been many such letters written to Susan — though not all of them had been posted — over the last year. The first sent to her after the torpedoing of the *Pluto* had opened with the remark, "Well, *that* will teach you to abandon *Leviathan* and take passage in another ship," and to her pleasure the tone of all of them had reflected the man himself — brisk, slightly impatient, observant, a little cynical, especially where motive was concerned, and, as always, shy of putting into words the depth of feeling she aroused in him and the extent to which she continued to live in his thoughts. In fact, since she had left, Susan had become almost an obsession to Mott, an obsession which seemed only to grow with the decreasing likelihood of even seeing her, except perhaps casually, ever again.

Yet no illusion can live without hope of some kind, and if Mott derived little direct encouragement from Susan's letters in reply, there was still solace in the fact that for one reason or another she had never married young Mr. Storm. Indeed as the year had worn on the references she made to Philip in her letters grew fewer and fewer.

To begin with she had been full of bright anticipation. After her experience in the *Pluto* she had expected him to arrive almost hourly despite all the wartime restrictions on movement, but there had been a hitch in his acceptance by the R.C.N.V.R., and each time he wrote new difficulties seemed to have been put in his way.

Then in February his father had died, and his mother, Susan's main enemy, had seized the opportunity to anchor him still more firmly to Boston. Responsibilities, which he had thought to shrug off on his uncle or his younger brother, proved in the event to be unshruggable. He was the eldest son and the principal heir to a considerable estate. But still he persevered with visits to Montreal until in April. Just when he thought he had everything fixed as he wanted it, he failed his eyesight test for the Executive Branch of the Navy.

This was an unexpected blow, and although he could probably have joined the Paymaster branch, and with his legal training would have been very acceptable to that branch, it did not have the glamour in his eyes, nor the possibility of command. So he hesitated and the chance slipped through his fingers for ever, since shortly afterwards the regulations were altered and it became virtually impossible for United States nationals to join the armed forces of the Crown. It had always been a back door approach and now the door had been shut. In the meantime Susan had joined the Wrens as she had intended and was employed as a cypherer in Portsmouth. She still wore the engagement ring he had given her but a frustrated — and censored — correspondence is no substitute for physical presence, and events were entirely against both of them that hot and disastrous summer of 1940.

Then in the autumn, as the Battle of Britain raged, a note of tetchy despair crept into their letters. By now Philip was wholly absorbed in the family law firm and had begun to suggest that Susan should wangle her way back across the Atlantic to Canada or New York. He did not react at all well to being curtly informed that in the first place such a maneuver was impossible, since the Canadians had plenty of Wrens of their own, and secondly, even if it had been possible, she would not dream of trying to get out of England at a time like this. If the Germans were going to come, she wanted to be there to help give them a hot welcome. It was beginning to be obvious, she said, that they saw things very differently and that if anything their viewpoints were diverging instead of coming closer together. In October she returned the ring and in January of 1941 Philip Storm got engaged to a young lady from Beacon Hill and the danger of his marrying "that stewardess," as his mother called her, had gone for ever.

Mott's knowledge of Naval officers led him to appreciate that Susan was not likely to suffer masculine neglect for any length of time, but boy friends in the mass did not worry him and it was only specific "steadies" he found he could really resent. If there had been another Charley Beecher hanging round the Wren quarters at Portsmouth, Mott might well have been jealous, but she made no mention of anyone special in her letters and Charles Beecher himself had now married his Veronique, duly installing her in a semi-detached house in the Wirral where she was sulkily expecting her first baby.

Yet, apart from her waning engagement to Philip Storm, there were other men who seemed to dodge in and out of Susan's life and who might have worried Mott had he known about them in detail. Principal among these was Alan Mitchell, whose pacifist ideas had carried him through a series of tribunals into an ambulance unit first in London and then, at his own request and as a sign of the change taking place in him, with the Expeditionary Force in France. He thus survived the cataclysm of Dunkirk, although his ideas did not. It began to be apparent to him that to believe in personal nonviolence was one thing, to be a pacifist in wartime another. After the evacuation from the beaches at Dunkirk, the change in Alan, which had begun with disillusionment over the Spanish Civil War, now came to a head, and while France fell and the invasion of England was actively being prepared, Alan decided it was better — or rather the lesser of two evils — to fight Hitlerism with force than to accept the creeping slavery which, politically, pacifism allowed in by the back door. In any case, he now wanted to fight. This shocked him a little, it horrified most of his friends, but at least he was honest about it. In June 1940, therefore, he applied to join and was accepted as an Ordinary Seaman in the R.N.V.R. Three months later, because of his Oxford degree, he was promoted Sub-Lieutenant and began to specialize in signals.

Susan had played some little part in this process. After her shipwreck in the *Pluto* she was sent home to recuperate, and there, over Christmas and the New Year, she met a number of her old schoolday friends, first among whom were the Mitchells. A lot had happened to all three of them since that night in the train so long ago when they had been going to *Leviathan*'s launch. At Christmas Alan's views about pacifism had already begun to waver. They came up against Susan's crisp outlook and the half-true, half-unadmitted charge that Alan's outlook was basically a rebellion against his home. Although Fabian was Fabian it was possible that some at least of his ideas might be right, Susan observed, and it was also possible to be patriotic without being either a Tory or a Blimp.

Although at the time her thoughts were centered on Philip Storm, Susan could not help noticing that Alan had turned into an attractive if intermittently morose young man. He certainly reacted to her as a woman. It was true that he took himself overseriously, but then he found himself having to fight his father every inch of the way as Susan had once had to with her own father.

However, Fabian himself was mellowing. Sooner or later he had always accepted things as they were — usually later — and by the time Alan joined the R.N.V.R. he had almost come to accept his son as a pacifist. In any case Joan had redeemed the honor of the younger generation by becoming a Naval V.A.D. Fabian was no nearer to understanding his children, but experience was teaching him that a strongly held opinion had an opposite point of view just as strong and possibly just as valid, the truth lying somewhere between the two.

As soon as Flint heard of Susan's adventures in the *Pluto*, he assumed she would have had enough of going to sea in war-time and would be eager to settle down in a cozy office ashore. He therefore renewed his attempts to entice her as his secretary, and Quilly was dispatched to reason with her privately over a very expensive lunch. Since Susan distrusted Quilly as much as anyone she knew, this move was a failure.

Flint then waited until Susan had duly joined the Wrens and by deftly pulling strings behind the scenes had her drafted to a Sea Transport Staff in Liverpool with the intention, later on, of asking for exceptional arrangements to be made and for her to be attached temporarily to his Headquarters staff. But Susan saw through this maneuver, and on being promoted a Third Officer W.R.N.S., elected to become a "cypherette." This effectively stopped Sir J. in his tracks and there was an abrupt and fatal little scene between them on a week-end she spent in London in November 1940.

"You'd be far more use helping me here," the old man said gruffly, "instead of dickering about in a herd of women at Portsmouth. You seem to have an inflated idea of your own importance and value."

"Well, of course," Susan retorted, "and who hasn't? The fact is you really want a sort of chess-playing companion at your beck and call at any hour of the day or night. I'm sorry, Sir J. That was all right when I was one of your employees, but there's a war on now and I want to do something a bit more useful than that."

"I don't need to remind you I'm a wealthy man," Flint said, the old foxy look coming back into his eyes, "most girls of any sense would jump at this chance."

"Oh, you can buy anything," Susan said airily, privately disgusted at his blunt suggestion. "As you say, most girls would jump at the chance of being bought for money — that's what we love." Her eyes sparkled and she felt the anger welling up inside her. "The trouble with being a rich old miser is that no one ever tells you the truth."

"I'm usually aware of what other people think," Flint said grittily, "but I've never paid it a lot of attention. Despite your obvious contempt and disdain, I've become very fond of you, Susan; I thought you'd enough of a business head on your shoulders to listen to a proposition from someone like me."

"No," Susan said firmly, "I'm sorry, Sir J., but — no, I won't, and that's that."

"Very well," he said both sad and angry at the same time, "the more fool you."

As she reached the door on her way out, she heard a sort of stifled cry and, turning, discovered the old man slumped back in his seat, his face twitching and a vacant look in his eyes. She rushed back to him in a panic and rang for help. She poured out a glass of water from the carafe on the desk as his secretary and Quilly both appeared from the room next door, but already it was too late. By the time the doctor arrived, another stroke had carried him off. Sir Josiah Flint, K.B.E., the renowned ex-Chairman of the Transoceanic Steamship Company, was dead.

The suddenness with which this had happened, following upon their short sharp battle of wills, was a terrible shock to Susan. If he had not died in her arms, he had certainly died in her presence with his gnarled fingers grasping her wrist as though even in death he had wished to have his own way and to take her with him if he could. For months afterwards Susan would wake up in the night to feel the touch of those vice-like fingers on her wrist, like the echo of a curse in the ears, a reminder of death itself.

But there were other shocks in store. The Press scented a story in the famous little man dying dramatically in the presence of the girl who had once dared him to give her a job as *Leviathan*'s first purserette, and this story burst into front page headlines when Flint's will was proved and it was discovered that he had left the bulk of his fortune to Susan and in particular his management shares in the Transoceanic Steamship Company. At first it was not legally certain that this provision in the will was valid, since Susan was not a director and would have to be made one for the shares to carry their power. The situation then became immediately complicated by Fabian and the company lawyers doing all they could to have the effect of this clause annulled; but Flint, unknown to any of them, had got one of the best legal brains in the City to draft the document. It had been deliberately calculated and deliberately phrased so that Susan, provided she consented herself, would find herself elected to the Board and in possession of a greater block of shares in the company than Fabian himself.

"I thus transfer into your young hands," Flint had written in a letter to Susan attached to the will, "a considerable power over the great ship *Leviathan* which, as I have learned, means to you something of the same mystery it has long meant to me. I realize that this will be considered the last eccentricity of a foolish old man, but it is not so to me nor should it be to you. I trust you and, indeed, impose upon you the duty of exercising this power now given you with responsibility and due regard for the opinions of those with greater experience than you. I cannot do more from the grave than place in your hands the power and commend you to be guided in its exercise by the good advice I have received for so many years myself from my co-directors on the Board and from the company Staff. You once asked for executive power: now it is yours. You will not find it as easy nor as pleasant as you have imagined, but it is a challenge which I am certain you will take up and beat."

This deed well deserved its description in *The Times* as "one of the most astonishing bequests ever to have been made in the history of the British Mercantile Marine." Under ordinary Company Law it would still no doubt be possible for the Board of Transoceanic to gang up in unison and, by altering the rules, dispose of Susan if they so wished, but Flint had made this as difficult as possible by bequeathing other shares to other directors with the express proviso that they give their support for not less than ten years to Susan.

Moreover the whole matter had received the most glaring publicity. Overnight Susan found herself in the news as a national figure and her arrival in this position was caused by such odd and questionable reasons that from that moment on very nearly the full Hollywood range of gossip, rumors, and accusations began to attach to her name.

She became subject, in fact, to the laws of notoriety to which any celebrity is bound whose arrival in the news raises more questions than it answers. Cartoons were drawn of *Leviathan* as the private yacht of a Third Officer W.R.N.S., nasty paragraphs speculating on her intimate relationship with Flint appeared in the bigger circulation Sunday papers, and for a few weeks she was even a music-hall joke. Whether Flint had foreseen any of this side of things would never be known, but if he had then, it was a more than adequate revenge for any latter-day frustration he might feel he had received at Susan's hands.

Repercussions to Sir J.'s death continued for a long time, most of them involving Susan. One of the first of these took place at the funeral, a surprisingly well-attended affair at Golders Green, and was between Fabian, who by that time knew the terms of the will, and Susan, who did not. Indeed, she had no inkling of the role she was so soon to play, and she had had trouble getting away from her duties in Portsmouth to attend the funeral of someone not even a relative. Except for the immediate newspaper stories of Flint "dying in the arms of his first purserette," there had been nothing to suggest the coming storm.

But Quilly knew, and Quilly had made it his job to see that Fabian was informed by indirect sources with the minimum delay. It was therefore a shock, and an inexplicable one, to Susan when she went over to Fabian outside the crematorium, as she would naturally have done, to find herself greeted with a cold stare of dislike and the traces of a barely repressed anger.

"Hallo, Uncle Fab, is Father here?" she said with the wan smile appropriate to the occasion. "I made it, you see, but only by the skin of my teeth. The Head Wren said . . ." then she stopped abruptly struck by his cold silence and the look on his face. "What's the matter? Have I done something wrong?"

"I don't know, Susan," Fabian said gravely; "only you and God can know about that."

"Only I and . . . I don't understand. Why are you looking at me like that?"

There was a pause. The large crowd of mourners was filing into the chapel, some of them giving Fabian and herself curious glances as they passed. There also seemed to be an unusually large number of Press photographers present, several of whom took photographs of herself and Fabian together.

"I've always stoutly defended your sense of honor and behavior, Susan. Whenever one of those unpleasant rumors about you and Sir J. has come to my ears, I've always scotched it right away. I've known you since you were a child. I used to believe you could never do anything cheaply commercial or deliberately calculated."

As with Sir J. himself, the sneering implication made her blaze up with rage.

"How dare you talk like that, Uncle Fab? *What* is it I'm supposed to have done?"

"I don't know, my dear, but it occurs to me — as I'm sure it will also occur to millions of others — that you must have taken things somewhat deeper than I imagined for Flint to leave you the better part of his fortune and all his management shares."

"I . . . I don't understand," Susan faltered. She felt dizzy and sick and very confused.

"Come, come, Susan," Fabian said briskly. "I can't believe you knew nothing of this at all. That's stretching credulity a little too far."

But for the first time in her life, and to Fabian's considerable embarrassment, Susan fainted, staggering and falling against him as she fell. For this reason Susan was not present as the small coffin containing the worn-out old body was lowered slowly to the furnace below.

"There you are," Ethel said to her husband, "I told you he'd leave her all his money, I told you he was mad about her. You never pay any attention to what I say."

"He's not only done that," Laban remarked, "he's made it almost impossible for her not to be put on the board without a first class public scandal — and he knows no one wants that. It's incredible. It's a kind of calculated malice."

"He was in love with the girl."

"Love? He was in love with one thing — himself and his power," Laban said sourly. "He fought his way up from nothing. Once there he never had any intention of letting go."

"He let Mitchell take over as Chairman."

"Only because Mitchell's a weak man and Flint knew he could still jerk him about from time to time — enough to keep him under control. Sir J. spent years being humiliated by Mitchell's father and he hated the son: he always hated 'father's sons.' Now he's devised a wonderful way of getting in Mitchell's hair — even from the grave. There's not much love for Susan in any of that — it's just a well thought out piece of spite."

"Perhaps the lawyers will find a loophole."

"Oh! sure," Laban said bitterly, "with every little wrangle blown up, distorted, and kicked around by the Press. That's going to do the company a lot of good."

"You always used to say any publicity was good publicity."

"Well, now I'm telling you, this isn't."

It seemed to Ethel that her husband's nose was out of joint not so much because of the old man's prank but simply because Flint had been removed from the scene and had in his going weakened or perhaps even destroyed the circuits of power by which things were habitually done. She herself was delighted by the news and wrote off at once to Susan to say so, and to wish her good luck and courage. A few weeks later she had a reply which put the effect of all this on the girl who was at the center of it into clearer perspective.

"I only wish this to-do could have taken place in New York," Susan wrote, "so that you and I could retire to a quiet corner and have a good laugh at it all. As it is I've been reduced to comparing notes with Quilly ('you can trust Quilly — trust Uncle Lenny') and reluctantly have had to raise my opinion of him. In fact the horrible little man has been a tower of strength, albeit a crooked one, and I've come to see the great use he was to Sir J. and the considerable help he's now being to me. Up to now my instinctive dislike of him linked up with Uncle Fab's pathological hatred of him as the sort of Rasputin of the company. I never did trust him in the way both Maxie and Sir J. did, because I always felt, as I think you did too, that if he thought he could get away with it he'd stick a knife in your back when you weren't looking. Maybe he still would. I don't know — but I do now see that he really doted on Sir J. and if he has a heart at all, it's broken because the old man is dead. Anyway he treats me as if I was a sort of visiting princess whom he has to advise as an elder statesman. I suppose because his life has very largely been the ferreting out of the inside story on most things, he's one of the few people I have to do with today who really doesn't think I was the mistress of a very old man. That side of things is horribly disagreeable. Some of the stories and rumors I hear about myself I wouldn't credit to my worst enemy and a part of the filth is very difficult to scrape off. Even Quilly said the other day, after hearing a particularly vicious rumor (in which both Sir J. and I were understood to be flagellants) that a time comes when it doesn't much matter whether I went to bed with the old man or not, since more people than not will believe anyway that I did. It's a bit scarifying when you find yourself right in the middle of something like this. Luckily I'm still at Portsmouth, so am both accessible yet not in London, and people who want to worry me are put to the trouble of an hour and a half's journey each way, and as much fuss as the Superintendent of the Wrens or the C.-in-C. Portsmouth's office chooses to make them (and I'm happy to say that a word with one of the Admiral's Assistant Secretaries can ensure the equivalent of a bucket of boiling oil descending on unwanted visitors' heads).

"How simple it all used to be in the good old *Leviathan* days, and how often I look back on them as though they were pleasant memories from another life! I get regular letters from Motty and can visualize the great lady as she now is 'stuffed full of pongos' (as the Navy here calls anyone connected with the Army). I wish I was back in her. I'm not enjoying this aftermath to Sir J.'s death one little bit."

Indeed no one was enjoying the situation, at any rate no one connected with the higher echelons of the company. The old man, in dying, had upset the applecart, and from a number of points of view it was fortunate there was a war on and the day-to-day operation of the company's ships had been taken over by the Government on a cost-plus basis. It was also fortunate that Susan, the heart and center of the trouble, should be safely in the Wrens and there could thus be no present question of her taking any sort of practical, daily interest in the company affairs.

The complications resulting from Flint's bequests were such that Fabian and the Board of Transoceanic were advised that it would be better to bend to the wind as far as possible, elect Susan to the Board and control her rather than stubbornly resist all along the line.

Over Christmas 1940, therefore, when Susan was at home, a kind of working peace was established once more between "Uncle Fab" and the new heiress. It was agreed that on the one hand she should be made a director with the full potential powers that were comprehended in this, and she on her side made a gentleman's agreement not to exercise those powers for the present, so that everything would go on much as before.

It was a Christmas when the two families were both reunited at Dorking — Susan with her parents and Alan and Joan with theirs. The previous one had seen Alan in France with the British Expeditionary Force, Joan up in the Orkneys as a newly fledged V.A.D. and Susan recuperating from her shipwreck. During the year the great changes wrought by the war in the outer world were reflected also in their personal lives. Susan was no longer engaged to her American, and had been turned by chance into a most eligible heiress. Alan had abandoned pacifism and was now a Sub-Lieutenant R.N.V.R., and Joan, the quiet, gentle, rather dull Joan, was half engaged to a young Irish doctor at the R.N. Hospital, Plymouth — a fact she kept secret from everyone except Susan — who turned out to be none other than Michael Kelly, sometime of the Transoceanic liners *Pluto* and *Leviathan* and now a Surgeon-Lieutenant in the R.N.V.R. "And he sends you special messages of 'Leviathanic' endearment," Joan told her friend, "and says if you ever find yourself in the vicinity of Stonehouse Hospital he can always offer you something approximate to the old mixture of coffee, cream, and Irish whisky in cabin No. 76 — though the cream, he says, is not up to *Leviathan* standard. He also says if any gossip column writer shows up within swiping distance, he'll bash him so hard on your behalf that the bastard won't know whether he's on his bottom or his elbow."

The old familiar aggressiveness, even filtered through Joan's hesitant choice of words, gave Susan a great warm feeling. It brought back the young doctor's smile and his hotheaded Irish outlook on life which had helped her so often in *Leviathan* to blow off steam. She visualized how he would be with Joan, seeing how his lively temper and her coolness and depth would complement each other, how he would quicken her and how she would soothe and comfort him.

"I can't think what Father would say if I brought him home," Joan observed as they sat by themselves like old times, in the nursery in front of a dying fire; "he's wild and Irish, and a Catholic of course . . . though that doesn't seem to trouble him much."

"He's a very good doctor."

"Well, anyway, I don't care," Joan went on with that stubborn look in the eyes which Susan remembered from the days when Jackson Levine had had to be stuck up for, "I'm mad about him and that's that."

She relapsed into silence and stared into the fire.

"We've given our parents some pretty rough times one way or another," she went on presently. "I used to worry about it a lot — what with Alan and all that nonsense at Oxford, and me larking about with my kosher boy friends in New York — and now an Irish Catholic to make things worse — but I can't see how we can ever be other than what we are, however we try, and what's more I don't see why we should try as hard as Nanny used to suggest. We're *us* and they're — well, they're in a different world, aren't they? and always will be. I suppose we'll be just the same with our children when it comes to the point."

"If we ever have any children," Susan murmured, lost in her thoughts. The fire flickered and as if to underline what she had just said, the air raid sirens sounded the "alert" in the distance. A mood of nostalgia possessed them both and a sudden feeling that friendship, especially when not put into words, was perhaps the strongest emotion to cling to in that troubled time. After a moment or so Susan looked at her friend and smiled.

"I'm not being gloomy," she said; "I just feel I'll never have a family with a comfortable Nanny bustling about and a settled life like our parents did — and of course to hear the way both yours and mine go on, you realize even they had none of that Edwardian security they were taught to expect. You know sometimes I'd lie on my bunk in *Leviathan* and wonder why I was there and what on earth would become of me. I suppose we all do that at some time or other."

"Yes," Joan agreed, "well — just look what has happened. You practically own *Leviathan* — in fact you do own it, or more of it than Father does — and all because one fine day you took it into your head to dash up to Liverpool and ask for a job. I'll never forget how Father went on about that."

"Uncle Fab's always thought me a bit of a tart," Susan said. "He really does think I was old Flint's mistress. He blamed *me* because Ethel Laban enticed you across to New York, and I fancy it's somehow my fault that Alan became a socialist."

"Poor Father! You mustn't be too hard on him," Joan said, more out of loyalty than conviction. Susan smiled and fell silent. She had never told Joan that Uncle Fab had once made a pass at her before she was quite fifteen. She'd been in very scant tennis shorts and for some reason they were alone — the others having gone on or not having arrived back — in the house in Cornwall both families were sharing for their summer holiday. She could remember to this day the fumbling gesture and the smell of cigar and something that looked suspiciously like a tear in the eye as she pushed him away horrified. She had never told anyone about that incident which had given her suddenly a most terrible shock, since it destroyed in one lascivious move the whole of her childhood trust in Uncle Fab, and put both of them into an entirely new position. It was shortly after this that Fabian had had a word with Susan's father suggesting that a sharper eye ought to be kept on her as she was becoming "a regular little flirt, giving anyone in trousers the glad eye," and clothing her so to speak in a reputation she neither deserved nor was fitted at that tender and changing age to bear.

There was a knock at the door and then Alan appeared, asking if he could join them. He brought a bottle of gin and some vermouth and suddenly Susan was reminded of that scene in the night train to Glasgow, now over four years ago, when all of them had vowed somehow or other to go to sea in *Leviathan*. What a press of events had taken place since then and how each of them had grown up and away from one another in different ways. . . . She looked at Alan now as he lit his pipe and sat down beside them on the nursery floor. He had turned into an attractive if slightly solemn young man with much of Philip Storm's intensity but also the beginnings of an urbanity which the signals branch of the Royal Navy was giving him and which was, perhaps, the chief quality possessed by Mott. Remembering Mott, she also visualized *Leviathan*, and as if both she and Alan were in the same stream of thought he suddenly said:

"I suppose the new Director of Transoceanic wouldn't be interested in going to sea in *Leviathan* all over again?"

"Well, of course I would," Susan answered, "just say the word — but you know as well as I do that Wrens don't go to sea, worse luck. They sit in a barracks so that the men can have all the fun and games."

"A few of Les Girls may make it yet," Alan said, "if this scheme I've just heard of goes through. The Navy's got to put a reorganized communications unit on board *Leviathan*, which means a signals officer, Naval telegraphist ratings, and a cypher staff. Normally the Paymasters would cope with that side of things, but there's a move on foot to break new ground and turn the cyphering over to the Wrens, if any volunteers come forward. What do you feel about that?"

"I can be ready in half an hour," Susan said. "When do we start?"

The Royal Navy being one thing and the Women's Royal Naval Service another and the Admiralty a third, the G.T.C.U. or Giant Transport Communications Unit, to give it its full title on Admiralty dockets, did not come into being for another six months. By then the war had taken several turns for the worse so far as Great Britain and her Allies were concerned. By June 1941 the U-boat campaign was being waged deeper and deeper into the Atlantic out of range of the Western Approaches flotilla escorts, denied, as they were, the use of southern Irish ports. The only land fighting of note was going against us in the Western Desert and, with Tobruk as a beleaguered enclave, the front was back to Bardia and Sollum on the Egyptian border. It was true there had been a great naval victory at Cape Matapan, and out in the Atlantic the *Bismarck* had been destroyed, though earlier in the same battle the world's greatest warship, the forty-two-thousand-ton battle-cruiser *Hood*, had been sunk in a matter of minutes with enormous loss of life. The Germans had moved into Greece, Crete had been abandoned, there had been a revolt in Iraq inspired by the Germans, and Vichy French bases in Syria were being used by German and Italian aircraft, thus directly threatening the Suez Canal Zone from the north. Then, at four A.M. on 22nd June, Germany formally declared war on Soviet Russia and the course of events took another incalculable turning.

At the end of that month, Lieutenant Alan Mitchell, R.N.V.R., with G.T.C.U. No. 1 joined R.M.S. *Leviathan* at Suez. Included in his party was Third Officer W.R.N.S. Susan Spicer, one-time purserette, present shareholder and director of the Transoceanic Steamship Company, and currently the senior of three girl cypher officers who would henceforth take over the coding and decoding of secret signals affecting the ship. Captain Banks received her with his usual abrupt formality but also with what Brynhild would have identified as an understanding twinkle in his eye. Mott, scarcely believing she was really back, seized upon her with almost indecent haste and kissed her passionately in his private office, and Jimmy Johnson, now reduced to control of the small stocks of wine and spirits kept for the officers, seemed to shine out with pleasure at seeing her again. During the first blistering hot week in the Red Sea and Indian Ocean, old friends still in *Leviathan*'s crew came knocking at the door of the cypher office, or catching up with her in the corridors, or on deck, all of them shaking her warmly by the hand and saying with equal sincerity but varying degrees of intelligibility how one and all were delighted to see her back in *Leviathan* once again. "Miss Leviathan" was back where she belonged.

As 1941 wore on the prospects for the free world steadily darkened. Despite President Roosevelt's help in every way short of war, the fact remained that the United States with her vast potentials remained uneasily at peace in a world tearing itself to shreds in Europe, in Africa and in Asia. American Embassies still functioned in the German-occupied countries of Europe, American ships sailed unmolested under their neutral flag, American naval power with a core of ten capital ships based at Pearl Harbor in Hawaii balanced any Japanese threat which could legitimately be foreseen, should Japan be unwise enough to declare war on the United States. Meanwhile Chiang Kai-shek, though heavily pressed, was still thought to be draining away Japanese strength in the vast heartland of China, much as the German thrust into Russia, though initially successful because of surprise, would eventually overextend itself into impotence with the winter yet to manifest itself on the Russian side. As it turned out, neither assumption was entirely valid but both were a slight comfort in the dark days of what was, from the point of view of the British Empire and her allies, the hardest and blackest year of the war.

During this period *Leviathan* continued to troop between Australia, New Zealand, Singapore, Cape Town, and Suez. The routine on board, now fully adapted to its wartime purpose, continued to turn day by day with the same silky ease as it had previously done in peace. The great ship in her gray war paint was watched and reported on by foreign consuls, agents, and other interested persons. But such intelligence as the enemy gleaned about her movements was never of what lay ahead but only of where she had been and what she had carried. This may have helped in assessing the build-up of troops in Malaya and the Middle East, but it was of scant importance to the German and Italian navies, since, in any case, there was little they could do, as things were, to hinder *Leviathan* in those parts of the world. This situation was to change instantly and completely when Japan entered the war, but during the first six months of Susan's renewed service in the ship, *Leviathan* came and went exactly as planned, without breakdown or incident.

Back in England Mr. Johns, the versatile Cardiff solicitor, now had another giant to keep an eye on, since *Leviathan*'s consort, the *Behemoth*, was nearing completion on the Clyde. He had so far engineered one successful attempt at sabotage while her engines were being installed; this had resulted in a delay of nearly six months. The organization's prime objective remained, of course, the total destruction of both ships. So far as *Leviathan* was concerned, however, there was no one aboard of the caliber of ex-Steward Llewellyn. Curiously enough Llewellyn himself after several changes of name was now operating under the name of Ray Banch in a dockers' union on the Sydney waterfront, where he was able from time to time to cause delay in the sailing or at any rate the loading of ships. But he kept himself, as always, in the background and took good care to stay out of sight whenever *Leviathan* visited Sydney.

On 1st December 1941 *Leviathan* was at Singapore. Something was stirring, something was in the air and it did not take a great depth of insight to realize that trouble could only come from one quarter — Japan. That something was about to burst was known by the President of the United States and the top circle of American officials, since for a year the Japanese cyphers had been pierced and their secret communications known. Moreover Prince Konoye, the moderate Prime Minister who had kept the Japanese Army and Navy in check for eighteen critical months, had been forced to resign in November, the aggressive General Tojo taking his place. But what was revealed by Intelligence in Washington and London was one thing; what was "in the air" at Singapore another. No one, not even the best informed nor those with the acutest insight suspected that the American Fleet thousands of miles to the east at Pearl Harbor in Hawaii would be attacked. But British Hong Kong, the Dutch East Indies with its oil, the American Philippines with Manila and its bases, and the Kra Isthmus north from Singapore, where a landing might quickly ensure the cutting of the Burma road, that one last lifeline to Chiang Kai-shek in China — all these rich plums were there for the picking. Indeed, the likeliest of all was an attack on the Dutch East Indies, since this would not necessarily or automatically involve the United States in war and would provide the oil of which the Japanese were starved.

Such was the mounting threat from Japan. As a counter-threat, the British had decided to build up a Far Eastern Battle Fleet, and on 2nd December 1941 H.M.S. *Repulse*, one of the Royal Navy's two remaining battle cruisers (now that the *Hood* had been sunk in the *Bismarck* action), and the very latest battleship H.M.S. *Prince of Wales*, arrived at Singapore.

"A nice solid comforting sight," Mott remarked to Susan and Alan Mitchell as they stood on the sun deck watching the equatorial evening change swiftly into night, while the lights of Singapore began twinkling in the dusk.

"Father always used to say the Japs wouldn't dare," Susan remarked. "They're all bluff and 'face merchants,' imitators without anything real of their own."

"They're islanders just as we are," Mott said, "and they certainly 'dared' so far as China was concerned. The Russians underestimated them in 1904; I shouldn't be surprised if we're doing it now." There was a pause as they stared at the peaceful scene.

"Nothing seems quite to add up," Alan said, drawing on his pipe. "We were always being told that modern war depends on steel, oil, and rubber. Japan's output of steel is about seven million tons a year compared with America's ninety million; she's got no oil and no rubber. Yet that hasn't stopped her for four years in China any more than it stopped Hitler in Germany or Musso in Italy."

"It could do in the end. In any case I doubt whether Japan would go directly for the States. That would bring in everyone against her. The Japs are much too clever for that. They know the President can make war, but he can't declare it — Congress has to do that — and Congress never will. After all the U.S. Army was only saved from reduction a few months ago by one single vote — and that in the middle of a world war. The Japs know all that, so they won't attack directly — thus allowing the President to act; they'll go for Sumatra where the oil and the rubber are and let Congress get into another wrangle about supporting the Dutch."

It seemed the likeliest thing to happen, the course of action suggested by reason after an examination of the facts. But reason is no match for a madness of the blood and, as Churchill remarked, governments and nations do not always take rational decisions. Already, as they stood there looking at Singapore, the decision had been taken in Tokyo. Already the Japanese Ambassador in Berlin had been warned to tell the Germans "in the greatest secrecy" that war might suddenly break out between the Anglo-Saxon nations and Japan and that this might happen "quicker than anyone dreams." Indeed, even as *Leviathan* and the great warships lay calmly at anchor in Singapore, even as the British Admiral was conferring with his American confrère at Manila, the Japanese Fleet was on the move, Japanese aircraft in Indo-China were preparing to strike and the Japanese Army to invade and seize the islands in the South China Seas according to a carefully worked out plan and aided by the one factor which gives an attacker the supreme advantage — surprise.

Less than a week later, with *Leviathan* at sea *en route* once more to Cape Town, the blow had fallen and the entire course of the war had changed. The Japanese had landed in Malaya; Hong Kong and the Philippines had been attacked from the air and the dastardly Sunday morning stab in the back at Pearl Harbor had taken place. In two terrible hours three hundred and sixty Japanese aircraft had attacked the eight battleships and the other eighty-six ships of the U.S. Pacific Fleet then present in the harbor, leaving the *Arizona* blown up, the *Oklahoma* capsized, the *West Virginia* and the *California* sunk at their moorings and every other major warship, except the *Pennsylvania* which was in dry dock, damaged. America was at war with Japan and "within the hour," as Churchill had promised, so was the British Empire and its allies. Two days after that Japanese bombers from Indo-China discovered, attacked, and sank H.M.S. *Repulse* and H.M.S. *Prince of Wales* in the Gulf of Siam. Japanese supremacy in the east was now absolute, and by the time *Leviathan* sailed away west to Boston where she was to be docked, everyone on board knew they would not see Singapore or Hong Kong for some considerable time to come.

⚓⚓⚓⚓⚓ XV ⚓⚓⚓⚓⚓

DURING the first six months of 1942, while the United States was gearing itself for war, *Leviathan*'s consort giant, the *Behemoth*, slipped quietly out of the Clyde and sailed, unmolested by German U-boats or from the air, to the United States. Except in detail she was an almost exact duplicate of *Leviathan*, both in hull and machinery, but none of the luxury fittings which she would require for her peacetime service — if ever there was to be peace again — had even been designed, let alone manufactured. *Leviathan* herself had been docked and refitted, as planned, in Boston and as this was being completed, the news arrived in the ship that both *Leviathan* and her consort were being turned over, on a decision of the War Cabinet, to the U.S. Government for fast trooping purposes. "*Plus ça change, plus c'est la même chose*," Mott remarked when he heard the news, "except that Uncle Sam may try to make us go 'dry' — certainly the troops will be. So we must offset the luxuries of a posh new American canteen against the tameness of a soft drink and hamburger routine."

Leviathan, however, remained a British ship under the Blue Ensign, so that although the troops embarked were allowed neither beer nor hard liquor, the arrangements for the ship's officers and the crew "Pig" continued to function as before. In March they were to load their first eight thousand U.S. troops. The great build-up in Northern Ireland was to begin, the object of which was to be a combined United States-British expedition to North Africa as a preliminary to the invasion of Europe. So once again *Leviathan,* aided now by her consort, would be back on the Atlantic run, back on a variant of the high-speed Western Ocean Service for which she was designed.

In the meantime the docking at Boston had meant leave for all of them. Banks, Mott and Alan Mitchell returned to England in H.M.S. *Duke of York,* the newest British battleship which had brought Churchill and his staff across the Atlantic for the first of the historic meetings between the British Prime Minister and the American President. Susan and the other "cypherettes" took passage in a so-called fast convoy from Halifax which traveled at under half *Leviathan*'s speed and from which in two U-boat attacks they lost seven ships. After her previous experience in the *Pluto* Susan spent the ten-day trip in a perpetual state of nerves. She supposed it to be straight fear and thus hated it all the more. But there was no escape. She tried making a joke of it to herself, telling herself that if it happened again she must consider herself accident prone, should she be left with anything to consider with, but this did not help set her at ease. She was ready for the big bang awake or asleep. However she reached home safe and sound, ready for her six weeks' relaxation, ready, in fact, for anything which might now be coming her way and glad of a time to herself in which to take stock, to digest and reflect on the experiences she had had since rejoining *Leviathan* in her new capacity. Boston, of course, had meant proximity to Philip Storm, but since he was now married, and since America was now at war and he was joining the U.S. Navy, there had only been a fleeting half-hour in the bar of the Ritz while they brought themselves up to date on each other's news and nostalgically skimmed over the "might have beens."

Although by now she had been several times through the process of falling in and out of love, it still surprised her to find how differently she felt both toward herself and the man she loved at different stages of the game. Instead of always taking herself as the same person, Susan had now begun dimly to understand that completely different personalities could take possession of her body at different times. Like succeeding tenants in a house, they did little to alter the outward appearance of the house, but the lives going on inside were distinct and separate.

The many tenants of the girl called Susan Spicer scarcely knew one another — or at best gave only faint signs of recognition. One or two were passionate and cried a lot into lonely pillows; others were dominant, angry and resentful; yet others were cool and casual and thought the whole business of falling in love a tedious bore; while the strongest and most frequently recurring group exhibited a kind of warm curiosity and an outflowing affection ready for any sort of surprise while not making precise demands on Fate, the Deity, or other human beings.

This last group of personalities was the easiest to live with and this was the one which Mott seemed to call up. With Philip there had been a passionate restlessness almost impossible to satisfy or dispose of and this had turned first into frustrated resentment and then into indifference. Quite how she felt about Alan Mitchell she could not be sure. Although she had known him through childhood and gawky adolescence, he seemed now to be someone of different caliber altogether. The slow smile and the pipe gave him an appearance of easy-going tolerance which she had soon found, through working with him, to be a defensive habit he had acquired in order to stand up to his father. In fact he had a temper and a drive which made life in the Giant Transport Communications Unit far from a sinecure. He did not tolerate the slightest stupidity, he seemed to have an almost religious faith in the socialist ideas he had picked up at Oxford and although Susan knew she attracted him, he was far more preoccupied with the daughter of an Oxford professor to whom he was unofficially engaged. Susan might be a director of Transoceanic and a thorn in his father's side, but to Alan Mitchell she was merely the senior W.R.N.S. officer on his cyphering staff.

With a little leisure to look back and reflect, Susan used this dark February of 1942 to do some personal stocktaking and to try and see where, if anywhere, she was going. Flint had once remarked that her independence would be her downfall but she had tossed her head and put this observation down to his soured frustration. Ethel Laban and Gloria in their different ways had both said the same thing. "In the end you frighten them off, you won't yield, you want to be both man and woman, and it can't be done." From time to time she caught a glimpse of their meaning, but there was nothing she could do to change herself.

This basic recurring restlessness would not leave her alone for long, and with the bombs dropping on London, the ships being sunk in the Atlantic, and the constant shifting around which seemed to take place among her friends and acquaintances each passing month as the war took them and used them, killed or maimed them, or left them to molder in deadly boring jobs in inaccessible parts of the world, it suddenly occurred to Susan that perhaps she was luckier than she thought. Her personality was matched to the time. Innately restless in herself, she could use these extraordinary war conditions with far less distress than, say, Joan Mitchell who longed to settle down with a husband and a home and a brood of children. In fact she was rather enjoying the war. It was an adventure she could not have had in any other way.

Perhaps this was what had originally impelled her to run away to sea. This urge to escape, to seek adventure, to be always on the move, was a deep bedded quality of the British. It was unfortunate she had been born a woman; it made difficulties and it added restrictions but, in modern times, she was merely expressing whatever force it was that for centuries had driven the British to leave their towns and villages and risk the unknown on the seven seas. You could not equate this with a settled English country life or its equivalent in a town.

Motty knew this. Motty knew and did not resent the things you could not have. He, too, enjoyed his life. He took pleasure in the changing human tide that flowed through the ship because he liked people, however similar, however much of a small range of types the cynic might prove them to be. Motty was aware that when his time came to retire from the sea, he would have nothing beyond an inadequate pension, and a sackful of memories of a full and active life. He was never sorry for himself. The sailor always on the move, always on some dockside or railway platform with his lashed-up hammock and his kitbag — a symbol, if ever there was one, of the impermanence of life — did not strike Motty as either pathetic or lonely. The transitory, unsettled conditions in which sailors live, a reflection of the sea itself, seemed to Mott — as he had revealed in odd moments to Susan — to be nearer to reality than the crystallized solidity of civilian life. Well — now, in this war, the crystallized solidity of civilian life was day and night being smashed to pieces in a way it never had been before. "Things" in quantity were being destroyed and those to whom "things" were important were having to suffer in a way in which sailors were already inured. So Susan consoled herself that perhaps after all her restlessness was not such a disaster in human terms as she had once thought it to be. If Motty could make a success of it, so could she.

During this leave she found herself thinking more and more of Motty. In the early stages a letter from him with a Bournemouth postmark arrived almost every day. He talked about how much he missed her, of the contrast of his home with *Leviathan;* he talked about his mother, indeed, he described his mother's life so sharply that she felt she had known the old lady for years, and one day on a sudden impulse she got into a train, went to Bournemouth and rang up to ask if she could come to tea. This took both Mott and his mother greatly by surprise, but neither showed the slightest trace of it and in five minutes she and the old lady were talking as though they'd known each other for years. After tea Mrs. Mott found an

315

excuse to send her son on an errand and when they were alone said to Susan:

"I'm delighted you came down to see me. I thought somehow you would. Now, we haven't much time. I know a good deal about you from Dudley, of course, but now I've met you I'm going to claim the privilege of a very old woman and say what I think."

"Motty tells me you always do."

"My son seems to tell you a lot of things," the old lady said with a smile, "and now I see why. He's been head over heels in love with you from the moment you joined *Leviathan* — but I suppose you think he's a confirmed old bachelor, set in his ways."

"No, it's not that."

"Then it's the difference in age."

"Well, partly, I suppose. And I'm not very sure of myself."

"You're more sure of yourself than any girl I've met in the last twenty years — and I mean that as a compliment. Don't rate that gap in your ages at more than it's worth. I was very much younger than Dudley's father; it never made any difference at all. Of course," she went on as though marriage was a foregone conclusion, an assumption so naturally made that Susan began to believe it herself in an almost hypnotic way, "of course it's unfortunate that old reprobate died and left you all his money and those embarrassing shares. I know Dudley feels awkward about that. . . ." How I hate the name Dudley, Susan thought, why on earth can't she call him Motty like everyone else. Aloud she said:

"I know. You brought him up to believe that the man should have the money in any marriage — and I think you're right. Women should spend money, never control it."

The old lady nodded curtly. She was not interested in Susan's theories but only in the girl as she was.

"However I fancy you rather enjoy a little awkwardness and embarrassment. It certainly doesn't seem to worry you very much. But now I look at you, I don't suppose anything does."

"My parents do," Susan said promptly. "If only I'd been a boy, which they wanted, I might have got along with them so

316

much better than I do. I've done so many things that either shock them or they don't understand. That whole business of Sir J. upset them — and I know how they'd feel about Motty's age. But I just can't marry one of the local chinless wonders — I'm not that sort of person — however many titles or estates may be dangled about as bait. If I hadn't run away to sea I'd have escaped somewhere else."

"Well . . ." Mrs. Mott said hesitantly, as if casting about for words, "I can see you're fond of my son and I can see most of the snags. It's not for an old woman like me to interfere — so I won't. I'll only say I'm glad you came down to see me, and I think you're every bit as nice as he's always made out you are. I think you're sincere with yourself, and if that's so you can't go so very far wrong."

Susan had made it clear when she arrived that this was just a day trip to the sea and that she intended catching the six-forty back to Waterloo. Both Mott and his mother urged her to stay. The spare bed was ready aired, there was plenty for dinner but Susan had the actress's sense of making both an entrance and an exit. She wanted to go and she went. As a general rule her temperament made her prefer a short high-voltage experience to a longer drawn out one at a low voltage — so, with a little smile because she saw that Motty's mother understood her ideas, she allowed Motty to get a taxi and take her to the station. The old lady and she liked each other without reserve. The visit had been a success.

She thought it a little odd that Motty neither kissed her good-by — except for a perfunctory peck on the forehead — nor waited till the train departed. But he excused himself by saying that he hated hanging around cold station platforms, especially in the blackout. So she settled herself in the corner of her compartment and got on with a book. There was still a restaurant car on this train but she decided not to have dinner. She was therefore very surprised when the steward came and told her her table was ready. She protested that she had neither reserved a place nor wanted dinner and was then even more astonished when the steward whispered in her ear, "It may not be up to *Leviathan* standards, miss, but this is something you shouldn't miss." Intrigued, therefore, she got up and went along to the dining car to find Motty sitting there in a quiet corner with, more extraordinary still, a bottle of champagne on the table and a bland smile on his face.

"You came to see me," he said, "the least I can do is to see you home myself, and it's remarkable what the Southern Railway Company can still produce *pour boire* if the *pourboire* forthcomes from the client. Anyway, they have long memories in this service and not everyone's been called up to the war." He smiled and nodded a dismissal to the steward who had brought her along.

"There's something more to this than meets the eye," Susan said wriggling into her seat, both pleased and suspicious; "I know you well enough by now, Purser Mott, not to take you at your face value. So don't hold out on me — what's behind it all?"

"Well, I was going to London anyway tomorrow; I merely did some lightning organization and made it tonight."

"Uh-huh — and what else?"

Mott paused for a moment, looking at her intently as though this was the moment, which indeed it was, for plunging off the highboard, the point of no return. Then very gently and sincerely he said:

"I want you to marry me, Susan. Just that and no more. Will you marry me?"

She looked straight into his kind, familiar eyes. Then she looked at the tablecloth, a feeling of panic for the moment clouding her thoughts, her heart beating very strongly as it seemed in her ears, a tingling in the tips of her fingers. Well, this was it! How strange to find herself cornered in a railway dining car taken utterly by surprise, although, as she instinctively knew, things had been working up to this point for some considerable time. After what seemed an age she looked up at him again.

"Yes," she said softly, "I will. Dear, darling old Motty, yes, I will."

She put her hand over his on the rocking vibrating table and for a moment or so they said nothing. When she next looked up at him, she found that his eyes as well as hers were suspiciously wet and this made her smile ruefully and tighten the grip on his hand.

"A fine state of affairs," she said, "to be blubbing away on the London train."

"I've done a lot of crying in my time," Mott said soberly as he began to open the champagne.

"I know."

"Do you? I wonder if you do."

"These things always show," Susan said. "I suppose it's a part of your being the kindest man I've ever met in my life. You poor innocent dear!"

"We can soon put a stop to that," Mott said cheerfully, recovering his usual poise, "once I've got you in my power, you'll find I change enormously for the worse. I can show you letters to prove it."

"Two can play at that game," Susan said, "as you'll discover to your cost." But her efforts to meet his familiar banter suddenly collapsed in a welter of tears, why, she did not know and she was certainly not feeling sad. He let this pass, as it did, while he opened and poured out the champagne. Then without another word they raised their glasses to each other in a silent toast.

"I never thought you would," he said eventually, "and yet in a funny way I always knew you would from the first moment I set eyes on you."

"I suppose I did, too," Susan agreed. "It's funny, though, the way things work out."

After a further pause while they consumed the champagne and the train rumbled on its way, Mott broke out of his reverie and said: "Now this is the way things should go, as I see it. You will proceed home tonight with me a few short paces behind in order to be on hand when you break the news to your parents. That done I shall take up residence in fitting style at the Savoy, procure a license, and we shall then get ourselves married just as soon as the law allows. A church wedding may take a bit longer but I expect that's what you'd like, isn't it?"

"I don't think I really care about churches," Susan said after a pause, as though she'd considered the question for the first time there and then. "If we get married I'd have to leave *Leviathan*, wouldn't I?"

"I don't see why. You own the damn ship."

"You know I can't alter the Company Regulations — well, not just like that, at any rate." She thought about it for a moment or two and then went on, "Why don't we get married in secret and keep it to ourselves for the present?"

"Because getting married's a public thing; it's bound to leak out especially with your notoriety in newspaper offices."

"But people do get married without publicity — even people the Press are chasing. I bet we could do it if we tried."

"Then we should have to go on just as we have up to now. That means telling no one — no one at all. You couldn't even tell your parents."

"Of course I could. It's only outside people we'd have to be careful of."

"Well . . ." Mott said dubiously, "I suppose a few well placed tips in the Register Office would take care of all that. The trouble is, after Sir J.'s death you're 'news,' especially if marriage was in the air, because that would also imply a certain control of the company's affairs."

Susan looked at him with that smoky smile in the eyes which for so long had made his heart leap with delight.

"But, Motty darling, that's one of the reasons I want us to be married, so that you could take all that side of things off my poor sloping shoulders. You see I know I'd never be able to stand up to Uncle Fab without having continuous, large-scale rows. If ever I took a practical interest in the company — in the way Sir J. envisaged — Uncle Fab would put hedgehogs in my path every step I took. I don't blame him in a way; but if I had you behind me I think I could do it without losing my head or making a mess of it."

"And keep a home and have a family?"

"Let's leave that till the war's over, shall we? Having a home as things are just isn't a practical proposition, and both of us know it."

By the time they reached London Susan had got herself

acclimatized to the idea of a secret marriage. Aided by the champagne both she and Mott had decided that their own personal lives were their own personal affair. They had decided that as long as they were together in *Leviathan* they would continue using their own names as before and they would behave exactly as they had done up to now, "Even in private," Susan had insisted; "which we must make an unbreakable rule — or sooner or later we'll be bound to be found out."

"I suppose there must still be something adolescent about me," Mott said, "even to consider playing such a game let alone enjoy it, which I shall. The thing is, my darling, we shall belong to each other and be at rest with each other and that's all that matters."

"Suppose another Charley Beecher comes along and makes a pass at me?"

"There's no supposing — another one will. I shan't lose any sleep over that. I know one thing about that for certain. Once you're married you couldn't be untrue to yourself without being something you're not — so that's all there is to it. It's really very simple. I wonder we haven't done it before."

She left Motty in London and caught the last train down to Dorking that night. When she got home she was surprised to find strange cars standing at the front door, and once inside the house she knew something was wrong, even before her mother, more white-faced and tremulous than usual, told her in a few breathless sentences that her father had collapsed and the doctors were with him upstairs. So all her carefully worked out plans for telling her parents the news had to be abandoned and instead she and her mother began a vigil which only ended seventeen days later.

In the meantime Mott hung about in London, seeing plays and his friends in the theater as he always had done before but continually putting off the highly secret and expensive arrangement he had made for their wedding. It could have been a period — indeed, from one point of view it was — of the utmost frustration but somehow or other both of them managed to rise above it. The date of their return to *Leviathan* drew steadily nearer, like the slow turning of a big wheel inside which both were imprisoned. It was inescapable if you lived on the rim of that wheel but had only secondary importance if you were alive to quite other movements, sort of to-and-fro pendulum movements, as Susan put it to herself, which took place in your consciousness inside that circle of time.

Awareness of that kind, a measure of which both Susan and Mott had been given, brought a kind of freedom from the outer chain of events, or rather allowed that chain to go on revolving without entirely catching them up in its links. Thus both achieved a detachment which neither confused with indifference but which both knew only instinctively and not logically with the mind. Most days and some evenings they contrived to see each other at least for an hour or so, but the doctors had given warning that her father might go at any moment and Susan did not care to be away from home for too long.

Then with their return to *Leviathan* only three days away, Mott forced the issue. Either they must get married the very next day or the whole project would have to be abandoned till another opportunity presented itself — if ever it did. He fully realized her father's condition, but he was also forced to point out that this could quite well go on for years. Perhaps now she would never tell her father, as she had planned, and now there could be no question of a honeymoon, but these details apart they should drift no longer or the chance might be gone for a very long time.

That evening Susan traveled home to Dorking trying to devise a way in which she could tell her parents she was to be married the next day without it seeming grotesque, but after dinner as she listened to a minute by minute description of her mother's day with every difficulty, conscious and unconscious, caused by her father's illness, laid out in detail and analyzed, Susan realized that her mother would never understand, could never understand, and perhaps was not intended to understand.

Then about ten P.M. the telephone rang. It was Joan Mitchell. Without a moment's delay she plunged straight in.

"Susan, I've just got home on leave about half an hour ago and the most awful thing has happened. They've rung up from

Liverpool. There's been an air-raid there early this evening, the Transoceanic Building's been hit, and Daddy's been badly hurt. Alan's managed to scrounge some petrol coupons and he's driving us up straight away. Isn't it awful?"

There was a slight pause then, "How's *your* father?"

"Just the same. I *am* sorry, Joanie. Is there anything I can do?"

"There's nothing anyone can do. But it couldn't be more awkward; you see Michael and I were going . . ." she dropped her voice and then said, "I can't talk now: look, can you pop over for a few minutes? I've something I must tell you — and I can't, like this, on the telephone."

A little later Susan was sitting on her bed as Joan threw some things into a bag. Alan was bringing the car round from the garage.

"Well, you see, the thing is Michael and I were going to get married," she said. "We managed to arrange our leave at the same time and he's gone to London to fix up the license and all that. He's a relapsed Catholic or whatever they're called so it was going to be Register Office. Now — this has to happen — and I haven't told my parents a thing about it."

"Neither have I," Susan said, suppressing a giggle.

"How could you? *I* haven't told a soul in the world except you, so how could you have told your parents about it?"

"Ah! Well, you see, Motty and I are supposed to be getting married tomorrow."

"No!" Joan sat down suddenly on a chair and studied her friend. "Well, what do you know?"

"Only I felt I really ought to tell Mother first and you know how it is with Father's illness. She'd just think it the height of bad taste, lack of consideration and all that."

"Which it is, of course, but that's what always happens," Joan went on despairingly. "It must be something about you and me. Whenever anything big happens to either of us there's always a whale of a complication in the offing."

"Yes: I was going to tell her tonight but when I got home there just wasn't a chance. Poor Motty's been so long-suffering, putting it off and putting it off."

"Why don't we all get married together — just the four of us witnessing each other and all that?"

"How can we? Motty and I have to go back to *Leviathan* the day after tomorrow, both our fathers are dying or at any rate *hors de combat*, Mike can't possibly get his license through in two days. . . ."

"You'd be surprised what he can do. I think he's got the license already; he made a flying trip to London about a month ago, dropped a suitcase at the Savoy and established residence or whatever it is —"

"At the Savoy?"

"Yes, we were going to spend our honeymoon —"

"Guess where Motty's staying."

Joan looked at her friend and then burst out laughing.

"Oh! no . . . then they'll be bound to meet . . ."

"Yes but I doubt Motty would say anything; you see, *ours* has to be secret because of our both being in *Leviathan* together and then —"

"Come on, Joan, hurry up," Alan's voice shouted up, "we haven't got all night."

The two girls looked at each other hopelessly and shrugged their shoulders.

"All night is just about all we have got," Susan said, moodily as her friend snapped her suitcase shut and began to go downstairs, "not a word to Alan, now, about this — please — not even in the strictest confidence."

"Of course not, Sue, I wouldn't dream of such a thing. Lordy, how I wish things could go our way just once in a while."

As if in answer to this prayer the telephone began ringing as they walked downstairs. Alan answered it and a few moments later, as his mother and sister were getting into the car, said to Susan:

"Well, that's something, I suppose. My return to *Leviathan*'s been put off a week. That was a telegram from the Signal School. I expect you'll find one waiting for you when you get home. Some delay in the old lady's completion date, I suppose."

324

Then without wasting more time he drove his mother and Joan off into the night, the masked headlights giving a feeble glow as the car swung out of the drive and away north on its journey to Liverpool. For a moment or so Susan stood on the gravel drive, the night dark and moonless about her, the February wind buffeting her cheeks, a kind of gambler's thrill coursing in her blood telling her urgently never to give up, never even at the last moment, when things were at their blackest. All that had happened recently had been unplanned and unforeseen, yet every event had its root in the past and a purpose of some kind in its manifestation. The right moment was always there if only you were awake when it came. "You're still alive," a voice in her said; "anything's possible while you're still alive. Hang on — all these obstacles are like the disasters in a fairy tale, they melt away if you don't compromise with yourself. The most complicated tangle *can* be unraveled if only you don't throw in your hand in a panic." She shivered and began walking across the lawn through the side gate. Past the familiar trees and the cold frame and the wattle fence she had known since childhood. She could not see a way out of the confusion at present. But there would be a way if she went on trying — at least it was a comfort to think so.

The telegram deferring her own return was there when she got back, and shortly afterward Mott rang up saying that he, too, had been granted another week's grace — had she yet talked to her mother? She snapped back unreasonably, knowing he would be hurt by her tone, and then told him about the Liverpool bomb and Fabian Mitchell.

"So you see, Motty . . ." she began.

"It's all off once again, isn't it?" his rather weary voice cut in. "I should never have listened to you in the first place. I should have come down and talked to your parents myself."

"That's not so. And don't ruffle up like that, it doesn't help either of us."

"I'm still free to talk as I please, Susan, you're simply being obtuse."

"Am I really? I can do without lectures, thank you very much — we're not on board *Leviathan* now."

She nearly rang off in anger but instead there was a lengthy pause.

"This isn't getting us anywhere," he said in the end. "I want to marry you, Susan, and I really believe you want to marry me. I think we ought just to go ahead and do it and to hell with everything else."

"Oh! yes, Motty, so do I," she said with sudden immense weariness. "I'm sick to death of living my life by other people's standards, of always thinking of someone else or of what other people will think. Why can't we ever do just what we want to — once in a while?"

"We can do," Motty's cool voice answered. "All this backing and filling has been on your side of the fence. I'm not getting at you, sweety. I quite see why. I've done all I can to help. Now I think you ought to take this last chance while it's there."

Another long pause ensued as the pips went.

"Would you trust Mike Kelly?" Susan asked suddenly.

"Yes, yes, he's all right."

"He's staying at the Savoy. He and Joan Mitchell were going to do exactly what we had planned for tomorrow."

"I know — I've been drinking with the old bastard tonight. He's really mad at the way things have gone."

"You didn't tell him about us?"

"Of course not, Susan. And to give him his due, he never asked. Mind you, he's a doctor. There are lots of things he doesn't have to be told."

"Because Joanie suggested we ought to have a mixed four-some and all be each other's witnesses. If you trust him, why don't we do just that?"

Again there was a pause as Mott thought it out.

"I'll sleep on it, sweety. Anyway, in the condition I left him Dr. Kelly's going to have a dirty big hangover tomorrow, and I'll be prescribing for him. Sorry I got yapping just now. Let's get on with chapter two hundred and fifty-six tomorrow."

"All right, darling, let's do just that. Sleep well."

"In this huge, luxurious, and lonely bed. Thanks very much; I'll love it."

As she put down the phone she realized that her mother must

have heard a part of the conversation, and on a sudden impulse she determined to have it out with her then and there. Thus in about ten minutes of straight discussion, the whole problem crumbled away into dust, the bogies and objections and falsities disappeared and for the first time she could ever remember, her mother never hesitated, never dithered, never ran away from the difficult problems involved as she had always done in every similar crisis before. Susan was so astonished, words failed her for a time and she began to see, with a clarity she had never before possessed, exactly what it must have been like to have been married all these years to someone as dominant, vain, and pompous as her father.

"Since we're being frank with each other, Susie," her mother said (and it still curled Susan up to be called by the hated sloppy diminutive), "I might as well tell you that I never liked him, and at times I've almost hated him. Ever since our bridal night he's always offended me with his gross insensitivity. I know I'm silly and weak. I know I've never been 'clever' — even clever enough for ordinary social purposes — but all he ever did was to sneer and make my inferiority complex a thousand times worse. Our family never had money as you know, and he never used to let me forget it. He had the money, the brains, the beauty — he had everything, according to himself. He's never been kind — in the way you say your — your Motty is — he doesn't know the meaning of the word. He thinks he's generous, big-hearted, with fine upstanding ideas — he's just a mean, selfish, posturing ass. Of course I'll stick by him to the end. Anyway, I never had any option. That's my duty and that's what I shall do — but love him? Never!"

There was so much pent-up force in her mother's thin wasted body that Susan for a moment or so was shocked into silence. She had always known her parents had never "got on," she had no idea it was as much of a pretense as this.

"I don't know whether you've chosen wisely or not," her mother went on after a pause. "You say he's understanding, and perhaps twenty years difference in age doesn't matter as much as it sounds. You've a good deal of your father in you, Susie, you're hot-headed and intolerant and you can be just as 'difficult' as he's always been, so he'll need to be understanding to take you on. I don't like the secrecy. I don't like you breaking the rules — as you say you will be if you're married and stay in the same ship — but after all that beastly publicity when that little man died and left you those shares, I suppose you'd be justified in keeping things to yourself. I don't know why you didn't come and tell me before — that's another way you're like your father — but if I were you I'd ring him up now and marry him tomorrow. Put the poor man out of his misery."

As if in a dream Susan went straight to the phone and rang the Savoy. She caught Motty just as he was going, dispirited, to bed. As she told him of her mother's reaction, she could hear his excitement growing — could almost see him coming alive. As soon as he could get a word in, he said he would hire a car and come down at once. A couple of hours later he was standing in the drawing room, his arm round Susan's shoulders, talking to her mother who, now that the decision was taken and the tension relieved, had reverted to her old habits and was sniffing moistily into a handkerchief. The only successful effort she had made at human communication for over twenty years had exhausted her energy and she had become once more the sad, drab, rather feeble creature Susan had known all her conscious life and who had clung so exasperatingly, as he thought, to the intolerant husband now lying inert upstairs, his explosive energy spent, waiting, a mere husk of a man, to die.

Susan and Mott were married in the late afternoon of the next day while the first dusk alert was sounding. Mott's mother came up from Bournemouth and Susan's from Dorking. The sirens wailed. The dingy Register Office, with its clinical spuriously cheerful briskness, seemed to glower malevolently about them. The civil servants calculating fees and extras, and the hangers-on ready to provide flowers and photographs and a ghastly sort of claque, if required, added to the grim banality of it all and it seemed to Susan at one time as if they had arranged to get married in a dilapidated station waiting room. Sworn to secrecy, Mike Kelly acted as best man. He seemed to be far more jumpy than either Mott and Susan and as the moment of the ceremony drew near dropped into a pit of gloom. Then five minutes before the short ceremony was due to begin, Joan Mitchell suddenly appeared in a breathless flurry, having caught the midday train from Liverpool. Alan and her mother had remained behind and in fact Joan had left without saying what she intended to do. They had driven most of the night but had none the less arrived in Liverpool too late. That morning at four o'clock Fabian had died without regaining consciousness.

As the A.A. barrage opened up and the first distant bombs fell, Dudley Fitzpatrick Mott and Susan Spicer became man and wife. Five minutes later, Joan Mitchell and Michael Kelly were also united in the eyes of the law. The bombs continued to fall and almost everyone cried.

⚓⚓⚓⚓⚓ XVI ⚓⚓⚓⚓⚓

BY THE time *Leviathan* began her transatlantic build-up of American troops in Northern Ireland, the lives of those most concerned with her had changed in a number of ways. Aboard *Leviathan* only Alan Mitchell knew that Mott and Susan were married. Susan had tried swearing him to secrecy but was not sure she had succeeded. His reaction had been cool and noncommittal and, to Susan, somewhat disturbing. Indeed, since his father's death and his sister's run-away marriage, Alan had "morose-ified" as Joan called it, and seemed to live in a curious, unpredictable state of mind. To call it shock and its aftermath was to oversimplify. Alan, in fact, was going through another process of rethinking similar to the one which had followed Dunkirk and his abandonment of pacifism. The secretly prepared, suddenly executed double marriages of his sister and the girl next door, with whom he had grown up and who, latterly, had been on his staff, had thrown a hard light on to a number of illusions he had long cherished, and had destroyed, at any rate for a time, some comfortable habits of thought. The rather earnest Oxford professor's daughter was one thing; at least he knew where he was with her. His sister and Susan were clearly another and, after so many years of easy-going familiarity, he now felt them to be strangers.

Moreover, on his father's death the mantle of Fabian's pomposity seemed to descend in some magical manner on the son, and Alan became ponderous, pontifical, and severe. Susan, as a member of his staff, found him more and more difficult to serve. His sense of humor seemed to have perished at some stage of the process and for some indefinable reason. Now, as the weeks went by, she began to realize with something of a shock that the emotion she was up against was resentment. How strange, she thought when she had worked this out, that someone like Alan, the open-hearted boy she had known all her life, the young man next door so taken-for-granted, so much liked, so familiar, how strange that he should now be jealous of her. Why? What had gone wrong? Where had both of them changed?

He began to find more and more fault in her work and to take pleasure in pointing it out. Before, it had all been something of a joke that they should both find themselves together in this great ship, pretending to be officers doing useful jobs, amateurs in a highly professional world. Now all that had altered. Now every mistake, every peccadillo, drew forth an almost sarcastic rebuke on the lines of, "You may be one of the principal shareholders in the Transoceanic Company, but that doesn't entitle you to cypher up this signal I hold in my hand with no less than five corrupt groups" — or whatever it was that had currently given offense. "And you can call me 'sir,'" he had snapped after another of his rebukes had bounced off Susan's back without making the effect intended. This had only caused Susan to burst out laughing and tell him to come off it — but she suddenly saw, with a chill, that he was in deadly earnest. From then on she avoided him on every possible occasion except for strict and inescapable duty calls.

Meanwhile, *Leviathan* got into her stride again as a military transport, embarking and disembarking eight thousand troops each voyage with clockwork precision, a drill which always excited Banks's admiration and praise. "I should like to record yet again," Banks wrote in one of his later reports, "the admirable efficiency with which these loading and unloading operations are completed. The Commanding General ascribes this, so he tells me, to the film which has been made of an embarkation and which is shown to all personnel in the marshaling camp. Whatever the reason, the speed with which the troops come aboard and go at once to their allotted stations without muddle or delay deserves and receives the admiration of all ship's officers whose duties bring them into contact with the present passengers we carry."

Now that the war was in its third year with Banks still in command of *Leviathan*, it was beginning to seem, at any rate to Banks himself, as if he had never been anywhere else except on the familiar curving bridge — now with its new magic eye called radar which enabled him, in fog or at night, to thread his way at speed through a crowded anchorage — and in his day and night cabins where he spent the always foreshortened hours of rest. In appearance but little altered except for a grayer head of hair, still of a girth in proportion to *Leviathan* herself, still bearded like the prophet Isaiah, and still with the Book of Rules instantly available in the left-hand pocket of his monkey jacket, Captain Basil Bellerophon Banks, D.S.O., D.S.C., R.D., R.N.R., had, while still in the job, acquired some of the properties of a myth, especially among those whose lives depended on his skill and judgment.

In company with the rest of *Leviathan*'s crew, Banks had spent his leave in the shivering austerity of England. Brynhild, more attentive than any wife, more understanding than any mother, had burned up her winter's ration of coal so that there could always be a large cheerful fire, and had thrown the contents of her carefully hoarded store cupboard into the formidable task of keeping the Captain fed. For the first ten days he had scarcely moved from the house. Then he got the Arrol-Johnson off its chocks and drove about Hampshire and Sussex as much as the exiguous petrol ration would allow, seeing old friends and shipmates. He took his usual pleasure in this, but it did not seem to allay the growing loneliness he felt more and more deeply these days. Indeed, if anything, it made it worse.

Even the oldest sea captains he knew had somehow or other been appointed into jobs connected with the war, and some of them had even contrived to get back to sea. When he met them they talked incessantly of the war, and he would have liked to have got away from it for a while. Wherever he went, whatever he did, the war, the grim all-pervasive war, was never more than a sentence or two away from any conversation, could never be forgotten for more than a few minutes at a time. *Leviathan,* for that matter, was never long out of his thoughts — *Leviathan* and the responsibility he had so long borne and would so soon be bearing again. But of course *Leviathan,* as he at once made it clear, was far more important than the war itself.

Indeed there was nothing unusual, to Banks, in this brooding about responsibility. It simply had to be borne. Such was the lot of any captain. It always had been that way and it always would be. Yet the weight he carried these days seemed to be heavier, the drag on his energy increased. Perhaps this was what it meant to grow old. He did not know, nor did he particularly care; and he did not resent this state of affairs. Pride in being the captain of the largest ship in the world came to his aid whenever his spirits flagged; pride in being the one man filling the one job from which there could be no out, since even when an individual captain came to be replaced, the necessity for having a captain at all continued as before, and a captain's responsibilities would always be onerous, inescapable, and unique.

But there had been other changes in Banks, some of which Brynhild had seen more clearly than the Captain himself. He was losing his gusto, losing that almost contemptuous mastery of the petty problems of everyday life, losing that sense of fun and frivolity which always seemed, incongruously, to lie behind his gruffest reactions and of which the only trace was often no more than a glint in the eyes. Now, in this early part of 1942, the twinkle had gone. Before, though he never encouraged the habit, a joke was a joke, and if it happened to be against himself it did not necessarily cease to be funny. On occasion he had even quoted the Book of Rules to his own discomfiture, though it had always been unwise for anyone to try and take advantage of this idea to any great extent. Now, however, such a notion would not be entertained for a moment. As with the outer world in which he lived, so now with the inner the darkness was creeping in closer. Life was real, life was earnest, and there was no time now except for the stern calls of duty which could, if one kept one's head down near the trough, comprise the whole of one's every day.

Back in *Leviathan* after his leave, the Captain's temper became noticeably worse. The smallest mistakes now provoked outbursts of rage which before would have been reserved for matters of greater importance. His list of *bêtes noires* had expanded prodigiously. For instance, no one was now allowed to smoke on the bridge and anyone caught doing so was apt to find himself doubling five times round the deck, a lighted cigarette in his mouth. Indeed, only fearless and unequivocal blame by the Surgeon for the collapse of an elderly quartermaster, blame which might well have led to a charge of manslaughter, caused Banks reluctantly to vary this particular torture. Long hair and idiosyncrasies in the interpretation of the uniform regulations also made him see red, and one young engineer with a splendid mop of dark wavy hair suddenly found himself sent to the barber and given what was later to be called a "crew cut." This was not a matter on which the Chief Engineer felt like making a stand, but it in no way eased the traditional antipathy between engine room and bridge. Incidents such as this occurred almost every day and affected almost everyone in the crew. In the aggregate they added up to a hardening fear and dislike of Captain Banks by the officers and men of *Leviathan*. He was becoming more and more "difficult" as the weeks went by. Always an autocrat, he was now turning into a bully and a petty dictator. People were saying he had been too long in *Leviathan* and it was time he went.

As against all this, the responsibility he carried was enormous. For *Leviathan* to embark eight thousand men was charge enough, for fifteen thousand souls to be crammed into one shell and then raced across the Atlantic at thirty knots was more than even Banks himself would initially accept. When the proposal was first mooted, Banks came out with a flat re-fusal to allow on board any troops in excess of *Leviathan*'s life-saving capacity. That decisions as to what *Leviathan* would carry and where she would go were settled at Cabinet level, Banks did not deny. Instead he concentrated simply and force-fully on the rights of any captain in command of a ship. "I still remain Captain of *Leviathan*," he told the Admiral and the Sea Transport Officers. "No one comes aboard any ship without the Captain's permission. If I sail knowingly over-loaded and the ship is sunk I shall have thousands of lives on my conscience and that, sir, is something I do not intend to allow."

The principle of a captain's absolute control over the ship he commands could not, of course, be questioned. But then, as Banks well knew, any centurion was himself set under au-thority and such authority must eventually always prevail. Thus there came about modifications in the life-saving equip-ment, a technical juggling with figures and a hint that even the Captain of *Leviathan* could find himself replaced overnight. In the end Banks bowed reluctantly to *force majeure*. The em-barkation of fifteen thousand U.S. troops would only be or-dered on the highest Pentagon authority, and then only after the risks had been freshly weighed in the light of whatever emergency was then taking place. Thus a compromise was reached and things went on as before. Only the brooding on the bridge deepened yet again as the Captain's responsibility had once more been increased.

Both Mott and Susan soon realized that their good luck in being together could not possibly last. It was illicit, and al-though both of them obeyed their own self-imposed rules, it was still, from the company and Service point of view, unde-sirable for man and wife to be together in the same ship. As neither took advantage of the position, Susan did not look on the keeping secret of their marriage as a particularly serious crime, but to her dismay Motty did. Just as Banks brooded over his responsibilities up on the bridge, so Mott now found his own personal state of affairs preying on his mind.

334

"It's the Puritan conscience, I think," he said one evening to Susan as they had a nightcap together before going to their separate cabins. "I've always felt guilty at breaking the law — even in a little thing like this. Perhaps it doesn't quite merit hellfire and eternal damnation, but there'll be retribution of some kind before we're through."

"But we're not harming any one else," Susan pleaded. "If we were depriving someone of something I'd agree like a shot — this is entirely between ourselves."

"Oh! I know. It isn't logical at all."

"You're too good to be true," Susan said tartly. "You can overdo this slavery to petty rules and regulations. You're a bit of a niggler." She wanted something to drive home her point but could only think of a habit of her own — the avoidance of paying a bus or train fare if she could get away with it. "I bet you'd go and pay your bus fare even if the conductor misses you out."

"Of course I would, wouldn't you?" She shook her head. "Then that's stealing."

"I would if the conductor owned the bus — or got a percentage of the fares. Then it's personal. Otherwise, if I get away with it I feel I'm beating the machine. And I hate great big machines — like bus companies and railways."

"And shipping companies?"

"Well . . . in certain respects." She hesitated a moment.

"I've always thought there's something piratical or anarchic about you," Mott said kissing the nape of her neck, "or is it only that women have completely different standards of honesty?"

"A woman can break any silly rule at any time provided she *feels* all right about it. It's only feelings that matter. I don't feel bad about us being together here like this. You do." She shrugged her shoulders and looked away slightly bored. "I didn't make that particular company regulation. I see there has to be a general rule of some sort, but so far as you and I are concerned I don't see its point. So it's not going to bother me that we break it and I'm not even going to worry unduly if and when we're found out."

It was all very well for Susan to go on like that, Mott thought to himself; her career was hardly at stake. It was different for him. In fact, ever since they had married his life had become more difficult and frustrated than ever before. The "game" of being secretly married to a former member of his staff in no way amused him. He discovered that his love for Susan was not controllable as he had hoped and imagined. Instead of being able to take her for granted and thus to a certain extent get her out of the way, she obtruded into his thoughts and his daily life more than ever before. Instead of an intermittent stirring, he now wanted her all of the time. She was becoming an obsession, and the occasional night ashore, whether in the States, Northern Ireland, or the Clyde, had perforce to be so clandestine and so fraught with difficulty that instead of relaxing him, it only seemed to make things very much worse. On these occasions he would lie awake most of the night, her naked young body in his arms, her head cushioned on his shoulder while she slept as artlessly as a child; and he, scarcely daring to move, lay absorbed by a love, by a gratitude, and by an astonishment that this fiery little creature should not only be sleeping with him but should also be his wife. Yet these brief experiences of her, keenly enjoyed while they lasted, left him restless and yearning for more time. Then next day they slipped away separately and rejoined the *Leviathan* at different times. Susan quite evidently enjoyed the unpredictability of their lives. She was almost totally non-domestic, whereas Mott was tired of "adventure." It took these first few months of their marriage to make him realize that what he really wanted now was a home — the one thing in war impossible to achieve, the one thing which even if it had been possible Susan showed no trace of wanting herself.

Fabian's death had naturally caused another major upheaval in Transoceanic Company affairs. The removal from power in a couple of years first of Flint and then of Fabian Mitchell made it fortunate, in one sense, that the company's ships had been requisitioned for war purposes and were not in ordinary commercial operation. A new "caretaker" Chairman was elected by the directors (though without consulting Susan) and Captain Masterton, the Chief Engineering, Catering, and Medical Superintendents continued as before to run the day-to-day affairs of the company's fleet.

As soon as Susan had rejoined *Leviathan* in Boston after her leave, Laban traveled up especially to see her. Since she was the one shareholder with enough management shares to make trouble if she wished, Laban had wanted to find out her views, and to urge her to let things take their normal course. She had never intended anything else, but Laban's open relief and the fact that he had seen fit to leave his busy wartime job in Washington simply in order to keep her quiet put new ideas in her head.

"*Could* I, in fact, take over if I wanted to?" she asked Laban, giving her imagination free rein for the moment. She found Laban giving her a curious look which she did not altogether enjoy. He seemed lately to be changing toward her, in a way she knew Ethel wouldn't like. Oh *dear!* she thought to herself, not that sort of trouble please, not from Maxie Laban of all people.

"You'd have one hell of a job," Laban eventually answered, "but I don't think they could legally stop you, and as they've put in another Chairman without consulting you I suppose you can make as much trouble as you like — but if I were you I'd wait. One of these days the war will end and we'll get our ships back into commercial service. Then I dare say you could exercise some of that power Flint put in your hands — if you want to, that is."

Laban himself had never been unduly worried about Susan *vis-à-vis* the company. She was no danger to him by herself. Indeed, she might well be an asset. But he went back to Washington much more disturbed by a subsequent talk he had had with young Alan Mitchell. This rather self-important young man, with Fabian's shares in his pocket, showed signs of being far more rigid and dogmatic than Laban thought good. He had already applied for a transfer from *Leviathan* to a shore appointment in Liverpool in order to attend to his father's affairs. If the Admiralty saw their way to granting such a request, as well they might, Laban could envisage a number of complications which might bedevil the company and his own plans and interests. He cursed the invention of management shares and the trouble they caused. When an autocrat as powerful as Flint died all sorts of snags and difficulties appeared. For instance, if young Lieutenant Mitchell took it into his head to do a deal with Susan Spicer, then control of Transoceanic might easily be at the mercy of two untrained adolescents — a possibility which gave Laban one of the worse nightmares he could remember. The prospects were ironic and, to someone like Laban who had given his life to the Transoceanic Company, appalling. He determined at once to initiate action with other directors to abolish the power of those management shares which Flint had been at such pains to create and on which, in fact, his own absolute control had depended.

Such, then, was the state of affairs in the beginning of July 1942 when *Leviathan* was to make her last trooping run to Northern Ireland prior to being sent once more to the Pacific. The build-up for what was to become "Operation Torch" — the invasion of North Africa — needed one more division to complete the assault force being assembled in Ulster. In view of the June figures for merchant shipping sunk by U-boats, a disastrous 627,000 tons sent to the bottom in one month, it was decided that this last division and its equipment would be conveyed *in toto* by *Leviathan*. Only Banks knew that this was intended to be the great ship's swan song in the Atlantic for some considerable time, and only Banks made another lone stand against embarking fifteen thousand men in his ship. But his single voice could not prevail — powerful though it was. Direct orders for this voyage had been given by the White House and the British War Cabinet. This was a moment when unknown risks must be accepted and margins of safety perforce ignored in high places. All Banks could do was to obey or ask to be relieved of his command, in which case, it was pointed out, a Captain of lesser experience would be found, causing a proportional increase in the risks, but the voyage would be made exactly as ordered. In other words, Banks might himself escape, standing on his principles and snuffing out his personal career; he could not prevent the embarkation of these thousands of men in *Leviathan*, he could not prevent or hinder the will of those who were directing the war — in fact all he could do was to make the execution of their orders more difficult and dangerous by the sudden removal of himself and his unique experience of the great ship at this highly critical time.

As always when some moral problem was particularly pressing, Banks sought guidance from the Bible. "Ask and ye shall receive: knock and it shall be opened unto you," had long been his comfort and his staff. But the chapter of Isaiah at which the Book of Rules lay open did nothing to allay his misgivings or to remove the instinctive warnings of danger which now, as never before, had begun to hammer in his consciousness. "We wait for the light but behold obscurity; for brightness but we walk in darkness," he read. "We grope for the wall like the blind and we grope as if we had no eyes: we stumble at noonday as in the night; we are in desolate places as dead men." This to Banks was only too painfully true. "For judgment is turned away backward and justice standeth afar off; for truth is fallen in the street and equity cannot enter." For nearly an hour, as was his wont, he went down on his knees in his night cabin praying for a sign while his "Tiger" kept the ship and the world at bay. Was he to accept this terrible risk of embarking these thousands of men, knowing full well that if anything happened not even fifty per cent were likely to survive? Was he to stand and refuse? What did the Lord God require of this, His humble servant? What sacrifice needed to be made? A deep and ominous misgiving possessed his soul; "I have trodden the winepress alone," his eye caught the prophet's words and his uneasiness seemed to increase, "and of the people there was none with me: for I will tread them in mine anger and trample them in my fury and their blood shall be sprinkled upon my garments and I will stain all my raiment. For the day of vengeance is in mine heart and the year of my redeemed is come." But no sign was given. No lightning flickered in the dark night of his fear and doubt. With a heavy heart, Banks got to his feet, sent for his Chief Officer and the Embarkation

Plan and began authorizing the detailed orders and local arrangements required for the sleeping and feeding of fifteen thousand men. When it came to the point you simply did as you were told. More and more the war was coming to mean a shrug of the shoulders and a blind eye to scruples which, at the Judgment Day, you would be called on to explain. The whole progress of the war was a descent from scruples and standards, some of which would never be regained, some of which perhaps were, in essence, what the war was about. Banks signed the orders and then took one of his prowls round the ship. An unfocused anger, muttering in his veins, gave way to a feeling of general distress. What was an individual man in a war except just another beast to be led to the slaughter. Was there no personal escape? No hope? The body must sooner or later die — that he knew and accepted — but must the spirit, too, be slowly submerged, slowly dragged down into the mire? Was the ark of the soul, when the flood was upon a man, no more seaworthy than the outer vehicle in which it was carried? He felt deeply uneasy about this coming voyage, and disturbed, in turn, at the helplessness besetting even a man high in authority such as the Captain of *Leviathan*. Ah well! When it came to the point you shrugged your shoulders and did as you were told.

The embarkation was scheduled to take twelve hours and actually took seventeen. Almost everything which could go wrong did go wrong. Gangways came adrift, couplings broke, hawsers parted, an armored car was dropped into a hold and nearly went through the bottom of the ship, a man in full equipment fell into the sea and sank like a stone, another broke his leg in one of the main alleyways and caused twenty minutes' chaos, a colored G.I. chose that particular time to run amok, and shot his sergeant in the thigh, a caldron of scalding soup got overturned and three cooks were burned, one of the main generators went on the blink, a small fire on B deck caused by illicit cigarette smoking had to be quenched and disciplinary action taken, the dimensions of a self-propelled gun had in some way been misread so that it could not be stowed as originally planned and this rearrangement, of course, affected everything else in that particular hold. By the time the division was aboard, *Leviathan's* officers were exasperated as they never had been before, the Commanding General had been treated to the rough side of Banks's tongue and was breathing brimstone and fire on anyone within range, a Congressman — and how *he* came to be aboard caused one of the biggest of the many storms that were to take place between Banks and the Commanding General — was forcibly ejected from the bridge, from Banks's cabin, and finally from the ship itself, promising as he went the most "goddamned terrible pack of trouble" in Washington and threatening to have Banks's head on a platter. Never before had an embarkation been less smooth, never before had more mishaps, misunderstandings, and inefficiencies taken place, never before had co-ordination been so totally lacking and the neutralizing force of good-will so nonexistent on either side. If the voyage started in this way, Mott commented to Susan, what would it be like if they ran into bad weather or a stray torpedo found its mark?

The voyage, however, did not even start for another twenty-four hours owing to the presence off the eastern seaboard of two U-boat concentrations, one of which had already accounted for two tankers and a storeship, and the other of which was believed to have sown a minefield in the fairway thus causing it to be swept yet again before *Leviathan* sailed.

"Looks as though the old lady's being reluctant and doesn't want to go, doesn't it, miss? She always knows when there's something she ought to avoid," Jimmy Johnson remarked to Susan as news of the third delay in sailing began to percolate through the ship, "or perhaps they're just saving us some lovely bad weather. It's time we were treated to a nasty storm; it's about all we haven't had the last week or so."

Meanwhile the colossal job began of providing fifteen thousand men with two good meals a day, of co-ordinating the smooth use of bathrooms and lavatories, of combining work and recreation for such vast numbers, of seeing that the Cox and Box sleeping arrangements were practical — whereby each bunk was used by two men in turn — and above all of en-

341

suring that life jackets were worn and that lifeboat drill was understood. On previous voyages these tasks had all been achieved with a certain "Leviathanic flourish," as Mott described it. No trip brought exactly the same problems but all had been solved with a mixture of energy, good will, and intelligence. This time, however, something seemed to be missing. Almost nothing went right the first time. Orders were misunderstood or wrongly obeyed, accidents happened at an alarming rate, complaints about the ship and her facilities flowed like a tide race in one direction and about the troops and their behavior in another, tempers were perpetually raw, and the whole thing added up to a most unhappy atmosphere in what up to now had been a most happy ship. To Jimmy Johnson, to Susan, to Mott, and even, in passing, to Banks himself there was something inexplicable and ominous in the way things were happening this trip.

At the last moment, and taking advantage of the delays caused by the embarkation, Max Laban arrived on board. He had been appointed as the President's personal adviser on Anglo-American shipping and was going to London for on-the-spot consultations with the Ministry of War Transport, where his old henchman Quilly was now installed in as powerful a position — from the point of view of knowing everything that was going on — as he had once been in the London office of Transoceanic. This suited Laban down to the ground. Apart from this wartime job with the President, for which he was uniquely qualified, he would now be able to study and perhaps come to control the new Chairman and Board of the company, reasserting himself and no doubt increasing the power he had enjoyed when Flint was in his heyday. Both Susan and Alan Mitchell were aboard *Leviathan* and during the voyage Laban intended coming to a working agreement with them over the use of their management shares. His only worry had been that he would miss the ship. He had White House and War Shipping Administration authority to take passage in *Leviathan* provided accommodation was available but his duties in Washington had at the last minute snowballed so that it looked very much as though he would miss the ship. Thus, from Laban's point of view, the troubles and delays the embarkation had caused were a blessing in disguise, as he was enabled to get on board just half an hour before *Leviathan* did finally sail.

His arrival on board, however, though it suited Laban, pleased no one else except Banks, who had great pleasure in turning a Brigadier out of his cabin and causing two Colonels to double up in what was, in any case, an annex to a stateroom. That Laban should be a civilian was bad enough, that he should be there on the President's personal say-so was worse, and that he should not only be a U.S. citizen but a director of the company owning and operating *Leviathan* was to the Commanding General the final straw. He retired angrily to his stateroom. He began writing vitriolic reports and he gave it out that he did not intend to emerge until disembarkation in Northern Ireland took place.

So the voyage began. A slight fog lay over the crowded anchorage as *Leviathan* sailed, her siren booming, her new radar in use, helping her to weave her way out at speed. Officers-of-the-watch in other ships, hearing but not seeing the giant, suddenly had the fright of their lives as *Leviathan* loomed out of the fog, apparently missing them by inches. These were risks which would not have been taken in peace time. Indeed, Banks hated depending on any instrument other than his own eyes, but as he watched that large minute-hand ceaselessly revolving round the little circular dial of the radar leaving behind, like a magician's wand, a trace of the harbor and its shipping which glowed for a second or two and then faded until the next passing of the wand, he was forced to drop his prejudices and marvel at the practical advantages of this "X-ray sighting gadget," as he had once scornfully called it.

Soon they were clear of the harbor and had picked up their escort of a British cruiser and two U.S. destroyers. The cruiser, H.M.S. *Antigua,* was to accompany them all the way across, the destroyers would peel off and return to their base that evening; then, a day before reaching the United Kingdom, more destroyers would meet the two ships and see them home. Such, at any rate, were the operation orders. A similar process

343

had taken place on most of their previous transatlantic trooping trips and there was no reason to think it would not happen many times again. Already those who knew the figures were saying that *Leviathan* and her consort were shortening the war by months each trip they made, and certainly to be able to transport a whole division with its equipment from America to Europe in under a week was to alter the strategic picture in new bold strokes, most disconcerting to the enemy. Sea power was once again proving itself a major asset to the Allies in this war, as it had done in the previous one. The Royal Air Force and the U.S. Air Force were gradually pulverizing the cities of Germany, but ultimately the war would end only when soldiers occupied those ruined cities. The German General Staff had evolved and perfected the technique of the *blitzkrieg* on land: the sudden, silent transportation by sea of large quantities of fighting men had already become an Anglo-American specialty, the flexibility of which was in the end to make it the more valuable weapon to wield.

The first two days passed uneventfully. Friction, which had marred the embarkation, seemed to have been confined to "the top brass" and the novelty of a round-the-clock eating and sleeping establishment appealed to the troops, as indeed did the quality of the food provided. Dinners might have to be eaten at five A.M. by the "night livers," but they were good dinners and an unexpectedly large number seemed to enjoy this upside-down kind of routine. Also, although the ship's officers knew they were running into bad weather ahead, the first few days saw *Leviathan* reach more than a thousand miles east of the States in calm summer seas incapable of upsetting even the worst sailor aboard. Everything so far was going as it should.

The presence on board of Laban, and the unsatisfactory stalemate between herself and Alan, drove Susan to reach very much the same conclusion as Laban himself — namely, that they must all make a settlement of some sort. They must extricate themselves from the situation in which Flint's death had placed them, and the time to do so was now. While at sea *Leviathan* naturally kept radio silence in order not to give her presence away, but she could receive messages and some of them, coded up by the British Mission in Washington, were for Laban. Thus Susan's daily work brought her naturally into contact with the American Director, and on the third day out she took the bull by the horns, after delivering a personal message from the White House, and said:

"Speaking as one director to another, Max, don't you think the three of us now aboard *Leviathan* ought to get together and pass a resolution or something? I mean we could creep up on the others, couldn't we, and declare a quick dividend, or sack each other or do *something*, don't you agree?"

"I was working up to that one, too," Laban answered with a smile; "sit down, Sue, and let's get after it now. What's especially on your mind?" He paused for a moment and then added, "Your secret marriage to Motty, perhaps?"

The shock of this casual remark stunned Susan for a moment. She sat down carefully, hoping her sudden blush had gone unnoticed and then looked straight into Laban's amused and calculating eyes.

"How long have you known about that?"

"Well, let's see, you were married on a Wednesday, weren't you? I think Quilly's cable must have arrived the following Friday, but how he found out I wouldn't know."

"And you never said a word to me — or to either of us."

"I thought your whole idea was to keep it secret; certainly it was your husband's idea — and for obvious reasons."

"Yes — well, there were a lot of reasons," Susan said briefly, "all of them personal and all of them valid at the time."

"I don't doubt that for a moment. Still, you must admit it also raises a problem or two. By the way, how is your father?" It was so like him to introduce an oblique issue into the conversation which had little if anything to do with what they were originally discussing. But it let Susan realize that Laban knew the background to her wedding, for what importance that had.

"Just exactly the same. The doctors say it could be hours, it could be years." She did not want the conversation sidetracked at this early stage and, as always, she went impetuously at the first obstacle she imagined she had seen. "I take it you don't approve about Motty and me."

"I don't know why you say that," Laban said blandly. "I've always liked Purser Mott and you've always been something special to me too, Susan. Something very special as a matter of fact." He went on with a look on his face she did not at all like. "It's your own life and what you do with it — that's up to you. Of course, officially speaking . . ."

"Does Ethel know?"

"Not from me — and I wouldn't think from anyone else. As I was going to say, officially speaking Purser Mott remains Purser Mott and the fact that he's now married to all those management shares isn't palatable from the company point of view and can't be tolerated. But you must have been aware of all that, Sue, before ever you went ahead and got married. And knowing Motty, I'd guess it has him a little worried too."

"Yes it does," Susan agreed. "In fact it's something which could mess it up for us both if things go on as they are at present."

"Oh! they can't do that," Laban said craftily, his hooded eyes suddenly reminding Susan of an Arab merchant in a book of fairy tales she had had as a child. She had always liked Maxie Laban, but those dark, cunning, calculating eyes were a warning never to commit herself entirely, never to put herself at his mercy without at least one way of escape. Well, she still had a trick or two up her sleeve; she still had those management shares. Then, almost as if he had been reading her thoughts, he went on:

"I think I should tell you, Susan, that one of the first things I hope the new Chairman will do will be to abolish the power of those management shares Sir J. was at such pains to create. If the Chairman does nothing about it then I shall. The present setup's absurd. I'm not sure what the old man had in mind, but if anyone knew about the use and misuse of power he did — so the way he left his shares is all the more surprising. This company runs on tradition — and I've spent a good deal of my life opposing it or trying to change it, so I ought to know. That's its great strength — its wisdom. For you and young

346

Alan Mitchell at your tender ages to be put on the Board other than nominally, for you — however charming your inexperience may look — to think you could run as old and involved a setup as Transoceanic is to affront all that wisdom and tradition. You can't do it and it won't work. In any case the company is a national asset and you just wouldn't be allowed to start wrecking it."

"Who's talking about wrecking anything?" Susan said hotly. "Perhaps I don't have experience. I can still always learn, can't I?"

"I don't think so, Susan," Laban said as quietly and gently as he could. "It needs a man, and a dedicated man at that." Again that curious almost lascivious expression came into his face. He looked yellow and tired and Susan did not enjoy the feeling there was in the cabin. He had been badly overworked in Washington, she knew, but that only explained his exhausted appearance — not this other inexplicable look.

"Suppose I don't agree? Suppose I do what Sir J. wanted me to do and —"

"How do you know what he wanted?" Laban interrupted with a touch of anger. "You think he left you those shares because he was fond of you and admired your qualities. Maybe he did. But it's also possible he was so goddam proud of himself and of what he'd built up, that he wanted to destroy it all when he died. That's possible, too, you know. He had a vicious sense of humor when he chose to let it be seen. I think he just wanted to go out with a bang and leave Fabian Mitchell a king-size headache. They always hated each other."

"I suppose the answer really is that you want control of the company yourself," Susan said shrewdly, but this unexpected dig produced no reaction other than a veiled smile and the immediate retort:

"I tell you what we'll do, Susan. I'll offer you the job you once wouldn't take from the old man. You can be my personal assistant. We needn't define your duties too far and I promise you you won't be just a secretary."

For a moment or so Susan said nothing, trying desperately to judge the implications in this offer.

347

"What about Motty?" she said. "I couldn't agree to anything that doesn't take care of him too."

"We shall have to think that one out when we come to it," Laban said easily. "In any case you're a Wren and I'm working for Uncle Sam — so for the present it's academic — but who knows? The war might end a whole lot quicker than anyone thinks. The smart thing to do is to be ready for that situation whenever it happens." He looked at her with that calm sardonic smile she had known for so long, that look which contained so much of the interplay between male and female which could never and should never be put into words — the possibilities, the dreams that dodged away into the shadows, the magnetism between two human beings of opposite polarity which in itself created the tensions, the invisible pressure which got things done. No wonder Max Laban was so good at business, she thought, as his seductive, mocking eyes seemed almost to stroke her. There was a power in him which she felt was only just held in check, and if it got loose she sensed there would be no holds barred. But so far he had made it all work for him — sex, charm, illusion, male domination — whatever the particular appeal for the particular person, Laban could always pull the right lever or play the right tune. So could Motty, she had decided a long time ago, but the purpose was different. Motty served. Motty was a good purser because he understood people's feelings, he considered them and helped them to obtain whatever it was they wanted. Laban operated, despite the many smoke screens he put up, solely and simply for the benefit of Maxwell Laban.

"I'll let you know tomorrow," she said. "A girl needs time."

"I don't think this one does," he said softly, "this one knows her own mind right away. This one can give her decision here and now." He paused for a moment and smiled. "Though, of course, a girl, especially an attractive impulsive girl, needs to keep her mouth shut — don't you agree?"

"You make it seem like a conspiracy, like a plot."

"No plot," he said, standing up and drawing her up from her seat, "just an understanding, a business understanding between us." Then, taking her quite by surprise, he kissed her full on the mouth. She struggled violently away from him but he was a strong man and the harder she fought the closer he held her. He smelled of an expensive after-shave lotion mingled with the Havana cigars he habitually smoked. A part of her was revolted and a part of her, a very compelling part of her, longed for his strength to prevail and for her to be forced into something she knew she would afterward regret. She continued to wrestle against him and at one stage kicked him hard on the shin, a blow which must have caused him some considerable pain but which seemed only to make him strengthen his grip. There was now a blind half-mad animal look in his eyes which made her very afraid. Gradually she felt her resistance melting away. Sobbing for breath, and both furious and afraid, she nevertheless felt a fire blazing in her blood, a fire which she knew instinctively could be both her strength and her downfall. For a moment she managed to get free, tearing her Wren monkey jacket and shirt in the process, but almost at once he had her again. She did not know how long she could hold out, and by now a wild panic possessed her, a panic caused by full instinctive knowledge of that primitive masculine violence which had lain for so long so carefully concealed beneath this easy, well-dressed, well-controlled exterior. Now, for the first time she saw the hairline that divides civilized man from the uncontrollable savage, the sudden blind lust which consumes a man and which afterwards makes such sorry and inexplicable hearing in a court of law. For a moment or so she felt that perhaps if she ceased to resist, became limp and pliable in his arms, then the civilized man in him might have a chance to regain control, but her nature was never to give in, especially to assault of this kind, and at the same time she knew that once she gave up the struggle she would never begin it again. By now she was crying helplessly and had begun to shout. This infuriated him and he clapped one hand over her mouth and began bending back her head. Now fear changed to terror and she started to fight with renewed effort, this time possibly for her life.

At that moment, the door of Laban's stateroom opened and Mott came in. For a split second he stopped paralyzed with surprise, the one word "Susan!" on his lips — then in an instant he had leaped across to her aid, got his arm round Laban's neck, releasing Susan, and with a strength he did not know he possessed, turned him round and smashed his fist as hard as he could into Laban's contorted face, following this up with a blow to the midriff which sent the other reeling across the cabin into the dressing-table mirror which broke over his head. Then it was over and Laban lay still, slumped among the broken glass, his nose beginning to bleed.

"Christ!" said Mott. "Are you all right, Sue?"

She nodded dumbly and then together they went to pick up Laban. For one terrible moment which seemed to last an eternity Susan thought he was dead but the heart still beat, and by the time they had got him across to the bed, he had begun to regain consciousness. Susan mopped up his face while Mott tidied the cabin and collected as much of the broken glass as he could. For a long time Laban lay staring at the deckhead without saying a word, then he shook his head slowly and painfully and looked into Susan's anxious face. "Don't know what got into me," he murmured thickly. "Just don't understand. Ethel never forgive me." Tears made their unlikely way into the hooded eyes and he began to shiver.

Susan took his hand and squeezed it gently.

"Ethel needn't know," she said. "You gave me a very bad fright. I don't know what got into you, but it's over now. You had an accident with the mirror, that's all, and you've been overworking — that's the usual excuse, isn't it? Anyway, Max, I promise you, Ethel will never know. Only I think we'd better discuss that proposition you made me some other time — when my husband can be in on it right from the start."

At that moment a long shuddering jar shook *Leviathan*, as though she had been struck up forward by some gigantic hammer. The reverberations of this lasted about ten seconds and before they had died away Mott had sprung to the door.

"We've hit something," he called out over his shoulder, "or we've had a torpedo. Come on, both of you, up on deck."

⚓⚓⚓⚓⚓ XVII ⚓⚓⚓⚓⚓

WHAT in fact had happened proved to be the worst accident which had so far occurred to *Leviathan*. Yet the great ship herself came out of it virtually unscathed. Moreover such was *Leviathan*'s speed and power that the whole thing came and went in a few desperate minutes. During that time, however, a terrible disaster happened and an even harder decision had then to be taken.

Earlier in the day there had been reports of increasing U-boat activity directly in *Leviathan*'s path. There was a fast Halifax-U.K. convoy a few miles to the southeast, and this was no doubt the U-boats' principal target. *Leviathan* and her escorting cruiser, H.M.S. *Antigua*, were overhauling this convoy obliquely from the south, zigzagging at ten-minute intervals in order to discourage any U-boat ready to risk a pot-shot at the twenty-nine-knots monster and her escort. Since a U-boat's submerged speed, or at periscope depth, was under ten knots, *Leviathan* was no easy target, especially with frequent alterations of course to contend with. Unless a U-boat happened to be waiting almost directly in *Leviathan*'s way, the chances of putting a torpedo into her were poor, and once out of range there was no hope whatever of catching her.

H.M.S. *Antigua*, an old six-inch-gun cruiser of just under five thousand tons, had been finding the pace heavy going. On leaving U.S. territorial waters she had taken up station ahead of *Leviathan*, but her old boilers were hard put to it to give her the twenty-nine knots she needed. In consequence Banks found himself constantly running up on her and urging her on from behind, so to speak. Thus the timing of changes of course on a zig-zag could be critical and the two ships had come uncomfortably close to each other on several previous occasions.

When it happened, it happened fast. Either the cruiser turned early or *Leviathan* was late, or it was a combination of the two. At all events H.M.S. *Antigua* was suddenly there crossing *Leviathan*'s bows in such a position that even though *Leviathan* had herself begun to turn a collision was inevitable. The knife-edge stem backed by the full power of two hundred thousand horsepower cut clean through the cruiser amidships with the tearing, grinding, convulsive scream of steel biting its way into steel. Hundreds of men below decks in the cruiser must have died instantly, hundreds more were to die in the course of the next few minutes. Even by the time Banks had raced up on the bridge (he had been washing his hands in his cabin when it happened), the two halves of the stricken ship were a couple of hundred yards away. Smothered in dense black smoke, the fore part of the cruiser was sinking to port as Banks reached the bridge. Away to starboard the after part was already awash to the base of the funnels. It was a question not of minutes but of seconds. Indeed, even as he studied the situation all that was left of H.M.S. *Antigua* sank to the bottom. There in the oily, swirling sea five hundred men were drowning in the most appalling conditions imaginable. There would be a few survivors, though not many, and the damage to *Leviathan* herself was so far unknown. What was he to do? Stop and pick up the men struggling in the water, numbering possibly a hundred, possibly very many less — and in so doing jeopardize *Leviathan* and the lives of fifteen thousand men on board? *Leviathan* was still driving on at twenty-nine knots, and so far as the feel of the ship was concerned appeared to be undamaged. Now unescorted, it was his clear duty to continue as before without in any way risking the ship, but this decision was, perhaps, the hardest one he had had to take in his life. Moreover, he could not break radio silence without endangering *Leviathan* more seriously even than by stopping. He went into the chart room and checked on the position of the convoy. By diverging from his route for two hours he could get into visual touch with the convoy escort so that the *Antigua* survivors could be picked up. This he decided to do as he turned *Leviathan* to circle the scene of the disaster. By now the bo's'n had come hot foot to the bridge to report that the ship's stem had been pushed back and the forepeak was awash. Banks reduced speed and at once sent the Staff Captain, the bo's'n, and the carpenter tearing forward to examine the damage. If the collision bulkhead, that watertight steel wall rising from the bottom of the ship to the main deck, had been pierced then *Leviathan* might well be in trouble herself, the more so since all the time the weather was worsening.

While this inspection was in progress, Banks turned his attention to the scene in the water. The *Antigua* by some miracle had been able to launch two of her boats before sinking and the few oil-blacked figures that were left were struggling to reach them. Banks considered lowering and abandoning to the survivors one of *Leviathan*'s own lifeboats, but to do that he would have virtually to stop the ship, in which case he might as well wait and pick up the lot. In those circumstances the stationary ninety-thousand-ton ship would be an irresistible sitting target to any U-boat there happened to be lurking in the vicinity. With a heavy heart Banks decided the men must be left and turning *Leviathan* on to a course to intercept the convoy, he awaited the damage report. Slowly the huge ship drew away from the dark patch of oil, strewn with wreckage and mangled corpses and the small pathetic clusters of men in the water who were still alive. "Help them now, O God!" he silently prayed. "Now in this their desperate hour. Help them, O Lord God Almighty, and help us all in our terrible need." His screwed-up eyes glistened and those on the bridge, studying him furtively had never before seen him look so scowling, so ferocious, nor so utterly and completely alone.

By now the Staff Captain had reported that the collision bulkhead was intact and that he was having it shored up with every balk of timber he could lay his hands on. So speed was again increased, and in just over an hour and a half *Leviathan* was flashing news of the calamity to the senior officer of the convoy escort, who detached a ship to go back and pick up survivors. Then in a freshening wind coming up astern from the west and as the twilight lengthened into night, *Leviathan* set course once more for the United Kingdom at her accustomed twenty-nine knots.

That night, which was a Friday, a storm overtook them from the west. It gave Banks no time to brood about the *Antigua* disaster, but also it allowed him no sleep. Speed was reduced as mountainous seas raced past from astern, forcing *Leviathan* into that corkscrew motion which is the most difficult of all to support in any ship. The scourge of seasickness began among the troops embarked, its clinging smell having a snowball effect on borderline cases, so that at one time it seemed as if all fifteen thousand men were going to be or already had been sick. As always, and despite the most stringent orders, some one had left part of his equipment not properly secured, so that on the first vicious roll it took charge, crashed against a bulkhead, causing broken wrists and local chaos.

When a ship the size of *Leviathan* begins to pitch and roll there is something so slow and ponderous about it that inescapability seems to be its dominant feature. Those on board are trapped. There can be no relief. Up—up—up—up—shudder—then down—down—down—down. There were times when Max Laban, wedged spreadeagled in his bed, bruised and sick and full of remorse, wondered if this was a form of torture imposed on him as a penance. His lapse of the previous evening not only distressed and disgusted him, it shook his spirits as fundamentally as the motion of *Leviathan* was now shaking his body. It was not the fact that he had forced Susan to kiss him, after pointedly revealing that he knew she was Motty's wife. A lot of wives got kissed by men who were not their husbands. Anyway, Susan was such a sexy young creature she could scarcely object when certain obvious reactions were provoked. Privately, he had always thought her a bit of a tart and also a tease. She caused these things to happen by the way she flaunted her sex. He did not worry too much about Susan.

What brought Max up all standing with a shudder was the animal violence which had gotten into himself. He had wanted to rape the girl. He had been perfectly capable of doing that, and then perhaps of strangling that slender neck. What had happened to him? Was this the middle-aged, respectable, long-married (and long happily married) man, now on his way to take up a Presidential appointment of great responsibility in

England? He shook his head in puzzled dismay as *Leviathan* heaved and creaked, swinging him up, up, up, and then down, down, down. What had become of him? What had possessed him? Where had a lifetime's intelligence and self-control disappeared to when most they were wanted? Above all, how could he, Maxwell Laban the Great, have allowed it to happen at all? He realized now that every time he had seen the girl, she had burned him up consciously and unconsciously. He had wanted to possess her from the moment he had first set eyes on her, but again there was nothing especially remarkable in that — that was the passing reaction of most normal men to most pretty girls. They would if they could, but since life was generally arranged so that they couldn't, the sexual drag remained what in essence it was — an illusion, a dream, harming no one except the dreamer himself. But this violence he had done to Susan was something baser than that, and to discover that there was that kind of thing in him at all was to Transoceanic's American Director a fundamental and horrible shock.

Susan and Mott, too, had had a bad half-hour with themselves.

"We've only ourselves to blame," Mott said despondently. "We were crazy to think we could cock a snook at convention the way we did. I knew it all along. I've spent my life watching people trying to dodge the laws our dear rotten society makes to protect itself and they never get away with it in the end. They always think they do at the time. I've seen wives slip away with their lovers and then come back and tell their husbands they've been to the ship's cinema. Some of them even bothered to look up the film they were supposed to have seen. Then the lover would get shamefaced and guilty. 'I can't accept a drink from him when I've just been seducing his wife,' or something quite unnecessary like that — then the husband's instincts get aroused and a dozen damning details they've overlooked suddenly come to light. Someone else went to the same show, and says, 'Wasn't it funny when they put a reel of the wrong film on by mistake halfway through?' and of course the wife and her lover knew nothing of that as they happened to be in bed with each other at the time. So then the husband knows exactly what's going on and proceeds to lay some fiendish trap into which they fall and from which none of them, including the husband, can ever get out. Well, we've been trying to do much the same thing, only in a different way. I knew all along it would end in disaster."

"You don't seriously think I've been having an affair with Max Laban all this time, do you?" Susan asked angrily.

"No, Susan, of course I don't. But it wouldn't surprise me to find out you had at one time or other."

"That's the most cynical thing I've ever heard you say."

"Is it? I wonder. There's something about you, Susan, which arouses extreme sexual violence in a man. It worked on Charley Beecher, on me, on Laban. But I know you, Susan, I know you very well. You're impulsive and generous and you act in the moment and for the moment. You *give* — and that's why you are the person you are. Anyway, the morning is the morning and the night the night. Never judge one by the other. The point is I love you."

"And I love you, too," she said, clutching him as tight as she could while *Leviathan* heaved and creaked up and down and all around them. "I think you're the most wonderful man in the world."

"Well, of course, I am," Mott said lightly, "but that doesn't get us out of this jam we landed ourselves in when we got married and thought we could see everyone off."

"We're not in a jam," Susan said, craning back from him and tossing her head in her old familiar way. "Before Maxie's little lapse he gave the whole game away. He wants control of the company himself — that's what he's after — that's why he's fixed this job over in London and that's why he wants me as his Personal Assistant, so that I won't make him any trouble. Well, he's going to find out it's not as easy as that."

But Mott shook his head sadly.

"No, darling, you can't do that. It *is* much too big a job."

"I could do it if you helped me."

"I'm a purser, my sweet, not a director of a vast steamship company. I haven't the talent, the knowledge, nor, if you want to know, the inclination. I've spent my life learning to be what

356

I am; I shouldn't like to start another job all over again, especially caught up in your apron strings, so to speak."

There was a long pause. Outside the cabin deadlight the storm howled and raged. They looked long and tenderly at each other and then Susan said with a smile:

"In the end it doesn't matter very much what we say, does it, Motty? It's what happens that counts. I wasn't going to tell you this till I was absolutely sure. But I suppose now is as good a time as any." She paused and smiled at him with a little sideways look. "I think I'm going to have a baby — so, you see . . ."

"Yes, darling, I see," Motty said taking her once more in his arms. "As a matter of fact, that's why I had such a great personal pleasure in disposing of Mr. Laban last night." She shook herself angrily free and gave a little jump of rage.

"Can't I ever surprise you?" she wailed. "Isn't there any one single secret a girl can have?"

"You once gave me the surprise of my life," Mott said, kissing her again, "you married me."

All through Saturday the storm grew worse. The misery among _Leviathan_'s passengers became acute and the Cox and Box system for the use of bunks was in danger of breaking down, since everyone wanted somehow or other to lie on his back. Seasickness, like a toothache, became one of those nagging tortures which narrows the sufferer's horizon down to the pain itself, and many thousands of those on board would gladly have settled for oblivion there and then if only the lethal dose could have been swiftly administered.

It was ironic and pitiful to Banks, who himself had not had any sleep since the _Antigua_ disaster, that so many of these men now so casually saying they would rather be dead, would in fact soon be dead when this division came to grips with the enemy. Now, like Job when his soul was weary of his life, Banks found as the storm progressed that his secret heart, which no one on board even guessed that he had, was overcome by pity or rather by its distillation, compassion. He thought about the drowning men from the cruiser he had had to leave in the water; he thought about these thousands of young American soldiers as yet unblooded, as yet unaware of the true grim nature of life, all of them about to be offered as human sacrifices on the altar of — what? An idea? Was this world holocaust now engulfing them all as easily explained as that? He doubted it.

He stared into the black raging night, balancing himself against the deep roll of the ship, and he brooded, like Job, on the meaning of it all. "Wherefore then hast thou brought me forth out of the womb? Oh! that I had given up the ghost and no eye had seen me! Are not my days few? Cease then and let me alone, that I may take comfort a little before I go whence I shall not return, even to the land of darkness and the shadow of death, a land of darkness, as darkness itself and of the shadow of death, without any order and where the light is as darkness." It was one thing to work out a comfortable philosophy of life in an armchair in front of a blazing fire; it was quite another in the heart of a storm like this or as the waters closed in choking back the screams of hundreds of your drowning messmates. Then how conscious could you be of your soul? The shocks of birth and death which, to Banks were identical in their meaning, being the same place in the great circle of one's life, could also, he realized, be accompanied by terror, panic, and the horror of nothingness. There were so many different ways of dying. He had long regarded death as a journey into loneliness, into a place where no one could reach you, however kind and compassionate the eyes which saw you go, but it was also possible that death was a further descent into yet more terrible conditions even than applied to life on earth. If Christ himself on the Cross could call out, "Lord, Lord, why hast Thou forsaken me?" what dire pit of nothingness was opening then in front of his eyes? And Banks could not clear his mind of the persistent idea that the Angel of Death was hovering near to all of them on this ill-starred, disaster-attracting voyage.

There was only one blessing to be offset against the storm and that was the impossibility of enemy attack. U-boats had been forced to stay submerged, aircraft — and they were now within striking distance of the long-range Heinkels based on France — would not venture in such conditions and, as far as was known, none of the German battle-cruisers or pocket battleships was then at large in the Atlantic. So by Sunday morning when the storm had abated and the gray rolling ocean was slowly regaining its blue, though there were pig-sty messdecks on board which would have to be cleaned up, *Leviathan* herself and her precious cargo had come through the ordeal unscathed.

"Let us give thanks," Banks said at the eleven o'clock service which it was one of his great pleasures to conduct, "for the passing of the tempest and the preserving of this great ship in which we serve or take our passage." Red-eyed from exhaustion and from close on to forty-eight hours without sleep, Banks would have jumped overboard rather than allow one of the many padres then on board to take this weekly service in what had once been the first class restaurant and was now a conveyor-belt type of cafeteria. Indeed, the holding this service meant an interruption to the round-the-clock mess arrangements. This disturbance had been strongly opposed, among other things, by the senior officer in charge of troops. But Banks would have none of it. "The food of the spirit, sir, ranks above that of our puny bodies," he had declared, "and as long as I am Captain of this ship a service to the glory of God will be held when I direct and where I direct." Those whose meal-time it was, therefore, at eleven A.M. on Sunday morning found themselves out of luck.

These weekly services were highly unconventional offerings of worship and usually derived from the parts of the Bible on which Banks had been meditating the previous week. Hymns and psalms were rarely selected by Banks until the service was under way, since it was one of his basic tenets that, although Pattern was all, Spontaneity in the tending praise to the Almighty was also of the essence. The organist, therefore, had to have his wits about him and woe betide him if he faltered or exhibited confusion in any shape or form. "Come along, sir, brace your ideas up," Banks had once called out when the organist had had difficulty with his stops, "you're not in the Palm Court now!" When *Leviathan* had been converted to troop carrying, Banks had done his best to have the electric organ in the main lounge held back on board for purposes of the Sunday Service. This organ made a noise like a musical stomach and was very appropriate to some of the more sentimental hymns Banks was wont to choose. But the authorities had decreed the organ must go with the rest of the peacetime luxury fittings, so Banks at his own expense had purchased a harmonium which now did duty in its place, and by a really involved piece of wangling he had managed to get the one-time pianist in the tourist class orchestra appointed to the ship as a temporary Hostilities Only Royal Marine Bandsman, an achievement made possible only because the Commandant General of the Royal Marines had a house in the same Sussex village as Banks and special exceptions which the Admiralty was never allowed to hear about had been made all along the line.

As a result of all this, and the sudden eccentricities of Banks himself, the Sunday morning service had already become part of *Leviathan*'s mythology. No doubt because of widely differing motives the "Church" was always packed, as it was on this last Sunday of *Leviathan*'s life. Sometimes Banks would merely read passages of the Bible and order bizarre hymns to be sung; at others he would launch out into ad-lib sermons and prayers of his own concoction. Whatever form the service took, the entertainment factor was high — though Banks himself would not allow such a thing to be said — and the result, not altogether surprising, was what Banks had always intended — a spontaneous uprush of joy and worship, pleasing, he hoped, to the Deity and sufficiently moving, in many cases, to tide those who took part through the trials and tribulations of the week ahead.

Spontaneous though these services were, Banks had his favorites to which he kept returning, and among those was Psalm 104. Simple-minded critics put this down to the delight Banks patently derived from roaring out the twenty-fourth to the twenty-seventh verses, "Oh! Lord, how manifold are thy works! In wisdom hast thou made them all: the earth is full of thy riches. So is this great and wide sea, wherein are things creeping innumerable, both small and great beasts." As he said this he would sweep his fiery gaze over his audience, dwelling on the word "creeping" as if it had special application to those then in his presence. Then with a broad gesture and a roar he would go on, "There go the ships: There is that leviathan whom thou hast made to play therein. These wait all upon thee; that thou mayest give them their meat in due season." There were other verses, too, which he fastened upon with dramatic relish such as "The trees of the Lord are full of sap; the cedars of Lebanon, which he had planted." He would declaim this aggressively emphasizing the word "sap" as he did another verse "He watereth the hills from his chambers: the earth is satisfied with the fruit of thy works," which was accompanied by a smack of the lips and an angry look around as if he expected some pawky denial from a critical member of his congregation.

There was no doubt about the old man, Mott thought, now watching him lead the hymn singing as if he were halfway through the charge of the Light Brigade. He would survive. He would survive even the end of the world itself. This present voyage might be studded with disaster of every kind, yet what visible effect did this have on the Captain of *Leviathan?* None other than to make him jut out his chin and resist the more ferociously. If Churchill was an emblem of national dogged tenacity in the face of catastrophe, then Banks could well double up for the Merchant Marine. Nothing could knock him off course for more than a second or two. The set of the shoulders, the paunch, the patriarch's beard, the glint of will in those red-rimmed eyes — all these different evidences of a wily toughness, a grip and a drive added up to the one word, "mastery." Banks was a master in every sense of the word. And because discipline first of himself and then of others had been the mainspring of his life, he was now free. He could do, and do effectively, whatever he decided on as a course of action.

The service proceeded on its grotesque and syncopated

course and after a time Banks launched out into one of his impromptu sermons. "For some of you," he began, "this is your first crossing of the Atlantic. Others no doubt have done it before. For me, this is my five hundred and seventy-first voyage across this great and dangerous ocean. You might say I know it a great deal better than you do. You would be right — I do. However in the storm we have just been through, and in the perils prepared for us by the enemy, you and I are literally in the same boat. We are in the same helpless but not quite hopeless position. We cannot prevent things happening — neither the tempest we have just survived nor the war in which we are all engaged. These things lie beyond our control. They are caused by Powers greater than ourselves which involve us at their pleasure for one simple and potent reason — namely, that mankind is asleep. When you are asleep you are at the mercy of your dreams: you cannot control them. But when we awake in the morning we think we become masters of our fate: we imagine we possess free will. If this monstrous illusion happened for a moment to be true would any of us be here now — arrayed for licensed murder as we are — purposing the destruction of our enemies? Of course we would not. Then why are we here? Why did we get ourselves involved? Where did we all go wrong? I will tell you why," here again he gave another of his dramatic pauses before going on. "We are here, gentlemen, because we are all fast asleep, asleep and dreaming in ourselves. We've forgotten why we were born — if ever we bothered at any time in our little lives to think out a reason. We've forgotten our aim and our purposes — if ever we had them. When we became men and put away childish things what did we set out to do with our lives? Drift helplessly along with the current? Do you imagine" — and here his voice rose in what was, to Mott, its double diapason roar — "do you imagine that if but a tenth of mankind were awake and alert that war would be possible? Of course it would not. What did Christ tell us to do?" He paused and scorched the assembly with a gaze like a searchlight beam, as if daring one of them to speak up in answer. "He told us to take heed, watch, and pray — for ye know not when the time is. For the Son of Man is as a man taking a far journey, who left his house and gave authority to his servants and to every man his work and commanded the porter to watch. 'Watch ye therefore: for ye know not when the master of the house cometh, at even or at midnight or at the cockcrowing or in the morning. Lest coming suddenly he find you sleeping, And what I say unto you, I say unto all — watch.'" Again Banks paused for effect. He would flail them, Mott surmised, and then wheedle and persuade them a little, and then finally lash them again. It was old stuff to Mott but the present audience from G.I. to Brigadier General seemed to be lapping it up, and Mott had to admit that the old man always put on an impressive performance. "Now, gentlemen," Banks continued. "What does waking up and watching mean in less general terms . . . ?"

At that moment a distant explosion could be felt in the ship and this was followed a second or two later by two others very much closer. Almost instantaneously action stations sounded off, and *Leviathan*'s multiple pom-poms could be heard opening up. Snatching up his tin hat and gas mask, Banks had vanished in mid-sentence, with that surprising cat-like agility he possessed, almost before his listeners were aware of what was happening. The weather they had endured was merely the overture; now the main trial had begun. A squadron of German long-range bombers had happened upon the richest target then on the high seas.

"I wonder if the porter was watching that time," Mott whispered to Susan as they made their way up top. "Because if he wasn't the old man's going to have something to say."

There were only three aircraft in the first attack and none of them scored a hit. What was much more serious, however, was the accidental discovery by the Luftwaffe of *Leviathan*'s whereabouts. Other attacks would be certain to follow and might even now be on their way. Moreover the weather was against them. The storm had been followed by clear, cloudless skies. There was still a heavy swell, the aftermath of the last forty-eight hours, and *Leviathan* still rolled and pitched to the misery of her passengers but now, unescorted and very much alone, she would be exposed to anything the enemy could put

363

in the air. No doubt also by this time a number of U-boats were altering their dispositions to intercept the great ship.

Since the enemy now knew *Leviathan*'s position, and since one unsuccessful attack had already been made, Banks broke radio silence to tell the Admiralty what had occurred and felt somewhat comforted to be told that two eight-inch cruisers were immediately being detached from the Northern Patrol and had been ordered to rendezvous with *Leviathan* at their full speed. However, the Admiralty continued, in a signal which Susan decyphered with an ominous sinking of the heart, it would be twenty-four hours at the earliest before these cruisers could be in company, and forty-eight hours before any form of long-range fighter protection could be provided. The next few hours, therefore, were likely to be *Leviathan*'s critical time.

They were not left long in doubt. By two o'clock in the afternoon another three bombers had attacked, all of them near-missing through a last minute high speed turn which Banks made in the nick of time. Then at five a force of twelve Heinkels arrived from the east, circled the ship out of range of *Leviathan*'s guns and began methodically and almost leisurely to attack from three directions at once.

"God help us now," Banks muttered to himself, as they all entered that timeless period between the beginning of an event and its inevitable end. As the planes came in to the attack and *Leviathan*'s pom-poms opened up on the profusion of targets, it seemed to Banks as though he were falling off a very tall building, falling fully conscious but none the less falling, falling, falling — waiting until the final sharp crack of his skull on a paving stone should bring it all to an end. But by dint of one high speed turn after another *Leviathan* still escaped a direct hit from the first attacking wave. Moreover the A.A. gunners forward and aft shot down a bomber each, to be rewarded by a shout of joy and congratulation from Banks on the bridge which was audible even above the din of the firing.

But the Germans had not flown all that way to give up after one attempt. The ten that were left formed up and again circled the ship out of range, as they had done before. Then, pairing up they attacked this time from five directions at once. This time they pressed home the attacks with a ferocity none of those on the bridge had ever experienced before. One of them, in fact, flew into *Leviathan*'s mast and then exploded in midair, while another could not pull out of its dive and continued headlong into the sea. But this time *Leviathan* did not escape. One 250-kilogram bomb fell on the forecastle, breeching the collision bulkhead so carefully shored up after the *Antigua* accident. Another, by some appalling fluke, went down the after funnel and exploded in one of the boilers. A third grazed the port side and burst on the waterline causing a ten-foot split amidships. Then the eight Heinkels, their bombs expended, returned to spray the decks and the bridge with machine-gun fire, and put out of action the forward pompom gun. Finally, no doubt satisfied with their results, they flew in formation back to the east, leaving the stricken ship making water forward and amidships on the port side, and seriously on fire in the boiler room, where a handful of badly burned survivors were scrambling to escape from an appalling shambles, and what was soon to become an uncontrollable raging inferno.

Now Banks faced the greatest challenge of his life. He had to endure another three to four hours of daylight when further air attacks were all too probable, he had a bad fire to control, a ship that was making water, a state of chaos in the boiler and engine rooms, a steadily dropping speed in an area peppered with U-boats and an unpredictable situation with thousands of raw American soldiers on board, some of whom had never been on or even seen the sea in their lives before, and all of whom were badly overcrowded, sleepless, and seasick from the previous forty-eight hours, and who, if pushed a little too far, might easily panic. And a panic down below, Banks thought grimly, was all he needed to round off the picture of catastrophe now building up steadily as he received each separate report on the bridge.

But although everyone on board knew the ship had been hit, *Leviathan* was so vast that only those immediately involved — and of course Banks on the bridge — had any idea of the extent of the damage. Susan, up top in the cypher office, was quite unaware that all of them were now in mortal danger; Jimmy Johnson down in one of the after store rooms knew the old lady had been badly shaken and that speed had been reduced, but otherwise there was no damage aft whatever.

By some miracle the forward boiler room was intact and thus there was still steam for the generators and for a speed of possibly eight to ten knots. But because of the split in the collision bulkhead up forward, Banks reduced speed to keep no more than steerage way on the ship while the bo's'n, the carpenter, and their working parties, tried to block the crack and shore up the bulkhead with more balks of timber. In this they were comparatively successful, since in any case the split was above sea level. The waterline gash amidships in the port side was a far more serious problem. Water poured in each time *Leviathan* rolled, the lights failed, and some twenty men were drowned in the darkness after being battered senseless by the inrush of the sea. The other men that happened to be down on D deck ran helter-skelter for their lives and a little panic of the kind Banks so greatly feared had begun. Luckily when they got up on deck the panic left them but this was a foretaste of worse to come. In the meanwhile the sea poured in through the hole and *Leviathan* began listing to port.

Due to the heroism of an engineer officer who lost his life shutting off the oil fuel supply to the after boiler room, the fire there did not immediately spread. But in the ghastly wreckage the bomb had caused, a wreckage of firebricks, boiler tubes, and fragments of human beings, what was not immediately realized was that a considerable quantity of oil had escaped into the bilges where it worked its way aft and awaited its time, explosively ready for the next disaster.

This then was the situation at dusk on the Sunday as *Leviathan* continued at about nine knots more or less directly into a pack of U-boats awaiting this most valuable prey of the British Merchant Marine. As darkness fell and the situation could be properly appreciated, the Admiralty diverted two battleships and their attendant destroyers to reinforce the cruisers already hurrying to *Leviathan*'s aid. But as Banks paced up and down the listing bridge and as every available pump was got to work to try and localize the damage on the port side, he realized with a chill that the odds were now badly against *Leviathan*'s survival. So night fell on the stricken giant.

⚓⚓⚓⚓⚓ XVIII ⚓⚓⚓⚓⚓

"THIS is the Captain," Banks said crisply into the public address system, "now listen carefully to what I have to say. . . ." All over the ship sailors and soldiers, officers and men stopped what they were doing and looked up blankly into the distance, waiting, some with intelligent interest in their expressions, some opaque and bovine, waiting one and all to hear what had to be said, waiting upon whatever it was that destiny had in store for each individual soul. "We were struck by three bombs," Banks went on, "all of which have done us material damage and cost us valuable lives. Our speed has perforce been reduced — and speed has always been this ship's main asset in avoiding attention from U-boats. I'm telling you this because we are all of us in a very grave situation — a situation which, if people lose their heads, may well be the end of us all. There is no need — and there never will be — for any disciplined man to panic. If the order to abandon ship should be given, you all know your boat stations, you all know where to go and what to do. Half the Home Fleet is racing to help us and for the next few hours we have the blessed shield of a moonless night. Now I want to tell you to remember this. Remember that nothing is lost until you yourself give up the struggle. We are all in God's Almighty power and in Him we put our trust. So let us face what is ahead with faith and with hope. Hope I can promise you: Faith is something for each one of you listening now. God be with us all and take us into His keeping."

Throughout the ship the final click as the microphone was turned off fell on an almost total silence. Troops and crew alike held the Captain's words in their attention and pondered the implications. Comments varied from a greaser who spat into a bit of cotton waste and said, "The old man's at it again. Can't wait to see us all there at the pearly gates," to Steward Wilkins, who promptly shortened the odds on the book he was running on the ship's survival. American comment seemed mostly to center on the wide range of interesting tortures that Herr Hitler would be subjected to if ever any of those then in *Leviathan* could get hold of him. Alan Mitchell put the whole thing out of his mind and after cautioning Susan for the umpteenth time about sloppy filing in a message she had decyphered, proceeded to bury his nose in the *Manual of Naval Signalling* in preparation for an examination he was intending to take. Concentrate as hard as he might though, the small severe features of the Oxford professor's daughter kept intruding on his thoughts and presently he put his manual on one side while he dealt with the absurd thought which kept recurring in his mind, the ridiculous idea that he might never see her again. "Nonsensical!" he told himself in the tone of voice he had so often heard the father of his beloved dismiss the theories of some hated university rival. But the more strongly he ridiculed the possibility to himself, the more annoyingly it plagued his thoughts. A deck below, Laban got on with a report on allied shipping he had hoped to finish on the trip. Elsewhere Susan and Mott carried out their respective duties but popped in to see each other as often as they possibly could.

Meanwhile an attempt was made to clear up the wreckage in the after boiler room. Surprisingly few had been killed, but seven of the engine room staff had such terrible burns that the surgeon did not give them till morning to live, and said frankly that from the victims' point of view it would be better if they died under the morphia. By midnight four of them had so died.

The watertight bulkheads which sealed off the split amidships seemed to be holding, and very little more water was percolating through the collision bulkhead up forward. At nine knots *Leviathan* would make a splendid target to any U-boat which happened to find her, but nothing had so far shown up on the radar and as Banks had forecast they were concealed by one of the darkest nights of the month. For the moment then they had a little respite.

368

While such was the state of affairs on board, the world once again had its eyes on the giant ship, and *Leviathan* was back in the headlines, this time by courtesy of the Germans. Just before Banks turned in for the first sleep he had had for nearly sixty hours, *Leviathan*'s chief telegraphist brought him Lord Haw-Haw's news over the German radio. "Dr. Goebbels has sunk us already, sir," he said with a grin; "we blew up with a tremendous explosion and sank in under a minute as the result of a brilliant Luftwaffe attack from which all aircraft safely returned after gallantly directing neutral shipping to humanitarian rescue operations. That's one of his biggest whoppers yet, isn't it, sir?"

Banks grunted and contrived to produce with difficulty an answering smile.

"Make to Dr. Goebbels from *Leviathan* 'keep your humanitarian rescue operations for your own concentration camps,' and repeat it to Hitler, the Admiralty, and the C.-in-C. Home Fleet."

The Chief Telegraphist never quite knew when to take his Captain seriously and in any case to send such a message, had it been possible, would have been against all regulations. He began to explain this fact, which of course Banks knew perfectly well, and then discovered that his Captain had gone fast asleep in his great hard uncomfortable oaken chair. The Chief Telegraphist shook his head sadly and muttered under his breath:

"Poor old bugger; I'll bet he could do with a good night's sleep." He felt a motherly inclination to cover up the great carcass with a rug but as he left the cabin he was brought back to normal and sped on his way by a gruff sleepy roar.

"Insubordinate remarks are punishable with *death*, sir, and don't you forget it. See that I'm not disturbed for the next two hours, and *don't slam the door*."

By now the succoring and saving of *Leviathan* had become a full fleet operation, watched with anxiety by Washington and London, and involving, as fleet actions do, a host of ships normally occupied on other duties. One of these, an escort destroyer called H.M.S. *Aquamarine,* happened to be commanded by Lieutenant-Commander Charles Beecher, R.N.R., who found himself ordered out of Plymouth at short notice and high speed to rendezvous with the Home Fleet cruisers coming from the north. Destroyer captains are not usually treated to the same information as admirals commanding squadrons and fleets but it so happened that Charles, too, had been listening to Lord Haw-Haw's news and the sudden receipt, a few minutes after, of orders to put to sea at his best speed, made him guess that Lord Haw-Haw had not, perhaps, been telling the truth. As he sped west through the night he wondered if it was to be *Leviathan* he would escort and whether she had in fact been damaged or whether this was just a precautionary measure. He had a sudden urge to signal *Leviathan,* "Don't worry, *Aquamarine* is coming," and at intervals through the night he relished his picture of Banks's expression had he not been bound by radio silence. He wondered what was going on aboard his old ship. He supposed George Stone would still be clicking his teeth and Jimmy Johnson tactfully rationing out the spirit supplies. Motty no doubt would still be making an ineffective pass at Susan (Charles had no idea of the truth) and she would doubtless be up to her usual teasing tricks with any male in the vicinity. Life, in fact, he reflected with a smile must be very much the same as when he had left *Leviathan,* and after he'd escorted the old lady in, he hoped there would be time to go aboard and make contact with his friends. In the meantime as ordered he cracked on west as hard as he could.

Thus, *Leviathan* became a point of focus for warships of all kinds both allied and German. Indeed, the known concentration of U-boats on the one hand and *Leviathan*'s reduced speed on the other set up a situation so potentially dangerous that during the night *Leviathan* was ordered to double back on her tracks, a procedure very little to Banks's liking.

That night aboard *Leviathan* almost everyone slept in their clothes. An uneasiness, arising principally from the ship's slow progress, hung like a cloud over everyone on board. They were crippled and a long way from home. The mystique of

370

the greatest and fastest ship in the world seemed suddenly to have deserted them and this crawling, first in one direction and then in another, the list to port, and the dent in the bows suggested more of a derelict than the *Leviathan* known to the world. Or perhaps, as Mott felt, coming events were casting a shadow ahead of them.

Not that many people slept either long or soundly that night. Every change in motion, every new creak, every roll a little more severe than usual brought people tensely awake and jumpily expectant. Halfway through the night Susan could stand it no more. Breaking every rule both official and self-imposed she made her way down to Mott's cabin, to snuggle into his arms. Though both were fully dressed and ready for the next emergency, the illusion of security they had in each other's arms helped them both and they were thus together like babes in the wood when, at dawn the next day, the fatal torpedo struck *Leviathan* twenty feet below the waterline on the port side aft.

Though the U-boat they had had the misfortune to encounter had fired all the three torpedoes she had left in her tubes, only one of them made its mark, but that one was enough. Not only did it blow a huge jagged hole in the ship's side through which the sea began pouring in, but it also pierced and ignited one of the oil fuel tanks and thus started a fire which began radiating outwards like a huge Catherine-wheel in every direction throughout the ship. Then things began happening at enormous speed.

Before Banks had a proper report of the situation, the worst thing of all took place — the one thing he and the officers in charge of the troops had tried at all cost to avoid — thousands of men below decks began stampeding up top and, what was worse, doing so on the port side thus making the ship's list far worse than it needed to be. Terrible scenes occurred in the melee, and such was the force of the stampede that those who fell had no chance of getting to their feet but were, in several cases, trampled to death where they lay. Moreover, once on deck, control was not established for some time. A madness was aboard, all discipline disappeared and numbers of men began jumping recklessly into the sea. Banks, in a rage there had never been the like of before, yelled and roared orders from the bridge which were totally disregarded. Then as the situation began to worsen and the ship's list increased, he told his Staff Captain to take charge on the bridge and seizing his revolver himself went down on deck.

It was an extraordinary sight. The angle of the deck made it difficult to walk and once in the crowd he found himself at one point in danger of being carried over the side too, in the rush. All the time he roared at them to stop, to get over on the starboard side, to stop, to listen and obey — but this was a mob and it had no time to listen nor anything to listen with. Wild primitive instinct was at large and this would only respond to force.

"The next man who attempts to jump I shall shoot," Banks roared out, and at last the huge bearded figure wedged against one of the davits was given a flicker of attention. But it was only a momentary flicker, and then once more the helter-skelter rush was on. So Banks took aim and shot, killing directly for the first time in his life. "Back! back! back!" he shouted and then as another man began climbing the guard rail he shot him as well. This in an instant had its effect. The first man had fallen into the sea but the second died there in front of them all. "Now do as I say!" Banks roared, following up the momentary hold he had on the mob. "Over on the starboard side — all of you now!" For a second or two it looked as though the pressure from behind would make this move impossible but miraculously it broke and turned and the hundreds of men pouring up on deck swirled forward and round on to the starboard side. By now the men's own officers, who to begin with had been caught up and submerged in the rush, began to fight their way out in front. Patches of order began to appear and the madness of the stampede vanished as quickly as it had come. All of a sudden a sheeplike docility took its place and everyone began to sort themselves out and make their way to their correct boat stations as they had so often practiced before. The list got better and although the sea was pouring in all the time on the port side, it was now making its way across, flooding the whole of the lower part of the ship, so that by the time Banks regained the bridge *Leviathan* was almost on an even keel.

The situation, though, was very bad. Both the vast engine room and the one remaining boiler room were flooding, and after hearing the Chief's report, Banks ordered them to be cleared. A short while after the generators stopped and the emergency lighting system came into use. Down below the chaos increased in the semi-darkness, though now there was no recurrence of the initial panic and most of the troops who were not trapped were moving in a more or less orderly fashion to their boat stations. Both the Staff Captain and the Chief Officer, who had made separate inspections on either side of the gash caused by the torpedo, and of the fire which was now raging amidships, told Banks they thought *Leviathan* could not be saved. The fire was out of hand, the sea was pouring in and it was only a question of time. For long seconds Banks looked at each of them, looked, as it seemed, through each of them, as if paralyzed with concentration. Then he walked to the side of the bridge and stared down at the sea. No one moved and everyone awaited his word. Then abruptly he made up his mind: "Very well, gentlemen," he said with his familiar crisp authority, "then we must abandon her. Order abandon ship."

Up in the radio room the dreadful news was being transmitted to the Admiralty and the C.-in-C. Home Fleet on the emergency batteries. In the cypher office Susan and her two assistants packed the lead-covered cypher and code books into canvas bags which they lugged to the side and then threw into the sea. Everywhere, as the lifeboats were manned and the floats and rafts were cut loose, there was now an exemplary order and discipline, as if somehow to make up for the initial stampede. But hundreds were already missing — perhaps over a thousand had been trapped below when the torpedo had struck. Others had been cut off by the fire and had been burned or roasted to death. Indeed, the fire had now cut the ship into separate halves, and communication between the two was only by means of the promenade and sun decks. As the sea poured in below, so the fire ate its way upward. Thus, by now, the whole midships of *Leviathan* was an inferno. The great lady was not going to go slowly like the *Titanic*, she was settling down in the water fast. Black oily smoke now obscured everything and down below the sound of explosions began. Even on the bridge the heat began to be felt, the fumes of burned paint and oil mingling in suffocating gusts.

To begin with the U-boat had surfaced and would have attempted to fire on the ship except that *Leviathan*'s after gun had engaged her first. Now that the great ship lay stopped and badly on fire and was now in process of being abandoned the U-boat surfaced again and began shelling the ship, aiming at the bridge. Banks had no means of retaliation other than raining Biblical curses on the U-boat captain's head and when two shells burst, respectively, on the bridge and in the Captain's quarters below — blowing to pieces the famous oak chair — Banks removed himself aft on the sun deck, where already the paint had started to blister. It was going to be quicker even than he or anyone else had thought.

About half the boats on the starboard side — each holding a hundred and twenty-five people — had been got away before *Leviathan* began once more to list to port. This made it impossible to lower away any more on the starboard side of the ship and it prevented the manning of those on the port side, except at the davits, since as they were lowered they fell away from the ship and could not be reached by those on the decks below. Thus it happened that both Alan Mitchell and Susan were trapped on the promenade deck as a new panic began. Mott's boat had been got away all right, but the one designed for the special communications unit still lay at its davits on the starboard side, and when it became apparent that people would have to jump for it a new wave of terror took possession of those who were left. It was still a formidable jump. The ship was still being shelled by the U-boat. The fire was all the time reaching up at them, and smoke which got in their eyes and their noses blinded them and made them gasp for breath. At one moment, as the ship lurched and Susan lost her balance, falling against a stanchion and cutting her forehead, it seemed as though there was no hope at all. Her bones turned to water as they had done on that other occasion in the *Pluto*. She thought of Motty. She prayed in a childish incoherent way and then Alan Mitchell was picking her up and smiling at her as she had not seen him smile for years, in the way he used to smile when they were children together.

"Don't give up, Sue," he said; "we aren't beaten yet. Come on, pull yourself together."

All the time *Leviathan* lay more and more on her port side, and soon it was impossible to stand upright on the deck. Then there was a lurch and hundreds of people were tipped helter-skelter into the sea. Alan had firm hold of the stanchion with one hand and with the other held on to Susan. The other two Wren Officers had been carried away in the avalanche and there were now only a few of them left on that part of the sun deck.

"Is she going to turn turtle?" Susan said. Alan shrugged his shoulders.

"She's very deep in the water for that. She might float on her side for a bit. We ought to climb up over starboard if we can."

This, slowly and with difficulty, they did, in company with a handful of others, to find themselves half on the side of the superstructure and half on the starboard side of the sun deck itself. Here they found Banks and the Staff Captain wedged grotesquely against the davits of one of the jammed lifeboats now itself on its side. Both were hacking away at the falls with jack knives so that the boat would be free and might possibly float away, if it could right itself, when *Leviathan* sank. Even now, like a great ape up a tree, Banks seemed to have shed nothing of that majesty of command which was his aura. Even now in these last few moments of the ship's life, and quite possibly of his own, he seemed to radiate a magnificent strength, and he had time to say to Susan as he reached down and yanked her up into a more maneuverable position, "You should have jumped for it, madam, a long time ago. But as you're here you'd better come up into the Royal Enclosure."

About a quarter of a mile from the ship Mott cruised slowly in his lifeboat, collecting together rafts and floats, taking on board the non-swimmers, the half-drowned and the injured, and all the time watching out for Susan in a state of acute anxiety. By now *Leviathan* lay almost on her port side, her funnels only a few feet above the sea, the fire in her quenched at last. He could see a handful of figures clambering up on to the ship's sloping side for all the world as if they were scaling some peculiar cliff in the sea. He could pick out the Captain and the Staff Captain and then suddenly his heart gave a great leap as he saw there was a girl with them and even at that distance he could tell from the stance that Susan was there and for the moment was still all right. But how long had she got? How long had any of them got? Would the old lady go in a rush, sucking down with her anyone still on her hull? or would she remain on her side, as she then was with just enough buoyancy sealed inside her to keep her afloat?

His attention was distracted by the U-boat which was now cruising among the survivors, its Captain declaring in gloating arrogance and clipped English that "humanitarian Germany had broadcast the position so that rescue operations could be undertaken. You have nothing to fear. Help is on the way. Heil Hitler!" and then, with a cynicism which even Mott with his knowledge of human nature would not have believed possible, proceeded to machine-gun every lifeboat within range. Thus the terror which had made their abandonment of *Leviathan* so chaotic still stalked them in the water. As the U-boat came near the instinct to run away, somehow or other to escape — though of course no real escape was possible — made people jump again into the sea. Mott made no effort to stop them nor could he have done so had he tried. Indeed, in these last few moments when he knew he was going to die, a great calmness and detachment possessed him, so that as the bullets fringed their way over the sea and into the boat, he thought only of Susan, thought of her with love and gratitude remembering the pleasure and the happiness she had brought him, remembering her smile and her gaiety and the joy of her eager young body in their lovemaking, Susan filled his whole consciousness and when the bullets ripped open his chest and the convulsive moment came, he died calling her name. A few moments of agony, a thrashing about like a hooked fish out of water, and then it was over and done with. The boat gradually filled with the sea and sank carrying with it the dying and the dead. "Help is coming. You have nothing to fear. Heil Hitler!" the guttural voice too died away and only the human wreckage in the sea was left.

The time for *Leviathan*, also, had come. By now only Banks remained. The Staff Captain, Alan, and Susan had simply walked into the sea and were now swimming as far away from the ship as they could. Banks, himself, knew he should linger no more. Once those ninety thousand tons began sinking to the bottom the downward suction would be fatal to anyone near, yet he could not master his reluctance to leave the great lady. An immense weariness enveloped him. He was now too exhausted in himself even to think. A sense that this was the end of it all, both of *Leviathan* and of himself, filled him with a kind of drugged apathy. He still had the Book of Rules in his left-hand pocket and he still mechanically prayed, but now it was different — now the end was near — the responsibility for it all no longer to be borne — the last of his commanding done. A tremor went through the great hull as he stood there rooted to the spot, staring unseeing at the wreckage all around and at the thousands of human beings dead and alive bobbing about like corks. So this was the end of it all, the end of this great, wonderful ship — the end, too, of his life. He heaved a great sigh and began slowly to walk down to the water. Into his mind came those verses of the psalm to which he had so often turned in perplexity and distress, "I will lift up mine eyes unto the hills from whence cometh my help, my help cometh from the Lord which made heaven and earth. He will not suffer thy foot to be moved: He that keepeth thee will not slumber," and then as he looked round at the sea which would so soon receive him and his ship the voice in him went on, "For they that go down to the sea in ships, that do business in great waters, these see the works of the Lord and His wonders in the deep. . . ." Still he could not make himself go. He paused once more to take a last look at the ship, and as if a signal had finally been given, *Leviathan* shuddered beneath his feet; and then suddenly she went, taking him with her, sucking him down swiftly and silently to the depths of the sea.